DISFIGURED

A Gothic Romance

by Wendy Coles-Littlepage

Acknowledgements

Many thanks to my friends who read this book multiple times in its various versions: Susan, Jeri, Janan, Lisa and my mom, Mary. Thank you all for your patience and constructive criticism. I'm sure it was tiresome at times. Special thanks to my friend Lisa for her excellent proofreading efforts on my behalf. I want also to thank my friend Janan Boehme; she is fluent in French and a skilled editor, and I could not have managed without her help with my French usage in the book, as well as her general editing skills.

My husband, Robert, gave me so much support, patience and encouragement as I typed away on my laptop night after night. Every time I hit a page number milestone, he was my cheering section. And he still is, to my great good fortune.

I want to make special mention of all the members of the female gender who, after watching a live performance of the musical, Phantom of the Opera or watching the film (and you know who you are) have said with a sigh, "I'd pick the Phantom. The heck with that wishy-washy Raoul." So thank you. This book is for you.

It would be very remiss of me not to make special mention of the actor Gerard Butler, who so memorably portrayed the Phantom, AKA Erik, in the 2004 POTO movie. He somehow managed to inspire sympathy and even a little empathy for a character who is essentially a sociopathic, misanthropic, obsessed stalker nut-case. Well, it doesn't hurt that he is a gorgeous hunk, but that notwithstanding, without a lot to work with he did a wonderful job. There's a scene near the end of the film when Christine has handed him back the engagement ring and walked away for the last time, and he is sitting there and a big tear runs down his cheek. It is that exact moment that my Erik sprang into being: I suddenly realized I wanted the Phantom to have a happy ending, regardless of whether or not he actually deserved one. So I wrote it.

Indeed I owe a lot to the POTO story in both its musical and movie versions. In particular I found the beautiful, sumptuous sets from the 2004 movie a real inspiration for my descriptions of Erik's cavernous home and of course the theatre above it.

I don't know if very many people nowadays have read the original book by Gaston Leroux; I did so in order to gather more information and background material for Erik's life before the Opera.

I must say, Andrew Lloyd Webber had his work cut out for him to piece together a musical based on this oddity of a book. And not just any musical, but one so beloved that it is always playing somewhere. For obvious reasons the character of "daroga" the Persian was left out of the musical, but I included him in 'Disfigured' because he plays a prominent role in the Leroux novel.

And finally, I give thanks to Mrs. Virginia Garrett, for her encouragement and support. Great teachers are never forgotten.

He whose game is the eagle
takes no heed of the sparrow.

The Three Musketeers,
Alexandre Dumas

Paris, 1870

CHAPTER ONE

'Never fear quarrels, but seek hazardous adventures'
A.D.

I entered the Cimetière de Montmartre with a deliberate stride, my fingers clutched around a set of heavy iron keys that weighed down the pocket of my winter cloak. It was a cold, crisp March day and the heavy cloak was welcome. The path was well known to me, but still I looked around with interest, admiring the bold, bare branches of trees not yet in leaf. I have always loved this cemetery. My father once told me that it had begun life as a stone quarry, but once it no longer yielded, it was transformed into a beautiful final resting place for the dead. When one walks down the flight of worn steps from busy Rue Rachel into the cemetery, it is like leaving one city for another. A city built for the dead, but the living can enjoy it too.

We actually lived not far from the Cimetière de Montmartre when I was a child; I lived in the same house all my life, until this very day. We used on occasion to walk here, especially in summer when all the trees were in leaf. It was a sweet, secret refuge from the summer sun; it even smelled nicer than the rest of Paris (which, truth to tell, does not smell very nice in the summer). I did not mind coming there even as a child, nor even after my father died and was buried in a quiet section, a simple granite slab covering his grave. This city of the dead held no terrors for me – in fact, quite the opposite. My mother and I visited my father's grave often, leaving flowers for him. I know that she came there sometimes by herself as well.

I was ten years old when my father died. He was seventeen years older than my mother, a respectable, kind and caring family physician, his small practice confined to the *quartier* where we resided. He toiled ceaselessly in his efforts to tend to the sick and injured, sometimes without accepting any payment for his time. My mother frequently contributed her cooking skills as well, providing nourishing food for those patients who had no means to provide it for themselves. Years of hard work and uncertain hours eventually took their toll, and my father died of a heart attack late one night while on his way home from tending to a consumptive patient. After his death it was only my mother and I for sixteen years (except for the one miserable year of my disastrous marriage). My mother had but recently

5

followed her husband into death and under the same granite slab. And so you see, Reader, that sad event is what set everything in motion: for if my mother had not died, my part of this extraordinary tale would not have happened.

I marched along the familiar paths, hoping a fast stride would keep me warm. Part of me was enjoying the peaceful scenery while the other part pondered my newly altered circumstances. I never wallow in self-pity, for there is nothing to be gained by such indulgences, but I confess to feeling just a bit irritated.

"If only I'd had the good fortune to be a widow!" I muttered to myself crossly, kicking at a pebble in my path. Instead of a *divorcée*, that is to say. *Quelle différence!* My present circumstances would be much improved by my having lost my husband in some war, rather than by the shocking action of booting him from my life. It isn't fair, but there we are.

I soon arrived at my destination, and found myself standing before the double grave of my parents. It was my mother I particularly wanted to talk to – *with*, to be honest. My father had been gone so many years now that he was a fond but distant memory to me. Though I had somehow absorbed some of his medical knowledge as a child, I could no longer recollect him very well. Frowning down at their wide, flat gravestones, I was not sure how to begin. So much had changed so quickly. What would my mother say if she could see what a change of circumstance I faced this day?

Whatever else I was expecting when I met with my mother's *notaire* shortly after her death, it certainly wasn't a marriage proposal. But it proved to be only the first of many strange things that happened to me.

Frowning, I cast my mind back to that awkward, uncomfortable meeting which had taken place a few weeks ago. M. Blanc the *notaire* was the reluctant bearer of bad news. Having gone over my mother's will with me, he carefully removed his *pince nez* and began polishing them on a large white handkerchief, something he habitually did without even being aware of it. I waited patiently, my gloved hands clasped in my lap, until he had finished. Satisfied the lenses were perfectly clean, he set the *pince nez* on his desk and regarded me seriously.

"Mademoiselle Bessette," he began at last, his voice grave, "I regret to inform you that although the family home is now solely in your possession, it will be necessary for you to sell it. I have gone over everything quite carefully, but I cannot see that you have a choice."

He frowned unhappily, and looked down at his plump hands on the desk. "The house itself is unencumbered, but unfortunately there is not enough money remaining in your mother's estate to maintain a house of that size, let alone keep the servants necessary to manage it."

"*Je comprends.*" I regarded M. Blanc without blinking; the news was not unexpected, after all. Calmly I asked, "What ought I to do?"

"I recommend listing the house with an estate agent as soon as possible, Mademoiselle. I can give you the name of one or two I know, both of whom are very respectable and trustworthy gentlemen. Once the sale is complete, you would be able to purchase a small apartment with the proceeds. Living on a smaller scale, you ought, *bien sûr*, to live in reasonable comfort on the income from the estate." M. Blanc's forehead had begun to develop a slight sheen of moisture, and as he spoke the handkerchief was employed to blot it away. He appeared suddenly rather nervous, which was quite unlike him.

I had always found M. Blanc to be rather distant and dry, in keeping with his profession. He was approximately of an age with my late father, and had managed our family's legal affairs for years as well as preparing both my parents' wills. His suits were impeccably tailored and hopelessly out of date, and he had for many years worn a very large, bristly mustache of which he was quite proud. He was, in fact, a classic example of a staid, well-to-do businessman. Why was he now behaving in such a peculiar manner?

"Are you quite well, M. Blanc?" I asked, studying him with concern. He looked rather flushed, as if he were about to be ill.

The *notaire* smiled a little and shook his head. "I am quite well, *merci*, Mademoiselle Bessette." A perplexing silence ensued, and then abruptly M. Blanc stood up and leaned on his desk, gazing at me earnestly.

"Mademoiselle Bessette," he began, his voice unaccountably raspy. Pausing, he cleared his throat. "Please forgive me, but I must...I would like...that is, would you do me the honor of accepting my hand in marriage?"

I stared at him, speechless with shock. How very awkward! It was the last thing I was expecting, and certainly not at all welcome, coming as it did from a man old enough to be my father. I told myself, however, that I would be wise to accept his proposal. M. Blanc was an established professional gentleman, honest and trustworthy, and I would be well cared for, *sans doute*. I would be safe, protected, and secure.

7

The life ahead of me if I accepted his rash and impetuous proposal flashed across my mind, and suddenly I had a vision of myself standing in a parlor, peering out at a quiet street from behind a lace curtain. My answer became instantly clear to me.

"M. Blanc," I said in what I hoped was a compassionate voice. "Do sit down, please. I cannot thank you enough for your proposal, for I know it was kindly meant, but I'm afraid I cannot accept it. Be assured that I am, however, greatly honored by it."

M. Blanc did not appear surprised by my rejection. He lowered himself back into his leather chair rather heavily, employing the handkerchief again and smoothing his mustache.

"It was not only out of kindness and concern for your welfare that I proposed marriage to you, Mademoiselle." He said after a brief pause. "You are a lovely, intelligent and lively young woman. You are your father's daughter, and you have a strong spirit. I have watched you over the last two years as you cared for your mother and managed all your family's affairs singlehanded. I have grown to admire you very much."

Blushing under his unwelcome compliments, I fidgeted in my chair. "Be that as it may, M. Blanc, my answer must still be no." I smiled at him in what I hoped was a kindly way. Standing, I began briskly tugging on my gloves. "Thank you again, and indeed I cannot thank you enough for all your help with my mother's estate. If you will send me the names of those estate agents, I would be most grateful." Having placed our relationship firmly back in the professional realm, I put on my hat and left his office. As I walked toward my home, I pondered M. Blanc's unexpected proposal. I hoped I had not hurt his feelings by refusing him, but surely his feelings toward me could not run very deep, as we had scarcely spoken two words to each other before this.

Returning to the present and to the cemetery with a shake of my head, I gathered my skirts and my winter cloak up over my legs and sat down on the chilly granite slab. Whatever life had in store for me, I would not meet it as the bored and lonely wife of a staid old *notaire*. Somehow I rather hoped there might be a little *adventure* ahead, even if just in a small way.

Sitting quietly, I surveyed my surroundings. Recent rains had washed away the little clods of earth and other tell-tale signs that a burial had taken place here only a few weeks ago. In this quiet, secluded part of the cemetery, there were only simple tombs and headstones. No great luminaries occupied this section, although the composer Hector Berlioz rested in eternal sleep a bit farther up the hill.

As my eyes wandered, they suddenly and unexpectedly met another pair of eyes, wary golden eyes that watched me closely. For an instant I experienced heart-pounding shock at this unexpected visitor, but then I saw that it was only a cat. Tucked away at the base of a statue just above me was a feral mother cat, with four multicolored kittens suckling busily at her. We stared at one another for a few seconds, blue eyes and gold studying each other intently.

"Don't be afraid, I won't hurt you," I murmured gently; as if she understood, the mother cat squeezed her golden eyes closed for a moment, then opened them and returned to cleaning her kittens. I could hear her purring from where I sat. Somehow, the little family was a welcome, even comforting sight to me. Looking away from the cat, I returned to my purpose.

"Well, *Maman*," I began, "I came here to tell you, I am moving into my new apartment today. I think you would like it…it is quite small compared to our house, but it is really very cozy. I do wish you could see it." I brushed my hand across the carved stone, my mother's name and dates standing out pale and new against the older undisturbed surface of granite. How I missed her!

"I brought your pianoforte with me – I must say it makes my new *salon* look like a dollhouse. You cannot imagine how difficult it was for the movers to bring it up those stairs." Suddenly my words caught in my throat; I rose, shook out my bunched skirts and pulled the hood of the cloak over my head. "*Adieu* for now," I said. I had intended to say more, but my throat felt tight and there was a burning sensation behind my eyes. And I knew there was but little point in asking advice of the dead, no matter how wise they might have been in life. As I turned to walk away the mother cat did not even raise her head to watch me go.

At the steps leading back up to the Rue Rachel's noisy bustle, I paused and looked back: such a lovely, peaceful place, I thought. After sixteen years apart, my parents were together again, but as for me, well, I was alone. Twenty-six years old and completely alone.

Turning away from the cemetery, I mounted the steps to the street and with a spring in my step, began walking. I like to think my own personal motto is the same as the one for Paris, the greatest city in the world: '*Fluctuat nec mergitur*' (she is buffeted by the waves but does not sink). It was a long walk to my destination, but I enjoy walking; *en plus*, I did not want to spend the money on a hansom. It would not do to forget that I was on a strict budget now.

Eventually my feet turned down a tree-lined side street, full of colorful striped awnings and lively commerce. About halfway down the block on the left side, I stopped at a door with a wavy glass panel set in it. The door was missing quite a lot of paint. I pulled the heavy ring of keys from my pocket, selected one and fitted it into the lock, opening the door to my new home, and my new occupation. As the door swung open to reveal a dusty, long-disused and outdated professional kitchen smelling of rodent droppings, a smile of anticipatory pleasure spread across my face.

Like my mother before me, my forte is preparing comforting, nutritious food for invalids, and I had decided to make it my profession. I learned to cook from *ma mère*, inheriting both her wonderful recipes and her compassion, which is why, I suppose, Celestine thought I would make a good cook for Erik. And if anyone needed comfort more than Erik, that person would be difficult to find. But I see I am getting ahead of myself; it would be better, considering the story I am about to relate, if I do *not* get ahead of myself. If I am to be judged (and I know I shall be), then let me be judged fairly; therefore I shall begin at the beginning.

Quite frankly, my present situation would have been most desperately precarious if it were not for my mother's prudent way of life. Thanks to her, I had a certain amount of freedom to choose my own future. My father's income as a physician had enabled us to live in a comfortable home in a good middle class neighborhood and to employ a few servants, but after his death my mother's efforts at economizing as much as possible were all that enabled us to remain there. After all, my situation could have been much worse, and I well knew it.

My only real mistake in life thus far was admittedly quite a serious one: the aforementioned, greatly-repented marriage. It was an all-too-familiar scenario: a young, overly protected and naïve girl, as I was at the time, swept off her feet by a dashing rake, handsome in his officer's regalia, but without the happily-ever-after. Against the advice of all and against the dictates of society, I divorced my husband within a year, when I discovered he preferred drink to everything else, including me. I learned a great deal about life in that brief year, most of it not very nice.

I would always regret that our brief marriage produced no child, because my fondest wish was to become a mother. In time I came to accept that it was for the best, since I needed to apply all my energies toward earning a living. The death of my mother only two years after the end of my ill-fated marriage left me completely alone in the world. It was a terrible blow to me, but at least I was not destitute.

Those last two years were difficult ones – my mother's failing health had demanded all of my time. But I felt myself ready to stand on my own and make my own way in the world. As a matter of fact, I had no choice in the matter. I no longer had the luxury to be naïve, and now that I had rejected the hand of M. Blanc, there was no one to protect me any longer except myself. They say misfortunes build character and I think it must be true. By this time I expect I possess enough character for two people.

There are not many employment opportunities for ladies, *respectable* employment, I mean. A respectable young lady of limited means (myself, in other words) might become a governess or a lady's companion, or confine herself to a convent for the rest of her life. Or she might decide to become a professional cook. Suffice it to say, no *unrespectable* options could possibly be considered. Lacking the proper education to allow me to be a governess, having too much independence to wish to become a shadow, and too much interest in the world to spend the rest of my life in a convent, I opted for the obvious; it was where my talents lay anyway. And what better place to earn a living as a cook than Paris; everyone knows that French cuisine is the best, the most sophisticated in the world – here, cooking is in the blood. Thanks to my mother, it certainly was in mine.

After several weeks of fruitless searching for something I could afford, I found the perfect location for my kitchen on the Rue de la Marché, in close proximity to an excellent *boulangerie*, a *charcuterie* and other necessary shops. It was not a fashionable address; rather, it was a serviceable one. A Market Day was held there every Wednesday, and had been for as long as anyone could remember. The space I found had once been a small confectionery, but was now closed and both upstairs and down was available to rent. The kitchen needed a considerable amount of cleaning and renovating, but what really tempted me was the small but comfortable apartment upstairs over the shop, with tall glass-paneled doors opening off the *salon* onto a small black wrought iron balcony overlooking the street. Here I could grow fresh herbs for my recipes, or sit with a morning cup of *café*. The wallpaper in the apartment was hanging in doleful tatters and generations of mice had nested happily in the *garde-manger*, but these were not insurmountable obstacles. There was even a place for my mother's old pianoforte in the *salon*. For the remainder of my furniture I had gleaned the smaller pieces from the home I was forced to give up. Larger pieces would never fit into my small apartment, with the exception of the pianoforte of course.

I sold virtually everything else that wasn't nailed down so I could purchase an utterly magnificent *Godin* professional cooking stove for my kitchen – the very latest model, which burned gas rather than wood – a true luxury. Everything else in my apartment might be out-of-date and genteelly run-down, but the stove was another matter entirely. I considered it a business investment.

In pride of place above the *divan* upstairs, I hung our reproduction painting of Constable's 'The Hay Wain'. It was my mother's favorite painting. My father had commissioned the copy as a gift for her shortly before he died. I suppose it seems incongruous that a painting by a well-known English artist should be such a favorite in a French home, but in fact John Constable had been more popular in France than in his homeland of England, which just goes to prove the English have no taste to speak of. 'The Hay Wain' even won a gold medal at the Paris *Salon*. My books went on the bookshelves, my clothes into the small armoire, and my mother's faded rose-print quilt went on my bed. From our old house I rescued the best of the white lace window curtains, cutting them down as necessary to make them fit the windows and door panels of my new apartment. The threadbare Aubusson hallway runner from our old home became the area rug in my new *salon*. Arranging these precious possessions around me made me feel as though my mother were near as well.

After settling in comfortably upstairs, I banished the mice, improved on the kitchen, bought my supplies, and placed a small ad in *Le Temps*. Two weeks and a great deal of labor after my visit to the cemetery, I was ready for business.

I confess I indulged in happy daydreams of bringing wholesome, healthy meals to delicate, picturesque invalids in nice private homes. In my imagination I could see a cart pull up outside my door and a servant step out to receive a delivery from my hands to take away to a shut-in. I could almost smell the delicious fragrance of some wholesome *potage* wafting from the covered dish. It was only a short leap of my imagination to see the delicate, wan invalid grow stronger and healthier by the day. I certainly could not expect to make many *francs* this way, but in my daydream it was adequate when supplemented by my small inheritance. Here, in busy, tree-lined Rue de la Marché, I would get to know the proprietors in the other shops and perhaps acquire some friends.

Et alors, the glass painter came, scraped away what remained of the old confectionery sign as I stood by watching, glowing with pride, and my new sign was painted in its place. I had given much thought to an appropriate name for what I intended to offer here. So the new name, in silver script with a thin black outline, read: *'Nourriture pour la Vie et la Guérison'*, Food for Life and Healing. 'Sylvie Bessette, Proprietress'. My fellow shopkeepers were welcoming and very pleased to have the empty and neglected store front filled again. If any of them thought it peculiar that an unmarried woman was setting up in business for herself, and *by* herself, they were too polite to say so.

I knew I was missing out on some of life's pleasures. Besides having to work for a living, a *divorcée* like myself, without family or connections, could not move freely about society without becoming the focus of unpleasant gossip and rude speculations. Parisian Society follows a strict code of rules. It is virtually impossible to make anyone's acquaintance here without proper introductions, and I had no introductions. The two years spent nursing my ailing mother had kept me completely away from the outside world. I therefore intended to keep to my cheerful kitchen and cozy apartment. Everything would sort itself out in time, I felt sure. I was in no hurry to marry again after my early misstep. I was well aware that I had nothing to offer a potential suitor, and I was not at all sure any potential suitors had anything to offer *me*.

A glance into my cheval glass tells me that I am not unattractive – not a raving beauty to be sure – but not repulsive either. I have a petite figure, being scarcely five feet tall. An inconvenience in many ways, but I do look rather well in a draped bustle. Although I have always attempted to keep *au courant* with the latest modes of fashion, I confess I absolutely *loathe* wearing corsets. Show me a woman who claims to like them and I will show you a woman who ought to be placed in an asylum for her own good. I much prefer being able to breathe. My upper half is unfashionably generous enough not to require *that* aspect of wearing a corset. My hair could be called blonde, I suppose, but such a dark blonde that perhaps that would be an exaggeration. It is almost exactly the shade of golden

13

honey. My face is, sadly, rounder than is considered desirable, and I have a tendency toward a rather stubborn chin. My mother used to tell me it looked like the prow of a ship when I was acting particularly determined about something, which admittedly occurred frequently. Well, I *do* have a fairly determined nature. I have been told that my blue eyes are my best feature.

In spite of my shortcomings and my advanced age, however, it should not have been difficult for me to make the acquaintance of a suitable male person and marry again, but this was not the case. There is a stigma against the divorced woman in our Society. Why this should be so is beyond my comprehension. If I were a widow I daresay I would be spoilt for my choice of suitors. So it was all to the good that none of that mattered to me any longer.

CHAPTER TWO

'In prosperity one should sow meals right and left,
in order to harvest some in adversity'
A.D.

To my growing dismay, my advertisement in *Le Temps* ran
for three weeks without garnering a single response. I
began to despair of ever acquiring business. I could not understand it.
Here was my lovely kitchen sitting ready, my gleaming black *Godin*
stove, my copper pots and pans hanging above it within easy reach, my
work table with chopping block waiting for the vegetables. Herbs
hung drying in fragrant bunches from wires strung along the ceiling,
and a big vase of peonies rested in the wide window. The larder was
laden with bags of flour and potatoes resting in its dark stone interior;
shelves were stacked with covered dishes, bowls, crockery, utensils and
wide trays for transporting food. A large wall clock that had once
hung in my father's medical office unnecessarily announced the time
every hour. What would I do with all this if no one ever answered my
advertisement? And how long could I afford to run it? I spent many
sleepless hours staring at my ceiling, wondering what was to become of
me.

One morning at the beginning of the fourth week my
advertisement ran, I was polishing my precious stove for the
hundredth time when suddenly the door bell rang. I was so startled by
the unfamiliar sound it took me a moment to realize what it was.
Through the wavy old glass of the door I saw two people standing on
the sidewalk outside. I drew a deep breath before crossing to the door
to open it, nervously smoothing my hair knotted at my neck and
praying silently, "Please let it be a client at last!"

It seemed that my prayer was to be answered. A gentleman
and lady were standing outside my door. The man held my
advertisement clipped from the newspaper in his hand – a very good
sign. He was a rather rotund older gentleman dressed in what had
once been a good quality suit of clothes, but now showing wear and
age. His face was wide, his warm smile wider. The woman was a nun,
instantly identified by her severe black habit. It was difficult to tell her
age, since I could not see her hair, but at a guess I would have said she
was around fifty. Bowing toward me, the gentleman removed his

rather shiny top hat. He had, I saw, very little grey hair plastered close to his head.

"Have I the honor of addressing Madame Bessette?" He inquired, while discreetly examining me up and down in the manner of a typical Frenchman. From the twinkle in his eye, I must have met with his approval.

"Mademoiselle," I corrected gently, inviting them in with a sweep of my arm. Maintaining an outer calm as befitting a professional cook whilst dancing with joy inside, I offered my potential new clients tea and showed them to chairs at my table.

Introductions were performed, and I learned that Doctor Gaudet and Sister Chantal ran a small private hospital a few miles distant, across the river on the Île de la Cité. I busied myself putting the tea things on a tray along with a little plate of *madeleines* from the *patisserie* nearby. The English habit of tea-drinking had been making in-roads especially in Paris, and I found I very much enjoyed drinking it in the afternoon.

It was really too bad I had not the wherewithal to employ a *domestique* on a daily basis, for if I had such a person in my employ she would be obliged to bustle about making tea, leaving me free to converse with my guests. Unfortunately, I made do with a girl who came in once a week to clean both upstairs and down. So I did the bustling while Dr. Gaudet and Sister Chantal waited patiently, looking around them at all the accoutrements of the kitchen. They seemed interested in everything, and apparently were satisfied by what they saw.

Presently I was able to join them at the table. "How may I be of service?" I inquired, pouring out cups of tea, hoping I sounded properly professional.

Dr. Gaudet placed my advertisement on the table, smoothing it repeatedly with his hands. "We are here in response to your advertisement, Mademoiselle," he began. Here he paused and exchanged a look with the Sister, who gave him an encouraging nod. He continued, "We currently have nine patients residing permanently at our hospital. I am responsible for their medical care, and the Sister supervises meals and housekeeping matters. We unfortunately have not the facilities to prepare proper meals, and it has been difficult to locate someone who would perform this service at the hospital. *Alors*, from reading your advertisement, we believe you are just what we need – you prepare the fare here in your kitchen, do you not?" Dr. Gaudet looked at me hopefully.

16

"*Oui*, as you see." I answered confidently. It was a small lie of omission, since I had not yet actually had any reason to prepare a meal in my kitchen.

"Excellent," he responded. "It would be a simple matter to transport meals from here to our hospital. We have a wagon that would be placed at your disposal. Our patients are accustomed to taking their main meal at mid-day, with a light repast of fruit or a sweet at the end of the day. We wish you to prepare their main meal daily, Saturdays and Sundays excepted, of course. On those days, we provide them with cold salads and meats. They take very little on Sundays as a rule. We are able to offer you an excellent salary for your catering, as well as providing the transportation for your deliveries."

Although inwardly I felt like dancing, I forced myself to speak calmly. "I see. Tell me about your patients, Dr. Gaudet, if you would. Are they invalids? Would they require special dishes?" I drew paper and my pen and ink set toward me as I spoke, trying to look businesslike, and prepared to make a few notes. There was a brief pause while my visitors exchanged glances again. Was it my imagination or did they seem somewhat apprehensive?

The doctor cleared his throat. "Our hospital is owned and operated by the Church, you understand, Mlle. Bessette." He explained. "Our patients are missionaries, struck down by illness while doing God's work in the most primitive surroundings." While he spoke, the Sister very quietly removed a rosary from the folds of her black robe and began running it through her fingers, her eyes never leaving the doctor's face. I suspected she was not even aware of what her hands were doing.

The doctor continued, "They were living and working in the most unsanitary and difficult surroundings and in a tropical clime, which we now know to be an exceedingly unhealthy environment. For the most part, we have had no problems but for some unknown reason, a few proved susceptible to some of the diseases prevalent in the tropics."

I considered this thoughtfully. While my father had been a physician, nothing about his practice had ever dealt with strange tropical diseases. Nevertheless, it was a job, and I needed it badly. Therefore I nodded encouragingly for Dr. Gaudet to proceed, but he seemed to have stuck at this point in his narrative and was having trouble going on. We were coming to the point at last, if he would only proceed and get there. I decided I would have to help him along a bit.

"*Alors*, you are saying that the nine patients at your hospital have contracted some sort of disease – something without a cure?" I prompted.

Sister Chantal nodded gently, as if to herself. "That is correct, you are very astute, Mlle. Bessette," said the doctor approvingly. "We thought it only right to bring them home where they might receive the best of care for the remainder of their lives, but because of the nature of their condition they must remain isolated from others. Here in Paris, however, they can live in relative comfort, even receiving the occasional visit from a relative, and they are able to attend services as often as they wish for we also have a chapel at the hospital."

There was more to this tale than met the eye, I was certain. The light was beginning to dawn. "Are you saying that…that your patients are…contagious?" I asked, frowning.

Removing a large white handkerchief from his coat pocket, Dr. Gaudet paused to mop his face with it. His forehead, I had observed, was beginning to break out in little beads of dampness. I was not stupid, and even I could see, or thought I could see, where this was leading. I certainly could understand his apprehension. If indeed all the patients at his private hospital were victims of some contagious tropical disease, it was small wonder he found it difficult to find a cook willing to spend time there. He must have seized upon my advertisement as the literal answer to their prayers.

Dr. Gaudet was now answering my question, so I forced myself to concentrate on what he was saying. "*Oui*, I am afraid that is correct. We do not know exactly how contagious, although thus far no one caring for them has been affected. We take all the necessary precautions, *naturellement*. But it is imperative they be kept away from the public in general and…in fact, their existence at the hospital must be kept a closely guarded secret. If you were to accept the position as our cook, you would be required to sign an oath of secrecy, Mademoiselle."

I stared at him, astonished. Had I heard him correctly?

"An oath of secrecy, did you say? But…why, if you do not mind me asking?"

Dr. Gaudet gazed helplessly at Sister Chantal, who now spoke for the first and only time during their visit.

"You must tell her," she said softly; "she will find out eventually." He seemed to derive some comfort from her serene countenance even as she drew comfort from her rosary. He nodded and turned back to me, setting down the teacup he had been holding.

18

"Very well. But you must remember, even if you decline the position, the existence of our hospital *must* remain secret. I must ask you to promise, Mademoiselle, before I explain any further." I could see no harm in this, and in fact was growing quite curious, so I promptly gave my promise I would tell no one. Satisfied, he went on, speaking carefully.

"Our nine missionaries have…have leprosy, Mademoiselle, in various stages. They are lepers."

I admit I was struck speechless – how could such a thing be possible in this modern age? Shock must have been writ across my face because Dr. Gaudet went on quickly and in a louder voice,

"*Bien sûr*, you understand, much research has been done and we no longer believe leprosy is particularly contagious if the proper protective measures are taken, and only to those of weakened constitutions perhaps. It is primarily to spare the general populace that lepers have been confined to colonies in isolated places. There are no cases to be found in Europe in our day, except a few in Norway, where Dr. Hansen is conducting his wonderful researches into the disease. I hope to go there one day…but I digress."

"I …I must confess I am quite astounded. I had no idea a leper colony existed right here in the heart of Paris," I admitted truthfully.

The doctor frowned slightly. "We do not refer to our hospital as a 'colony', Mademoiselle Bessette. It is properly called a Leprosarium, but we usually just refer to it as a hospital. But surely you can comprehend the importance of secrecy, there is such a stigma attached to the disease. There is no danger to the populace of Paris, since our patients never set foot outside its walls. There is a courtyard in the center where they can take fresh air and a little exercise. I believe the fresh healthy air by the river to be good for them. You see, although the missionaries contracted the disease in far-flung places, it is a great comfort to them and their families that they should be allowed to live out the remainder of their lives at home, here in Paris."

I could see that Dr. Gaudet was devoted to his nine patients. I thought it most fortunate that they should have such a dedicated physician to attend them. "Do your patients have special needs for their nutritional requirements?" I asked, returning to my previous line of questioning.

Now that the worst was over, Dr. Gaudet relaxed considerably, especially since I had not recoiled in horror at his shocking revelation. He assured me that the patients had no special requirements, but he himself was of the opinion that plain, wholesome foodstuff was best, simple preparations such as *pot-au-feu*, stews and braises – in short, exactly what I excelled at making. I could not see a reason *not* to take this job; it sounded absolutely perfect for me. But while the excellent salary was tempting, and the danger of exposure to the disease appeared to be minimal, I knew very little about leprosy (well, to be honest, I knew absolutely nothing about leprosy). I fought off a twinge of concern about the appearance of the patients; would I be affected as adversely as they seemed to affect others? I could only hope that my sense of compassion would override such shallow considerations.

I made a few quick notes and then gave them both a confident smile, more confident than I was feeling at that moment. "It sounds perfect for me, Doctor. But I need to see your facilities before I commit myself, and then I would better be able to give you a price for my services." I held my breath, wondering what Dr. Gaudet would say to my request. But his answer was immediately forthcoming.

"*Mais oui*, Mademoiselle," he said promptly. "We can go there now if you wish – our brougham is waiting on the corner. I am afraid I cannot say a great deal in favor of our kitchen facilities, but you will see for yourself." As he spoke, Sister Chantal tucked her rosary back into a fold of her robe, her face serene. I briefly left them sitting while I dashed upstairs for a hat and gloves, my heart beating with anticipation.

Making embarrassed apologies for the advanced age of the hospital's brougham, Dr. Gaudet handed me in and then helped the Sister to climb in beside me. The leather seats were indeed quite cracked and weathered, but I did not mind. We were soon on our way toward the Seine. It was only a few miles from my apartment and presently we were rattling through the Tuileries Palace gardens toward the Pont Royal Bridge. In the distance to our right could be seen the long shady parterres before the palace, looking green and inviting in the soft April morning light. The palace itself, although a royal residence, had not much to say for itself in my opinion – the buildings composing it were too long and low to lay claim to any architectural grandeur. But I had not been this way in some time so I gave myself over to enjoying the trip.

Once across the bridge we made our way to the Boulevard des Invalides, turning south. It came as no surprise to me that the leprosarium that was our destination should be located off this road, since there were a number of clinics and hospitals located in that vicinity of the city. Dr. Gaudet and Sister Chantal spoke but a little during the journey – no doubt they were pondering how this visit would turn out, as was I.

Presently the horses slowed almost to a stop, and I saw we had drawn alongside a tall wrought iron fence. The brougham turned into a long circular drive. As we passed between large black spear-point gates, they swung closed behind us. Now avidly curious, I peered out the age-dulled glass window to catch my first glimpse of the hospital.

I was pleasantly surprised to see that it did not resemble a hospital in the slightest; it was, in fact, a very old cloister, made of red stone, so that at a distance it gave the appearance of having been built of red brick. It rose three stories, with massive, ancient wood doors, and the tall, graceful spire of a chapel soared above the *façade*. It was a beautiful old building, full of character, and the grounds surrounding it, though small, were abundant with trees and flowers. But in spite of its ancient beauty, the building carried an unmistakable aura of secrecy about it. There was nothing about the *façade* to give away the residents within. Above the arching double doors was a sandstone plaque; as we drew closer I saw that it read: 'St. Giles Hospital founded 1860'. Dr. Gaudet saw me studying the carved plaque and smiled.

"St. Giles is the patron saint of Lepers," he explained. "There was once a hospital for lepers in London with the same name."

"What a lovely old building – was it a church?" I asked.

"This was a nun's cloisters for many years," he explained. "It is at least 400 years old. It was abandoned as a nunnery long ago and stood empty until the Church granted it to us for use as a hospital. As you will see, it suits our needs perfectly." We mounted the worn stone steps and Dr. Gaudet reached for a large, ornate door knocker, giving it three loud raps. Almost at once we heard the sound of a bar being pushed back, and one of the doors swung inward. We stepped inside.

My first impression was of spacious, ethereal beauty. We stood in a large, open room, obviously the chapel where services were conducted, and had been conducted for hundreds of years. The large, flat threshold stone had been worn smoothly into a dip in the middle from centuries of feet passing over it. On either end of this room a series of stained glass windows in brilliant colours gave the effect of being underwater. The windows appeared to depict scenes from the Crusades – knights on horses, heraldic images and similar scenes seemed to float across the walls. I caught my breath in admiration of their stunning beauty. Dr. Gaudet followed my gaze and nodded, acknowledging my reaction with pride.

"*Magnifiques*, are they not? We are very proud of our windows."

The nun who had admitted us now bowed and departed. Dr. Gaudet indicated a corridor through which he guided me with a hand respectfully under my elbow. "This is the hour our patients take their outdoor exercise, Mlle. Bessette, so they will be in the courtyard. I would like to show you first where we take our noon meal, if you will come with me."

We proceeded into a refectory room with several long tables and chairs, all clean and tidy, with small bouquets of flowers here and there along the tables. Books, mostly bibles and other religious tomes, were strewn about the room. My eye was drawn to a smoke-darkened, naïve painting of the Last Supper that inevitably covered one wall. It was surely several hundred years old, and it seemed to me that the apostles were sitting down to a rather abstemious meal. A wooden pulpit below the painting, with a bible resting open on its stand, indicated that the patients would be listening to a reading while they ate. It was a tranquil room in which to take a meal.

The small, dark room that housed the cooking facilities, if they could be called that, was quite another story. It was sadly lacking in modern conveniences, looking, in fact, as if not much had changed there in the last 400 years. Opening off the refectory, it was a narrow, dark, windowless room with a very ancient open fireplace at the far end. A squat black cook stove nestled into the soot-blackened fireplace opening was too small to be really useful. Everything, even the walls, was black with ancient soot and very dingy. It even smelled old. I looked around the room with a critical eye, finally turning back to the doctor.

"I can certainly understand why no one would want to cook here. Under these conditions it would be next to impossible to turn out anything remotely palatable," I said crisply.

The doctor gave an emphatic Gallic shrug. "*C'est ça*, Mademoiselle, as I have told you. But unfortunately there is no room to expand and as it is a historic building, impossible anyway. That is why we require a service such as yours."

We continued our tour through a few other rooms, including one that functioned as a clinic for the leprosy patients. This was Dr. Gaudet's domain, and he pointed out all its amenities with understandable pride. It was quite clean with a pervasive odor of antiseptic and carbolic soap, scents which pungently reminded me of my father's clinic. There were a great many bundles of cloth bandages

22

stacked on open shelving. Seeing me eyeing the bundles curiously, he explained they were used to wrap the hands and feet of the patients.

"Leprosy is seldom fatal, but over time, the patients lose all sensation in their hands and feet. We keep them bandaged in order to protect them from further damage." He continued to talk, and his talk began to take on the attributes of a lecture. By this time Sister Chantal had faded away, returning to her duties with a polite murmur to me, and we were alone. I began to sense that Dr. Gaudet was avoiding what was to me the most important part of the tour.

"May I meet some of your patients now, Doctor?" I interrupted finally, growing weary of hearing about the confusing-sounding scientific researches being conducted by Dr. Hansen in Norway. Dr. Gaudet obviously revered this paragon. He even had a framed portrait of him on the wall of his clinic.

Brought up short by my interruption, the poor doctor could no longer find excuses to postpone that part of the tour he was most hesitant to perform. "Oh yes, *certainement*, Mademoiselle," he said reluctantly. "Please follow me and I will escort you to the courtyard." We made our way rather more slowly back through the refectory toward a side door leading to the outside. As we went, Dr. Gaudet began to speak with feeling of the cruelty and prejudices of healthy people toward lepers throughout history, undoubtedly hoping to inspire my sympathy before I met his patients. I would have assured him this was unnecessary had he given me an opportunity to speak, but he carried on ceaselessly until we were outside.

Moving from the cool dimness of the cloister into the bright sunshine of the courtyard made me blink. Dr Gaudet abruptly fell silent. I looked around interestedly, and just a trifle apprehensively, I must admit. The idea of actually coming face to face with a leper victim here in the heart of Paris was so *bizarre*. I saw that the hospital courtyard was a simple square of paving stones and earth, dominated by an ancient sycamore tree rising from the middle. The trunk of the tree must have been five feet thick. It was planted underneath with mint and other aromatic herbs. Painted wooden benches were placed randomly about, while little beds of flowers and herbs flourished in the sun. The fragrant air of the courtyard was heavenly. A few nuns moved slowly across the open space, pushing patients in wheelchairs, but most of the other patients were ambulatory, strolling about holding their faces to the sun. I saw that those in wheelchairs appeared to have no toes at all, their feet were so foreshortened. All the patients had the carefully wrapped and bandaged hands that Dr. Gaudet had told me about.

As we stood in the courtyard looking around, we were approached by one of the more ambulatory patients, a kind-faced, round little gentleman whose hands were bandaged and whose countenance bore evidence of the ravages of the disease. His nose was flattened across his face. Around his forehead and mouth were several red, distressed-looking nodules. He was mostly bald, but had a fringe of wiry black and grey hair circling his head. He took me in with alert eyes that were black as a bird's, and then he smiled with that grotesque mouth. Under Dr. Gaudet's watchful eyes, he performed a graceful little bow before me.

"Mlle. Bessette," said Dr. Gaudet, "allow me to present Father Stèphane Barbier, one of the missionaries who reside here. Father Barbier worked in Africa for many years." He explained. "Mlle. Bessette is considering our offer to cook for us, Father."

Father Barbier fixed me with his bright, intelligent-looking eyes and steepled his thickly wrapped hands together in front of him, as though praying. "You will forgive me, my dear, if I do not offer you my hand, but please imagine that I have done so and we have just shaken hands heartily. It is indeed a rare pleasure to have such a lovely young person visit our home." He possessed a resonant, warm voice, and clearly an abundance of charm. Such sweet words uttered in a kindly voice, issuing from such a distorted countenance. I liked Father Barbier at once.

Dr. Gaudet smiled affectionately toward the short, rotund figure. "Father Barbier has always had the gift of speaking well; he was one of our most popular soldiers of God in his day," he said.

"I can well imagine," I said, "and thank you for the compliment, Father." I turned back to the good doctor. "I believe I will accept the position, Dr. Gaudet. I am sure we can arrive at agreeable terms for my contract." I offered him my hand, which he accepted, pumping it up and down eagerly. He was glowing with delight now that the outcome of my visit was all he could have hoped for.

We took our leave of the charming old missionary and strolled around the courtyard, where I was introduced to the other eight patients, and several attendant nuns. I am afraid I never did learn the names of all the nuns at the hospital, besides Sister Chantal. They were all rather interchangeable in their black habits and kindly attention to their patients. The patients were in various stages of the disease – for some, it revealed itself only in their carefully bandaged hands and a slight flattening of the nasal appendage. The sick missionaries all seemed in good spirits no matter what stage of the disease they were in. Finally Dr. Gaudet steered me back to the refectory where we sat at a long, scrupulously clean wood table and discussed meals, quantities, methods of preparation, bread and other comestibles. We settled on what seemed to be a very generous sum to be paid monthly, and I prepared to depart in the brougham which was to return me to my apartment.

"I shall have a contract drawn up and delivered by messenger as soon as it is ready, Mademoiselle," Dr. Gaudet assured me. "Do not forget, it will include your oath of secrecy, as the contract is contingent upon that very important matter," he added seriously as we walked toward the heavy wooden doors.

"*Bien sûr*. I understand completely. Shall I plan on beginning next week?" We settled the remaining details satisfactorily while waiting for the brougham to be brought around, then the doctor handed me in. The horses were whipped up; we trotted out the black gates and down the street. Swiveling around in the seat, I peered out the window and watched as they were pulled shut again with a loud clang. What a place!

The return trip was most enjoyable. I settled back against the stiff leather seat and indulged myself by feeling quite complacent and satisfied with the outcome of my meeting. I could go directly to the newspaper office this afternoon and cancel my advertisement, for this job would satisfy all my financial needs as well as take up a fair portion of my working day. The morning that had begun on a low note was ending on a high one, so I allowed myself a little time to enjoy the moment, and the beautiful spring afternoon. I would be very busy soon enough.

The contract with St. Giles Leprosarium was duly delivered and carefully perused over my afternoon tea. Finding it all in order, I was pleased to dip my pen into the inkpot and sign my name below the signature of Dr. Gaudet.

The secrecy clause was nothing, really, because there was no one to whom I could tell my secret even if I so wished. It certainly would not be likely to come up in casual conversation with the butcher down the lane, I thought wryly. I decided a little celebration was in order, so I slipped out and with a spring in my step, turned toward the *boutique de vin* for a split of champagne.

CHAPTER THREE

"I am not proud, but I am happy; and happiness blinds,
I think, more than pride."

A.D.

The following Sunday found me hovering over several large,
steaming pots as I busily prepared the chicken and beef
stocks that were to be the foundation of my soups for most of the
following week, and my first deliveries to the Hospital. Making stock
has always been one of my favorite activities. It is a peaceful, almost
meditative act, very soul-satisfying, creating so much goodness out of a
few odd bones, some onion, carrots and celery, a few herbs. Making a
mirepoix is almost a mystical process. I used my own dried herbs to
make little *bouquet garni*, two for each large pot. Steam covered the
glass of the windows and the kitchen was enveloped in fragrant
warmth. My hair kept trying to escape its net, sending damp tendrils
curling around my flushed face. Nevertheless, I was absurdly happy,
for at last I was doing exactly what I wanted to do.

I had already determined that I would accompany my first
delivery on the morrow, rather than simply see it loaded into a wagon
and sent on its way to St. Giles. No one expected me to come, but I
knew it would give me even more satisfaction if I could be there in
person. If necessary I could certainly walk home should a wagon or
brougham not be spared for a return trip. It was a journey of only a
few miles and I was in excellent physical condition.

I made arrangements with a local *boulangerie* on the Île de la Cité
to deliver a quantity of fresh-baked rolls first thing every morning, and
later today I planned to make two or three fruit tarts to round
everything out – it was to be their main meal of the day after all.

As I worked, stirring the stock and slicing the mushrooms and
onions that would be sautéed and added to the pots later, my thoughts
strayed, as they often did, to memories of my mother. Not of those
last two terrible years of her declining health, but of my childhood and
happier times. I spent many happy years at her side in the kitchen,
watching, learning and studying her recipes, now it felt as if she were
here with me. I could almost hear her reminding me not to let the
stock boil too hard. When my *papa* was alive we employed a cook, *bien
entendu*, but even so *maman* was often to be found working in the
kitchen right alongside her.

27

She had prepared these exact same recipes on a regular basis, delivering them to invalids and shut-ins not for monetary purposes, but out of the goodness of her heart. Eschewing the elegant restaurant cuisine prepared by the likes of M. Escoffier, my mother returned again and again to simple French peasant food. It was, she often said, the healthiest food in the world. I had not, alas, the luxury to be as generous as she, but I felt sure she would understand. As for myself, I found I was anticipating the next day as much as if I were going on a pleasure outing, not to a leper col…that is, a Leprosarium.

How odd that here in the heart of Paris such a place should exist, I mused to myself as I added finely chopped carrots and celery to the pots. One could not help but wonder what other peculiar things and people must exist in this sprawling old city, unknown and secret.

Had I but known, fate was already plotting to bring me face to face with the most peculiar person of all.

Monday morning found me putting the finishing touches on a pot of thick, creamy chicken mushroom soup and one of beef with rice. Two pretty fruit tarts, looking like gleaming red jewels, rested on the worktable. Spring meant raspberries and strawberries arriving in the markets from the country, a short but delightful season, so I had used these to make the tarts. This completed my first offering for St. Giles, and I was confident it would be satisfactory.

In due course a wagon drew up in the street beside my door and the driver dismounted, coming to the door with cap in hand to introduce himself as being in the employ of the Hospital. I recognized him at once as the man who had opened and closed the Hospital gates on my first visit there. His name was Robert, he told me, and he was here to fetch the meal. Robert was a dour, gloomy-faced man who appeared to be well into his fifties, roughly dressed in the manner of a workman. He was quite taken aback when I explained my intention of returning with him to the hospital. He did not appear to be particularly pleased about it, either.

Ignoring this, I assisted him to load everything into the back of the wagon. Exhibiting a practical turn of mind, Robert had fitted it up with wooden boxes to hold the pots firmly, thereby minimizing any splashing of the soup when the wheels hit a rut or drove over a rough patch in the road. I complimented him on this clever arrangement, receiving a grunt from that taciturn individual in return. The rest of the trip was made in complete silence. It was a silence I was soon to grow quite accustomed to.

My entrance into St. Giles behind the pots and baskets of food created quite a stir. Today, instead of drawing up to the front door of the cloister, Robert drove the wagon on around the building, stopping at a side door leading into a service area and thence to the refectory, so that I was able to walk directly into the refectory. Here I found eight of the leprosy patients seated at the long wood tables while the ninth, none other than my new friend Father Barbier, leaned on the pulpit I had noticed before, reading to them from the Bible. I comprehended at once why it was he who read aloud to the others: his voice was deeply timbered, resonant, commanding – so incongruous coming from that short, round figure. Sunlight streamed in from the open doors leading to the courtyard beyond. Vases of tulips decorated the long tables. It was a soothing, peaceful scene, but as soon as I entered Father Barbier stopped reading and stared at me blankly, causing all eyes to turn in my direction. At that moment I perceived Dr. Gaudet hurrying up to me, so I turned to greet him with a smile.

"My dear Mademoiselle Bessette, this is an unexpected pleasure! How is it that you have come here?" He asked, bowing over my hand. "It is not required of you, I hope you do not think you were expected to attend our meal as well as prepare it." He looked at me with a puzzled expression.

He could not imagine that anyone would actually desire to attend the meal, to sit at table with nine patients suffering from leprosy, but he was too good to say so out loud. He was not, however, dealing with just anybody, he was dealing with *me*.

"*Bonjour*, Dr. Gaudet, it's very nice to see you again. Do not worry about me, I come because I wish to, not because I thought it was required," I explained calmly. "Will you be serving the meal from that kitchen?" I pointed to the dim little medieval room I had seen on my first visit. This was obviously the case, because I had seen Robert carrying my pots into it.

"Yes, but…" Dr. Gaudet was so taken aback by my unexpected arrival, he could scarcely finish his sentence. I reminded myself how unaccustomed they were to having strangers here.

"*Merci*. I will just see if I can be of any help. Please do not worry about me." Smiling at him reassuringly, I proceeded directly to the kitchen. Here I found my pots and baskets had been set out on a very old mahogany trestle table, scarred and pitted from a century of hard use. Two nuns were preparing to serve the food, so I offered to assist them. Although both registered surprise at my abrupt and unexpected appearance, they were grateful for the help and we made short work of ladling up bowls of hot soup and plates of rolls. The soup's fragrance soon filled the little room, causing the nuns to cast longing glances at the contents of the pots each time they filled a bowl.

"You will have some too, will you not, Sisters?" I asked.

"Oh yes, we sit down to eat after the patients have eaten. Some of the patients cannot eat without help so we need to attend to them first," one of the nuns explained as she passed out into the refectory with a steaming bowl of soup in each hand. I had not thought of that. A quick vision of all those thickly bandaged hands, some appearing to be without digits, came into my head. It would be impossible for some of the poor things to even hold a spoon, much less carry it from bowl to mouth.

"I would be very pleased if you would allow me to help," I said cheerfully, following the second nun out of the kitchen with a happy heart.

On my way home that afternoon (the silent Robert acting as my chauffeur again so my worries of having to walk home came to naught) I was conscious of a feeling of satisfaction, of a job well done. I had assisted two of the patients in their repast, and found them to be gentle souls, very appreciative of my help, and everyone in the Hospital refectory appreciative of the food. Dr. Gaudet had been a bit shocked by my reckless behavior at first, to be sure, but he soon recovered himself. Taking me aside, he quickly explained what I should do to protect myself from undue exposure. Mainly, I was not to actually touch the patients, and before leaving for the day, I must stop at his clinic to have alcohol poured over my hands. I assured him I would follow his instructions when I returned the next day. Father Barbier, ever charming, paid me several compliments, especially about the berry tarts, of which he had two slices. He claimed he only wanted to see which he preferred, the raspberry or the strawberry.

After Robert and I had carried in all the empty pots and baskets, I turned to him with a friendly smile, tea kettle in hand. "I am going to have a cup of tea, Robert." I said. "Would you care for a cup before you return to St. Giles?"

Robert gave me such a horrified look, you would have thought I had just asked him if he would like to walk on hot coals. Shaking his head, he departed with such alacrity that I had to laugh. He must have thought me quite improper. Or perhaps he disliked tea.

My days soon fell into a comfortable pattern. I was busy much of the time, a state I much preferred over the previous weeks' inactivity, and I knew I was doing something worthwhile. It was such a good feeling to be needed. Mornings would find me downstairs, having had my *café* and a simple breakfast, apron on, hair bundled into a net, busy with my cooking. By late morning my pots would be full of rich, delicious *pot au feu* or stew, or sometimes meat pies and salads would be resting on the worktable.

Midday found me at St. Giles, helping those who needed help to eat. Dr. Gaudet had instructed me quite thoroughly on the precautions I needed to take when helping the patients, in order to protect myself from possible infection. After the meal, I would often sit near Father Barbier, enjoying a little wine while listening to stories of his days as a missionary in Africa, where he had been afflicted with this terrible disease. Afternoons were spent back in my kitchen, washing up and getting ready for the next day's work. Then I would put my feet up with a cup of tea or *café* before going out to do any necessary shopping.

On Saturdays and Sundays, I took long walks in a wide radius all around my apartment, often venturing as far as the Louvre and other museums and art galleries. I had never been to this *quartier* prior to moving into it, so I wanted to familiarize myself with my new neighborhood. I never ventured to attend church on Sunday – I disliked having to do so alone, and I had nothing appropriate to wear. Sometimes I browsed the musty old bookstore I had discovered a few blocks away. Reading was my greatest pleasure and since I had not an opportunity to further my education, I read to fill up some of the empty spaces in my head with knowledge. Occasionally, however, I would succumb to the lure of a novel instead, although not without a certain sense of guilt over the wasted time. My favorite novelist was Alexandre Dumas. I devoured The Three Musketeers, Count of Monte Cristo, and the Man in the Iron Mask. All of France eagerly

31

awaited the completion of his next novel, but alas, it was not to be, because Dumas was fated to die before the year was out.

It was a pleasure to escape from my quiet existence into such tales of romance, intrigue and dashing swordsmen from times long past. I particularly felt for poor Kitty, the ladies' maid who loved the handsome, dashing D'Artagnan, though her steadfast love availed her naught. His heart had already been pledged to another, and Kitty never had a chance. What hope could a mere ladies' maid have with D'Artagnan, after all? He would have considered her as being beneath his notice.

CHAPTER FOUR

'Oh, pray do, for heaven's sake, tell us all about -- is he a
vampire, or a resuscitated corpse, or what?'
A.D.

It was on an ordinary Market Day in that extraordinary summer of 1870 that I made the acquaintance of the woman who was fated to usher in all the strange events that would change my life forever. I only met Madame Celestine Giry in the first place because I was trying to do her a kindness. If I had not stopped to assist her...well, it did not seem to be a particularly momentous meeting at the time, but it certainly turned out to be one, for myself and for a number of others as well.

I had been working at St. Giles since early summer. I suppose because the life I led was so quiet and uneventful, my favorite day of the week was Market Day Wednesday, when I could browse among the vendors selling meats and poultry, herbs and spices, vegetables, flowers and fruits. Our street was a little hub of domestic commerce, and the street market had been held there every Wednesday for untold years. All I had to do was walk out my kitchen door to be surrounded by activity and all sorts of good things. This was one of the primary attractions of my location. It meant being awakened very early on Wednesday morning when the vendors came from the outskirts of the city to set up their stalls and wagons, but I didn't mind, even though not all the smells emanating from them were pleasant ones. At first light I could step out onto the balcony with a cup of *café au lait* to see which vendors were setting up who had something I wanted for the week's cooking, and admire the brightly colored awnings, signs and displays. I became acquainted with most of the vendors, and it was quite pleasant to wander from stall to stall, exchanging greetings and listening to them extolling the silvery freshness of their *poisson* or the perfection of a little punnet of *fraises*.

The Wednesday street market was also the best day, from an economic point of view, for me to obtain my weekly supplies for St. Giles. It was expected that one would haggle a bit with the vendors over prices, whereas it would have been rude to haggle when buying from the shops. I was an excellent negotiator; if I could save a bit for book money out of my monthly salary, so much the better.

33

As I made the rounds of the stalls that morning no premonition came over me that my life was about to be altered completely and forever, or that darkness and danger were so close at hand. It was a beautiful morning, warm and inviting. The shade of the plane trees lining our street was welcome and the vendors clustered their open wagons under the spreading branches as much as possible. I had a wide wicker basket over my arm, and was selecting ripe tomatoes from a cart when I heard someone give a shout of warning. Looking up sharply at the cry, I was just in time to observe one of the donkeys, having been kicked by a compatriot, accidentally knock a woman down flat in the street. She was unable to catch herself, owing to having a bundle in her arms, so it was a hard fall onto the cobblestones.

The owner of the donkeys was completely occupied in getting them back under control. Since I was closest to the woman, I hastened to her at once.

"Are you injured, Madame?" I asked, bending down to her.

"Only my pride," was her surprisingly composed reply. I saw that she was an attractive lady, perhaps in her late thirties, with fair, fresh skin and big blue eyes, with thick auburn hair bundled into a net at the nape of her neck. She wore an unstylish, rather loosely cut grey silk dress. She reminded me of a governess or a teacher.

As I helped her to sit up, I noticed that one of her black stockings was torn at the ankle, revealing pale skin beneath scraped raw. She must have caught it on the rough stone curb when she fell.

"Oh dear; you *are* hurt!" I exclaimed. At the sight of her wound, I made an impulsive decision. "I live just there, where you see the flowers in the window," I said, gesturing with my free hand. "Come in for a moment and I'll make you some tea and you can tidy up."

She considered my offer while scowling formidably at the small crowd that had formed around us, including the profusely apologetic owner of the donkey, then rose to her feet gracefully, imperiously declining any assistance with rising.

"Thank you, that would be very kind," she said, accepting my invitation. She brushed off her skirts while I held her bundle – it was full of flowers and various items she had already purchased at the Market that morning. Exhibiting remarkable *sang-froid* under the circumstances, she grasped her bundle in one arm and extended her other hand to me.

"Permit me to introduce myself. My name is Madame Giry, and I am on my afternoon off from the Opera House." She inclined her head toward where the massive bulk of that unseen structure would be located.

I took her hand and smiled. "My name is Madame Sylvie Bessette and I am very pleased to make your acquaintance, Madame Giry." Taking her arm, I steered her to my door. "I suppose I must be Madame Bessette, although to be quite truthful, I prefer to think of myself as Mademoiselle." Naturally my new acquaintance had no idea how to respond to this odd statement so she prudently kept quiet.

Once inside the kitchen, I invited her to take a chair while I carefully placed my lovely tomatoes in a basket and put the kettle on for tea. Madame Giry looked around the room interestedly, taking in everything, her bright blue eyes seeming to miss nothing.

"Do you own a *café* by any chance?" She asked at last.

"Not exactly – it is more like a catering business. I prepare meals here and transport them to a small private hospital nearby. I live in the apartment above," I explained, punctuating my words by pointing up at the ceiling. "If you will remove your stocking, I have medical supplies upstairs and I can help you clean and disinfect your ankle."

Madame Giry took a moment to examine a gold watch pinned to her jacket lapel. "*Très bien*, if it would not be too much trouble. I believe I am still bleeding."

Dashing upstairs, I returned shortly with my medical kit and alcohol and gauze to clean the scrape. I always keep such supplies on hand in case I should have an accident in the kitchen. Burns and knife cuts are the common injuries of cooks and I have had my share.

Kneeling before my guest, I carefully tweezed a few bits of gravel from the scrape. "I am sorry, Madame, but this will sting a bit," I warned as I prepared to place a gauze pad with alcohol over it. While disinfecting the scrape with alcohol, I felt compelled to elaborate on my rather incongruous comment about my marital status. "Please allow me to explain my wish to be addressed as 'Mademoiselle'. You see, while I was once married for a short period of time, I no longer have a husband. He did not pass on, however; I...I divorced him. After that I reverted back to my original surname, and I have endeavored since then to forget that entire part of my life. And so I really do feel as if I were Mademoiselle Bessette, *vous comprenez*. To be addressed as a Madame makes me feel as if I were still married." At this repugnant idea, I shuddered involuntarily. I was a little discomfited to have revealed such personal information about myself to a virtual stranger, but something about Madame Giry's calm, alert face made me feel comfortable with her.

"Ah, I see," she said, giving me a shrewd glance. "It was not a happy marriage, then. I understand about that, probably better than you think. Do not trouble yourself further with explanations, Mademoiselle Bessette." She smiled at me in an understanding way, and I found myself warming to her as we talked.

"There," I said, having cleaned the scrape and secured a clean piece of gauze over it. "You will be as good as new. I will serve the tea while you put your stocking back on."

"You are a very efficient nurse, Mlle. Bessette," said Madame Giry, examining her ankle.

Placing the tea tray on the table, I smiled. "My late father was a family physician, Madame. I am very familiar with basic medical procedures. At one time I thought of training as a nurse, but then my father passed away unexpectedly and there was no money for the training."

Having dispensed with the formalities, we were now at liberty to enjoy our tea and a little conversation about less personal topics. We were soon talking as easily as if we were old friends. I was fascinated to learn that she both lived and worked at the Opéra Populaire, being a girls' ballet instructor at the Conservatory. She liked to walk to the Wednesday market on her morning off to buy flowers and pick up a few trifles for herself and her young daughter, Meg, also one of the student dancers. I recollected that from my balcony I could see the rooftop of the Opera House, so it was actually fairly close by. I had not, however, ever had cause to enter it.

"It has only been open for ten years," Madame Giry explained. "I have been fortunate indeed to have worked there from the beginning. I know it well after all this time. Did you know there are seventeen stories in all, of which seven are below ground level?"

I confessed I did not know.

"Why are there so many underground?" I asked, genuinely curious.

"Oh, for storage mostly. The first levels are for the dormitories, sleeping apartments, dressing rooms and so on, but as you go further down, it is where many props, equipment and stage furniture are stored. I do not myself venture to the lower levels except occasionally to see…to see that none of the girls go wandering about there by themselves." It had sounded as if she was about to say something else, but changed her mind at the last instant.

We shared an enjoyable half hour chatting about her work and mine, before Madame Giry, noticing the time, rose to take her leave. As I walked her to the door, she turned impulsively back to me.

"This has been a most pleasant conversation, and I thank you again for coming to my assistance this morning. Would you like to join me for a coffee at the Opera Café one day soon? It is but a few blocks from here, next to the Opera House, on the Boulevard des Capucines." I was quick to accept the invitation, and we soon fixed on the forthcoming Friday to meet for coffee. I returned to my kitchen with high hopes that I had just made a new friend. It seemed to me that my new life was sorting itself out nicely.

From that point on, I and Madame Giry (or Celestine as she asked me to call her when our friendship had progressed) met almost weekly at either the Opera Café or in my kitchen for afternoon tea and gossip, and now and then I would invite Celestine and her daughter to my apartment for dinner. Meg turned out to be a very pretty girl of fifteen, with long blond hair and a tendency to be almost as curious about the world as myself. Celestine doted on her with obvious pride. Like myself and my own mother (while she lived, that is), they were alone in the world, Celestine's husband having been dead for many years. Celestine had herself been a ballet dancer in a travelling troupe when young, but she had long since turned to instruction as a means of supporting herself and Meg.

Although Celestine had what one might call a formidable personality, away from her work at the Opera she could be very amusing. She was a mine of stories and little snippets of gossip about the people who lived and worked at the Opera House, from the singers, performers, dancers, backstage hands to even the Manager himself. She had little respect for the business acumen of the manager. She seemed to know everything that went on upstairs and down. And always she complained about her pupils: the young girls training to become ballerinas on the stage. Of her own sweet daughter, upon whom she utterly doted, she would complain the most.

Although I did drop rather obvious hints from time to time, Celestine did not seem inclined to offer me a tour of the Opéra Populaire, nor was I invited to dinner or coffee with her there. I puzzled over this as it seemed rather antisocial behavior, but it would have been rude to inquire, so I said nothing. Perhaps she did not have the means to entertain guests, and was too embarrassed to say so.

All her colorful stories about the Opera House and its denizens naturally ignited my curiosity about the place, especially the underground storage cellars. Most fascinating of all, there existed, if her stories could be believed, a lake of water deep underneath the building. A lake! When I asked her if she had ever seen it, her expression became suddenly guarded.

"I have not," was her short and succinct reply, and then she changed the subject. I did not renew my question.

The one difficulty in my blossoming friendship with Celestine was my own work. I had by now told her all about my life prior to our meeting, and she was as understanding and sympathetic as any friend could possibly be. But she was naturally curious about my catering business (as she thought it was) after spending time in my kitchen and seeing how cooking occupied my days until each afternoon. She was also a very appreciative recipient of my dinners.

Perhaps because our occupations were so different, she was as interested in my work as I was in hers. I dislike having to tell a lie, but I had to stretch the truth a bit when, in answer to her question about what sort of hospital I catered for, I explained that it was a small private hospital for victims of fire. I had to tell her *something*, and it was the first thing that came into my head. Since I was bound by oath to preserve the secret of the Leprosarium, I thought this presented a reasonable explanation for why the patients did not venture out and their meals had to be brought to them. They were, I explained, badly disfigured, some crippled, and preferred not to mingle in society because rude people stared and made comments about their appearances. I carefully avoided telling her the hospital's exact location, giving her a vague direction on the Île de la Cité that seemed to satisfy.

All in all I was rather pleased with my slight alteration of the truth. It certainly seemed to strike Celestine. After her first, politely interested inquiry, she gave me her full attention, expressed sympathy for the poor patients, and asked a number of additional questions regarding the extent of their injuries. She inquired particularly about how badly disfigured their faces were. This required further exaggerations on my part, but having committed myself to my fire story, it was necessary to continue as I had begun. I had no way of knowing at the time why she was so particularly interested in my mythical burn victims and their injuries, but I was soon to learn her reason. Celestine had her own secret to keep.

We were sitting over coffee at one of the Opera Café's outdoor tables a few days later. It was a warm June afternoon and the sunshine was making me sleepy, so I had ordered a cup of the strong coffee they served to help me wake up. It was the first time I had seen Celestine since I had been forced to produce such a pack of lies about my work, and I had to conceal my dismay when she began asking me yet again about the patients. What did the most disfigured one look like?

I could not fathom her fascination with this unpleasant subject, or why she insisted on talking about it, but she was regarding me alertly, waiting for my answer. Frankly puzzled over her morbid interest in disfigured faces, I considered how I ought to respond. The *most* disfigured of the leprosy patients was Father Didier, an older missionary no longer able to walk or feed himself. His face was terrible to look at – nose flattened completely, lips virtually gone, his face covered with unsightly and painful red nodules. In spite of all Dr. Gaudet's efforts, these nodules never seemed to disappear, only increase in size and number. The problem was how to translate Father Didier's face into one of my mythical burn victims. I must make an effort to do so, for clearly Celestine would not give up until she knew.

"Well," I began after a moment's thought, "one poor gentleman lost his nose and has scars from burns over most of his face. He also lost most of his hair, and his hands were almost burned off, so he needs help to feed himself. But in spite of his dreadful appearance, he has become a favorite of mine. In fact all the patients have become rather dear to me."

Celestine gazed at me speculatively. "But Sylvie," she asked after a moment, "how can you bear to be around them, if they are so dreadful to look upon?" An odd, almost calculating look came into her eyes as she spoke. She watched me intently while waiting for my reply, as though it were of great import.

Her obviously sincere interest made me try hard to explain, but it was difficult to put into words. "Oh, well," I said with a little hand flutter, "they are not beautiful, indeed they are not. But that is of no matter to me - they are only human after all, and are not to blame for their terrible affliction, only pitied. I feel for them, Celestine." I hoped she could understand.

"Besides, my salary is so generous, it more than makes up for any discomfort I might be supposed to feel," I added with a gay smile. It was a little ruse on my part to distract sharp-minded Celestine from asking any more questions about my patients. It would be nice if she would let this subject drop away and take up another, any other, subject that did not require further fabrications on my part.

She set her cup down in its saucer with care, and studied me for a moment. "I wonder…" her voice trailed off; she was lost in thought. "You must think me very odd, asking you all these questions, but I have a good reason, I assure you." She paused. I *did* think her odd, but I was too polite to voice my thought.

"Why are you being so mysterious this afternoon, Celestine?" I asked her instead. "This isn't like you."

She gave a little nod, as though suddenly making up her mind at last to tell me something. I was inwardly relieved, for I did not like the idea that she was keeping secrets from me.

"Yes, yes I believe you would be perfect, Sylvie. You are compassionate, and you would not be…put off. You would be just the person. It is almost like a gift from Providence that we met and became friends! But I must…" again she paused, thinking. I waited, watching her, puzzled. Finally she went on.

"Well, I have a friend, he has a…a disfigurement that prevents him from coming into society. This is why I asked you all those impertinent questions, Sylvie. I help him when he needs things, and I have been taking meals to him when I can but I am so busy now – those girls, they take so much of my time. *You* could do it, though; you spend time among those fire victims every day. It would be highly unlikely that you would ever see him, but if that should happen, rest assured he always wears a mask." She stopped and drew breath. I had never heard her talk so much at one time. "I must speak with him first, and tell him about you. You would have to be presented to him very carefully or he would very likely refuse the suggestion. He is so very cautious about strangers. But I think if I recommended you, he would be amenable. He trusts me; he knows I have his best interests at heart. And he would reward loyal service generously, I assure you." Celestine leaned toward me across the table.

"Would you consider it, Sylvie?"

Ah, now we came to it. My ears had perked up at the word, *disfigurement*, at least I now understood the intent of all her pointed inquiries. Smiling gently, I said, "I had no idea you had such a friend. Why have you not mentioned him before? That is an odd coincidence indeed. Does he live nearby the Opera?"

"Yes, he does. It would only be a daily dinner, delivered to…delivered nearby. And I am sure he would pay handsomely for your time and trouble. But let me speak to him first. And you must promise...promise never to tell a soul about this." With this last sentence her voice became urgent, serious.

"Not tell anyone – but why?" I asked, feeling slightly exasperated that all my clients seemed to require oaths of secrecy. Weren't there any normal invalids in Paris? But if I am to be completely straightforward, my exasperation was tempered by her hints of a handsome salary. She well knew it was my weak point; something or other was always needed for the kitchen, after all. Celestine was attempting to answer my question, so I returned my attention to her.

"As I told you, my dear, he is disfigured, rather badly I believe. Unfortunately, it is on his face. I do not know in what way exactly, or how, but I believe it was some dreadful childhood injury. It has made him reclusive in the extreme. People have treated him badly, scorned him, even tormented him for it. People can be so shallow and stupid!" she added fiercely, her eyes flashing. "That is the reason I have not told you of him before. I have to respect his wishes and his privacy."

"And you care for him, I can tell," I said sympathetically, patting her hand. What a sad circumstance. Unlike my patients at the hospital, this poor man had endured his misfortune since childhood. He had endured a lifetime of torment and loneliness, and all because of something he had no control over: he was disfigured.

Celestine gave me a rueful little smile. "*Oui, c'est vrai.* I have known him for years and he is always good to me, always kind. But you must understand, he hates most people, shuns them and only wants to be left alone, in peace. He is a recluse. I must warn you that he would never want to see you, or want you to see him." She looked at me intently. "Will you promise?"

I took a moment before answering to ponder this sad, pathetic and disfigured man. Of course my interest was piqued, my sympathies aroused. Poor soul! I certainly knew how callous and insensitive 'normal' people could be to those who were different, for Dr. Gaudet had spoken very passionately to me about that very thing.

My mind made up, I said, "*Très bien*, Celestine, I will agree to try it and see how it works out. Do speak to your friend. I would be happy to cook his evening meals and deliver them, and I promise to keep your secret. But what is his name? How will we communicate with each other?"

Celestine gave a sudden start and stole a glance at the little gold watch pinned to her bodice. "Oh, la, is that the time?" She stood up quickly, adjusting her hat. "I must get back to the Opera. I have a lesson in a few moments. I dare not be late; I am always after those girls about tardiness." She smiled at me. "Thank you, Sylvie my dear. I will speak with you again soon." Collecting her bag and parasol, she paid for her coffee and hurried from the café with rapid, graceful strides.

Perplexed, I watched her rapidly retreating form and then sat lost in thought for a little while longer, finishing my now-cool coffee. Why had Celestine bustled off without answering my questions? My curiosity was definitely aroused. She was hiding something from me. Someone so disfigured that he felt compelled to wear a mask even when alone must be very damaged indeed.

CHAPTER FIVE

'...Now hovered like a phantom...'
A.D.

Several days passed before I heard again from Celestine, and then I received a surprising note from her inviting me to visit her at the Opera House at long last. She even went so far as to offer me a little tour. If I arrived early in the morning, none of the theatre people would be at work yet so we would be able to move about freely. She was looking forward to being able to introduce me to her home and place of work as I had introduced her to mine. Naturally to refuse was out of the question. I had always wondered why Celestine never reciprocated my invitations for tea or dinner. I suspected her purpose in doing so now was to convey news to me about her friend. I eagerly accepted her invitation for the next morning, therefore, and then prepared myself for a very long day.

In order to make everything work out, I toiled late that evening in the kitchen to prepare for the following day. Though I was rather tired the next morning, I still managed to be up, appropriately gowned, gloved, hatted and out the door in good time. If I was eager to experience the imagined pleasures that awaited me at the Opéra Populaire, I would not admit it to you, Reader. You may infer whatever you like.

I had decided to walk, for it was a lovely day, and I had not yet ventured in that direction. I was taken aback, however, by how broad and busy the boulevards were surrounding the Opera House. It was some time before I was able to cross the Boulevard Haussmann without fear of being knocked over by a carriage.

The main approach to the building was along the appropriately-named Avenue de l'Opéra, which led directly into the wide, sweeping forecourt of that imposing structure. It had to be wide, in order to accommodate the many carriages that would line the long entry way every evening before a performance. This morning, however, the forecourt was empty save for a few people coming and going to purchase tickets.

Entering those doors for the first time, I was conscious of growing excitement – how curious I had become about this place after listening to all Celestine's stories. I found myself standing in a huge foyer, with a soaring ceiling, grand, sweeping staircases, ornate candelabra and gaslights that must produce a magnificent spectacle at night when all would be afire. There was a vast quantity of marble, gilt and statuary. The intricate inlaid parquet floors were amazing works of art in marble and colored stone.

As I stood gaping about me like a sightseer from the country visiting the Louvre for the first time, I beheld Celestine walking up to me with a welcoming smile on her face, her hand outstretched to take mine. She escorted me to her and Meg's rooms first, where we took coffee and croissants together, since I had not had breakfast yet.

"Where shall we begin?" I asked eagerly once my breakfast was finished.

"I am going to show you the theatre itself, Sylvie. This is the only time of day when the stage is empty, so we will not be in the way of any preparations. After that, if you like we can go up on the roof. I assure you the view of the city is well worth climbing all those stairs."

I was a little disappointed in her response. "Can we not venture down into the underground levels?" I asked. "I would love to see the underground lake you told me about." The idea of the dark water far below was so delightfully eerie and mysterious, like something out of a gothic novel. I looked at Celestine hopefully.

"Not today," she replied firmly. "There is nothing to see down there. It is dark and dusty." Taking a little peek at her watch, Celestine rose briskly. "*Allons*, Sylvie. It won't do for us to be late."

"Late for what?" I asked, concealing my disappointment as I followed her to the door.

Celestine looked a trifle disconcerted when she answered me. "Oh, I only meant, we must go now so that we will not be in anyone's way on the stage. After that, it is of no matter where we go."

I followed her through a maze of corridors and rather tatty-looking rooms full of props, costumes, and building supplies. It was not particularly clean and I could not help but notice one or two people appeared to have collapsed and fallen asleep in the hallways. The prostrate bodies had a pervasive odor of stale alcohol clinging to them, an odor with which I was unfortunately all too familiar. I made sure to keep my skirts held well above my ankles.

Presently Celestine led the way up a set of sturdy but worn wood stairs. We slipped past a wave of heavy wine-colored curtains that hung suspended from far above us yet brushed the floorboards, and she led me out into the middle of the stage. Taking my arm, she held her other arm out in an expansive gesture, inviting me to gaze out over the stage with its unlit footlights and into the vast, shadowy expanse of the Opera House itself. Dust motes floated through the still air on a beam of sunlight coming from somewhere far above, giving that enormous space a magical, mysterious appearance.

"Well, Sylvie," she said proudly, "here is where I work and here is where my heart is. What do you think?"

I looked, wide-eyed and fascinated, out over row upon row of plush upholstered seats.

I had *never* seen anything quite like this – the ceiling rose above all into a far away dome, painted to look like the blue sky of day, with little white clouds floating in it and angelic cherubs bearing banners twisting in the wind. It reminded me of how the ceilings of cathedrals were sometimes painted. From the very apex hung the most enormous, glittering, fabulous chandelier I had ever beheld. On the other hand, I tried to avoid looking at the gigantic, golden statues of well-endowed females that adorned the theatre balconies. They were in a shocking state of undress that made me blush. I found myself self-consciously glancing down at my own endowments, realizing that proportionately they were quite similar. A little movement far up on one of the balconies caught my eye: squinting, I made out two rather bulky cleaning women busy dusting and tidying to make the theatre ready for that evening's performance. I could only imagine how long it would take to clean every aisle and seat in that enormous space.

Celestine's voice interrupted my wide-eyed gazing. "It is beautiful, *n'est-ce pas?*" She said proudly.

I turned at once and smiled at her. "It is a magical place, Celestine." I answered warmly. "How fortunate you are to be able to live and work in such a magnificent building. I have never seen anything like it."

The silence around us was profound. Our steps as we wandered here and there on the stage were loud on the floorboards, and sent an echo throughout the empty theatre. What acoustics it must have! I laughed a bit nervously at the loud sound of our steps. As we strolled, looking about, I noticed that Celestine glanced up several times into the shadowy space over the stage where we stood. Following the direction of her glances, I beheld what looked like rope and wood bridges spanning the open space above, with cat walks, ropes and pulleys everywhere. It was dark and dim, but the space appeared quite large to me. Thanks to the clever placement of a short fringed curtain hanging at the top edge of the stage, it would be completely invisible to anyone seated in the audience.

"My goodness," I murmured, staring up into that dark expanse.

"*Je sais;* you see, that is the realm of the stagehands who work the curtains and some of the props that descend from above during performances," she explained. Celestine took my arm to draw me away, but we were suddenly interrupted.

A tearful young girl appeared from the wings and called to Celestine hesitantly. She was obviously one of her younger ballet students. Excusing herself apologetically, Celestine hurried to her. Left to myself, I turned back to look out again over the vast, empty Opera House, wondering what it would be like to stand on this stage in the evening, when it was packed with people, the lights were all lit, the magnificent chandelier glowing brilliantly, the orchestra pit overflowing with music. Clasping my hands together in front of me, I gazed, imagined, and sighed a little wistfully.

All at once as I was standing there, I felt the hairs on the nape of my neck rise. I could feel eyes on me, I was sure of it. Someone, somewhere close, was watching me. I looked around quickly, but Celestine was still talking to her distraught student. No one else was in sight except the cleaning ladies busy in the upper aisles, and they were not looking in my direction. My sense of unease grew and I took a few steps back toward Celestine.

I could not help myself - my eyes were drawn back up into the dark recesses above our heads. There was something about that space that made me ill at ease, but I could not say why exactly. Even as I raised my eyes upward again, searching for my unseen watcher, I caught a quick glimpse of something moving there in the shadows: a flash of white, a blacker shadow against lighter ones. Not out on the rope bridge directly above, but along one side of the wall, where it was darker. A little thrill of fear went down my spine. I stared harder, trying to make out what was lurking up there, but nothing could now be seen.

The feeling of being watched passed, but a strong sense of unease lingered. I shivered, hugging myself even though it was not cold.

Celestine sent her student on her way and took my arm. "Such a fuss over a torn costume," she said ruefully. As she led me back the way we had come, she gave one last quick upward glance.

Seeing her preoccupation with that dark space, I seized the opportunity to ask, "What is it, Celestine? Is someone up there?"

She shook her head. "No, my dear, no one would be up there at this time of the day. It is too early."

"But I thought I saw something moving up there, just a moment ago. It was something dark."

Celestine waved her hand dismissively. "If you saw someone up there, it would only be one of the stagehands, Sylvie. Come, I want to show you the view from the roof." And with that, we departed the stage. I was not sorry to go. We duly visited the roof, enjoyed the stunning view, and then I took my leave of Celestine in order to get back to my kitchen. Not once did she mention her friend and the possibility of my cooking for him.

Which was perplexing, because why else had she invited me today?

Several days passed. Busy with my own occupations, making the most of summer's bounty, and taking long, pleasant walks along the Seine, I forgot about the matter of Celestine's friend until I looked up to see her hastening toward me as I was making my way through the stalls next Market Day.

"*Bon matin*, Sylvie!" Celestine called out cheerfully. "I have good news. Let us go inside where we can talk." She took my arm, steering me rapidly back to my door, her face glowing. She had been shopping, and held a small pink paper parcel of sweets from a confectioner's shop that I guessed were a treat for Meg.

I had just purchased a quantity of lovely red cherries fresh from the south and perfect for filling a clafoutis, so I was glad to be able to put them down in the cool of the kitchen *garde-manger*. Perfectly ripe cherries have a tendency to grow overripe in the blink of an eye. After seeing them safely tucked away, I turned to Celestine.

"Good news? About your friend?"

"*Oui*, but of course," she replied. "I have had a letter from him this morning. He is perfectly satisfied with you - he has agreed to pay you forty *francs* a day for his evening meal, but you will need to deliver it to him, as he will not leave the...will not venture out, as I have told you." She stopped to catch her breath, looking at me expectantly.

"Forty *francs*?" I exclaimed. "That...that is more than I dared hope for." I was astonished, but pleased. "He must be quite comfortably off then," I added deliberately, hoping Celestine would take the hint and elaborate a bit, but she did not.

"Well, I told him you will require a carriage for the delivery since it is too far for you to walk, so he wished to make sure the amount would cover such expenses. He is invariably kind and generous to those who are loyal to him, and who follow his instructions."

I looked at her blankly. "What instructions?"

Celestine smiled at me reassuringly. "It is nothing, Sylvie. You remember I told you he would not want to see you? That is an important part of his instructions. Don't be concerned, *ma chère*. I am certain he will be pleased with you."

"Oh yes, *bien sûr*." Recalling our previous conversation, I remembered the particular emphasis she placed on his desire not to see or be seen, as well as the need for secrecy in general. "But I thought he might wish to give me instructions about his meal preferences. *Et aussi*, you said he lives near the Opera House. Where exactly am I to go?"

Celestine, looking satisfied, rose at once and reached into a pocket of her black silk gown. "Everything you need to know is here, Sylvie. Just follow the instructions and all will be well. As for his preferences, he told me to say, he is indifferent as to what you prepare as long as it is delivered promptly. I must be going now." As she was speaking, she pulled a crisp envelope from the folds of her gown and placed it carefully on the table. It was edged in black, like a funeral notice. The outside of the envelope was blank, containing no direction whatsoever.

She was halfway out the door when she stopped and added, "He expects you to begin tonight; I hope that is all right. *Au revoir*, my dear." And then with a rustle of her skirts she was gone.

I was much struck by one of the things Celestine had just told me: her friend was indifferent to what I made for him? It was possible that what he had been given thus far was indifferent in quality, or perhaps he had a poor appetite due to his injuries, whatever they might be. The poor man. I would, I vowed, do my best to do away with that indifference. All at once I thought of something – I dashed to the door and looked out, but Celestine had already disappeared around the corner. Stamping my foot in frustration, I closed the door rather more forcefully than necessary. I had forgotten to ask her his name! *Bien*, no doubt I would find it appended to the bottom of his note to me.

Glancing up at my clock, I saw that I was behind schedule, so I picked up the envelope and tucked it carefully out of the way. I had no time to open and read it now. It was past time to start the mid-day meal for St. Giles, and I was going to have to hurry to get everything ready in time. I turned my complete attention to making the pastry for the cherry clafoutis and making *pistou* with the fragrant green bunches of fresh basil I had acquired at the market that morning.

The letter from Celestine's friend lay forgotten for the rest of the day, until I returned from the hospital, when I finally sat down and opened it while I had my tea.

After tea I went back downstairs to begin preparing my first dinner for my new client. I had devoted much thought to this as I went about my day's duties. I had perused all my mother's tattered recipes as well as some new ones I had set aside to try when the opportunity presented itself. I wanted my first meal to be nutritious, *naturellement*, but something else as well. I imagined that, for someone forced to live away from the world, in self-imposed isolation, there would not be much time out of doors, in the sunshine. So perhaps something warm and spicy would do the trick.

I found the perfect recipe tucked away with some others *ma mère* had collected but never attempted, for they were all exotic and foreign. I had no idea where she found them, but the one called Moroccan chicken tagine caught my eye. The ingredients it called for made me think of sunshine and exotic climes. It was necessary, *bien sûr*, to adapt the recipe because it required a special kind of pot. It was served with an exotic ingredient called *couscous*, apparently some sort of grain. I decided rice would do nicely in place of that, whatever it was. The chicken would be wholesome and the preserved lemons redolent of sunshine and warmth. And there were lovely olives resting in a crock in my larder. Welcoming the chance to try something so unusual and interesting, I slipped my pinafore apron over my head, put a net over my hair and started browning the chicken.

Once the covered casserole dish containing my tagine went in to the oven I could relax a bit. Removing my apron and hair net, I poured myself a small glass of sherry and stood at the shop window looking out. Although I was ostensibly watching people come and go down the lane, I was actually pondering my odd instructions for the delivery of my first dinner. Strict instructions, Celestine had reminded me, penned by her friend himself in an elegant but rather peculiar script, in blood-red ink. The note was now lying open on my worktable. I picked it up and read it again for at least the tenth time.

"Dear Madame,

Please follow these instructions to the letter and we shall have no difficulties. Deviate from them, and there will be difficulties.

You will bring a meal to me each evening at six p.m. It cannot be later. Mark that if you please. You are to proceed from Blvd. Haussmann down X Street [1] *until you reach a large window on your left which will have some red paint on the glass. You should have no difficulty identifying it. You will pass through the window and leave the tray on a shelf on the opposite side of the room. The room is unoccupied so there will be no impediment. You will then depart <u>at once</u>. Do not linger, and do not attempt to penetrate further into the building. To do so would be quite dangerous, I assure you.*

I look forward to a successful association with you. Madame Giry assures me you are an excellent chef.

Best Regards, O.G."

It was an unsettling missive, to be sure - politely worded, but containing several veiled threats. I tried to shake off my vague forebodings, however. I reminded myself that Celestine was his friend after all, and would never have suggested this arrangement if there was any real danger to me. Still, what a peculiar place to leave a hot meal: in an apparently vacant building. Part of me rather looked forward to solving this little mystery.

---

[1] *Note to the reader: It must be stated that I have deliberately made these directions vague. Many years have passed, and it would not do to have people trying to find their way to such a dangerous and long-abandoned place.*

I sipped my sherry and daydreamed while a warm, lemony fragrance perfumed my kitchen. In my mind I conjured up a pleasing image of my new client. He would be an older gentleman, clearly

wealthy judging by the generous amount I was being paid for my services. He would probably be like my patients at the Leprosarium, sweet, kindly, suffering in solitude, hidden away from the cruelty of the outside world. Much like dear Father Barbier, I supposed.

Most healthy people were afraid of lepers and those carrying physical deformities, and quite often acts of cruelty and forced isolation were born of this fear. It is as if people believe that somehow a physical deformity could be contagious. Even in these modern times, such notions still persist. Celestine's friend must have suffered similar treatment. It would certainly explain why he had become such a dedicated misanthrope, and one could hardly blame him. My heart went out to him; he would receive only kindness and understanding from *me*, as well as delicious dinners.

But what was his name? The note had not, after all, proved very helpful. What did 'O.G.' stand for? Was he a Frenchman? I really must remember to ask Celestine again.

The sun passed behind the shops on the opposite side of the street, sending long shadows creeping into my window. As I rose to turn up the light, I glanced at the clock. It was now five p.m. and time to take out my tagine. It was such a pleasure to make something exotic and spicy like this. My patients at the hospital required milder food, simple, wholesome dishes such as my usual *répertoire* of soups and stews. But now I had someone to cook for who was not ill. It would be a nice change as well as giving me a chance to be a bit more creative.

The tagine came out of the oven and I stole a little taste of the thick sauce. Happily, it lived up to its delicious aroma; it was rich and warming, and the chicken was falling-apart tender. I put a small portion aside for my own dinner while making up the tray. I was worried about being able to keep the food warm until it was wanted – did my client have a way to warm it up? I couldn't be certain, not knowing what his living situation was like. In the end I warmed a ceramic dish in the oven then wrapped it up well in a cloth after filling it. For a final touch I added a nice fresh *baton* of bread from the *boulangerie* down the lane and a small wedge of delicious aged Gruyère cheese to make a simple cheese course. Finally I secured everything on a large tray with deep sides, throwing a cloth over it.

When the hired hansom pulled up outside to carry me to my destination, I was ready, having exchanged my apron and hair net for a light cloak. I was so excited and eager to begin my new venture that I all but danced out the door.

I was not *quite* so eager when I found myself standing alone at the mouth of a narrow, shadowed alleyway between two rows of tall buildings. My enthusiasm had rather waned, in fact. Behind me on the boulevard my hansom waited, a safe haven I was now sorry to leave; ahead of me I could see nothing but an empty, derelict-looking side street. A biting wind blew between the tall buildings, surprisingly cold for the time of year. I was in the right place, I was sure; I just wasn't feeling particularly happy about it. It was not the sort of place a young lady ought to be wandering alone, with night well and truly falling now. However, there did not seem to be any miscreants lurking about, so I took a deep breath and warily entered the alleyway, scanning the windows along the left side as I did so. The alleyway curved somewhat, so that once I had walked a short distance, the street was hidden from my view, adding to my sense of isolation.

I was concerned that in the growing gloom I would not be able to see the distinguishing mark I was told to watch for. I need not have worried, however. About half way down the block I came to a tall casement window with a ledge only a few feet above street-level. I could just make out a small oval of red paint on the lower right hand pane of glass. Leaning closer, I saw that it was... a *skull*. Now that was odd! Why a skull? This was more of a warning than a 'welcome' sign.

Disconcerted, I set my tray down and examined the window to see how it opened. My hand had barely pressed against the frame when it silently swiveled inward. Anxious now to make my delivery and depart before darkness was complete, I picked it up and rather clumsily slid through the window. I found if I sat on the sill, twisting myself around, I could get my legs and skirts inside. It was awkward, and I had to exercise care.

Looking around alertly, I saw that I was standing in a long, narrow room with high ceilings. I made a mental note to bring a candle and matches next time, for the room was dismayingly dark and gloomy.

The floors were of marble, dulled with dust. The room was entirely devoid of any furnishings or decorations excepting one floor-to-ceiling woven hanging of some kind, tattered and age-darkened. The room smelt of dust and disuse and I wrinkled my nose against the musty odor. On the other side of the room I was relieved to observe what I had been looking for: several built-in marble ledges in the wall. They were ideal for resting my tray; I was glad not to have to leave it on the dusty floor.

Quickly I crossed the room and placed my tray on one of the ledges, observing as I did so that the flat surfaces had been recently cleaned. I stood for just a moment looking around in the gloom, listening for any sounds, but all was utterly silent – not even the scurry of a mouse could be heard. A sense of abandonment lay over the room, as though no one had been here for years.

I hoped my client would come soon to collect the tagine before it grew cold. What a strange place to pick up one's dinner! I had no desire to linger in this lonely place any longer than was necessary. Anxiously I went to the window, climbed out, and drew it carefully closed behind me. The dark street was empty and silent.

I all but ran down the alley back to the busy boulevard and my waiting hansom. Leaning back against the cushions as we made our way back to the Rue de la Marché, I pondered my new commission. I was having serious misgivings. For all I knew, each time I ventured down that gloomy side street my life could be at risk. Some ruffian might be lurking in the shadows and come upon me inside the empty room, where I would be beyond anyone's help. The street was narrow, so I could not ask the driver to pull down there – and besides, that would violate my promise of secrecy. I reminded myself that after all I only agreed to try. The next day's visit would tell the tale, so I would have to make this unsettling trip one more time at least. I pondered Celestine's friend, my new client, as well. Would he enjoy his first dinner? And where was he now eating it? Would *he* wish to retain my services?

I was thankful to reach the warm, safe environs of my little apartment after my unsettling expedition. I had my dish of tagine while sitting before the fire, wrapped in a warm shawl. Something about the cold, dark place I had just come from made it difficult for me to feel warm, but the tagine helped, as did another glass of sherry.

The vexatious problem I faced the next day, was deciding what to prepare for my new client's second (and possibly last) dinner. I had no way of knowing how well the tagine went over, although I had enjoyed it very much myself. At last I settled on a proper French dish, another warm and comforting one, *Boeuf en Daube en Casserole*. It would not require an expensive cut of beef, and I already had most of the vegetables in the larder. And again, I could make a little one for my own dinner.

And so the next evening found me once again stepping into a hansom bearing a covered tray, but in a much-altered mood. To say I was feeling wary was an understatement.

Once again I made the trip down the alley, all the while looking about me apprehensively. I now expected to see sinister figures lurking in every shadow, but as before, I was completely alone there. At the window with its ominous red emblem I stopped, as before, and pushed it open. Tonight, with all my senses on the alert, I noticed the faint smell of oil. The hinges must have been very recently oiled so that there would be no difficulty in opening it. I made my awkward way through the opening and stood looking around cautiously. There, resting on the ledge on the opposite side of the room was the tray I had delivered yesterday evening.

I crossed to the ledge quickly, rested my warm burden next to the empty tray and reached into my pocket for the candle and matches I had placed there before departing. Lighting the candle made a great improvement in the room. I fixed it to the ledge with a drop of melted wax and examined the empty tray. The cover was set neatly in place and both tray and dish appeared to have been cleaned. There was no sign of the forty francs that had been agreed upon as my payment, but there was only one place it could be.

Quickly whisking off the cover, I looked underneath. On the clean plate rested a small black velvet pouch, and under the pouch, a folded piece of paper. Eagerness to investigate the contents of the velvet pouch and read the note warred with my knowledge that I was not supposed to linger in this room, but curiosity won over any other concern and my fingers closed over the little bag. The hard shapes of coins could be felt inside.

With fingers trembling ever so slightly, I untied the silk drawstring and opened the little bag, holding it to the candlelight, allowing the contents to spill into my open palm. Sixty *francs!* Thrilled,

I tumbled the coins into my coin purse and placed the empty pouch next to the tray I had just delivered. My eager fingers plucked up the folded note; by the light of the candle I read it anxiously.

The message contained therein was brief and succinct:

"Madame Giry was indeed correct in her assessment of your cooking skills. I will be pleased to consume anything you care to bring me. Please remember my other instructions and obey them to the letter, and any potential unpleasantness will be avoided.

Regards,

O.G."

Upon reading the note I was seized by a fearful panic! I must depart *at once;* there was no time to lose. My new client was happy with my cooking and generous as well, so it would not do to disobey those other instructions now that we had got off on such good footing. The note followed the money into my skirt pocket, and the candle was blown out. Hastily I snatched up the empty tray and in another moment I was sliding out of the window and closing it behind me. I was feeling much more sanguine now – certainly the beef stew in its succulent pastry crust would be as well received as the tagine had been.

Again I almost ran down the alley to my waiting hansom, but it was happiness that gave my feet wings, not fear this time. Sixty *francs*!

CHAPTER SIX

"What is it that we really desire?
That which we cannot obtain."

A.D.

I must confess, Reader, that against my own better judgment I was seduced by that very generous sixty *francs* into retaining my new commission. And it was a very curious, indeed fascinating, situation. As I went about my (now much busier) daily activities, I found my thoughts returning again and again to my new client and his mysterious circumstances.

Celestine was not forthcoming with additional information about O.G., which I thought odd. She could not even tell me what sort of apartment he lived in. She always referred to him as a friend, and yet she appeared to know very little about him. It was quite frustrating; speculation could only take me so far. I finally decided there could be no harm in satisfying my curiosity about one thing, at least. I was eager to discover how the mysterious O.G. came and went. Was it by the window, or was there some other entrance I had thus far overlooked? Therefore, on the third evening of my employ I contrived to arrive at the empty marble room a few minutes earlier than necessary, in order to give myself a little time to explore it uninterrupted.

I had prepared a simple dish of lamb stew for the patients that day, and I set some aside to bring to my reclusive new client. It would save me some cooking time as well as money if I could occasionally make the same dish for both clients. I also included a generous slice of *tarte tatin*, made from my mother's recipe. The patients at St. Giles were quite fond of my *tarte tatin*, so I made it for them often.

I resolved not to waste any of my precious time. As soon as I placed my tray on the ledge I lit a candle and began walking about the empty room, examining it carefully for any signs of recent activity. As I already knew, there was not a stick of furniture in it, and the walls were bare except for niches that once held sconces for light. The cobweb-festooned remains of once-ornate chandeliers hung from the ceiling. From the appearance of it, the room must at one time been a place of business, but long unused. As I looked around me, my eyes kept returning to the moth-eaten hanging near the left corner of the back wall, not far from the built-in ledges. Since there was nothing else remaining to be examined, my feet turned at last toward the hanging.

Closer inspection by the light of my candle revealed it to be a woven tapestry of the sort one sees often used as wall hangings: faded clusters of roses and wide bands of ribbon could be made out on its age-darkened surface. It looked as though it had been hanging on the wall forever. I wondered curiously why it was still there, the only ornamentation left in this otherwise empty and forgotten room. Could it conceal something? A door, perhaps? The instant this possibility occurred to me, my hand was eagerly lifting the tapestry aside. Then I gasped and dropped it, jumping back quickly as though the floor had opened beneath my feet.

For the floor *had* opened up.

I stood still for a few seconds, getting my ragged breath and thumping heart under control. The candle had blown out when I made my precipitate leap back from the gaping hole, so I had to relight it. This took several tries due to the trembling of my fingers, but once it was relit, I cautiously approached the hanging and lifted it again, holding my candle out in front of me to illuminate the darkness beyond.

Upon closer inspection, what had seemed on first glance like a gaping pit in the floor was in fact an opening in the wall, a door frame without a door. Dark, narrow stone stairs descended directly downward into stygian depths, closely walled on both sides. I could make out only three or four of the steps, beyond which the dim light from my candle could penetrate no further. How far down the stairs went, or *where* they went, could not be ascertained.

I stared down into that dark passageway while numbing fear curled around me like a cold mist. Indeed, I was not imagining that – it *was* cold - damp cold air seemed to emanate from the opening behind the hanging. It was like a nightmare, or something from one of Edgar Allen Poe's horror stories. I found myself repenting my insatiable curiosity. I knew that from this moment on, every time I came here I would be terrified that some unspeakable horror would creep out from the blackness. It wasn't enough that I was afraid to walk down the street, now I would be afraid of the inside, too.

Finally I released my grip on the tapestry. I hurried away and gathered up my things while the hanging was still falling silently back into place. Casting nervous glances back over my shoulder, I hastened to the casement window. I was about to clamber through it when I was suddenly struck by the sure and heartfelt knowledge that *this* was what I had been looking for: this was the way my new client came. Not through the window from the outside, but up those stairs, up from the darkness below. The realization stopped me in mid-step as a new thrill of fear ran down my spine. What sort of man, recluse or otherwise, would shut himself away in a dark, damp tomb? My comfortable vision of an older, kindly and infirm gentleman was seriously shaken by this discovery. Such a man should not be capering up and down long, dark stone staircases. Once again, I found myself wondering if this commission was one I ought to keep.

A sudden sense of urgency propelled me through the window, fueled by the desperate need to put a vast deal of distance between myself and that room. Gripping my tray firmly, I walked with brisk steps toward the boulevard. Settling back in the hansom, I released my pent breath and wondered what Celestine had got me in to. I had every intention of finding out.

Upon arriving home, I wasted no time in penning a note to her with an invitation (rather insistent) to come for tea the next afternoon. I had a number of questions about her mysterious friend that could wait no longer. The vaguely threatening notes, the red skull, and now this: the horrid knowledge that he dwelled in some deep, dank underground cellar. How had Celestine ever come to meet and befriend such a person? And beyond all this, what did O.G. stand for? I vowed I would have answers to my questions before another day had passed, most certainly before I ventured back to that empty room. As I dispatched my invitation to Celestine at the Opéra Populaire with extra money paid for an answer by return messenger, it occurred to me that I had a little more of a mystery on my hands than I was really prepared for.

St. Giles appeared all the more peaceful, wholesome and safe to me the next day, in comparison to my previous evening's dark discovery. I welcomed the chance to sit quietly listening to the murmured prayers in Latin that began the mid-day meal. But I was only half-listening; the rest of my mind was already anxious for my afternoon appointment with Celestine. Clearly, she had deliberately withheld some things from me, and I was not going to let her leave until she gave me more information about this mysterious 'O.G.'. I tried not to allow my distraction to interfere with my time with the patients, but even Dr. Gaudet noticed something was not quite right. I finally told him a little white lie about a non-existent headache so that I could leave the hospital early.

Back home, wiping down the stove and work tables, I watched anxiously for Celestine's arrival. She was a few minutes late. When I admitted her into my kitchen she wore a sheepish expression and avoided meeting my eyes. The tea was ready. I knew by now that Celestine actually preferred coffee, but the English habit of tea had become *en vogue* in Paris, and I had succumbed to its soothing qualities. And as I was feeling cross with her at the moment, she was going to get tea. I poured for both of us, pushed the sugar bowl toward her and sat down at the table. She thanked me and then fell silent, and I saw she was watching me apprehensively. It was obvious she had been expecting something like this to happen.

"Celestine," I began gently, "there are things about your 'friend' that you have been keeping from me, aren't there?"

She looked at me beseechingly. "Sylvie, you must understand, they are *his* secrets, not mine. I have to be very careful."

I could not repress a little edge of anger in my voice when I answered her. "You protect him, your mysterious O.G., but what of me? There is something strange about that place, Celestine, and about your friend. I am afraid to go there again; I do not believe it can be safe in spite of what you say."

"Oh no, Sylvie, you have nothing to fear, I assure you. You are perfectly safe as long as you do not..."

Interrupting her, I exclaimed bitterly, "Yes, yes, I know – as long as I do not linger in that room or venture down those stairs! As if I would! I looked behind that tapestry, Celestine; I saw the stairs going down into darkness. I am no coward, but it is like something from a nightmare! He lives under there somewhere, doesn't he?" I set my cup down rather hard in the saucer and we both jumped.

She was silent for a moment, looking down into her cup. When she looked up at me again, I could see in her eyes that she had resolved to tell me the truth.

"Yes, he does," she said at last. "He lives beneath the Opera House. That is a...a secret exit he seldom uses. But it was perfect for your deliveries."

Although I had suspected something of the sort, her confirmation of it came as a shock nevertheless. *"Mon Dieu,"* I whispered. "Does he ever see the light of day?" Had I stumbled into a gothic tale complete with a vampyre sleeping in a coffin deep under the streets of Paris? My fancies of Edgar Allen Poe tales did not seem so far-fetched after all. A chill swept over me, and I shivered in spite of my warm kitchen.

"Please Sylvie," Celestine pleaded. "Remember what I have told you about him. I believe he…he hates the light, because he can be seen, and he hates to be seen by anyone, even me. He doesn't want to always have to hide his face!" That note of maternal fierceness crept into her voice as she spoke.

I sat back in my chair with a long troubled sigh. For a few moments all that could be heard was the steady ticking from the clock on the wall, and the faint but familiar sounds of commerce taking place along the street outside. Celestine, her face slightly flushed, picked up her teacup and took a sip; when she replaced the cup in the saucer it rattled ever so slightly. I sighed again. She loved her friend, I was sure of it. She would protect him from me or anybody else.

"Tell me something, if you please. What does O.G. stand for? What is his name?" I asked, determined to learn this piece of information from her, at least. Celestine's expression became instantly wary. I was not going to like this, it was written all over her face. This was something she had done her best to avoid telling me, but I would stand for it no longer.

"Tell me, Celestine. I have the right to know," I said firmly.

"*D'accord"*, she said resignedly. "I do not know his real name. He has never told me and I do not ask. But he calls himself the…oh dear." She paused, making a little, helpless fluttering gesture with her hands. "He calls himself the Opera Ghost," she finished ruefully.

I stared at her, thoroughly bewildered. "You are saying O.G. stands for…*Opera Ghost*? What kind of name is that! I do not understand, Celestine. What is his connection to the Opera?"

"Oh, Sylvie, this is so difficult to explain! And I don't want to frighten you away. I have told you that he lives deep under the Opera building, far below all the cellars and storage levels. But I have not ever been that far myself, so I do not know exactly. That is why I could not take you down there – it is his domain. It is a place he found years ago, where he could hide from the world and be safe. He writes music, he composes there. He is a genius of music and he plays and sings beautifully." She stopped, watching me for my reaction. I was still staring at her, and suddenly realized my mouth was open, so I closed it.

"*Alors,* your friend lives beneath the Opéra Populaire, and calls himself the Opera Ghost. Well, that is all perfectly normal I am sure." I said bitterly. "And does he haunt the place, frightening people like a real ghost?"

She hesitated, a frown creasing her forehead. I had been attempting a little joke to lighten the tense atmosphere, but her expression warned me this was not a joke. "Good heavens!" I exclaimed. "What else are you keeping from me?"

Seeking to placate me, Celestine spoke in a rush. "He knows that place as no one else does. He comes and goes by ways unseen, and sometimes, if someone catches a glimpse of him, they say it is the Ghost. People tell stories and invent things. Whenever something goes wrong there, they blame it on the Ghost. He encourages that sort of thing; it makes people afraid of him, because if they believe he is a ghost, that he possesses magical powers, they will not go looking for him. I know better, *naturellement*, but I say nothing." Celestine looked sidelong at me, her expression thoughtful.

"Have you never heard of the Phantom of the Opera?" She asked. *Phantom of the Opera?* The idea of a vampyre did not seem so far-fetched to me all at once.

"N-no, I can't say that I have." I responded slowly. "Why?"

"That is a *sobriquet* he uses sometimes. They are one and the same man. He will not be happy with me for telling you all this," she said resignedly. "But please, Sylvie, do not cease cooking for him; he enjoys it very much, he told me so. You have nothing to fear from him."

Phantom? Ghost? I found I was looking doubtfully at her. It was as if she were discussing fairy tales, except....

Thinking over what Celestine had just told me, something suddenly stood out in my mind. *A darker shadow moving in the shadows, a flash of white.* The watcher above the stage. My chin came up and I stared at her accusingly.

"Last week when you invited me to the Opéra Populaire and so obligingly gave me that tour: I wondered about that at the time, because you had never been inclined to invite me before. There *was* someone up above the stage, wasn't there? You knew, because you brought me there on purpose. *He* was there. Your Ghost." Anger sharpened my words and my expression. Celestine had deliberately put me on that stage, at that particular time, so that her 'friend', lurking in the upper shadows of the theatre, could spy on me. The thought made my skin crawl.

61

Celestine at least had the decency to blush. "I am sorry, Sylvie. But he wanted to be able to see you before he agreed to employ you, so he asked me to bring you there. It was the only way he could see you without being seen himself. But no harm was done."

"So you keep saying, but I am not sanguine about that. That place I have to go frightens me. Do you know that he marked the window I was to use with a blood-red skull painted on the glass? What kind of man is this?"

She made another helpless fluttering gesture with her hands. "Oh, but you must understand, that business with the paint is all part of the mythical persona he cultivates to protect himself! It does not mean he is a killer or dangerous, at least not to you or me." She dismissed the ominous red skull with a wave of her hand.

I stared at her. "And this is meant to reassure me?"

She clasped her hands together as if praying. "Please Sylvie. Just try again. Everything will be fine, you'll see."

Alas, I could not resist her desperate pleading, or her stubborn desire to protect her reclusive friend. Before Celestine departed, I agreed to continue my deliveries, but I vowed I would cease them permanently if anything untoward were to happen, whatever that might be.

Later that evening, as I prepared for bed, I turned over at length in my mind everything Celestine had told me. Before she took her leave, I had asked her how she came to meet this so-called Ghost. Her eyes softening, she told me a disconcerting, yet rather sweet story.

She had just come to the Conservatory of Music to be the dancing mistress. It was soon after the Opera had opened. One evening Meg, five years old at the time, became very ill with a case of *le grippe*. Celestine did not want to leave her the next morning to teach, but the manager refused to grant permission for her to remain with her daughter. He was new to the theatre business and very strict. That evening Celestine was sitting by Meg's bedside in the girls' dormitory watching her by the light of a candle. She could not help but shed a few tears as she sat, and one of the older girls tried to comfort her, offering to sit with Meg the next morning so Celestine could conduct her lesson. The offer was kindly meant but inadequate as far as the worried mother was concerned.

But very early the next morning, the manager presented himself at her rooms, looking pale and frowning in consternation. He held a piece of paper in his hand, and on it could be seen a few lines written in red ink. It was a letter from the Opera Ghost, the first one he had ever received but it would certainly not be the last. He had found it lying in the middle of his desk when he arrived at the Opera early that morning. The writer, after politely introducing himself as the Opera Ghost, instructed him in no uncertain terms to allow Madame Giry as much time off as she needed to nurse her sick daughter, with her full pay, or the manager (Monsieur Poligny) might or might not live to regret it.

Veiled threats are much more terrifying than ones that are spelled out, and M. Poligny was rather shaken by this suavely threatening letter. He gave Celestine the time she needed, and not another word was ever said about it. From that day forward, Celestine was devoted to her 'Ghost', and M. Poligny never dared to cross her for fear of the consequences.

During Meg's lengthy convalescence, the little girl awoke one morning to find a box wrapped in black paper on the table next to her bed. There was no note or card. Upon eagerly tearing it open she discovered a beautifully carved wooden toy inside: a dromedary camel with head, neck and legs all articulated, looking virtually life-like, carefully carved and painted. She had it still, on a shelf in her room, though the paint wore off long ago from constant handling. After all these years Meg no longer remembered where the camel came from, but she loved it dearly. There was no doubt in Celestine's mind that the toy had been made by the Ghost to help cheer the little girl during her recovery.

Celestine's story helped me understand her fondness for O.G., her trust in him, and her wish to protect him. I must admit it even softened *me* toward him a little. He could not be so very bad, after all, if he had taken an interest in the mother and her sick child. I began to forgive him a little for living underground in a dark hole, and painting red skulls on things. The poor old fellow, living apart from civilization in general, had perhaps forgotten what it was like to interact socially with others. I should not, I decided, be so quick to condemn him. My sympathy helped to lessen the resentment I still felt over being so blatantly manipulated by the both of them – I forgave Celestine for her part in that as well. I fell asleep that night trying to picture the wooden camel in my mind. I must ask her to show it to me some time.

CHAPTER SEVEN

'You are very amiable, no doubt, but you would be charming if you would only depart'

A.D.

And so, Dear Reader, I kept the commission, pocketed my forty *francs* a day (and sometimes a bit more when I happened to prepare something O.G. especially enjoyed), and kept far away from the dark doorway concealed behind the tapestry. I avoided even looking at it. Two uneventful weeks passed in this way. Celestine wrote me a note thanking me for carrying on with the work and reassuring me once more of my client's satisfaction with my cooking. From him, I heard nothing.

I asked Celestine when next we met what the O.G. looked like, but all she would say was that he wore a mask and had dark hair. She explained that he preferred to communicate with her via letters, so she seldom had a chance to really look at him. My curiosity seemed to grow with each evening's delivery, and once or twice I found myself deliberately slowing my steps to delay my departure from the marble room on the chance that he might appear. I still envisioned someone older and rather frail, unintimidating. I imagined what it would be like to actually meet him – surely I would be able to convince him that he need not avoid seeing me. I wished for an opportunity to reassure my client; a chance to show kindness and compassion. I dared not discuss this desire with Celestine. She would be adamantly against it, I knew. It would be a direct violation of my instructions.

It was difficult for me to reconcile the client of my imagination with this misanthropic individual who wanted to be thought of as a phantom. He was most certainly real, if his enjoyment of my dinners was any indication. Finally I formed a plan. After I made my evening delivery, I would simply retreat to a corner of the marble room and wait for him. When O.G. appeared, I would step forward and introduce myself as his cook. I would of course apologize for intruding on his privacy. The fact was I longed to make friends with him as I had with my patients at the hospital. There could be no difficulty about this, surely. I was, after all, perfectly harmless and had the best of intentions toward him. He need not fear me. And besides, he had made a point of seeing *me* in the flesh, why should I not do the same? If all else failed, I had my food itself to fall back on as a conversation starter. It would offer an excuse for me to linger and talk. Celestine need not know anything about it until the deed was done. It certainly seemed like a good plan, a perfectly reasonable plan, at the time.

It only remained to decide when to put my plan into action. There was nothing to be gained by delay, so I decided to do it that very evening. I made the O.G. a lovely tomato and *courgette* tart and arranged the dinner tray with cheese and fruit for dessert. It was high summer, after all, even though the poor old soul seldom saw the sun. As I busied myself preparing the tray and dressing to go out, I felt excited and eager. In a short time I would be face to face with my mysterious client. We would soon be on the way to becoming friends. Did I even spare a thought for the agreement I had made, did I even consider, by so deliberately and willfully violating my instructions, that I might lose this lucrative contract that very night? No, I did not. I can only say in my defense that anyone can behave foolishly on occasion, even a sensible person like myself.

The room was, as always, empty when I arrived. I deposited my burden on the ledge and after a moment's deliberation decided against lighting a candle. The days were long, and there was a rectangle of pale light falling obliquely on the floor from the casement window. It illuminated the middle of the room adequately for my purposes, so I retreated to a shadowed corner near the tapestry to wait for my O.G. Perhaps, I mused as I waited, I would learn his real name at last. He could hardly avoid telling me his name once I had told him mine.

Anxious and agitated at the same time, I engaged in a whispered rehearsal of what I would say to him when we met. *Excuse me, s'il vous plaît*...no, no, that sounded as if I were about to ask him directions to the *gare*. Hmm. Ought I to offer him my hand? My foot tapped impatiently on the stone floor. Soon, very soon, I would see the tapestry lift and he would be here. How long would I have to wait?

The answer was: not long. My ears, straining to hear a sound in the pervasive silence that would herald his approach, suddenly picked up the staccato rhythm of rapid, bounding footsteps. I was expecting to hear a slower, more sedate tread, so I was caught off guard by the rapidity of his approach. I felt my pulse speed up as though to match those rapid steps. I held my breath and turned, my eyes riveted on the hanging that so effectively concealed the dark opening behind it. The sound of approaching steps grew louder, and louder still. The tapestry was abruptly flung aside. My breath caught as an enormous black shadow suddenly materialized in the room!

For an instant I thought I really *was* seeing a Ghost, an actual ghost I mean, so large, black and amorphous did the shadow appear. But then it moved purposefully into the square of dim light, crossing the room toward the ledge. As it moved, the huge shadow resolved itself before my staring eyes into the form of a tall, broad shouldered man, enveloped in a long black cape. It was the swirling movement of the full cape that had made him appear even bigger in the darkness. I saw that he carried no lamp or candle; he came and went in the dark. He must have eyes like a cat. I caught a glimpse of a long-nosed, imposing profile. The hands that were now resting an empty dinner tray on the ledge were sheathed in black leather gloves. I was suddenly petrified; I saw now that there was no possibility that he would be intimidated by *me* – it was actually the other way around.

I found myself frozen in fear, with nowhere to hide, rooted to the floor where I stood. I hadn't realized he would be so tall, so dark, so *dangerous* looking. His broad-shouldered form seemed to radiate danger, from the top of his dark head to his booted feet. Danger, and something else…my pulse stuttered as the beat of my heart reacted to his dark presence. I longed to somehow hide myself, to disappear from this spot before it was too late. But it was already too late. In a few seconds he would turn and see me standing there wide-eyed in fear. I would have to face what I had started.

At that moment he lifted the cover from his dinner tray and studied it closely, and I heard him make a little vocal sound of satisfaction. It was that small human gesture that gave me the courage I needed. I drew my right hand out of my cloak and stepped forward to join the Phantom in the dim rectangle of light.

"*Bonsoir*," I said softly.

The man known as the Opera Ghost whirled around to face me so quickly his cape flared out and swirled around him. He instantly started toward me with hands extended and then froze, staring, utterly speechless, while a look of severe consternation appeared in his eyes. It was obvious that I was not whatever enemy he was expecting to find, and as for me, I was rendered speechless also. I stared back at him in amazement while the frail, older client of my imagination dissolved like smoke in the wind.

In his place stood a different creature altogether. I was prepared to see a mask covering his face, for Celestine had told me more than once about it, but it was startlingly white against his skin and hair. His eyes were grey or blue, it was difficult to tell in the faint light, but in spite of the stark white mask covering one side of his face,

I could see they were cold eyes, glittering with anger. His hair was dark, brushed straight back from a high forehead. I hadn't expected he would be handsome, but he was. He was dressed like a gentleman, in finely tailored waistcoat, black trousers and an impeccably tied black silk cravat. I found this somehow reassuring, but I ought to have known that just because a man has an outward appearance of being civilized doesn't mean he really is. In my current state of innocence, however, I took one slow step toward him, and held out my hand. It only trembled a little.

"My name is Sylvie Bessette," I said. "I am your cook."

The O.G.'s glance flew rapidly to the covered tray and then back to me again, understanding appearing on his face. At last he spoke.

"I know who you are," he said coldly. "I thought it was agreed you were not to linger here. You were to leave, at once." He did not look at my extended hand, or move to take it; awkwardly I dropped it back to my side, embarrassment and burgeoning fear warring in my breast. Fear was beginning to win.

"I am sorry," I said hesitantly, "but Celestine…Madame Giry I mean, who is my friend, has told me a little about you, and I…I wanted to…" I was babbling like a brook, which abruptly went dry. I could feel sweat forming under my clothing. This was a really stupid, foolish thing I had done - what was I *doing* here? Why, *why* had I thought this was such a clever idea? How I wished I could take it all back! My heart was thumping in my chest and breathing was a bit challenging, but I took a long, almost gasping breath and forged ahead.

"I only wanted to meet you. To see if you are happy with the food." It was necessary to clear my throat before I could finish speaking.

Those hard eyes seemed to grow harder still, and a calculating glint came into them. He smiled a little, a sneer really. He seemed to be looking down his prominent nose at me. I couldn't understand it, until he spoke again.

"I see. I begin to comprehend. You want more money, is that it?" His voice was filled with scorn.

It was the sneer that did it. What was wrong with the man? A hot wave of anger swept my fear away, and without realizing it, I took another step toward him. We were facing each other now only feet apart, and I had to look up to see into his forbidding countenance.

"*Mais non!*" I said crisply. "I am perfectly content with the terms of our arrangement – they are most generous. I wanted only to...to see you, and talk to you, that is all."

"And now you have seen me. I hope you are satisfied. Allow me to apologize, if I misunderstood. You should leave now," he said, pausing to fix me with a menacing stare, "while you still can."

I was so irritated by his inexplicably rude behavior that I completely overlooked the threat implicit in his voice and words. Resentfully, I said, "May I remind you, Monsieur, that you have already seen *me*. You spied on me, in fact, when I thought I was merely receiving a tour of the theatre."

Not bothering to deny it, he made an impatient gesture with his hand. "That is completely different. I cannot afford to take chances on being seen or discovered. I must safeguard my privacy at all costs...a privacy which *you* have now willfully violated." His eyes narrowed as he studied me. "How did you know I was there that day? I took pains to ensure you would not see me."

I frowned, remembering the way the hairs on my nape had prickled as I stood upon the empty stage that morning. "I felt your eyes on me," I answered reluctantly. "And yes, you are right, it *is* different. *You* were hiding in the dark, spying on me while I was unaware. But I have come here and introduced myself to you directly, because I wished to make your acquaintance." I cannot even now say where I found the nerve to speak so to this dangerous stranger.

He did not appear the least bit chastened by my effort to put him on the defense. "I must be slipping, if I allowed you to actually catch a glimpse of me that morning," he muttered crossly. "But as for you, you nosy little shrew," he suddenly took a menacing step toward me, closing the distance between us, and I found myself taking a small step back. "I don't care to meet *you*. You exhibit a great lack of respect for my privacy. Understand this and mark it well: I prefer to be left *alone*." The last word emerged as a menacing whisper. "You knew my terms...I will overlook this one transgression, but as from now you have no excuse. You are showing intolerable disrespect for me and my orders, which I never allow. Do not linger here again. I warned you – you really ought to listen to me. You know," he paused, glowering down at me, his gloved hands clenching into fists. "You are lucky to still be alive, Madame. I could easily have killed you for this transgression."

I supposed he could have, but he had not. In fact, he had not even touched me. Emboldened by this realization, I put my hands on my hips and returned his glare with interest.

"I wonder, *Monsieur*, at your finding anyone willing to work for you if you threaten to murder them whenever you chance to meet. It wouldn't be easy to replace me, you know."

The O.G. stared at me. His mouth opened and closed twice, and then he sputtered a little and unclenched his hands. I had apparently rendered him speechless. Was that a brief flash of amusement I saw in his eyes? The crackling energy in the room seemed to recede a bit, and I began to consider that I ought to acknowledge I had been in the wrong and make what amends I could.

But before I could speak and offer an apology, however insincere, he abruptly turned away toward the tapestry, saying to me over his shoulder, "You have been warned, Madame Bessette. There should not be a next time."

He was about to depart as he had come, down the long flight of stairs into darkness. I moved toward him again without thinking what I did.

"Wait! Please." I said urgently. "You must know that you can trust me…not to say anything, not to give you away. I mean you no harm, *Monsieur le Fantôme*." I felt a little thrill of fear and excitement course through me as I pronounced that strange *sobriquet*. "I will forgive you for spying on me that morning if you will forgive me for this. I promise you I will not do it again." Once more I extended my hand toward him.

"Will you not shake hands with me?"

His wary eyes moved from my face down to my hand, and he stared at it for a long moment while I held my breath. His mouth suddenly twisted into a grimace, as though my gloved hand were a dead rat he had stepped on in the street. Then he whirled away without another word, and vanished into the darkness below.

I stood rooted to the spot, listening to the staccato sound of his retreating steps until I could no longer hear them. After the footsteps had faded away there was only silence, and the loud beating of my heart. It took several seconds for me to recover from my astonishment, but when I looked around, I was dismayed to see that he had left his dinner on the shelf. It was a good thing I had made something that could be enjoyed cold, I thought ruefully. Thoroughly ashamed and despondent, I picked up the empty tray and walked to the window.

I had met the Phantom, the 'Opera Ghost' at last. He was *nothing* like I had imagined he would be from the things Celestine had told me. I had no idea he would be…well, so compelling, so frightening and fascinating at the same time. And he was not old! He was, in fact, a handsome man in the prime of life. As I hurried toward the boulevard clutching the empty dinner tray, I felt absolutely on fire with wonder and curiosity. I decided to write and invite Celestine for *café* the very next day. Not only *café*, but also perhaps I would get a slice of Napoléon from the *patisserie*, as it was her favorite. I hoped to encourage her to be more forthcoming about her *soi-disant* friend.

Unsurprisingly, I found it impossible to sleep that night. I had an extra glass of wine, and a warm, lavender-scented bath. I went to bed with the most soporific book I could think of – a volume of English poetry translated into French. But all to no avail. I was too excited and over-stimulated to sleep. I had experienced so many conflicting emotions in such a brief span of time: curiosity, fear, frustration and anger, to name but a few. And it seemed that all I could see in the darkness of my room was a pair of cold pale eyes glaring at me.

Over and over again my mind replayed my strange encounter with the Opera Ghost. There was so much to ponder and puzzle over: why, for instance, had I felt no fear when he threatened me with death, yet felt chills chase down my spine when I spoke his name? And who was he? *What* was he?

There was something rather endearing about the way he had eagerly lifted the silver cover from his dinner tray to see what awaited him. Almost as if his anticipation of the contents made it impossible to wait until he sat down to table with it. And that made me happy.

Eventually I calmed down enough to finally fall asleep, but not before my little mantel clock in the *salon* had chimed twelve.

CHAPTER EIGHT

*'His eyes were full of melancholy, and from their depths
occasionally sparkled gloomy fires of misanthropy and hatred;
his complexion, so long kept from the sun, had now that pale
color which produces, when the features are encircled with black
hair, the aristocratic beauty of the man of the north; ... and he
had also acquired, being naturally of a goodly stature, that vigor
which a frame possesses which has so long concentrated all its
force within itself.'*

A.D.

Alas, there was in fact no need for me to invite Celestine,
for she arrived at my apartment in person early the next
morning, in a state of perturbation. A hollow feeling settled in the pit
of my stomach when I beheld her outside my door, vigorously ringing
the bell. Belatedly, a sense of guilt over what I had done came over
me. Why had I acted so foolishly? Celestine had every right to be
vexed with me. Feeling hot and ashamed, I tried to compose my face
while I hastily wiped my hands on my apron and let her in; she began
to talk without preamble as soon as the door closed behind her.

"Sylvie, what were you thinking? He is *very* displeased with
you, very displeased. He came to my chamber this morning on
purpose to tell me what happened last night, and he was in such a
state! He is very angry, not just with you but me as well. Oh, why did
you do it, Sylvie?" She pulled off her hooded cloak as she spoke, and
dropped heavily into a chair, having run out of breath. Her heart-
shaped face was pale, her eyes accusing.

I stared at her in wide-eyed alarm. "He has not...he has not
cancelled the agreement after all?" I asked, her agitation and distress
making me think the worst.

"*Pas encore*, but if it should happen again..." she paused,
twisting her hands together in her lap, "you must understand, Sylvie,
the Opera Ghost is not like other men...he has not, he does not
have...oh, I don't know how to explain! Perhaps I have made a
mistake; I never intended that harm should come to you because of
me."

"Harm come to me – from him, do you mean?" I stared at
Celestine, shocked. "Why on earth would he harm me? I only
introduced myself and inquired how he enjoyed the dinners thus far."

Celestine shook her head in exasperation. "You must not try to see him again, promise me you will not. He will cancel the agreement if you do not obey his commands. The Opera Ghost is accustomed to having his orders and instructions followed to the letter." She looked at me pleadingly before going on. "If his orders are not followed, sometimes…sometimes bad things happen, over the years there have been strange accidents…" her voice trailed off.

I felt a little *frisson* of fear at her words. "What do you mean? Are you saying, he *makes* things happen there, at the Opera?"

She nodded. "*Oui*, nothing terrible, *vous comprenez* – sometimes a curtain may fall, a rope break, a trapdoor open that should have remained closed. I am not even sure myself sometimes if it is the Ghost or just an ordinary accident. Because you see, accidents do happen, quite often. I told you, remember, M. Poligny the owner, pays him 20,000 *francs* a month, and the Ghost has given him good value for that over the years, with advice and instruction, so M. Poligny has learned to follow his advice. But I think also, he pays him the money so that things will not go wrong." As she spoke, her worried eyes never left my face.

I sank slowly into the chair across from Celestine, pondering her words. "It did not seem as though he intended any harm to me," I said thoughtfully. "He was not happy to find me there, to be sure, but he made no threats against me. Well, not *exactly*…I was only afraid because…well because he was so intimidating. For some reason, I expected he would be older, perhaps infirm. I don't know why I thought that," I admitted, feeling foolish.

Celestine looked surprised. "Infirm he certainly is not! Quite the opposite, in fact. I do not know his exact age but I believe him to be in his late thirties."

I asked her one of the questions that had been nagging at me since my encounter of the previous evening. "Celestine, have you ever seen him without that mask?"

She shook her head emphatically. "*Non*, never. He usually communicates with me by letter, remember, so I seldom see him. That is why this morning when he actually came to our rooms, I knew he was terribly upset." She could not repress a shudder at the memory.

I rose and went to my stove. "I'll make you a cup of *café au lait*, shall I?" We could both do with a restorative – I certainly needed something. Regrettably it was far too early in the day for spirits.

"Does he not have a real name?" I cast an inquiring glance at her while setting the copper kettle over the flame. "Surely it cannot be

Opera Ghost or Phantom. I intended to ask him but he did not give me the chance."

Celestine shrugged and gave her long red braid a twitch, tossing it over her shoulder. She had apparently come away in such haste that she had not taken time to put up her hair.

"I am sorry, Sylvie, but I do not know him by any other name. He stays away from people and does not wish to interact or be seen by anyone, so I respect his privacy." She looked at me pointedly. "I do not ask questions of him, and neither should you, *ma chère*. He has been very good to me over the years. He has made me many little presents of money." Her voice had taken on a softer tone as she spoke.

I placed a cup of milky coffee down in front of her, pushed the sugar bowl toward her and touched her arm gently. "You care for him, as I have said before. That is plain to see. But..." I hesitated, not sure how to proceed. I could not help but wonder if the 'little presents of money' were simply his way of insuring Celestine would willingly do his bidding whenever he asked.

"*You* do not fear him, do you, Celestine?" I asked finally.

"Not for myself, no," she replied promptly. "But I do not know how he will behave toward others sometimes, when he is displeased with them. It is difficult to explain but...I do not believe he has a clear understanding of right and wrong. I suspect he could be dangerous if he did not get his way." She sighed heavily, and murmured in a softer voice, "He has led a strange life."

We sat sipping the hot coffee in companionable silence, each of us lost in our own, no doubt quite different thoughts. "He must be very lonely." I realized I had said out loud what I had been thinking, and felt my cheeks color.

"*Oui*, I think he is lonely, but I do not know if there is any other way for him." Finishing her *café au lait*, Celestine turned to me. "I should get back, we are rehearsing a new dance today and those girls will be lazy if I am not there." She rose, reaching for her cloak. "Thank you for the *café*, *ma chère*. Do you promise you will not wait for him again? You will not try to see him again? I told him I would secure your promise." She gave me an anxious, entreating look, waiting for my response.

"I promise," I said sincerely. And I actually meant it this time.

Satisfied, she patted my arm. "*Merci*, Sylvie."

I saw Celestine to the door and watched her walk swiftly away down the street, before turning slowly back to begin my day's work. I found it difficult to concentrate, however. I was taken aback by the swift, furious response from the Opera Ghost; I confess it gave me pause. I was also sorry to have been the cause of ill-will between Celestine and her mysterious friend. It was not her fault, it was mine, so I pondered how best to repair the damage. Several ideas came to me, and I decided to act on one of them without delay. Glancing at my clock, I was happy to see I had just enough time to do a little shopping before beginning the day's cooking.

That evening, as I made ready to depart, feeling rather tired from a busy afternoon in the kitchen, I sat at my desk to pen a note of apology to the O.G. I had thought the matter over all day while going about my duties, so it was to be hoped that my effort would garner the desired result.

"My dear Sir," (It began respectfully)

I wish to apologize for my unforgivable intrusion upon your privacy, although in fact I do hope you <u>will</u> forgive me for it. My curiosity sometimes carries me away, but I see I ought to have resisted in this case. I hope you will not blame Madame Giry, for she is completely innocent and was, in fact, quite shocked at my improper behavior.

And now I have a small request to make of you. I wonder if you might leave an oil lamp in our meeting place for my use – the days are getting shorter and it is now almost perfectly dark when I arrive. I would very much appreciate that kindness if it would not be too much trouble.

It was a pleasure meeting you, Monsieur Ghost. Regretfully, the pleasure was all on my side. Perhaps if you were to be there another time when I arrive, we might try again. I do not believe we got off on the right foot, but the fault is mine.

Yours Sincerely,
Mlle. Sylvie Bessette."

Voilà, I thought, putting down my pen and carefully blotting the wet ink. Upon reading it over, I felt 'pleasure' was a bit of an exaggeration, but I would leave it in nevertheless. It was the best I could do; the rest would be up to him. I had given my promise to Celestine and I meant to keep it, so this was my only recourse. I cannot even now say why it mattered so much to me that I should see him again. It also mattered more than it ought that he was angry with me, very angry; for of course he was in the right, I in the wrong.

Perhaps because my life was rather dull and well-ordered, the attraction of this mystery was all the greater. I longed to discover all his secrets, and find out who he really was. For now, I could pretend I was involved in exciting intrigues, just like Madame Bonaceiux in Dumas' Three Musketeers. It was to be hoped, however, that I would not end up like she did.

Apprehensively making my evening delivery, I left my penitent note prominently next to the covered dish where the O.G. could not miss it. A wonderful fragrance emanated from under the silver cover. Hoping to return to his good graces and get our association back on the right footing, I had recreated my first dish, the Moroccan chicken tagine which had gone over so well with him. I was confident he would not miss the underlying message: that I understood I had been in the wrong. Then I followed through on my promise to Celestine, leaving the room without even so much as a glance at the faded tapestry. Well, perhaps only a quick glance!

Later that night, sitting up in my bed with a book resting forgotten in my lap, I visited that room again in my imagination, seeing the tall, masked man lifting the tapestry, crossing to the ledge and finding my note. Saw him holding it in black-gloved hands. I could not suppress a little thrill of excitement – what expression would be on his handsome face if I could see it somehow? Unsurprisingly, I slept restlessly that night.

At St. Giles the next day, Father Barbier, whose intelligent black eyes missed nothing, noticed my preoccupation and remarked upon it. I could not, of course, explain it to him, so assured him that all was well with me. We were sitting on a bench in the courtyard as it was a fine summer day, the mid-day meal being finished. Father Barbier's eyes twinkled at me as he smiled. Nothing ever seemed to disrupt his happy nature; his very presence gave comfort.

But now he had decided to tease me, for he went on, "No, no, Mademoiselle, I do not believe your assurances. Something has definitely captured your thoughts today, and it is not my humble self. I venture to say it must be a matter of the heart. Have you been crossed in love, Mademoiselle?"

His innocent *bon mot* made me smile – how far from the truth he was!

"No, Father, I promise you, this is not an affair of the heart. Indeed, it is only that I feel a certain amount of guilt. I did something I should not have done, and I feel rather low because of it." It was a relief to say the words, even though they were only partially true. For to be perfectly honest, I was not entirely sorry for my behavior.

Father Barbier shook his head in disbelief. "*Pardon*, Mademoiselle? I cannot imagine such a thing! You are surely mistaken."

"*C'est vrai*, Father. I behaved in a rude and inconsiderate manner to someone last night, but I have taken steps to repair the wrong. I have apologized, so I hope all will be well."

He gave me such a look, I could see that he did not believe me in the slightest, as his next comment confirmed. "I am certain it will be, *ma chère*, although I cannot imagine you ever exhibiting such behavior as you describe. When I see you tomorrow your melancholy will have been replaced by your usual good cheer, mark my words."

"I sincerely hope you are right," I said feelingly. What I did not venture to add, was that the answer would be waiting for me this evening, and I was both eager and filled with dread over what it would be.

I took heart in the fact that I had not yet been dismissed by my client – surely this breach of the most important aspect of our agreement would be grounds for such an action on his part, yet it had not taken place. He had threatened and intimidated me, to be sure, but apparently he was not willing to part with my cooking skills. This gave me some hope of being able, eventually, to repair the damage my foolhardy behavior had caused. I set out that evening, therefore, with more curiosity than dread, to see what awaited me in the marble room.

As soon as I reached the casement window, I could see something was different. A warm, soft glow emanated from the other side of the glass. Upon entering, I observed a small glazed pottery oil lamp resting on the shelf next to the empty tray. Its wick burned low, only a gentle glow giving out just enough light to show that the lamp was there. Crossing to it, I turned up the wick and at once the room brightened, taking on a warmer, more welcoming air.

One sweeping glance was enough to assure me that I was alone, so I immediately turned to the tray; with clumsy fingers I raised the silver cover of the dish, and my eyes fell at once on a folded piece of crisp paper lying next to the black velvet pouch containing my fee. My heart leaped. Opening it, I read it rapidly, and then read it again, having failed to comprehend it the first time due to my state of mindless agitation.

It read:

"Madame,

Here is the lamp you requested. Accustomed as I am to darkness (indeed I prefer it), I forget that others require light. Remember, you have nothing to fear in this place, except myself.

As for your charming apology, I will consider it, but do not expect me to accept it. And as for our meeting again, I do not think that is something you should desire to happen.

The tagine was superb, and the gesture appreciated.

Regards,

O.G."

It could have been worse, I thought pensively as I made my way home. He did not sound *quite* as angry as on the previous evening; additionally, he had been kind enough to leave me the lamp. I would have to be satisfied with this enigmatic missive for now. It contained, as did all his correspondence thus far, several only lightly-veiled threats, all designed to cause me to wish to avoid the Phantom, not desire to see more of him. Instead, the magnetic pull he exuded on me only grew more powerful. There was, perhaps, something not quite right about my reactions, especially in light of what I had learned about him from Celestine. The Phantom was dangerous and unpredictable, without a clear sense of right from wrong, according to her. But at the time, I did not comprehend the danger; all I really wanted was to see him again.

Matters returned to their normal routine after this; that is to say, I did not lie in wait to take the Opera Ghost by surprise, and I received no further communications from him.

The days sped by. I was busier than ever, and soon managed to recover from the discomfiture caused by my *faux pas*. Summer began to fade toward autumn, and the days gradually grew shorter. The warm light of the pottery lamp was more welcome. As day followed day, I began to wonder if perhaps the darkly dangerous man I had met that night was an image from a dream, not a real man at all.

The empty dishes I collected each evening were all that I had to confirm that he was, in fact, real. Things might have gone on like this for some time if I had not been so clumsy.

One evening I was a few minutes late arriving, and my lateness caused me to be in an anxious hurry. I feared that I might inadvertently violate my instructions again, thus incurring the wrath of my Ghost. Unfortunately, the hospital staff at St. Giles was short-handed that day, so I had been needed more than usual to help serve the midday meal. Once I reached the window, I had a little difficulty getting it to push open – it must need fresh oil. I would have to leave my *soi-disant* Phantom a note about it.

But somehow, my foot caught as I was swiveling across the ledge, I lost my balance, the dinner tray went flying and I fell to the floor inside, striking the back of my head sharply against the stone ledge as I landed.

Dazed, my hair loosening from its neat chignon, I sat where I had fallen, my back against the wall beneath the window, one leg curled under me, almost losing consciousness from the blow to my head. After a moment, I came to my senses enough to look around me. By the dim glow of the oil lamp across the room I could see the contents of the dishes scattered on the floor. The tempting fragrance of roast pork with apples filled the room. *Quelle* disaster!

The breath knocked out of me, I must have sat without stirring for several minutes before reaching up to gingerly feel the back of my head. Immediately I regretted the action. My chignon had cushioned the blow but it was still very painful. I would have a lump there *sans doute*. 'Now I've done it! I am going to break my promise – he will dismiss me,' was my one coherent thought, but there was not a thing I could do about it. Thanks to my ungainliness, there would be no dinner for my O.G. tonight, only spilled food and scattered dishes.

I felt the sting of impending tears, but there was no time to indulge myself in weeping, so I blinked them back. I had to get up and clean the chaos before he arrived. I dreaded to think of how furious he was going to be. Spurred by this terrifying thought, I straightened my leg and tested it cautiously. I was relieved to find that my leg and foot were undamaged, although my ankle was a trifle tender from being twisted at an odd angle as I fell through the window. Taking a deep breath to steady myself, I attempted to rise.

I was bracing my hands against the floor in order to lift myself when suddenly, *he* was there. I had not heard his approach although I was listening for it with trepidation. All at once the tapestry lifted and he stepped into the room, looking exactly as he had the first time I saw him. Not a dream, then. Not a product of my overactive imagination. No, I could never have imagined such a dramatic vision.

At the sight of his tall, menacing form standing there my heart lurched and I sucked in such a gasp of air that I almost choked myself. I was doomed. He did not speak; his glittering eyes swept the room, taking in first me, frozen with my back against the wall, looking absolutely terrified, then the chaos on the floor, then they fixed on me again. My heart began to thump uncomfortably. Silently I cursed my cursed clumsiness.

"I am very sorry…" I began, but before I could finish, the O.G. moved. As gracefully and swiftly as a cat, he darted to the lamp, snatched it up, and came to kneel on one knee directly in front of me. Before I had time to register fear regarding his intentions, I was startled to find his face inches from mine, his eyes studying me intently. I could feel myself blush under that cool, steady regard.

"Are you injured, Madame Bessette?" His voice was full of concern, no discernible hint of anger there at all. Devoid of the scornful tone it had carried on my first encounter with him, I realized he had a very pleasant voice. Encouraged by the absence of the anger I was expecting, I ventured to respond to his question.

"My…my head. I lost my balance climbing in, and I hit my head on the ledge." I whispered shyly. "I think I can…" again I made an effort to rise, but he stopped me with a commanding gesture. Eyes wide, I stared at him in surprise.

"No. Do not attempt to move yet," he said firmly. I could but obey such a strong command, so I did as he asked. It was, perhaps, the only time.

He pulled off one black glove and reached toward me with his bare hand. "If you will permit me…" he murmured, pausing, waiting for permission before touching me. I nodded, suddenly unable to speak. My mouth had gone dry. Leaning closer to me, his fingers probed the back of my head carefully. He was so close now I could feel his warm breath as it fanned gently across my cheek. Unexpectedly, I noticed that he smelled nice: a manly combination of leather, spice and something else I could not identify. I suppose if I had given it any thought at all, I would have expected someone who lived in a tomb to smell like death.

"Oh." I could not help but flinch a little when his fingers found the bump and gently probed around it.

80

Lowering his hand from my head, he said, "It is not bleeding, nor is the skin broken. Look at me," he commanded.

I realized I was squeezing my eyes shut, so I opened them and raised my head to look into his masked face. Holding the lamp in his hand, he lifted it to shine the light directly into my eyes. I blinked.

"Your pupils are not unduly dilated; I do not believe you have concussion." He said after a moment. "Can you stand now?" Resting the lamp on the floor, he rose to his feet in one fluid, graceful movement.

"I think so. And it is *Mademoiselle* Sylvie Bessette, not Madame, *s'il vous plaît*." While this bit of information was of absolutely no importance to the situation, I felt compelled to give it to him anyway.

"Quite. Permit me to help you." If he thought my correction odd he was, rather unexpectedly, too polite to show it. After pulling on the black glove once more, he put his hand under my arm and helped me struggle to my feet, then promptly dropped my arm and stepped back. Finding my backside close to the window ledge, I sat on it gratefully and straightened my disarrayed skirt. I was suddenly so overcome by embarrassment I was unable to meet his gaze.

"It was my fault, I was running a little late tonight and I was careless." As I spoke my eyes went to the chaos on the floor. "I cannot believe I did that. Your dinner is ruined. I will go back and…"

"Do not be absurd." His voice cut across mine curtly. "I will not starve; I managed not to starve here for years before you came along. You are to go home and rest." Clearly, the O.G. was accustomed to having his orders followed with alacrity. Now he began to gather up the spilled dishes, placing them back on the tray.

"I take part of the blame myself," he muttered as he did so. "I am well aware that you must think my rules very odd. Please do not hurry again if you are late, I do not wish you to harm yourself on my account." I looked at him then, unnerved by this unlooked for display of kindness. I was not sure what exactly I *had* expected from him, but it was certainly not this. It was as disarming as it was unexpected.

"*Merci*. I will be more careful after this." I rose then and prepared to depart.

"See that you are. Can you manage getting back out?" He had gathered everything up neatly, somehow not getting any spilled food on his immaculate attire. He now stood before me, over a head taller than myself so that I was compelled to look up to see his face. Once again I was struck by how handsome he was. I wondered in passing

81

what the masked side of his face looked like: the disfigured side. Well, it didn't matter, since I was not likely to ever see it.

He was ready for me to leave, clearly. With care I maneuvered myself through and out, but when I turned to retrieve the tray from him, I saw he was climbing out after me, his long legs making little of the casement window.

"What are you doing?" I asked, perplexed.

"I am escorting you back to your hansom, *bien sûr*. You received a hard knock on the head. It will feel worse tomorrow."

There was no arguing with the O.G.'s masterful attitude. Throwing one side of his cape back over his shoulder, he offered me that arm to hold like the perfect gentleman he was not. I was rather glad to have it, as I was still a trifle shaken and my ankle was tender. He walked at a slow pace, trying to accommodate me, I knew. He did not speak. Shyly, I cast a quick glance up to look at his face, but it was the masked side, revealing nothing. He stopped just before we had reached the main boulevard however, choosing not to be seen in that busy place. My carriage stood waiting not far away.

"Can you manage from here?" He asked. His tone was polite, but it was clear he did not intend to come any farther, whether I could manage or not.

Reluctantly releasing his arm, I turned to face him. "Yes of course. You have been…very kind. I was afraid that you would be angry with me, after my unforgivable behavior the last time we met." Shame at the memory of my last folly brought additional colour to my cheeks.

I thought I detected a fleeting look of sadness in those pale eyes. "I am not entirely devoid of humanity, Mademoiselle Bessette, in spite of appearances to the contrary," he said quietly.

I felt my own expression soften in turn. "I can see that, Monsieur. I would be happy if you would call me Sylvie." Once again, as I had done a month before, I held out my hand to him.

He looked down at it, his expression serious, a little frown creasing between his eyes as though he were contemplating a puzzle of some sort, or a chess move. At least he did not appear to be looking at a dead rat this time. I realized I was holding my breath as the silence drew out. Slowly, very slowly, like someone performing a gesture for the first time ever, he extended a black-gloved hand and placed it cautiously in mine. We shook hands formally while a triumphant glow of pleasure washed through me. His grip was firm and strong, as I knew it would be.

Releasing my hand, he offered me my tray, saying, in an odd, rather bleak voice, and sounding as though his thoughts were far away, "When I needed to have a name to go by, I used...Erik. I have not used that name for a long time. It isn't my real name; it is just a name I picked at random. You are welcome to use it, however, if you wish, just *entre nous*."

I was caught completely off-guard by this unexpected gift of a name, and I was utterly beguiled by it, and by him. Right then and there, he ceased to be a 'phantom' or a 'ghost', and became real to me: he became Erik. And thus, also, my undoing, although I did not know it at the time.

Still formal, his face grave, he made me a slight bow, turned with a swirl of black cape, and walked swiftly back the way he had come. It seemed that even the most ordinary gestures assumed the air of drama when *he* made them. Fascinated, I watched his retreating form until it disappeared into the night. *Entre nous: just between ourselves.* I turned almost reluctantly toward the busy street. For some inexplicable reason, I felt elated, happy. Grateful. A great chasm had just been closed, and all due to my unusual clumsiness. I had been privileged to see a softer side of the Phantom – indeed I would never think of him again as anything but 'Erik'. I walked along in a warm dream, seeing only a pair of mesmerizing blue eyes.

"Mademoiselle! Mademoiselle Bessette!"

Hearing someone calling my name, I turned quickly to find myself gaping at the driver of my carriage. Lost in my thoughts, I had walked right by it.

Erik was right about my head; it was indeed very sore that night. It was necessary for me to sleep on my side. When I slept, I dreamed. I was back in the empty marble room, alone. It was terribly cold. The lamp had gone out. I was struggling to relight it; in the usual way of nightmares the simple act of lighting a lamp was amazingly difficult, but the room was full of shadows and I was afraid. I finally managed to light the lamp, but not all the shadows fled before its light. One remained: a tall, dark shadow. When I turned toward it in terror, I beheld the man now known to me as Erik standing silently, unmoving as a statue. He did not even seem to breathe. I froze where I stood, unable to look away from him, for what seemed like an eternity. But slowly I felt my fear drain away and I was unable to resist approaching him.

"Erik." I said, as if trying out the strange, very un-French sounding name. I reached my hand out to touch him, to assure myself that he was real, but before I could place my hand on his arm, he moved. With a sudden, unexpected gesture he raised his arm as if warding off a blow, swirled around, and vanished in a flash of fire and smoke. I was alone once more.

I awoke from that dream with pounding heart and feeling very bewildered – what did it mean? Why was I reaching out to touch him? It must be the blow to my head, I decided finally. Turning over, I fluffed my pillow and sought sleep again, though I found those words, *just between ourselves*, repeating in my mind.

CHAPTER NINE

'Curiosity prevailed over prudence.'
A.D.

Thanks to my accidental fall and the resulting *détente* between Erik and me, things soon took a very interesting turn. When I arrived with my delivery the next evening, the man formerly known to me as the Opera Ghost was already there waiting.

My heart gave a great lurch of fear when I saw him there; it reminded me so strongly of my dream of the night before. He stood perfectly still, cloaked in darkness, as expressionless as in the dream. Everything on my tray rattled together. Seeing that I was in danger of dropping his dinner yet again, he moved with alacrity to relieve me of my burden and set it safely down.

"*Pardon*, I did not mean to startle you, Mademoiselle. I thought you might require assistance because of your injury last night," he said politely. It was almost as if tonight he were making a real effort not to frighten me. We stood facing one another, separated by the open window. The stark white of the mask molded to the side of his face seemed to glow in the dim light. There was, I noticed, an attractive dimple in his chin. It made him seem a little less forbidding somehow.

I was not so disconcerted that I failed to notice he had remembered my unnecessary correction from the previous evening; it told me that he paid attention, that he was very observant. So I ventured yet another inconsequential correction.

"Please call me Sylvie," I murmured as I handed his dinner tray across the window ledge. "And thank you, I believe I could do with a little help. You were right about the fact that my head would hurt today. I had rather a time of it at the hospital." I admitted sheepishly.

"Hospital?" He asked, looking at me alertly. "Surely you did not require medical attention after all?"

"Oh no, no indeed. Did not Madame Giry tell you I cater the noon meal for a private hospital?" I would have expected her to mention it to him, so I was surprised he did not know.

He shook his head. "No, she did not," he said, clearly vexed to find there was something he did not know. "We discussed these arrangements only briefly. Do you do this every day?"

"Only on weekdays. I have Saturdays and Sundays off. I could have wished to have my accident on one of those days, but I expect my head will feel better tomorrow."

Erik frowned. "All that cooking must take up a lot of your time," he said, sounding slightly annoyed. "Why must you do it?"

"It is how I earn a living." I said simply. It did not seem like the time or place to go into a lengthy explanation of my bereavement, divorce, and lack of funds. I did find his interested regard rather disarming. However, his next remark explained all.

"As long as your work for this hospital does not affect your ability to cook for *me*. I could increase your salary to compensate, and then you could give them up altogether."

I shook my head in astonishment at his incredible self-centeredness.

"Under no circumstances, Monsieur, would I do that." I replied crisply. "I will not allow my cooking for the hospital to interfere with your dinner, you may rest assured."

"Hmmm," was Erik's response. He looked thoughtful; no doubt he was trying to think of further ways to convince me. "How many do you cook for at this hospital?" He asked after a moment.

"There are nine patients, and also a few staff members. But of course it is not the same as what I do for you, Erik. They have different dietary needs. That is one reason I accepted this position for you – it gives me a chance to try different things." I felt an absurd little thrill course through me when I spoke his name out loud for the first time.

"But surely…" He stopped abruptly. His curious face abruptly closed down and became unreadable again. "Forgive me; it is rude of me to ask you all these questions. You will want to be getting home and I am detaining you. Do you require any assistance back to your carriage?" It was only a perfunctory offer; he obviously did not intend to accompany me to the street today.

"N-no, I can manage," I said reluctantly. "Thank you for your help tonight. I hope you will enjoy what I made for you." Our incongruous conversation was at an end and it was time for me to go. He was clearly ready for me to make my departure.

"I am sure I shall. You have not disappointed me yet; at least, as far as your *cooking* is concerned. *Bonsoir*, Mademoiselle." There was a subtle glint in his eyes as he produced this little prodding reminder of my past misbehavior.

"Sylvie." I murmured, ignoring his little jab.

"Sylvie." And having said my name irritably, he closed the casement window in my face and turned away.

But from that night on, when I arrived at the marble room, Erik was usually there waiting for me. If I arrived before him, I could expect him to come bounding up the steps shortly after. After the first few times, I stopped being startled and unnerved to find him there, and began to eagerly anticipate it instead. Usually he spoke very little; we would merely exchange a few words while he assisted me with my delivery and climbing through the window. Unsmiling, distant, he frequently appeared preoccupied, as though his thoughts were elsewhere. But slowly, by fits and starts, we got to know one another. My mysterious, reclusive client, although still just as mysterious and reclusive, gradually transformed from a cold-faced stranger into a marginally warmer and more approachable person. I looked forward to our brief interactions each evening with far more pleasure than they really merited, but after all, he *was* the most interesting and exciting part of my day, or even of my life.

A week and a few days passed in this way, and I confess to dawdling just a bit if he was not there when I arrived, so that I would not miss seeing him. None of this assuaged my raging curiosity about him, however, and I found myself drawn frequently to those stairs diving down into darkness. As much as I had once avoided them, they now interested me greatly. Knowing that Erik lived down in those subterranean depths was as compelling as it was strange to me. I could have simply asked him about it, but something told me he would not be amenable to such a personal question. He guarded his privacy with fierce determination.

I cannot even now say why I had to know where he had been before climbing the stairs, or where he went when he departed down them again, but it soon became my obsession. Consumed by curiosity, one day I formed a plan to act on it. One would think, after the outcome of my last plan, I would know better. Sometimes my mind shied away from it out of fear of his reaction (which, in truth, could not possibly be a good one) if he were to discover me, but *most* of the time I was convinced my plan was rational and sound. It would be simple really: I would make my preparations in advance, and secretly follow Erik down the stairs.

A pair of soft slippers and a candle or two would be all that was required to carry out my exploratory foray, and I assured myself he need never know. Of course, if I had any idea at that time about Erik's proficiency with the Punjab lasso or his tendency to lay deadly traps for the unsuspecting, such a mad idea would have seemed suicide. It was only because he was so secure in the knowledge that this secret entrance was known only to himself and now, me, that there were no such traps set along the way, but I could not know that at the time. I blame my own pitiful naiveté and the powerful fascination I felt for him. I could not stop myself.

So yes, my little plot seemed quite simple, sensible even, right up until the night I decided to attempt it. *That* night, for some unaccountable reason, my mouth was dry and my heart pounded harder than usual, but I was nerved and determined to see it through. When I arrived at the window, slippers carefully rolled up in one pocket and candles in the other, the lamp was lit and Erik was there watching for me. I found I was too nervous to experience my usual warm pleasure when he took the tray from my hands so that I could pass through the window unencumbered. There was also, I must confess, just a small guilty feeling over what I intended to do tonight.

"*Bonjour*," I said, my nervousness making me breathless. "I hope I am not late." I realized I must sound as if I had been running.

"You are not late, I am early. What have you brought me *ce soir*?" He was dressed, as always, formally in tail coat, waistcoat and perfectly arranged cravat, and as always I was not unmoved by his sartorial perfection and well-knit form. As my mother would have said, he was a fine figure of a man. Fortunately Erik was always oblivious if it took me a moment to reply to a question from him. And I preferred him to think me stupid rather than speechless with admiration.

"*Poulet rôti*," I got out at last, exasperated at myself.

He lifted the cover off the dish and leaned over it, drawing a deep breath. "Mmmm. This smells delicious. I feel quite spoiled. Madame Giry made an excellent choice for me when she found you." My heart quickened a little at his words, but he was only referring to my cooking, as his immediate actions showed. He replaced the cover briskly, picked up the empty tray from its place on the ledge and made to hand it over to me. He was in haste then, and perhaps eager to attack his portion of roast chicken.

"*Merci*," I whispered, in response to his compliment (about my cooking). Erik gave me an odd look, finally noticing I was acting rather peculiar tonight.

"You have not caught a cold, have you, Sylvie?" He asked, moving to the window as he spoke. "You sound hoarse."

"I am fine." I said, summoning up a stronger voice, wishing inwardly that he had not chosen this particular evening to suddenly become observant. Not wishing to linger, I went to the window and not very gracefully slipped through it, turning back to take the empty tray from Erik. He was all business now, bidding me a perfunctory good evening before pushing the window closed after me.

As I prepared to walk away I glanced back through the glass and saw that Erik was already extinguishing the lamp. This was all to the good - if he was in a hurry to depart he would not linger and I would be able to follow him without arousing his suspicion. I knew he trusted me now, and I did feel a little pang of unease over the fact that I was about to violate that trust a second time, simply for the sake of satisfying my curiosity. But I did not feel *quite* guilty enough to change my mind.

On the pavement again, I turned and walked away in the gathering dusk as I always did. After walking a few yards I stopped, pressed myself against the wall and very quietly crept back to the window. Peeking cautiously through the glass, I saw the room was already empty. The tapestry hung limply, not moving. Giving thanks for the now well-oiled and silent window, I pushed it open and entered, closing it behind me. Quickly and quietly I set down the tray, pulled out my slippers, put them on and left my street shoes on the floor. Then I crossed the room to the tapestry, noting with satisfaction how silently I moved. Cautiously I lifted one edge of the fabric and peered down the stone stairs. Nothing could be seen except darkest night; not a sound could be heard except my own shallow breathing. Nevertheless, I listened for another long minute before taking a candle and match out of my pocket. I managed to get the candle lit on the second try.

Sucking a long draught of air into my lungs to calm myself, I slipped behind the tapestry and started down the stairs. This journey into the underground was, had I but known, the most foolish thing I ever undertaken in my entire life. But since I was ignorant of the potential danger, I carried on in relative fearlessness. The stone steps were very old and worn in places into smooth dips, but I soon saw indications where broken or badly worn stones had been skillfully repaired with cement and smaller pieces of stone. The walls were close enough on either side that I could reach out and touch them. By the dim light of my candle I could see, at intervals along the walls, rusty metal brackets where candles must have once given light to this gloomy pathway, but they were empty now and coated with cobwebby dust. The atmosphere was decidedly gothic, doing nothing for my peace of mind. As I descended I did worry a bit about possibly encountering a rat (I absolutely *loathe* rats), but fortunately nothing of the sort was seen.

Finally I came to the last step and found myself in a small, musty-smelling room, apparently once used for storage, for it had a worn flagstone floor with a few old casks piled in one corner. This was certainly not where Erik lived, for it was quite small and clearly had not been used for eons. At first I was puzzled and disappointed, for I could see no exit anywhere. Where did he go from here? Holding my candle high, I examined the opposite wall and saw that in fact the wall stopped before reaching all the way, making an almost invisible opening on the other side. The space between was so narrow and the walls so similar in appearance, they gave the impression of being one solid wall. It was a clever ruse. I crossed the room and looked around the half-wall, holding my candle out ahead of me to illuminate the space. It was a short corridor, and beyond was another opening. I took two or three such winding, mazelike turns before the last opening brought me to something that really gave me pause.

The space I now entered was far larger than the ones I had just passed through. A high, vaulted ceiling disappeared into darkness above me. I could hear the gentle splash and catch the scent of water nearby, could feel a rush of colder air on my face, but what really caught my attention was a long, straight stone causeway directly in front of me. It seemed to run on a gentle decline downward in the direction of the water, which I could now observe glittering darkly ahead of me and on both sides of the causeway. I wondered curiously if it was a boat ramp leading to the underground lake I had heard about from Celestine. I stood gazing at it, a little afraid, giving serious thought to retracing my steps out of this dungeon-like place. My former fascination with seeing the underground lake was rapidly vanishing. But somehow, I found myself stepping bravely on to the causeway.

The atmosphere grew more oppressive the farther I progressed; though I had encountered no other living thing, I felt as though eyes were on me, unfriendly eyes. Only the thought that I must be nearing the end of my journey spurred me onward. I was, in fact, much closer to that final destination than I realized.

The causeway did indeed cross over dark water, but it was not as long as it first appeared to me, for I soon came to the end of it. Water gently lapped the stone sides and I now understood that the causeway had been purpose-built to allow crossing of the water here. All along the landing where the causeway came to an end, were ancient-looking pillars with thick metal loops in them for tying up boats. In years long past, this would have been used as a dock for the unloading of casks and crates – there must have been an underground warehouse here at one time. Such things were not uncommon, though seldom used now that trains were preferred for transport more so than the river in these days. What the rest of the space looked like I could not tell, for my little candle could not penetrate that vast darkness.

Reaching the end of the causeway, I found myself stepping on to a well-maintained but very old wooden landing. Before me rose a solid brick wall with no window or door to be seen. Mystified, I stood studying it, puzzling over what to do. This *had* to be right; there was no other way Erik could possibly go. I was sure I had not missed a turning along the way. Looking the wall carefully up and down, I observed at last a faint pale line of yellow light along the bottom of one section, seeming bright only because it was so dark around me.

Emboldened by this discovery, I leaned closer to the section of wall directly above the faintly glowing line and ran my fingers over it gently. My careful examination revealed a cunning false door in the wall, in fact an actual wood door, marvelously painted in the *tromp l'oeil* style to blend in with the surrounding brick facade. If I had not touched the door, I never would have been able to discern that it was not actually part of the brick wall. Erik must have done this as a precaution on the very unlikely chance someone might find their way here via the ancient waterway.

I knew I had arrived at last at Erik's home, and I was certain he was on the other side of that door, enjoying the p*oulet rôti* I had brought him. I wasn't *very* afraid of Erik, but I was sufficiently afraid that, though I reached out to run my hand gently over the invisible door, I could not make myself learn how it opened. If he found me lurking out here on the landing he would surely cancel our arrangement and I would never see him again, or (and here I could not suppress a shudder) worse.

Behind me the cold black water lapped at the ancient causeway, a continual reminder of how easy it would be to dispose of someone in this lonely place. Well, perhaps I was more afraid of Erik than I cared to admit. It was his fault if I was, I thought glumly as I retraced my steps, the way he was always swirling dramatically around in that black cape and living in such a dismal, cold place. *But how lonely he must be.*

I was thoroughly relieved to arrive back at the top of the stairs without mishap, and I made haste to change into my proper street shoes so I could be gone. The hansom driver would wonder what had become of me, and it would not do to have him come searching for me, so I hastened down the alleyway and went home.

That cold, dark, lonely place should have been the stuff of nightmares, but to my extreme surprise and consternation, I had a very different kind of dream that night. It was really extraordinary. And I assure you, Reader, I am not in the habit of having dreams of such a...*personal* nature.

In my dream, Erik and I were lying together in a bed, in a state of complete undress, wrapped in each other's arms. His body was partly over mine, and he was kissing me passionately. Nothing else seemed to exist except the bed, Erik's lips on mine, and our two entwined bodies. My arms were around him and I could feel the warm, smooth skin of his back under my fingers. He was not wearing his mask, but in the dim dream light I could not see all of his face. It made no difference to me; all I was aware of in the dream was my flaming desire for him, and his for me, and the fact that I was utterly, blissfully happy – happier than I could ever recall feeling in my life. I was shocked into sudden wakefulness by the sheer intensity of my own joyful passion, and found myself sitting up in the dark gasping for breath, one hand pressed against my wildly beating heart. I could feel myself flushing hotly from my head to my feet.

The dream felt so real that I actually put my other hand out half expecting to find Erik there next to me. My fingers seemed to tingle from the warmth of his body. But no, I was here, alone in my own bed, and I was sure it was not the same bed as in my dream. I shook my head to clear away the last wisps of my dream-passion. How strange! I could not recall ever having such a realistic dream, and why would I dream of kissing Erik of all people? I was afraid of him most of the time, in awe of him for the rest. I decided it must have been the extra glass of sherry I had taken before bed. Slowly, I lay back on my pillow and pulled my quilt up to my neck, seeking sleep again, but sleep was slow to return.

CHAPTER TEN

'Really I have nothing to complain of,
for what I see makes me think of the wonders of the Arabian
Nights.'   **A.D.**

I did my best to put that strange dream out of my mind,
although the next time I saw Erik, I was extremely grateful
for the dimness of the room because it prevented him from seeing the
hot blush spreading across my cheeks. I found it impossible to forget
the intense desire that had coursed through me in my dream, especially
when confronted with the object of that desire in the flesh. My eyes
would dart to his lips of their own accord, and I would drag them away
and then begin blushing all over again. I was indescribably thankful
that Erik could not read my thoughts. Fortunately, I experienced no
further dreams of such a personal nature, and after a few days I was
able to meet with, talk to and actually look him in the face. I was
relieved when enough time passed that I was able to forget it. *Of course*
I forgot it.

Moreover, I had a new worry to occupy me. Father Barbier
caught a bad cold, no doubt from one of the few family visitors who
came occasionally to the hospital, and was bedridden. Dr. Gaudet was
really worried, and so was I. Illness was a particular risk for the leprosy
patients, for they were more susceptible and more likely to succumb to
complications than healthy people were.

I recalled that my mother had a very nourishing chicken soup
recipe that she used to make especially for the sick; I had never made it
because the stock took a long time to prepare and there were quite a
few ingredients. Driven by a sense of urgency, I now hunted until I
found the recipe in her collection and made a pot to take with me to
St. Giles.

Unable to remain downstairs in the refectory and allow one of
the nuns to take a bowl up to Father Barbier's room, I insisted on
doing it myself in order to check on his condition. What I found
shocked me. He was worse than I expected; so ill he scarcely had the
energy to sit up, much less eat. Standing near his bed, I cajoled,
coaxed and threatened until I had forced him to finish the bowl.

It was, *naturellement*, the first time I had ever seen his little
room, for generally only the caretaking nuns were permitted into the
patients' rooms. I was not surprised to see that Father Barbier's room

was as bare and pure as the cell of a monk, with a beautiful old crucifix over the bed and a religious print hanging over the small fireplace. The worm-eaten mantle was lined with his books, and what I knew must be some carvings in wood from his days in Africa, for they were executed in an outlandish and primitive style.

When he finished the soup, he lay back on the pillow, pale and exhausted, and closed his eyes. "My dear Sylvie," he whispered weakly, "I had no idea you possessed such a forceful personality."

Setting the bowl and spoon carefully aside, I said worriedly, "Father, you need nourishment if you are to get better, and I insist upon your getting better." I leaned over him as I spoke, unable to keep my concern from showing in my voice.

He opened his dark eyes and looked at me. I was alarmed to see how lacking in their usual bright, intelligent sparkle his eyes were. He really did not look well. I longed to be able to give him a comforting touch, even to be able to tuck the heavy brown blanket up around his chin, but I could not, so I must be satisfied with just standing near him for a bit.

"You are a dear girl; I do not understand why someone as young and vibrant as yourself should want to spend time with a decrepit old man like me." His voice was weak, but his eyes took on a little of their usual twinkle as he spoke. "You should go *maintenant, ma chére*; there is no need for you to expose yourself so."

"Do not worry about me," I said reassuringly. "I find your company very comforting, Father. I am fond of everyone here, of course, but you are special to me – I feel sometimes as if I had always known you."

"Well, my dear, if I had not been a priest and had had a family instead, you would be exactly the sort of daughter I would want. Perhaps God has given us to each other as a gift for being good sorts of people. I would like to think so, anyway."

I was so moved by his tender declaration that tears sprang to my eyes. In my heart, I felt the same. But I could see it tired him to talk; *et aussi* he was right, I should not stay. Hastily dashing the tears from my eyes, I rose, saying, "I had better go now, so you can rest, Father. I will be back tomorrow and I expect you to eat your soup with some bread next time."

"*À demain*, my dear," he murmured, his eyes already drooping closed. The effort required to swallow some soup and talk a little had exhausted him. I slipped quietly out of the austere little room and then stood outside his door for a moment, trying to collect myself. What if

Father Barbier should succumb to his illness? It was certainly possible given his compromised health. What would I do without him? I knew that in some way, he had come to take the place of my own father in my heart.

Dr. Gaudet was waiting for me at the foot of the stairs, looking concerned. "My dear, you should not have…" Then he saw the empty bowl in my hands and a look of pleased surprise crossed his broad face. "You were able to get him to eat for you, Mlle. Bessette?"

I nodded, frowning. "*Oui*, but he is very weak. It would be good if he could be persuaded to take a little more later today."

"We will try. I won't deny that I am worried about him. I have never seen him so ill. I only hope it will not spread among my other patients." He shook his head, his eyes full of concern that mirrored my own.

We walked to the kitchen together where I left the bowl and spoon with a nun to be washed. "Let us hope he will be a little better by tomorrow when I return. I will force-feed him if need be." I said determinedly. If there was anything *I* could do to keep him in this world, I would do it.

Dr. Gaudet gave me a small, tight smile. "If anyone can convince him to eat, it is you, Mademoiselle. He has a real *rapport* with you. I appreciate your help."

I was disconsolate and worried as I made my departure homeward in the wagon next to Robert. I had grown so attached to Father Barbier in such a short period of time. I loved his irrepressible cheerfulness, his kindliness, his sweet nature, and *bien sûr*, his charm. I sighed. Robert glanced over at me but said nothing, as usual. I was thankful for his silence tonight, for I did not feel like talking.

Even Erik, who seldom paid any more attention to me than was necessary (except when I did not want him to), noticed when I saw him that night that my spirits flagged. Normally, I was excited and eager to see him, but tonight, preoccupied with Father Barbier's condition, my steps dragged and I could not muster a smile when Erik, immaculate and handsome as always, assisted me through the window. Fixing me with a penetrating look, his eyes examined my face carefully.

"Is something wrong, Sylvie?" He asked.

"No. Yes. No." I stammered. "Yes."

"Well, I am glad we have cleared that up," he said wryly. We were standing by the ledge, illuminated by the oil lamp resting there, and I could see his lips turn up slightly at the corners. Then, in one of those abrupt *volte-faces* he was capable of, his voice became unexpectedly kind.

"Something is worrying you. Your face is like an open book, you know."

I had not intended to say anything, but, emboldened by his kindness, it all came out in a rush - I told him about Father Barbier, about my fondness for him, and how worried I was because he was so ill. I even found myself telling him about the special chicken soup recipe. I said more than I intended, no doubt encouraged by his unexpected appearance of concern, and my relief in having someone I could unburden myself to. Erik listened attentively, saying nothing, letting me talk until I was finished. I found myself feeling a little embarrassed and foolish.

"*Pardon*, I did not mean to go on so," I said apologetically. "I am just so worried."

Erik turned away and began helping me to gather up the empty tray. He said, in a cool, businesslike voice, "Your soup is a good idea, but I recommend adding fresh lemon juice to it next time."

I stared at him, startled. How could he possibly know anything about cooking?

"Why, Erik?"

He fixed me with a rather stern look. "Just try it. Go home *maintenant* and stop worrying. I doubt very much that your Father Barbier would have the nerve to die while you are looking after him. Or he may welcome death just to escape your badgering." This rude comment was delivered slyly as he was helping me out the window, but before I could respond he added, "If for some reason you are unable to come tomorrow evening, send a message to Madame Giry. She will see that I receive it."

I stopped, half in and half out, sitting on the window ledge. Moved by his unexpected show of kindness, impulsively I reached out and rested my hand on the arm that was grasping mine to steady me.

"*Merci*, Erik. You are very kind. But I pray that I will find Father Barbier better tomorrow, not worse."

I saw his eyes drop down to look at my hand on his arm. Gently, but firmly, he removed it with his own gloved hand and pushed me through the window. I swung my legs around and stood up. He handed me the tray and then looked at me, his face austere.

"You pray then, do you?" Erik asked finally.

I felt myself blush a little — feeling shamefaced because I seldom, in fact, did pray or even attend services. I replied, somewhat flippantly, "In Father Barbier's case, it seems appropriate, don't you think?"

Erik was unamused. His upper lip curled back disdainfully, baring his teeth. "I do not believe in *le Bon Dieu*, and he does not believe in me." He answered curtly. Giving me one of those frighteningly feral smiles, he added, "As a matter of fact, there are those who believe I am in league with *le diable* himself, and perhaps they are right."

I scowled at him. If I had not been holding something, I would have put my hands on my hips just like my mother used to do with me when I said something saucy or impertinent to her.

"Well," I said sternly, thinking in particular of the red skull painted on the window, "you certainly seem to do everything in your power to make people believe that. However, I refuse to believe it myself, in spite of appearances to the contrary."

"Just give me time," he said ominously. "*Bonne nuit*, Sylvie, and do not worry about your friend. I expect he will be better tomorrow." With that enigmatic comment, Erik closed the window, leaving me standing outside alone and perplexed. It was odd the way he managed to be both frightening and gentle at the same time. I doubted I would ever grow accustomed to the complexities of his personality.

More slowly, I followed suit, and walked away. It had been an odd conversation, but in some inexplicable way, I was comforted by it. I slept peacefully that night, undisturbed by dreams, nightmares, or even worry about Father Barbier. Erik had said he would be better, and somehow I believed him.

And mysteriously, Erik was proved right: Father Barbier *was* better the next day. I could tell as soon as I entered his austere little room to find him sitting up in his bed with all appearances of being on the watch for me.

"Father! You are looking much better today!" I exclaimed, awash with relief. Dr. Gaudet had intercepted me in the refectory and informed me of the improvement, which he was pleased to attribute to my special chicken soup. One of the nuns had persuaded Father Barbier to take more soup in the evening. Today his colour was better, his eyes looked clearer.

"I feel better today, Sylvie," he said when he saw me. "I believe I am on the mend, thanks to you. Dr. Gaudet has just taken my pulse and he thinks it is stronger today."

"I am very glad to hear it," I replied sincerely, carefully offering him the bowl and spoon. The wonderful, healing fragrance of the golden broth filled the room with its wholesomeness. Father Barbier took the bowl in his hands. After the first spoonful, his eyebrows shot up and he gave me an enquiring look.

"What is that I can taste in the soup? It is different from what you brought me yesterday."

"Do you like it?" I asked.

"*Oui*, it is delicious, and fresh, somehow."

"It is lemon juice, added just at the end, when the soup is nice and hot. A …friend gave me the suggestion." He did not notice my little secret smile. I had tasted it myself, *naturellement*, and it really was a good addition. I vowed to ask Erik where he had got the idea.

I stayed until Father Barbier had finished every spoonful, just to be sure. Handing me back the empty bowl, he said, "This is the best soup I have ever tasted. You should open a *café*, my dear."

"*Non, merci*, I am happy with things the way they are." I smiled down at him. "Perhaps tomorrow you will be strong enough to come downstairs."

"We shall see. It is God's will, and yours too, I daresay."

I left the hospital in a much happier frame of mind. Perhaps Erik was right – Father Barbier would not dare to die with me looking after him! God would have something to answer for should that have happened.

That night I was eager to see Erik and tell him my good news. I am not sure why I thought he would be interested; but he had seemed concerned so I wanted to let him know the old missionary was out of danger. And that I had taken his advice about the lemon juice. In a rush, I actually arrived several minutes ahead of schedule, flushed and breathless with anticipation.

Upon my arrival at the marble room I found it empty. I was not discouraged at first, for it was not unheard of for Erik to arrive after I did. I cast several surreptitious glances at the faded hanging as I made my exchange of trays. I dawdled as long as I reasonably could, but still he did not come. Disappointment warred with worry; eventually I went to the tapestry and lifted it aside, peering down the staircase, half expecting to see him emerging from the darkness. I could almost hear him greeting me with a sardonic remark to express his displeasure at catching me on the watch for him. The stair, however, was dark and empty; my listening ears heard only a profound silence. Now I really *was* disappointed. Dropping the tapestry and letting it fall back into place, I had turned halfway back toward the ledge when I suddenly froze in the midst of my turn. I was suddenly seized with a mad idea.

Since Erik was not here, why not deliver the warm tray myself and save him a trip? I knew where to go now, having explored those depths once before, unbeknownst to him. I need only leave it on a convenient table (did Erik *have* a table?) and depart. How could he consider it anything but a kind and thoughtful gesture? How indeed! I have no idea why this seemed so reasonable to me at the time, when it was obviously a clear violation of my instructions: *'Do not attempt to penetrate further into the building,'* he had commanded, and there was something else about danger, but I had already violated that command without encountering anything more dangerous than black water lapping at the stone causeway. My worst fear, encountering rats on the stairs, had proven an unfounded one. Somehow in that rash moment it did not occur to me that the only real danger I faced was from Erik himself.

I did worry that I might actually meet him along the way. The thought of how furious he would be made me go cold all over. And there was the not inconsequential problem of how to hold a candle to light my way while also holding a loaded tray containing a bowl of hot soup. I could not possibly manage. Clearly the sensible thing was for me to go home.

I suppose my growing fascination with Erik colored my judgment somewhat. In the end I hesitated only briefly before carefully tucking the tray under one arm and grasping my candle high with the other. Then I took my first step downward. Drawing a deep breath, I went on.

A dozen times during my progress a voice in my head cried, "Go back, go back, you idiot!" but I heeded it not, having set my feet upon my chosen path. In truth, I was tired of speculating about it: I wanted to see where and how he lived. I suppose by that time I was beyond rational thinking where Erik was concerned. I never stopped to consider this could, and probably would, spell the end of my contract with him, and possibly have even more serious consequences for me.

By the time I negotiated the mazelike passageways and the causeway it was too late to turn back. My progress was much faster now that I knew the way. I found the false door in the brick wall easily – by blowing out my candle and standing quietly in the dark, I could just make out a faint strip of light seeping from under it. Heart pounding, I raised my hand into a fist and bravely rapped on the door, calling to him as I did so.

"Erik, are you there? It is Sylvie." Who else would it be, I thought with a little hysterical bubble of laughter, the tax collector perhaps? Only an ominous silence answered my knock. I stood perplexed for a moment, but the only sound was the dark water as it lapped gently against stone. It seemed the Phantom was not at home.

Emboldened by Erik's absence, I drew a long, calming breath and cautiously pressed on the door, for there was no indication of how it opened. To my dismay, nothing happened; the door remained tightly closed. After running my hand gently over it several times, my eager fingers finally found a tiny catch. I pressed the catch; the door abruptly, silently opened outward, rotated around in a circle and shut again. I was so startled I made no move to enter, and so had to press the catch again. This time I was ready and slipped through when the door made its silent and smooth revolution. It was perfect for stepping through while carrying something, I mused. He must have designed it specifically for this purpose.

At first I could not tell what sort of room I was standing in. This small room was not the source of the light; the faint glow, brighter now, was emanating from beyond this place. Ah, he used this outer room for storage – by the light of my relit candle I could see wooden crates and casks stacked neatly around the perimeter, and a large box of white candles of various sizes, some quite large. A watery dark green sparkle caught by my light showed wine bottles shimmering as they lay on their sides in a rack. A small wooden table against one wall held a little pottery oil lamp that was a duplicate of the one in the marble room upstairs. The rough walls appeared to have been carved out of the very stone of the earth.

Satisfied that there was nothing of interest for me in Erik's tidy storage room, I made my way across it to another sort of door. At least I surmised it was a door. This one was tall and smooth, in a large gilt frame. Anxious now, my fingers fumbled as I tried to find some way of opening it. At last I realized it was quite simple: this door slid to one side on a little track. I promptly pushed it to the side, frame and all, holding my breath expectantly, but still could see nothing. Directly

100

in front of me hung a heavy damask curtain thick with gold fringe, completely blocking my view of what lay beyond. With trembling fingers and pounding heart, I lifted aside the heavy fabric and stepped at last into the Phantom's Lair.

Vraiment, it was like stepping into a waking dream. I had never in my life been in such a strange, otherworldly place! There was water, a lake or a pool disappearing into distance – part of the underground lake? My gaping eyes took in what appeared to be a hundred candles of various sizes in ornate gilt candelabra and candlesticks on every surface, pools of hardened white wax puddled at their bases and dripping down their sides. A few of them were lit, providing the light I had observed from under the door. There was also pale, indirect light falling on the water.

To my left, on a raised stone dais, stood a pipe organ, the great pipes rising beyond it looked as though they should be in a cathedral, rather than what seemed to be a large natural cavern cut into the very foundations of the earth. Beyond that, I could see pieces of furniture, tables, and large swaths of fabric draping the walls of the cave. There were even some old etchings of Paris streets and landmarks attached to the walls. I felt my lips quirk into a little smile as I recognized an old lithograph of the Arc de Triomphe. If this was Erik's attempt at making the vast space seem home-like, he had most certainly failed.

Pages of hand-written music lay scattered about or rested on gilt music stands. I had never seen so much ornate, gilt furnishing in my life – it was absolutely *trop grand*. There was something almost *Persian* or Bedouin about the place, like a sultan's tent in the desert hung all about and underfoot with rich carpets and woven hangings. I gazed avidly about me, blinking with astonishment. It was so *incroyable*; I almost pinched myself to make sure I was not dreaming this Arabian Nights setting.

One quick scan of the large open cavern assured me I was alone in Erik's extraordinary home, and I breathed a sigh of relief, for he would surely be furious with me if he found me here. That frightening recollection sent my heart pounding again and galvanized my frozen feet into moving. I scurried across the stone dais, down the other side, toward a table I could see beyond.

On my way a curious sight caught my attention and I paused to examine it: a beautiful miniature of a theatre stage, complete with a perfect little chandelier hanging overhead. I recognized it as an exact reproduction of the stage far above, in the Opera House. I wondered if Erik had made it himself. The little replica possessed a certain charm, especially the tiny doll figures that must represent performers on the stage, creating a little *mise en scène*, but I tore myself away from the model and pressed on, finally resting my dinner tray on the table I had seen. The soup was still hot and smelled divine, and most of it was still in the bowl. I did hope he would be back soon to partake of it before it grew cold. I could not imagine what was keeping him away for so long.

I was curious as to whether or not Erik had any means of warming food, or of warming himself for that matter. I had not yet observed a fireplace, hearth or anything like it. What a dismal place this must be without any fire for warmth! With this in mind, I started back the way I had come, determined to see the rest of Erik's home before leaving. I knew I ought to depart immediately, but diffused light glittered like green jewels on the water's surface, catching my eye and making me pause. For the first time I noticed there was a large portcullis opening framed dramatically by heavy dark drapes, and beyond them the water continued through a long, narrow canal before disappearing into the distant darkness. This watercourse must be how Erik came and went, since he never used the window in the marble room. The water was peaceful, unmarred by even a ripple, with little curls of mist floating on its calm surface. It was rather attractive in fact, like viewing a fairy's pool in the moonlight. Erik's entire home was like a giant stage set for some mythic production. What a strange place to live!

I carried on past the sliding mirror door through which I had made my entrance, looking about me curiously. There were several large hangings covering similar tall frames, and when I peered behind one I beheld yet another mirror. Inexplicably, all the mirrors were covered. More stone steps led up to another part of the cavern, thence to another sort of room cut roughly into rock. I climbed the steps and made for the opening, thinking that I might discover a fireplace or something of the sort.

Looking into the opening, I beheld a bed. At least, I supposed it was a bed. It was in the shape of a huge winged bird, its tall golden head raised proudly as if surveying the water beyond. More candelabra and other furnishings could be seen beyond, and on a little table nearby, rested a hideous music box in the shape of a rather wizened monkey. As a result of an unpleasant childhood experience I have always disliked monkeys, and this one was particularly unattractive. It looked like a real one had been killed and stuffed (Much later, I would learn that Erik had made the thing himself, and composed the little piece of music it played as well). A brass dish sat next to it, holding a small molded piece of some dark substance, from which an exotic fragrance was faintly emanating. Bending close, I breathed in the heady, spicy scent I had first noticed when Erik knelt to examine the bump on my head. I had not recognized it at the time, but this was surely the source: incense. It was like nothing I had ever smelled before, and it made me think of the Orient and all the exotic places I had never been but read about in books.

My eyes were drawn back to the golden bird. I was pulled toward that intimate object as if by an invisible cord. It was opulent and plush inside, big enough, I noticed, for two people to recline. The seductive memory of my dream flashed unbidden through my head, and with that very improper thought, I felt myself burning with embarrassment and shame. And it was at that moment, that *extremely* inopportune moment, a voice, a *very* angry voice sounded right behind me.

"Did it ever occur to you to do *anything* I asked you to do?"

I gasped and whirled to see Erik standing *right there*, his face livid with rage, looking as if he wanted to grab me and shake me apart. Horror at my position seized me. Oh, how I wanted to sink into the earth, to vanish from this spot! I felt myself flush scarlet to the roots of my hair – indeed it felt like my head was about to burst into flames. That he should find me here at all was bad enough, but to find me standing by his *bed*! What must he think of me? Shame threatened to overwhelm me; how could he not feel the heat radiating off my face? And how the devil had he arrived here without my hearing him?

"I am so sorry, Erik," I stammered pathetically. "I didn't intend…that is, I don't know…I wanted to see where you lived, that is all. I meant no harm. I…I was only going to leave your dinner here and see if you had any means of keeping it warm." I was acutely conscious of babbling incoherently and forced myself to close my mouth to stop the flow of words. I could scarcely bring myself to meet his eyes, so great was my mortification at that moment.

He was so furious he practically spat at me, "I live here precisely because I need to be left alone. No one else has ever been here except you. Don't you understand that anyone I found trying to reach this place would never leave it alive?" He was glowering down at me fiercely, his black-gloved hands clenched into fists. He looked absurdly handsome standing there, quivering with fury, his pale blue eyes like twin shards of ice in his flushed face.

My shame and embarrassment at being caught in Erik's bedroom was beginning, belatedly, to give over to a sense of fear. He was far angrier with me now than he had been the first time I met him, to be sure.

Hoping to placate him, I stammered, "B…but Erik, no one knows I am here, no one has ever seen me enter the window, and I promise you I would never betray your secret." To my chagrin, my voice shook. This turned out to be the wrong approach. At my words a cunning look came in to his eyes, dimming the anger but no less disconcerting.

"No one knows you are here, that is true," he murmured softly, almost to himself, in a voice now purring with menace. He took a silent, catlike step toward me. "I can do whatever I like with you," he added thoughtfully, his hands unclenching.

Truly terrified now, I had to conjure up all the nerve I possessed to keep from taking a matching step back. My chin went up.

"You would not harm me, Erik," I said, trying to sound calm and confident when I was quaking inside. How I hoped I was right.

"And what is to stop me? Certainly not you, Sylvie." Another step. He looked at me with deadly intent. His arm stretched out, reaching toward me. What was he going to do to me? Were these my last moments on this earth? I could feel the blood slowly draining from my face. Unable to stop myself, I took that backward step; something hard pressed against the small of my back. It was the beak of that absurd golden bird. I could retreat no further. Beads of sweat broke out on my forehead.

"Give me one good reason why not…" Erik murmured in a menacingly soft voice.

Fortunately, I was able to think of one. "You…you would miss my cooking." I said reasonably, as if this made perfect sense.

Erik paused in the act of reaching for me, tilting his head to one side as if seriously considering this. Then he shook his head regretfully.

At first I thought he had rejected my argument and was about to throttle me, until he said wryly, "I suppose you are right, I *would* miss your cooking, especially the tagine." As he spoke, his hand closed over my upper arm, his hard fingers biting into my flesh. I winced, but he did not soften his grip. The glower still firmly in place, he pulled me none too gently out of his bedroom and down toward the pipe organ on its raised dais. It was impossible to resist his firm hold on me, so rather than try to pull away I simply followed him rather precipitously down the stone steps, trying not to trip over my own skirts. He stopped at a massive wood table and shoved me unceremoniously into a chair, where I landed with a gasp and an audible thump. Several loosened pins fell out of my *chignon*.

I found myself seated at the same table where I had set down my tray and candle, and I was conscious of a pleasant but incongruous fragrance of rich *soupe à l'oignon* emanating from the covered dish. Erik noticed it, too. He raised the cover, took a long, appreciative sniff, and gazed sidelong at me, his eyes glittering with malice.

"Are you frightened of me, Sylvie? You should be, you know. Did you think I was going to wring your neck?" His beautiful lips curved up in a wicked little smile. "I could have. I wouldn't have used a rope, either," he added conversationally.

I stared at him round-eyed, my heart thumping so hard he ought to hear it. "You are terrifying me, actually," I whispered, my mouth as dry as dust. There was no point in denying the fact; he must have seen me go white to the lips with fear. Smirking slightly, Erik replaced the cover on the soup.

"I had to teach you a lesson, you foolish creature. You never follow my instructions, you fearlessly invade my privacy. If your cooking were not so sublime, I would put an end to our agreement this very night. And you are very fortunate indeed that I find you harmless and trust you well enough not to kill you. You have no idea how fortunate."

I could think of nothing to say in response to this statement, so I refrained from speaking. My eyes were glued to his, and my breath came in shallow little gasps. Meanwhile, an idiotic little voice inside my head was singing happily, *he thinks my cooking is sublime!*

Erik gazed at me thoughtfully for a moment, and I knew his eyes were missing nothing. Finally, he sighed, and it was a profoundly sad sound. "You don't know me very well, Sylvie." He said. The teasing note was gone from his voice.

I cleared my throat before responding. "No, I do not. But that is your fault, not mine." I said crisply.

"*My* fault!" He exclaimed exasperatedly. Any trace of lingering sadness vanished in a trice. "Because I prefer to guard my privacy, because I ask only to be left alone – a request which you, I might add, have willfully disregarded on more than one occasion."

"I am sorry, but I cannot seem to help myself," I admitted reluctantly. "I *would* like to know you better, Erik." Erik stared at me, his dark brows drawing together.

"Why?" He demanded. And it was clear from his scowl that he had no idea how fascinating he was to me.

I considered his question carefully before answering. I wished to be honest, but not *too* honest. I would rather he did not realize just how compelling, how *interesting*, I found him to be, even now, when he was frightening me out of my wits.

"I suppose because I have never met anyone like you before," I finished lamely. That much was certain, I thought wryly.

Erik shook his head, a grim expression on his face. "I should have known your insatiable curiosity would get the better of you eventually. But you have no idea what a risk you were taking by coming down here, Sylvie. If you had tried to reach this place a different way, you could easily have fallen into one of a number of traps, any one of which would have resulted in a very unpleasant death. You should not have come here."

His words stung. He was right, of course; I should not have come, but it hurt to hear him say it. It sounded too much as if he were saying he did not *want* me here: a very different thing entirely. Not wanting him to see the naked disappointment on my face, I looked down at my hands folded tightly in my lap and said nothing. I could feel his eyes on me.

He sighed again. "Are you feeling better now?" He asked in a gentler voice after a few seconds of silence.

I wasn't certain – I was still feeling the pain of rejection, but perhaps I *was* feeling a little better now that meeting death at Erik's hands did not seem quite so imminent. I nodded, looking up at last from my contemplation of my folded hands, lacing my fingers together tightly so that he could not see that they were trembling. I also owed him an apology (*another* apology!), so I drew in a breath and gave it to him.

"I am so very sorry I disobeyed you, Erik. I know it was wrong of me. But I do feel fairly confident that you are too much a gentleman to harm a lady."

"Hmmm. I may possess some of the instincts of a gentleman, but I would not rely on that if I were you," he said. "I have lived as an outcast for so long I have become a law unto myself." Rising, he went to a side table pushed up against the stone wall of the cavern, returning with a bottle and two long-stemmed wine glasses.

"I think a little of this will restore the colour to your cheeks before you leave. It is an Imperial Tokay, one of the few luxuries I can have." He poured a half glass, pushed it toward me, and then poured out a measure for himself before continuing. "I have never harmed a woman, *c'est vrai*, but do not push me too far, Sylvie. There is always a first time, and you do not always behave like a lady." This threat was delivered slyly, accompanied by a sidelong glance of amusement.

"Drink your wine." He added gently. Picking up his glass, he drank deeply, set the glass down and smirked at me. "Go ahead, Sylvie. It is not drugged." Why did I feel like a mouse being tormented by a large cat just prior to being dispatched?

I took a small sip of the wine, and it was sweet and delicious. I had another, larger sip, feeling the warmth from the wine moving through my body. I had never tasted Imperial Tokay, it being far out of my price range. Erik watched me, the smirk lingering on the side of his face visible to me, and it occurred to me that all along he *had* been playing cat and mouse with me, as my punishment for invading his domain. A warm flush of embarrassment spread across my face, but I really could not blame him. It had been wrong of me; I had been willful and inconsiderate of his privacy yet again. I decided this was a good time to change the subject.

"Why didn't you ever tell me the Moroccan tagine was your favorite? Had I known, I would have made it for you again."

He shrugged. "I enjoy everything you bring me, Sylvie. It is of no matter. But I believe I like the tagine because it reminds me…of places I have been…but as I said, it is of no matter." More secrets, more questions for me to file away for future reference. I was determined to winnow them out of him eventually.

Feeling more relaxed now, thanks to the wine and Erik's abandoning his game of terrifying me, I looked around the cavernous space with avid curiosity. I had not had time to take it all in before.

"Where on earth did you get all this furniture? I have never seen so much gilt since I toured the Palace at Versailles!"

"You don't care for my *décor*? It is opulent, I admit, but beggars can't be choosers as the English say. These are all props, 'borrowed', if you like, from the lower storage vaults of the Opera." He gestured upward as he spoke. "At least, most of them came from there." He gave me a wry look. "In case you failed to notice, I have a theatrical nature, and living here allows me to indulge myself."

"*Oui*, I can see that." My eyes fell on a huge, ornate chair, more like a throne for a king than a mere chair. It must, I thought, have featured in a play on the stage far above. I could picture Erik sitting there brooding over his dark domain. "You said most of it came from here – what about the rest?" I asked.

"A few things, a very few things, I brought with me when I came here."

"Why only a few?" I asked interestedly.

He gazed away toward the water, where a little mist curled across the calm surface. Following his gaze, I now observed a little boat tied up at the water's edge. What was that on the prow? I frowned, peering at it harder. Ah, I ought to have guessed. It was a skull, cast in some sort of metal.

At first I thought he wasn't going to answer, but then Erik spoke at last. "It was necessary for me, once or twice, to depart in haste from where I was living, due to circumstances that were beyond my control," he said in answer to my question. His tone closed the door firmly on further questions. Abruptly he turned to look back at me.

"Now," he said in a brisk, business-like voice, "It's time you went home, Sylvie. I have just received some rather vexing news, and I must consider the ramifications." As he spoke, he removed a letter from the inside pocket of his tailcoat and placed it on the table. "I am a creature of habit; I dislike change, especially when the change affects me directly."

"Most men are creatures of habit," I murmured, speaking my thought out loud.

Erik glanced up from his letter. "And how would *you* know?" He asked acidly.

Unoffended by his sarcastic tone, I shrugged and began collecting my fallen hairpins and pushing them back into the somewhat disarrayed knot at the back of my head.

"I was married once; I am not completely without experience in the ways of the world." *Not necessarily good experiences, either,* I thought to myself, this time prudently not speaking my thought out loud.

"You were married *once*," he said, emphasizing the last word. "You are a widow?" He sounded only mildly curious.

This was not a conversation I wished to have, so I merely answered "no."

Erik opened his mouth to say something else, then closed it again, and turned back to his letter. Regretting my curt response to his innocent question, I gestured toward the letter in his hand, saying in a normal tone of voice, "I hope it is not bad news." I wondered if he would confide in me.

Perhaps he did feel the need to unburden himself to someone, for he went on, "It is from Monsieur Poligny, who manages my theatre." I frowned, mildly irritated. I knew perfectly well Erik did not own the theatre. I remembered Celestine telling me once what a proprietary interest he took in its operations, however. "He kindly informs me that he and his partner are retiring and are bringing in a pair of new owners." He glanced over at me. "Have you ever been to a performance or a concert there?" He asked. I shook my head. I had never been able to afford such a luxury, nor had I an escort to take me. "A pity. It is a beautiful building. The architect, M. Garnier (who employed me, by the way) designed a real masterpiece here. The acoustics are quite superior." As he spoke he proceeded to read his letter over again and reluctantly I rose to make my departure.

Erik slapped the letter down, making a little noise of derision as he did so. "They are apparently bringing a wealthy backer along with them, which is a good thing for them. M. Poligny promises to inform the new owners about me and let them know my rules and requirements, that is all very well but I daresay I shall have to break them in myself." He gave me a sharp look as I was collecting my shawl. "If they are anything like you, they will ignore my instructions and I shall have to make a little trouble for them."

I could not repress a quick, involuntary shudder, recalling how menacing he could be, and had been, only moments before. My shawl slipped from my suddenly clumsy fingers to the floor. Erik was picking it up for me with one of his swift, panther-like movements before I could even recover myself to bend and retrieve it. In an unexpected but rather sweet gesture, he reached around me to drape the shawl over my shoulders. I was unprepared to find his face so close to mine; that unexpected proximity did strange things to my heart that had nothing to do with fear. I found myself gazing up at those well-formed lips only inches from mine as if mesmerized. They looked so soft and appealing when not drawn into a hard line from anger. I had no such tender effect on Erik, however.

He pulled the ends of the shawl over my arms and stepping away, said, "What is the matter with you, Sylvie? You look like a bird hypnotized by a snake. I hope you are not still afraid that I would harm you." He returned with a candle in one of the smaller gilt candlesticks and handed it to me. He was frowning again.

"Nothing is the matter. I am fine." Accepting the candle, I quickly averted my gaze to my hand as it wrapped around the holder. I did not want Erik to see my expression at that moment. It made me sad, the way he could so willfully misunderstand his affect on me. And it hurt that, instead of inspiring similar sentiments in him, I only managed to vex and annoy him.

And he was clearly annoyed with me now. "Allow me to remind you, you have no one to blame but yourself if you are afraid. I did not invite you here – you willfully trespassed. Come, give me the candle and I will go with you as far as the window. If you stumbled and fell on the steps you would probably say it was my fault." Sounding exasperated, he reached for the candlestick. As he plucked it from my hand, his warm gloveless fingers accidentally brushed against mine and a jolt of pure pleasure ran through me. But when I glanced up at him, he was already turning away.

Sighing, I tied the ends of my shawl into a knot and attempted to put a more light-hearted tone into my voice. "I *said* I was sorry, Erik, but I still think it was a mean trick to frighten me like that."

"You will get no apology from me," he said in a self-satisfied manner. "In fact, I thoroughly enjoyed it." Leading the way to the tall mirror that disguised the secret entrance behind its enormous gilded frame, he lifted the heavy drapery out of the way. He then waited, a slight smirk visible on his face, but ever the gentleman, for me to go first. Which I did, mustering as much dignity as was possible under the circumstances.

The return trip to the marble room was made in heavy silence. Erik fell into a brooding quiet, thinking about his letter from M. Poligny I supposed. For my part, I was mulling over our recent conversation and everything that had happened. When he was assisting me to climb out the window, he spoke at last, catching me completely off my guard.

"Don't assume I have forgiven you your trespass tonight, Sylvie. One day I may decide you have not been punished enough."

Startled, I looked up at him quickly, but his expression was unreadable. His face looked austere and stern. The cursed mask hiding half his face made it difficult to read his moods at the best of times. But I was not about to let him think he had got the better of me.

Recovering from my temporary alarm, I gave my head a toss, replying, "And don't *you* be surprised that I will do it again. I could not help but notice that beautiful pipe organ you absconded with from the Opera House, *sans doute*. I expect you can play it. I should like to hear that some time." Brave words, now that I was outside in the street looking back at him, with a window ledge between us.

"Would you?" His face brightened; he looked almost pleased at the idea, but then his brows drew together. He frowned. "What a sly creature you are. You think you will gain admission to my home by legitimate means next time. *Très bien*, I will play for you one day, but I assure you, it will cost you, Sylvie."

Speechless, I watched his dark figure retreat from the window, until he vanished behind the tapestry. I did not feel quite so brave now. What did the cat have in store for the hapless mouse, I wondered?

CHAPTER ELEVEN

'When one loves, one is only too ready to believe one's love returned'

A.D.

How tired I felt the next morning! I blamed it on a restless night's sleep, tossing and turning and experiencing a nightmare or two. Additionally, I had gone to bed without any dinner, for when I returned from Erik's cavern, I felt too overwrought to eat. After my misadventure of the previous evening, it was not surprising.

At the Hospital I was pleased with Father Barbier's progress. He gained strength each day but was not yet strong enough to come downstairs to eat with the others. Dr. Gaudet was still concerned about preventing his illness from spreading to the other patients, so I continued to bring him his meal myself. But it made for a long day; by the time Robert delivered me back to my kitchen I was feeling quite done in.

Rather than prepare a separate dish for Erik that night, I brought back a portion of the *jambon* and leek pies I had baked for the patients. I hoped he would not mind, but I simply did not have the energy to cook again that night. I decided to go upstairs and lie down to rest a bit before it was time to make the delivery. I was certain a cup of hot tea and a rest would set me to rights before I undertook the journey.

I was not exactly looking forward to seeing Erik tonight; he had been so displeased with my inexcusable intrusion upon his closely guarded privacy. I would not put it past him to have thought of another way to punish me by now. Oh well; it would have to be done, although I really did not feel up to the trip, or to facing him.

I was doggedly going through the motions of tidying the kitchen and putting things away when a wave of dizziness swept over me and I was forced to sit down. I suddenly felt uncomfortably warm. Pressing the back of my hand to my forehead, I felt a fine sheen of moisture on it. It was necessary to face facts: grimly I had to admit to myself that this was more than mere tiredness - I was not well at all. My thoughts flew to Father Barbier. Was there a chance I had caught his terrible cold? I was so thirsty, so hot, and my head was beginning to pound.

I must have some water, I thought hazily. The water pitcher suddenly seemed far away. I rose from the chair and started to walk rather unsteadily toward it, but almost as soon as I stood up my head swam, and tiny flashing sparks of light danced before my eyes. Black clouds swirled around the room and then everything vanished into nothingness, as though a thick blanket had been thrown over my head.

A few seconds later, I was dismayed to find myself lying on the cold flagstone floor. I had fainted, I realized with shock. I *never* fainted. How strange. But the cool stone felt so good against my hot skin, I decided to stay there a little while longer. I was not certain I could get up just now anyway. I closed my eyes, my cheek pressed against the cold stone of the floor.

I do not know how long I lay there; I must have slept, I suppose. I was brought back to consciousness by the awareness of a peculiar sensation, as though I were floating. I was certainly moving - my eyes were closed, and my face was against fabric. I could feel it rasping against my cheek in a little scraping motion. I comprehended that I was being carried, limp and boneless, in someone's arms. Before I could register alarm at this circumstance, I breathed in the unique scent of spice and man that I knew belonged to Erik. What was he doing here?

I was not afraid; I might have been under other circumstances but at the moment I could not spare the energy. I had been hot before, but now I was cold, terribly cold. Shivers were running uncontrollably through my body. My head ached; in fact every part of me seemed to ache.

Erik's breathing was labored and I knew he was carrying me up the stairs; he paused at the door to my *salon*. I struggled to lift my heavy head from where it lolled on his shoulder. Opening my eyes with an effort, I found myself looking into his worried face. I brought my dangling arm up and weakly wound it around his neck to help redistribute my weight, while my other hand came up to grip the lapel of his coat.

"Erik…" my voice emerged as a scratchy whisper. A violent chill swept through me and my teeth started chattering. "I'm c-c-cold. So…cold…"

"I know, Sylvie; you will be warm soon, I promise." He sounded agitated and breathless. "I *knew* something was wrong," he muttered as if to himself, while pushing open the door with his foot. He carried me in, kicked the door shut behind him, and crossed the room quickly to deposit me gently on my *divan*.

113

"It wasn't like you not to come without sending word," he said. "I began to think that perhaps I had frightened you away last night. I wish now that I had not amused myself so much at your expense." While he was speaking he gently tucked a cushion behind my head. Glancing alertly around the room, he saw the door to my bedchamber and darted in there, coattails flying, returning almost at once with the quilt from my bed. He draped it over my shivering body and pulled it up to my chin.

"H-how…how long…" but my teeth chattered too much for me to finish my question. Unable to hold it back, a little moan of distress emerged from between my clenched teeth.

"I think you must have been lying on that damned floor for two hours at least, Sylvie. You gave me quite a shock when I found you there." While I pondered this information Erik, a frown of worry creasing between his eyes, tugged off his gloves and rested a warm hand on my forehead. It felt wonderful.

"You may feel cold, but you are running a fever. I do not like this." He muttered distractedly. Another uncontrollable chill coursed through me, I could feel my body tremble all over. I subsided back against the cushion and closed my eyes; I could not summon the strength to keep them open any longer. How odd; the hansom driver must have rung my bell when he came to collect me for my evening delivery, but the sound had not been able to penetrate my swoon.

"I…I think I must have f-fainted…" I whispered.

"Shhh. Try not to talk, as difficult as that is for you." His warm hand left my forehead and I felt a pang of loss while new shivers overtook me. As if from a far distance, I heard Erik moving around the apartment; he went in to my little *garde-manger*, returned and soon I heard the sounds of a fire being laid. In a few minutes it was crackling and burning brightly and I could feel warmth growing in the room. Then he was next to me again, shaking my shoulder to get my attention. When I cracked open my eyes, I saw he held a steaming cup of tea.

"Here Sylvie, take some of this." He commanded. The fragrant tea smelled wonderful, but when I reached for the cup, my hands trembled so that some of the liquid spilled over.

"C-can't…" I whispered miserably. Erik cursed quietly but with feeling, then sat next to me and held the cup to my lips. The first taste was heaven: hot, strong, sweet. A sigh of pleasure escaped me. With Erik's help the rest of the tea went down quickly. His gentle ministrations only added to the sense of unreality I felt. Could this be

114

the same man who had blithely threatened to throttle me with his bare hands the night before?

As soon as I had finished the cup, I felt a little better, and the bone-chilling cold receded somewhat. "*Merci*," I murmured, gratitude welling up inside me until tears burned at the corners of my eyes. Without any conscious thought, I reached out and put my hand over his where it rested on the quilt next to me. I felt him stiffen at the touch, but he did not pull away.

"Were you worried about me? Is that why you came here tonight?" I asked weakly.

"Of course not," Erik replied promptly. "Don't be absurd. I only wanted to find out where my dinner was." But we both knew better. His other hand, so nice and warm, came to rest on my forehead again. Erik was full of surprises - when I did not bring his dinner, he had been worried enough to come here to find me. He must feel some remorse over his enraged behavior last night. I never would have expected him to concern himself with my welfare to that degree, but I was thankful that he had, because otherwise I would probably still be lying downstairs on the cold kitchen floor. I wondered how he knew where I lived. Weakly, I turned my head a little to look at him. Another frown was creased between his eyes.

"Were you by any chance exposed to that sick man you were telling me about?" He asked, his hand still on my forehead.

I nodded, and the movement made my head hurt even more. "I have been helping him to eat."

Erik made a groaning sound of profound exasperation. "Why am I not surprised to hear that? You would try the patience of a saint, which I most definitely am not." He pulled his hand from under mine and passed it over his dark, smooth hair in a frustrated gesture. "I do not know what I am going to do with you, Sylvie. What a great deal of trouble you are. First you are mercilessly invading my privacy, and now *this*," he growled, but beneath the growl was a note of worry. "You require a doctor. I am going to go for Madame Giry and have her fetch a doctor back here to see you."

I knew he could not go for a doctor himself, but I did not want him to leave me. "*Non, non*, I do not want a doctor, Erik. Just need rest...I cannot be sick. They need me...I have to...have to..." He stopped me with two fingers pressed to my lips.

"You are going to stay right here and rest, Sylvie. For you to get up tomorrow and cook will be impossible. Even you must realize how ill you are." He tucked the quilt up around my neck a little tighter and rose to his feet. As large a man as he was, his every move was full of natural grace, even simply standing up. I sighed. He added a few pieces of coal to the fire, and then turned back to me.

"I am going to fetch Madame Giry for you. *And* a doctor. I will send her to you as quickly as I can." He gave me a stern look. "Do not move from that *divan!*"

I had no energy with which to argue, so I simply watched him go, and then I was alone, staring at the closed door. What an enigma he was! From being so furious he was threatening to murder me one day, to rescuing me off a cold floor the next. There was a wealth of goodness hidden away somewhere inside that extraordinary man, I was certain.

Slowly my eyelids drifted closed and I concentrated on absorbing the warmth of the fire into my aching body. Although I hated to admit it, Erik was right; there was no possible way I would be able to get up tomorrow and prepare the mid-day meal for the Hospital. But I was too exhausted to think what to do.

While all these chaotic thoughts ran through my mind I must have dozed off again, for the next thing I knew, Celestine was there in the room with me.

"Try to get her to take another cup of tea, or even better, a little broth, Madame," said a man's voice from somewhere above me. Opening my eyes, I saw a thin, stoop-shouldered, seedy-looking man standing beside me, reeking of stale tobacco and garlic. He grasped my limp wrist in his hand and was taking my pulse. When he saw that I was awake he gave me a cheerful grin, exposing teeth stained yellow from tobacco.

Although he must be the doctor Celestine had brought, he did not look much like a physician to me. A physician ought to resemble Dr. Gaudet or my own father, whose neat, tidy demeanor tended to inspire confidence. This fellow was not even wearing a cravat. He was, I later learned, the physician who was on call for the denizens of the Opéra Populaire; he lived not far from that building. Perhaps that explained his seedy appearance and casual demeanor.

Celestine bustled into my *garde-manger* while the doctor continued his examination. He pulled a thermometer from a black bag on the floor next to my *divan* and put it under my tongue, and he then studied my eyes intently, lifting the lids and peering under them.

"I see you are awake now, my dear. *Bon.* When did this first come on?" He asked me a number of questions and I answered as best I could with a thermometer in my mouth. I was not feeling cold

116

any longer, but my head hurt and all my joints ached. I was so weak I could barely lift my head. Celestine returned then with a cup of tea and helped me to drink it. She looked anxiously at the doctor.

"Do you know what is wrong with her, Doctor? Will she be all right?"

The doctor was taking something else out of his little black bag. "She has a fairly severe case of *la grippe*, Madame Giry. It is making the rounds of the city, unfortunately. I am leaving some aspirin for her; it will help with the pain, and also this laudanum to help her sleep. Get her to take tea and clear broth as much as possible, and rest. She ought to be better in a few days, but send for me if the fever increases. These things must run their course." He patted me gently on the shoulder. "*C'est la vie*, Mademoiselle," he said philosophically, and departed, the scent of garlic and tobacco trailing after him.

Celestine closed the door behind him and came back to sit near me. I drifted in and out of uneasy slumber; at one point I became aware that she had taken all the pins out of my hair and was tenderly brushing it out; she then braided it into a neat side braid for me. Her gentle touch reminded me of my mother and I took comfort in it.

"Do not worry about a thing, Sylvie," she murmured reassuringly. "In the morning just tell me where and I will send a message to the Hospital to let them know you are ill." I was not happy about this; I had never wanted to tell anyone the exact location of St. Giles, but it could not be helped. At some point she brought me some beef broth she had found in the kitchen downstairs, and then I slept again.

I awoke from that restless slumber with shocking abruptness. I was having a terrifying dream that my little *salon* fire had somehow escaped the fireplace and spread to the *divan* where I lay. I felt as though I were on fire. Flinging the quilt aside, I sat up in mindless panic, heart pounding. Firm hands were instantly on my shoulders pressing me back down, and I was too weak to fight against them.

"No you don't, Sylvie," said a stern voice I recognized. I cracked open my eyes to the dim light of early morning, and saw Erik sitting next to me.

"But I am so hot! I...I was dreaming I was on fire." I protested weakly, my hands fluttering up to grasp his arms, as if I had the strength in me to dislodge them.

"It is the fever – you feel as though you were burning up." Releasing my shoulders, he pressed something to my forehead and I

117

realized he was holding a cool cloth to my face. I wondered how long he had been doing that while I slept. "Here, drink this." I was able to hold the glass he placed in my hands; it was water, which I drank greedily.

Fully awake now, I looked at Erik worriedly. "The doctor said I have *la grippe*, Erik. You should not even be here; I might give it to you. Where is Celestine? I hope she will not fall ill too." My voice sounded thick in spite of the water; I had to stop and clear my throat before I could finish speaking.

"She returned to the Conservatory of Music to teach her ballet class, so I came to sit with you, at great inconvenience to myself, I might add." Erik frowned. "You are in no condition to be alone, Sylvie."

I felt so feverish and light-headed, I knew he was right. I felt damp and clammy all over. I was still wearing the same gown from the night before, now badly wrinkled, and my muslin chemise was wet from sweat. The dampness should have cooled my hot skin but it seemed to have the opposite effect. I felt like a steamed pudding. Plucking ineffectually at the folds of my gown, I tried to lift it away from my body.

"Help me walk to the bedroom, Erik. I cannot bear to be in this room, it is so hot. I do not think I can..." once again I struggled feebly to sit up. How frustrating it was to be as weak as a kitten.

With an exasperated sigh, Erik assisted me to raise myself off the *divan*. Ignoring my protests, he gathered me up in his arms again as easily as if I were a child and carried me into the bedroom.

"You need to get out of that gown," he muttered as he placed me gently on the side of my bed. It was so much cooler in here, I felt better at once. "Have you a nightgown to change into?" He glanced around the small room with a perplexed expression, obviously having absolutely no idea where to look for such an intimate item.

"The...the *armoire*." I said weakly. I began to unfasten my wrinkled gown but my fingers were unequal to the task. In a flash Erik was at my side. He put my white embroidered nightgown on the bed and pushed my weak and trembling hands away, and in a trice the gown was undone and sliding off me. The cool rush of air on my skin was heaven and I sighed in relief.

Although I was now clad in my muslin chemise, a modest, knee-length garment, Erik was clearly discomfited. Averting his eyes he said in a low voice, "I wish Madame Giry were here." It occurred to me rather belatedly that he probably had not had very many

118

opportunities to see ladies in their undergarments, and he was embarrassed.

I slipped my white ankle-length nightgown on over the damp, wrinkled chemise and pulled it down to cover myself, then wriggled out of the chemise and discarded it - the effort to do so used up all the energy I had. Exhausted, I slid under the cool sheet and into my bed with a grateful sigh. The cool linen sheets and soft pillow were comforting and my eyes closed almost instantly. Erik brought me more water and then I must have drifted off for a few minutes. When I opened my eyes again I saw that he had settled himself into a chair by the window and taken up a book.

"Erik," I whispered raspily, "You should not be here alone with me in my bed chamber; it is not proper." When I thought of the intimacy of him seeing me in my wrinkled undergarments, I felt a blush burn my cheeks in spite of how ill I felt. I knew that by the time I was feeling better, mere embarrassment would become utter mortification.

He made a noise of scornful amusement in his throat. "Believe me, Sylvie, even if I were the kind of man who would take advantage of a sick woman, you do not look particularly appealing at the moment." He replied drily. Certain that he was correct about that, I prudently remained silent. The truth was, I found Erik's still, watchful presence strangely comforting, and soon I drifted into heavy slumber. When I next awoke morning was far advanced, my fever had broken, Erik was gone and Celestine was there.

I spent the entire day in bed. She brought me soft eggs and broth and tea. By the afternoon I began to feel marginally better, enough to sit up in bed and pepper her with questions. One of the first things I had asked her to do for me was send a messenger to St. Giles to let them know I was ill; Father Barbier would feel terrible about giving me his illness, but it could not be helped. Now I had another pressing question for Celestine.

"How did Erik find out where I lived?"

Celestine was sitting on the window seat mending one of her stockings. She shrugged. "I had to tell him, Sylvie. I hope you don't mind. When you did not bring his dinner last night, he was certain something had befallen you; he came to my rooms demanding to know where you lived and would not take no for an answer." She glanced at me apologetically. "You know how he can be. He was quite agitated. I believe he has grown rather attached to you, my dear. I am very thankful that he was concerned enough to come here. I cannot bear to

119

think of you lying on that cold floor! You might not have been able to get up the stairs. You would have been much more ill if he had not found you, I am sure." She shuddered involuntarily, and so did I, remembering that bone-chilling cold.

Celestine looked at me curiously. "I have only ever known him as the Opera Ghost, but you call him 'Erik', Sylvie. Is that his true name?"

"No, it is not. It is just a name he has assumed at some time or another; I do not know when or why that particular name." I studied my teacup thoughtfully. "I do not know his real name, and I am not sure that he even remembers it himself."

"It is extraordinary, though. I do not believe he has told anyone that name except you. You are the only person he has allowed to be that close to him." I could not miss the slightly wistful tone of her voice. He had tried to keep me at arm's length, too, as he did everyone else, but I ignored his edicts and did as I pleased. I smiled a little at my own impertinence.

"In fact, I try his patience exceedingly, Celestine," I said truthfully. "Erik finds me very vexing, I am sure."

Night had gradually been falling while she sewed and we conversed companionably; suddenly there was a soft noise from the *salon* and then the object of our conversation was standing framed in the bedroom doorway. Had he heard me speaking of him? I felt myself blushing at the thought.

Erik looked me over critically. "You are looking better, Sylvie," he pronounced. "You have some colour in your cheeks." His observation only made my face burn hotter. He glanced over at Celestine. "I thought I heard my name; were you talking about me?" He did not sound pleased at the idea.

"*Oui*, I was just telling Sylvie how you happened to find her last night." She said composedly. "Well, *ma chère*, I ought to be getting back to check on Meg. She will not have a proper dinner if I do not scold her about it." Celestine rose, tucked her mending away, gave my shoulder a little pat, and departed. Apparently, she and Erik were taking turns watching over me. I was touched, I admit. This was what it was like to have friends.

Erik turned back to survey me again, crossing his arms across his chest and scowling. "You *do* vex me, Sylvie. It is what you do best, next to cooking." So he *had* heard me. I groaned and slid down under my quilt.

It was an entire fortnight before I felt well enough to resume my duties for the Hospital. During that time Dr. Gaudet came to visit me twice, brought by Robert in the wagon. I was very happy to see him. On examining me himself, Dr. Gaudet's reassuring assessment was the same as the Opera House doctor's diagnosis: *la grippe*, or what the English call 'the influenza'. He clucked his tongue sympathetically and assured me that this was *not* the same as Father Barbier's recent illness; *la grippe* was spreading through the city so I might have been exposed to it anywhere.

I was rather taken aback when Robert actually came up the stairs behind Dr. Gaudet, removed his faded old cap, and peeked around the doctor's broad back at me. He spoke not a word; only nodded his head and then retreated to wait downstairs. Checking to be certain to his satisfaction that I was really ill and not simply malingering, I imagined.

Early in my convalescence, Erik spent several evenings watching over me. Although he would never admit it, I thought he found my cozy apartment a comforting place to be. It was certainly an improvement over his cold, empty subterranean home. He discovered my mother's pianoforte, and I discovered his unorthodox method of gaining access to my apartment. It startled me excessively the first time he manifested himself in my *salon*, having scaled the plane tree from the street outside, climbed on to my balcony, and let himself in through the French doors before I was even aware he was in the room.

One evening I was sitting quietly on the *divan*, having reached that bothersome stage of convalescence where one feels well enough to be bored but not well enough to actually do anything about it. I had brought out my sewing basket, turned up the lights and took out a long-neglected needlework project. I was concentrating on pushing the needle back and forth through the thick fabric, wondering if in fact I would ever actually finish it. It was a floral-patterned cover for a footstool. I no longer owned a footstool, but it was good to have something to do with my hands. When it was finished, I planned on giving it to Celestine, who did have a footstool. I had been sitting there, my head bent over the work, for perhaps half an hour when some little movement or stirring of the air made me glance up. A tall dark figure was standing inside my French doors.

For an instant I was gripped with absolute terror – all I saw at first glance was a darkly-dressed man wearing a low-brimmed hat standing in my room, apparently having materialized out of thin air. My heart seemed to stop and I felt the blood drain from my face. The needlework dropped from my hands to the floor. Recognition, when it came, only served to calm me a little.

"Oh!" I said, with my hand pressed over my heart, restarted now and pounding frantically. "How you frightened me, Erik!"

He removed the hat with a theatrical flourish and followed that with his cape, which he dropped casually to the floor. "Did I startle you, Sylvie? I should have warned you before. I could not very well be seen breaking into your apartment, *vous savez*."

"But how…oh, of course. You climbed the plane tree." For someone in Erik's fit physical condition, it would be a simple matter to climb the plane tree and gain access to my balcony. I never bothered to lock my balcony doors *because* I was on the second floor.

As though reading my mind, he said, "You really ought to lock those doors. It's very easy to climb that tree. Anyone might do it."

My heartbeat was beginning to return to normal. "No one ever has except you." I replied tartly. "And besides, if I did keep them locked, it would have been that much more difficult for you to get in when you came looking for me that night." *And quite possibly saved my life,* I thought to myself. And it certainly was preferable to having my neighbors see a strange man in a cape coming and going at all hours. My reputation was on shaky ground as it was.

"*C'est vrai*," Erik crossed the room and stopped by the pianoforte. He ran his fingers gently over several keys on the keyboard. "This is a beautiful instrument, by the way. I am pleased to see you keep it well tuned. Do you play, Sylvie?" He glanced up at me inquiringly.

At that moment I wished I could say yes. I shook my head, regretting the abandonment of my childhood lessons. "No, I do not. It was my late mother's pianoforte; she did play, reasonably well. Sometimes she gave lessons to supplement our income after my father died."

His graceful hands picked up the small stack of faded sheet music on the bench and riffled through it rapidly. "That explains why this music is somewhat dated; it must have belonged to your mother," he murmured, almost to himself. His eyes took in the miniature portrait of my mother resting under its little glass dome on the pianoforte. He picked it up and examined it closely, asking: "This is she?" I nodded. "There is a little resemblance," he said thoughtfully. "You have her eyes. What was her name?"

"Marie," I spoke the name softly; it hurt to say it out loud, reminding me of how much I missed her.

"How long ago did she die?" He asked, carefully placing the glass dome over the miniature again.

"She had only been gone a few months when I first met you," I answered slowly; only a few months, but somehow it seemed much longer.

Erik said nothing, only regarded me thoughtfully for a moment. Then, brushing the tails of his coat out behind him with a graceful gesture, he seated himself on the music bench and ran his fingers gently over the keys, testing them and teasing out little melodies. He directed a mischievous look in my direction.

"A *cognac* would be delightful, by the way. I think you owe me that much after all the trouble you have caused me lately. I know you have some because I saw it on the shelf in your pantry."

Smiling a little to myself, I put aside my embroidery, rose obediently and went to the *garde-manger*. After a bit of rummaging on the shelves I retrieved my only bottle of *cognac,* gave silent thanks to its being a very good bottle, and pulled a dusty snifter down from a shelf. I gave it a quick wipe and poured a measure of *cognac* into it. Lighting a candle, I held the glass over the flame for a few moments, warming the dark amber liquid until it released its fragrance, the way I had seen my father do in the evenings when I was a child. By the time I returned to the *salon* with the snifter and a small sherry for myself, Erik had put down the music and was looking around him interestedly.

"I like this room," he said sounding almost surprised. "It suits you, just as my home suits my own nature."

"Yours being prone toward secretiveness and theatricality." I said. "But you know very little about me, Erik."

"I know more than you think I do, Sylvie. I am more observant than most. This room, for example, is restful and warm, like you. I think that must be why I don't object to your company now and then. And that," he said gravely, staring at me over the pianoforte, "is paying you a real compliment."

"I am glad that you find my apartment restful, considering the amount of time you have had to stay here of late." I replied ruefully. Back at my place on the sofa, I picked up a cushion and held it in my lap, plucking at it idly with my fingers. I glanced up at him with a warm look.

"You have been very kind to me, Erik."

"A grievous error on my part, I expect, but I do not intend to make a habit of it." He replied cheerfully. "You will be spoiled. Do you mind if I try this instrument? I did promise to play for you some time, if you will recall." As he had made himself quite comfortable at the instrument, I suspected it was what he had in mind anyway. I therefore graciously granted him my approval and settled back to sip my sherry and listen. I had always wanted to hear Erik play for me.

Erik's fingers began moving gracefully over the keyboard in a moody rendition of the first movement of Beethoven's 'Moonlight' sonata. It was one of my mother's favorite pieces, and I had not heard it for a long time. She had ceased to play at all in the latter stages of her illness. Erik gave the music a slow, almost dirge-like quality, so that it sounded, not just pensive, but downright sad.

Listening to him play gave me an excuse to watch him, to study his face without appearing to stare rudely. Intent upon the music, his expression was serious but not severe, and he was so handsome, so perfect to my eyes. He did not look up from the keyboard so was unaware of my rapt regard. When he drew to a close, I had to wipe away a little moisture from my eyes.

"That was beautiful, Erik. *Merci,*" I said sincerely. "I knew you would play well."

Unmoved by my heartfelt appreciation, Erik merely shrugged and took an appreciative sip of his *cognac*. "It is a simple piece if you like that sort of thing, not difficult to learn. I could teach you to play it in time (my heart gave a little leap of pleasure at the thought of all that time), but I don't expect to have very much free time in future." He gave me a rather odd look, and a dreamy light kindled suddenly in his blue eyes.

Before I could ask him why, he shrugged, saying, "I may as well tell you, because it will affect our business arrangement. You see, I have hopes of marrying in the not-too-distant future, and when that event occurs, I expect to be very busy. In fact, it is highly likely I will leave Paris for a time. But you must not tell anyone, Sylvie, it is not for common knowledge."

Having dropped this statement upon me matter-of-factly, he returned his attention to the sheet music. How glad I was that he could not see my face! Even as Erik began another movement of the sonata, I remained quietly seated, head bowed under the weight of terrible new knowledge. Being ill had drained me, but suddenly I felt alive again. Alive and in agony. Furious, overwhelming fire seared through my veins like a green consuming flame. *Our business arrangement!*

Until that moment, I never knew my own heart. It was as if a brilliant firework had exploded in my head and heart, illuminating all so that at last I could see inside myself. Jealousy, horrible jealousy of this unknown and heretofore unsuspected rival burned so hot my insides were on fire. My fingers twisted together over the cushion in my lap as I fought to control my rampaging emotions. And why? The answer was now clear to me.

"Ah, *bon Dieu*," my lips silently formed the words illuminated in my heart, "I love him."

Why hadn't I seen it coming? How could I have been so obtuse about my own feelings all this time? When did my growing fascination with Erik turn to love? Perhaps because my own past experience with love was so disappointing and small, only an illusion in the end, I simply didn't know how to recognize real love when I felt it. But I knew it now, now that my heart had been painfully illuminated by the green flames of jealousy burning therein. I loved Erik, and I wanted him for myself. He should be *mine.*

But what madness this was! Was I now to discover, at the advanced age of twenty-six, that I was in reality one of those silly young girls who fall in love with mysterious, romantic figures in absurd gothic romances? Heretofore, I had always derided and made fun of those insipid creatures. It was so *stupid* of me, I could scarcely believe it. I, who had always taken pride in my sensible, practical nature! I, who only recently resolved to be through with love forever! I realized my fingers were still clenched fiercely in the velvet fabric of the cushion, so I forced them to relax and then carefully set it aside. It had been my mother's, after all. I did not wish to ruin it.

By the time Erik's fingers stilled on the keys, I had composed myself, and felt up to the task of making some sort of polite response to the bolt-from-the-blue he had just delivered to my heart. I must not give myself away – he must not guess my true feelings! But what to say? I was treading on unsure ground here, I knew. I forced myself to look at him and speak, and somehow my voice and expression were neutral, but it cost me dearly.

"I...I had no idea you were betrothed, Erik. When may I offer you congratulations?" I asked, trying to keep my tone light. In fact I was burning with possessive curiosity, for since meeting Erik I had not observed him to have any other acquaintances of the female variety besides Celestine, nor had he ever mentioned the possibility.

He did not answer at once, but sipped a bit more *cognac* and made a show of staring into its amber liquid depths, thus avoiding my eyes. At last he spoke, hesitatingly.

"I have not...yet...pressed my case with her...there are obstacles, certain obstacles to be overcome."

Erik's hesitation was perplexingly unlike him. Pondering his mention of obstacles, I was on the point of asking him to clarify when it struck me. With a sudden flash of intuition, I knew that the greatest obstacle, which I had given no thought to at all, was what lay behind that stark white mask. I had never seen that, and wondered if his intended ever had. I was afraid to ask, not wishing to invite the bite of his quick temper, or to inadvertently say something that would injure him, especially as ever since my illness we had been getting along so well.

But that mask! It was another one of those gothic novel props. Why hadn't it ever occurred to me to want to see behind it? Here was I, besotted and beguiled by his blue eyes, well-shaped lips and broad shoulders, and his swanking about looking dashing in elegant clothes, but in all possibility, one look behind that mask and my regard might melt away like smoke from a blown-out candle. Hadn't Celestine told me he was badly disfigured? How badly, I wondered. All this passed through my mind in the briefest instant, and while I was reaching the determination that I must see behind that mask before another day had passed, I was also forming my next question.

"May I ask who she is?"

"She is a soprano at the Opéra Populaire, and a very gifted *chanteuse*," he replied promptly. Ah, of course. As Celestine once told me, music was his passion.

Curious in spite of myself, I blurted out another question without thinking. "But Erik, what does she think about your...er...living arrangements? Surely you would not expect her to live under the Opera House!" Somehow it was difficult to imagine a new bride experiencing domestic felicity in such a cold, dreary environment. I certainly would not find it particularly appealing.

A flash of irritation crossed his face and his lips compressed into a tight line. "It is where I live," he said in a tone of finality. "But in fact, I have not brought her there, *yet*. I will though," the last words were spoken in a softer voice, and I saw that he was staring into the distance at nothing. "Very soon."

Hoping to return to a safer line of inquiry, I asked hesitantly, "How...how long have you known her?"

"You and your questions – always questions. I grow weary of them." Erik rose with fluid grace from the music bench and drained his glass, and I knew he was leaving. He crossed the room, picked up his cape and with a theatrical swirl put it over his shoulders, removing his black gloves from a pocket and deftly pulling them on. I got up and followed, picking up the hat and handing it to him, and now it was my turn to avoid making eye contact, as I could not trust that my eyes would not give away my inner turmoil. I concentrated on the floor instead.

"I am resuming my cooking schedule tomorrow, Erik. Will you be there when I arrive tomorrow night?" I asked, my voice tentative. "Will I see you?"

"Only if you do not ask me a thousand questions. You are supposed to be my cook, not an interviewer from *le Temp*." He paused and frowned at me. "Are you quite sure you are well enough to manage the work?" He asked, his voice changing from irritated to concerned-sounding in a heartbeat. I nodded firmly. The wide-brimmed hat was pulled down low over his right eye, casting the mask into shadow. This would make it easier for him to pass unnoticed in the streets I supposed.

"*Bonne nuit*. Thank you for the *cognac*. Do not forget to lock that door." A mocking bow, and then he was gone. I caught my breath at the suddenness of his departure.

When I stepped out onto the balcony a few seconds later, it was empty. A few leaves on the plane tree trembled gently in the still night air. There was no sign of Erik anywhere. Disheartened and dejected, I returned to my *salon* and closed the balcony doors, this time throwing the bolt firmly into place. By reminding me to lock it, he was telling me in his own subtle way that he would not be coming to check on me again; I was well enough that it was no longer necessary. And of course, I thought bitterly, he would not want to spare the time.

127

I went to bed that night in a state of absolute wretchedness, my mind in such turmoil sleep did not come for a long time. I lay staring up at the dark ceiling wondering how I could have been so…so *wrong* about him. And about myself! In addition to being utterly suffused with jealousy toward my unknown rival, and feeling quite sorry for myself, I was also conscious of a sense of…shame. I was ashamed of myself because all along, I saw Erik as being completely alone, in self-imposed exile to such a degree that an object of love would never be available to him. I believed, and I am disgusted with myself to even admit it, that there was no woman who could possibly be in his life. I longed to be that one who could, and would inspire his love. He had gone out of his way to show me kindness and concern, and I had allowed myself to hope…but I was too late. He had not been as alone as I thought.

As I stared up into the darkness, my thoughts slowly coalesced down to one, unyielding and unequivocal: if Erik were ever to win and wed this girl he desired, our association must come to an end. Lying there alone in my bedchamber, a nightmarish vision came to me of myself, being forced to deliver a nightly dinner tray to Erik and his bride, seeing their happiness, and knowing they were lying together at night in his golden bed. He would barely spare a glance for me as I crept forlornly down the steps like a shadow, and then back to my apartment, my heart filled with bitterness and despair. Tears burned in the corners of my eyes when I pictured how it would be – I could not bear it, I *would* not. I knew I would have to walk away from Erik and never see him again.

CHAPTER TWELVE

*'All falsehood is a mask; and however well made the mask may
be, with a little attention we may always succeed in
distinguishing it from the true face.'*

A.D.

I went about my duties with less than my usual energy the
next day. Unsurprising, really, given that part of me was still
reeling from the blow dealt to my heart the previous night. All the rest
of my thoughts were bent on finding a way to persuade Erik to take
off his mask so I could see his whole face. This had become
overwhelmingly important to me for several reasons, not least of
which was my own private need to see how badly he was disfigured. I
saw it as a kind of test of my love for Erik: was it real, was it deep
enough to survive what I would see, or was it only a passing fancy, a
silly girlish crush on a mysterious, romantic figure out of fiction? Had
I read too many novels?

It was also a test of his trust in me, and *vraiment*, what had I
done but violate that trust at every turn? It was astonishing that he still
seemed to trust me at all. And finally, I would see what the singer
from the Opera would see when Erik unmasked for *her*. If the sight of
his face was really horrible, would he stand a chance of winning her
regard? Was I a bad person for harboring a hope, however forlorn,
that this would be the case? Well, too much self-inspection is bad for
the soul, so I abandoned the effort and forced my mind back to my
cooking.

Everyone at St. Giles was happy to have me back, although I
was not allowed to help serve the meal in spite of my assurances that I
was perfectly capable of doing so. Instead I was made to sit while
Sister Chantal waited on *me*. She was quite stubborn about it. Father
Barbier informed me that he had prayed for me every day. He seemed
to take full credit for my recovery – that is to say, Father Barbier and
Someone Else. I must admit that I was glad to be able to just sit
quietly, for though I was still rather tired, my mind was busy with my
whirling thoughts. Robert had stopped the wagon in front of my door
before I realized we were back; I had made the entire trip home in a
fog.

I had made up my mind on the previous evening that I was
going to see Erik's face, and nothing could deter me from my purpose;

the only question was, *how?* How to persuade him? He would think me mad, *sans doute*. Finally I decided to simply take a direct approach. It might catch him off guard. I decided, therefore, to come back to Erik's home with him that night. I thought he might feel safer and more comfortable about removing his mask for me if he were in his own familiar surroundings. I ran the risk of incurring his ire yet again, but as that occurred on a fairly regular basis anyway, there was no point in worrying about it. If I had not yet been sacked, it was unlikely to happen now.

I informed Erik of my plan to accompany him to his home after he had assisted me to climb through the window. He did not take my announcement well; he dropped my arm as if it burned him and glared at me ferociously. That frigid glower no longer intimidated me as much as it once had, however, now that I knew he possessed a softer side, seldom seen. I lifted my chin and gave him back stare-for-stare.

"There is something I must talk to you about, and this," I said, indicating the empty marble room with a sweep of my arm, "is not the proper *ambience*."

"You have unbelievable nerve!" He sputtered furiously. "I would think, after the last time you invaded my privacy, you might have learned your lesson." His lips set in a firm, thin line, a sure sign he was vexed with me. "What could you possibly have to say that cannot be said right here?"

"Something important." I answered. Full of righteous determination, I reached around him and pulled the window closed, then started toward the tapestry. Stopping, I looked back to see him standing in the exact same place, staring at me.

"You might just bring the lamp. I cannot see in the dark the way you do," I added.

Erik ran a hand over his dark hair in an exasperated gesture, smoothing it, although not a hair was out of place, and shook his head. "I do not have time for this," he muttered, almost to himself.

"It will not take long. The sooner we begin, the better." I paused next to the tapestry, still holding his dinner, and gave the hanging a significant nod. Finally, Erik moved. Rigid with indignation, muttering under his breath, he nevertheless went to the lamp, picked it up, and approached me. I was certain I heard the word *shrew* quite clearly. Without looking at me, he lifted the tapestry and I passed under it, waiting for him on the next step down.

130

"*Mon Dieu!* What is wrong with you? Perhaps your recent illness has affected your mind," he said brusquely. "Here." He removed the tray from my hands and gave me the lamp to carry instead, and we started down. The rest of the trip was made in silence – the sounds of our footfalls and breathing made the only noise. I hoped Erik was not too angry with me; not too angry to comply with my request. There was only one way to find out.

Once more I found myself entering that sepulchral, dream-like place, this time with Erik behind me, practically walking on my heels. The candelabra were all lit and there was a pretty greenish glow on the still water. It felt chilly to me, however. I shivered, and the flame of the lamp in my hand trembled. We made our way back to the table where we had sat the last time I was here, and put down our burdens. He turned to face me, his countenance forbidding, his pale eyes cold. He did not speak. I supposed he was trying to intimidate me.

Thinking it would be extremely awkward to launch immediately into my reason for being here, I hastily thought of something to say to fill the uncomfortable silence between us.

"I have been meaning to tell you, by the way, that Father Barbier did recover from his illness. I took your advice and added lemon juice to the soup I made him. He liked it very much...and so did I. Where did you learn that?" If I hoped that the introduction of this harmless subject would soften him or remind him of his recent kindness toward me, I was wrong.

Erik made an impatient gesture with his hand. "It is not important. That was not what you wanted to talk about, was it, Sylvie." A statement, not a question. His icy gaze bore relentlessly into mine.

I sighed, shoulders drooping a bit, discouraged. "I am sorry you are so vexed with me. This is not an auspicious start. I hoped...are we not friends now, Erik?" I looked up into his face, my voice unintentionally pleading, imploring it to be true.

He was not expecting that particular question. His expression left off being icy and became guarded. After a long pause, he said, "I do not have friends."

Having anticipated what his answer would be, I had my response ready; I shook my head in disagreement. "You must know that is not true," I answered firmly. "Madame Giry is your friend, and I rather think that you and I have become friends, if you will admit to the fact. You have not yet sacked me nor murdered me, and I consider that a hopeful sign."

131

Erik turned his face away from me to stare out over the water, and sighed in his turn. "If I do end up murdering you, it will most certainly be in hot blood, not cold. You would try the patience of a saint, Sylvie Bessette."

"*Oui*, Erik, you have told me that before." His remark did not frighten me, even if that was his intention. I could tell by the tenor of his voice that he had resigned himself to my annoying presence. He was no longer angry; perhaps only a little exasperated. I squared my shoulders, therefore, and put my hand on his arm to pull his attention back to me. I let go as soon as he had turned back; by now I knew he did not like to be touched.

"There is something I want to ask of you, Erik. As a friend - as someone you can trust." And I wanted him to trust me, in spite of the fact that I knew I did not deserve it.

"Well, what is it?" He demanded curtly. "I am waiting. And if you are going to ask me if you can stop cooking for me, the answer is no."

I was almost diverted from my purpose by his brusque comment, but only for a moment. "No, Erik, that is not what I wanted to ask of you." I felt my voice turn soft, pleading. "I...I want to see your face...your entire face. Would you please remove your mask for me?"

"*What?*" His voice was a hiss of shock and surprise; he appeared utterly horror-struck. This was clearly the last thing he was expecting. He actually took a step back away from me, as if he thought I was going to snatch his mask off his face. This made me feel slightly cross; as if I would do such a rude thing.

"I already know you wear a mask because you are disfigured on that side of your face. It is part of who you are. Now that we know each other better, what harm can there be in removing your mask and showing me?"

He gave a sharp, humorless bark of laughter. "What harm!" He studied my face incredulously, trying to read my thoughts perhaps. "My dear Sylvie, allow me to explain. It is highly unlikely you have ever seen anything as repulsive as I am. You would scream and run, and then you would trip and break your neck on the stairs. At the very least, I would lose your cooking and I would miss that." He sounded as proud and sarcastic as ever, but I saw a tremor pass over him briefly and it wrenched at my heart.

"I give you my promise I am not going to scream and run. You ought to know me better than that; *en plus*, I've almost certainly seen worse." I hoped I sounded more confident than I felt when I gave him my assurances, because in truth, I could not be sure. It would break his heart if I did scream and run blindly away from him. It had happened to him before, I was certain. But it was *me* standing before him, not just any silly female. I had fallen in love with him somehow or other, and whether he knew it or not, his heart was now in my care.

Erik gave me a penetrating look. "Do you intend to clarify that remark? For I find it hard to believe." He placed both hands on the table and leaned on them as though in need of the support.

"Well," I said carefully, "you already know that I prepare and deliver meals to invalids at a private hospital here in Paris;" I paused, and Erik shot me a brief nod, a wary sidelong look. "I also sometimes assist them to eat. Some of the patients...some of them are unable to feed themselves, and the nuns are very busy." I paused once more, and could see he was growing both impatient and curious. He was watching me sidelong, still turned away from me, leaning on the table. I hesitated now because, for the first time, I was about to break my oath of silence, not a thing I took lightly. I was certain, however, that I could trust Erik to keep the secret.

"Pray continue," he said, impatient for my answer.

"It is a special kind of hospital, Erik. No one knows of its existence here in Paris besides me. I break the oath of silence I took in order to tell you this, because I trust *you*. It is a...a Leprosarium." Watching his eyes, I saw understanding dawn in them.

"I see," he whispered softly. "Yes, I see. Lepers – so your Father Barbier is a leper – hmmm. Interesting. That makes perfect sense knowing you as I do: always rushing in where angels fear to tread. And you are curious, always curious, Sylvie." I said nothing, just stood waiting expectantly, steeling myself for what I would see when the white mask came off, which I now knew was imminent. Although I was not as sanguine as I was letting on, I would rather have cut off my own tongue than do something to hurt him at this moment: the moment he was about to show me the source of his secret sadness.

"This feels strange," he murmured as if to himself. He straightened to his full height and faced me, a challenge sparking in his pale eyes. "Let me satisfy your curiosity then, and get it over. I hope what you see will not mark the end of our arrangement. I wasn't joking when I said I would miss your cooking."

Slowly, while I watched and held my breath, he reached up, grasped his mask in both hands and pulled it away, bringing me face-to-face with the real Erik.

"You asked for this, do not forget," he said grimly. "*Regardez.*"

Oh, I had been wrong, so very wrong. I had *not* seen worse. Never in my life had I ever seen anything like this. The entire right side of Erik's face was sunken in places and hideously scarred. Some areas looked red and livid, others pale as death. The strange scarring seemed to retreat under the perfect edge of dark hairline. The right eye socket had melted downward, like sagging wax from a guttering candle. In fact, the entire right side of his face looked as if it had partially melted and then solidified again, almost revealing the bone underneath.

I was accustomed to the facial deformities commonly caused by leprosy, such as the flattening of the nose until there seemed to be no nose, but Erik's face was a terrifying sight. And yet out of that ghastly, scarred visage his pale blue eyes gazed at me with their customary intelligence. The same eyes, the same face, the same Erik: he was the same man he had always been. I could see wariness and even pain in those eyes as the seconds ticked by and he waited silently for my reaction. He appeared to be braced for the worst, and that gave me the courage not to fail him.

I did not gasp, shriek, swoon, or scream, but I came close. Only my strong desire not to hurt him held me together in that terrible moment of truth. I clamped my jaws together tightly, blinked once, looked down at the floor for an instant, composing myself, and then I returned my gaze to his face in relative calm. A corner of his mouth turned up wryly.

"Are you happy now? Or are you sorry you asked?" His voice was soft, but it carried an edge, as though he was fully aware of what it cost me to retain my composure.

My poor Erik! Now I understood everything Celestine had tried to explain, why he lived in self-imposed exile; why he shunned every human connection. He was confronted every day of his life with the knowledge that, were both sides of his face like his good side, he would have been handsome indeed. The world would have been at his feet. He could have had any woman he desired. His brilliance, talent and wit would have been appreciated by all who met him. But instead...I found myself wanting to reach out and touch him, just a hand on his arm, to demonstrate that I felt no revulsion, but I knew such a touch at this delicate moment would be unwelcome. I forced

134

my arms to stay at my sides, though my fingers twitched with a powerful sympathetic urge to reach toward him. I took a step closer to him, looked up into his eyes, and found my voice.

"*Non*, of course I am not sorry, but oh, Erik, I don't know what to say. Does it...does it give you any pain?"

He gave another harsh bark of humorless laughter. "Only of the psychic variety, not the physical, I assure you."

"What caused it, do you know? Madame Giry said you told her once something happened when you were a child..."

"I was born this way," he replied curtly. "An infection when my mother was carrying me, I believe. No one was sure. You remember I told you recently that I do not believe in God – now you see why." He gestured roughly toward his face as he spoke. "What benevolent God would do *this* to an innocent child?" It was a rhetorical question for which I had no answer, only sympathy. I tried to imagine Erik as a small, helpless child, born horribly disfigured, dependent, at the mercy of others, but I could not. His tall, powerful presence made too strong an impression on me. That he could ever have been small and helpless seemed impossible.

I was peering at him carefully, and without conscious premeditation I found I had moved quite close to him. Suddenly he closed his eyes against my intent regard; he did not like it, I could tell.

"But there is more, isn't there?" I asked gently. "That is a wig you are wearing, is it not?" As I studied his perfect hairline, I realized that the scarring must continue under it. It had never occurred to me that Erik's smooth dark hair might not be his own.

His eyes flew open, his lips firmed into a thin line of vexation. He sighed. "How curious you are today. I should not be surprised by now. You are asking me to stand before you and reveal the full extent of my repulsiveness. And why should I comply, answer me that." His tone was sharp.

"You are not repulsive to me, Erik, you never have been and you still are not, and I want to see *you*, who you really are. I trust you, and you ought to know by now that you can trust me. I have told you my own secret, Erik," I said, referring to my work at the Leprosarium.

"Oh very well," he said resignedly. "I do not know why I bother arguing with you, Sylvie. You always get your way. You won't like it, but you may as well see the full extent of my hideousness, I know you won't rest until you do." The self-loathing in his voice tugged at my heart. Erik whisked the wig away with an abrupt gesture.

I studied him interestedly. There was less hair on the right side, the scarring did carry on as I had suspected. His own hair was fine and soft, a lighter shade of brown than the dark wig he always wore.

"Hmmm," I murmured thoughtfully, "I think I prefer your own hair colour to that dark wig. It suits you somehow." Erik gave me a speaking glance, but made no reply.

Just between us, Reader, I found Erik shocking in the degree of his disfigurement, and the contrast between that side of his face and the undamaged side was great. But as I studied him, I realized that I much preferred seeing him this way than with his disguises. With nothing to hide behind, without the artificial perfection of the mask and wig, he was much more real, and somehow younger looking. Erik's vulnerabilities were clearly visible, while the Phantom kept his hidden away. However, to my regret Erik did not give me much time to study the man behind the mask.

"Enough," he said curtly. Swiftly he turned away, replacing the mask with a smooth, practiced gesture, adding matter-of-factly, "even my own mother could not bear to look at me. It was she who gave me my first mask. It wasn't quite as sophisticated as this one." I was speechless at this casually heartbreaking remark, and he took advantage of my silence to fit the wig neatly back into place, smoothing it down with his hand. The darkly handsome man I was familiar with had returned, and with it his confidence, and the barriers between us. He picked up his tailcoat and shrugged into it.

"Don't feel sorry for me, Sylvie. Pity is something I neither need nor want." He began pulling on his black leather gloves, and turning back to me, gave me a sardonic smile that held more than a hint of mockery in it. Along with his disguises, his equilibrium had also returned.

Reaching up, I gave his perfectly neat cravat a little adjustment, just because I could not help myself. Studying the silky black cravat intently, I murmured, "I do not pity you, Erik. Pity and compassion are not the same thing." I inhaled discreetly, so that he would not notice. How good he smelled, like leather and spice, and that exotic incense.

"Aren't they?" He asked softly, almost to himself, as I stepped back from him.

"Where are you off to?" I asked. "You have not had your dinner."

"I have a singing lesson to give – I must hurry or I'll be late, thanks to you. My dinner must wait tonight. Can you see yourself out?" His voice was brisk now; he was already moving toward the boat moored in its stone slip. "Take the lamp."

"*Certainement*," I replied crisply, turning away and picking up the empty tray to hide my disappointment. I could not help but notice the softening of his voice and expression when he mentioned his lesson. I could guess with whom he had this lesson, and I could feel the green fire smolder in my breast. Still, we had made progress today. On impulse, I turned and looked back at Erik. He was standing in the boat, holding a pole. He had already forgotten my presence. Turning away, I continued toward the heavy curtains concealing my passageway.

Afterward, I was to become so completely comfortable viewing that grotesque face that I never gave it any thought at all. Reality is always preferable to subterfuge and artifice, in my opinion.

On my way across the causeway I thought about what had just happened. I felt a strange, elated joyfulness, and I all but floated up the stairs. Erik had just given me a gift – the gift of trust. Perhaps, just perhaps, we really had become friends. And the next day, I received a more tangible gift from *Monsieur Le Fantôme.*

CHAPTER THIRTEEN

'I cannot for one instant believe you so devoid of gallantry as to refuse a lady your escort when she even condescends to ask you for it.'

A.D.

It was my day to make stock, an involved procedure but one I usually found very satisfying. I was making several pots of chicken stock today: the basis for all the *potage* and *ragout* I was planning to make for the hospital during the week. I was, however, going about the process with less than my usual attention because my thoughts refused to remain here in my kitchen. Every now and then I became aware that I was simply standing, my normally busy hands stilled, blind to what was before me because in my mind I was back in the cavern with Erik, reliving that momentous occurrence. I was still trying to come to terms with what I'd seen and how my new knowledge had changed me. I had the unsettling feeling that I was never going to be the same.

Despite these distractions I miraculously managed to finish cutting the vegetables without doing myself an injury, and was adding them to the stockpot when there was a tentative knock on the door. Looking through the rippled glass, I saw a young foot messenger on the other side clutching an envelope in his hand. A note from Celestine, I guessed, inviting me to meet her for coffee. Smiling expectantly, I wiped my hands on my apron and opened the door, confirmed I was indeed Sylvie Bessette, and accepted the envelope. The boy seemed very glad to rid himself of it; he kept glancing at me oddly, almost apprehensively. I wondered if there was something not quite right with him. Then I turned the envelope over and saw what was on the flap. It was small wonder that the boy was apprehensive.

Frowning with annoyance, not at the foot messenger but at my correspondent, I reached into the pocket of my skirt for the coin purse I usually kept there, and distractedly handed him a coin. He barely tipped his cap to me before he ran off down the street without a backward look. As I stared at the black-edged ecru envelope in my hand, I felt a thrill (or perhaps it was a chill) race up my spine, and my heart beat faster, for I knew who had sent it. There was only one person of my acquaintance who was obsessed with skulls.

I slipped back inside and closed the door, pulling down the shade. Alone in my warm kitchen, redolent with the scent of wholesome vegetables and a simmering chicken carcass, this crisp envelope was incongruous. For the back of the envelope carried a macabre seal, an enormous, blood-red sealing wax skull, staring back at me as if it were a messenger from Satan himself. I gave an involuntary shudder. I knew it was all part of the mysterious aura of evil and supernatural that Erik worked tirelessly to cultivate: 'The Opera Ghost'. I did not approve. No one seemed less like a ghost to me. And what was his strange fixation with skulls? Skulls on his boat, skulls here, skulls there. As if he lived in a graveyard. I made a mental note to ask him about it soon.

Regardless of my distaste for Erik's trappings of wickedness, I was happy no one could see with what eagerness I slid my finger under the envelope flap to tear it open. I could not command my trembling fingers to be steady. I must know *at once* what Erik had written to me. It was too much of a coincidence not to be related somehow to yesterday evening, when I had persuaded him to unmask for me. Having had time to think about it, had Erik determined to be angry with me? Was I about to be cast off? I drew out a single folded piece of stationery, and in my haste to open it missed a small rectangle of pasteboard that had been inside. It drifted softly to the floor at my feet.

The notepaper was covered with neat, elegant script written in (what else) dark red ink. A brief vision formed in my mind of Erik seated at his massive wooden table dipping his pen into a bottle of ink, surrounded by candelabra. I could almost smell the hot sealing wax he would use to press the seal into place.

"My dear Sylvie,

Since you informed me yesterday that you had never had occasion to attend a performance at my theatre, I have taken the liberty of enclosing a ticket for you. There is a very special performance this Saturday evening and I think you will enjoy it — an important occasion which I have been working toward for some time. Should there be any difficulties when you give your ticket to the staff, show this note. I am giving permission for you to sit in Box Five, which is always reserved for my use. I hope you will enjoy the performance.

Best Regards,
O.G."

Slowly, I bent down and picked up the fallen ticket, and replaced both ticket and note carefully in the envelope. I stood for a long moment, holding it in my hands, running my fingers gently over the glossy red seal, no longer thinking of it as a sign of evil, but instead thinking of Erik making it and placing it there.

What did he mean by it, this unexpected gift? A happy thought came to me: perhaps he wished my attendance so that I might share this special occasion with him! I permitted myself the luxury of a little glimmer of hope that some invisible threshold had been crossed. He must care a little for me, if he desired my company at the performance. It was a good sign, for there was always a chance that the singer he hoped to marry would refuse him once she saw what he looked like behind that mask. As for myself, I thought I might get used to it in time. This was an opportunity I could not neglect. One never knew what might happen. At last I gave myself a little mental shake and tucked the envelope away in the pocket of my apron. It was time to get back to work.

Absently picking up my wooden spoon, I went back to stirring my simmering pot of chicken stock. My thoughts, however, roamed elsewhere, along a familiar path. Erik was always foremost in my thoughts now. My fascination with him seemed to grow greater after each meeting, and now that I had seen him undisguised, I felt myself drawn to him even more. I had passed the test I set for myself: I had seen behind the mask, and, if anything, found myself even more in love with him than before.

All at once my arm froze in the midst of my stirring. I had suddenly thought of an even more pressing concern: I had nothing even remotely suitable to wear!

Contrary to what you may think, one's attire is serious business in Paris – to see and be seen is all important here – at least to some. Not, needless to say, to cooks and other young ladies who must fend for themselves, but here was a cook who was in possession of a ticket to the opera. And moreover, with a man to impress. What did *dames à la mode* wear to the Opera nowadays? All the gowns I owned had become rather threadbare and all were hopelessly outdated. They dated, in fact, from the early days of my ill-fated marriage, before my mother's death and my fall from fortune. They had been part of my *trousseau.*

140

Any formal gowns I had possessed were given away during my mother's illness. Although I could ask Celestine for help, even if she could tell me what *en vogue* was now, there was no time to have a new gown made up. The theatre performance was only a few days away. *Typical man*, I thought grimly. Men never understand these things, but another woman certainly would. I ran upstairs and hastily penned a note inviting Celestine to tea. There was no question of my not attending the performance, for it had crossed my mind that perhaps Erik planned to share the box with me. A thrill of anticipatory pleasure ran through me at this happy thought, but the possibility made having a proper gown of paramount importance.

Celestine was indeed a great help. Once she had got over her initial skepticism that Erik would not only send me a ticket but also give me permission to sit in Box Five (which she confirmed was always kept empty for the Opera Ghost), a thing which had never happened before, she had a marvelous idea.

"Let me take your measurements, Sylvie, and I will see what we have in the costume department," pulling a measuring ribbon from her pocket as she spoke. "We always have modern gowns on hand and some of them are quite pretty." She tilted her head and regarded me thoughtfully. "Something blue I think, to match your lovely eyes."

Excited, I replied, "*Merci*, Celestine. That would be wonderful!" Shaking my head, I glanced down at the outmoded gown I was wearing and added ruefully, "I really do need to have some new gowns made up, now that I have a little income to work with, but I haven't had time. And there is not much need for pretty gowns when one is stirring pots all day."

She frowned, still puzzling over Erik's unprecedented behavior. "It is very unusual, nonetheless! I cannot understand it, it is so unlike him," was her final pronouncement. I dared not share with her what my own hopes were for the evening, so I prudently remained silent as she took my measurements with brisk efficiency. "I hope I can find one that will fit you in the bodice, she murmured. "The *décolleté* is quite low this season, and I am afraid..." Celestine made a little clucking noise as she spoke, her words bringing a blush to my cheeks.

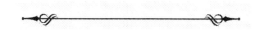

141

True to her word, late the next afternoon Celestine sent Meg to my apartment. She carried a costume bag from the opera in her arms, so bulky it practically overwhelmed her petite frame. I hastened to relieve her of it, laying the bag over the back of a chair in my *salon*. Meg, ever curious, pushed back the hood of her cloak and began peppering me with questions about the Opera Ghost. I sidestepped her questions as best I could, simply telling her that he had sent me the ticket because he was so pleased with my cooking. I had to smile, though; it was clear from the direction of her inquiries and the sparkle in her big blue eyes that she had a young girl's romantic fascination with the mysterious Phantom.

"Have you ever actually seen him, Mlle. Bessette?" She inquired hopefully. "*Maman* will say nothing about him. She grows quite cross with me if I ask her too many questions."

Turning away, I pretended an interest in something outside the window. "No, Meg, I have not. I'm afraid I can tell you no more than your mother can."

She sighed, looking dreamy-eyed. "I should like to see him some time." She said, fingering the costume bag as she spoke. I did not think she would enjoy it as much as she imagined she would, but I said nothing. Wandering toward the *salon* door, she looked at me conspiratorially, her eyes wide.

"Please do not tell *Maman*, but once I and another of the girls accompanied a few of the stagehands down to the lower storage levels when they went to get some props. She has forbidden us to go down that far, and she would be very angry if she knew we had done it…but while we were down there, we heard… *music*!" Eyes round, her voice dropped to a dramatic whisper.

Fascinated in spite of myself, I asked, "What kind of music?"

She frowned, trying to remember. "It seemed to come from far away, but I am sure it was organ music, like they play in church. It sounded…strong and loud, soaring, as if he were playing his heart out. It was so thrilling! I wanted to see where it was coming from, but the stagehands were afraid. They gathered the props and made us come away quickly."

"That was probably for the best, *chérie*." I said gently, concealing a shudder at the thought of the two silly girls stumbling about in those subterranean recesses, until they fell into one of Erik's many traps.

"You won't say anything to *Maman*, will you, Mlle. Bessette?" Meg asked anxiously.

142

"*Bien sûr que non.*" Taking her by the arm, I led her to the doorway, and pulled the hood of her cloak up over her head, adjusting it so that it would keep her ears warm. "But you must listen to your mother, Meg. Stay away from the lower levels. Run along home now, dear, before it is dark." Of course, I couldn't really blame her for her girlish interest in the Phantom. I knew that *sans doute*, I would have done the very same thing had I been in her position. For myself, Erik generated both fear and attraction in equal measure.

Once I managed to send the inquisitive Meg on her way (with strict instructions to go straight back to the Opera House), I snatched up the costume bag and carried it into my bedroom, impatient to see what Celestine had chosen for me. When I opened the bag yards of pale blue satin and frothy white lace spilled out onto my bed. It was a confection of a gown. I was rendered momentarily speechless by its beauty, and I could hardly wait to try it on. I only hoped I would be able to fasten it up by myself.

Eventually, after much struggling and several inappropriate words, I stood before my cheval glass, gazing, astonished, at my own reflection. I had missed a few of the fastenings, but for the most part, the blue gown was on. I scarcely recognized myself, for it had been a long time since I had cause to wear such a lovely gown. Celestine had been right about the *décolleté* neckline; I found myself tugging at the lacy neckline and at the little cap sleeves that seemed perpetually about to slide off my shoulders. Perhaps I could add a little more lace?

The ruffled underskirt was of pale blue satin, matching the bodice, with a darker blue satin and lace overskirt that flowed gracefully over the bustle in back. A number of ruffled petticoats would cause the skirt to fill out nicely. The bodice was trimmed with draping strands of *faux* pearls. I had to admit, I looked rather pretty in it – the blue colour made my own blue eyes sparkle, or perhaps it was anticipation.

It would be nice to have Erik see me in such a flattering gown, I thought to myself dreamily as I studied my reflection. He was undeniably a man; therefore he ought to find the revealing *décolleté* attractive. He never seemed to notice me that way, but after all, he was not yet engaged to his soprano, so there was no harm in trying to look my best. I went to bed that night full of hopes and happy dreams, but all my romantic dreams were doomed to disappointment. More than I had any idea.

When I saw Erik that Friday, it was only a disappointingly brief meeting in the marble room. Since showing me his face a few days past he had made no mention of it again, and behaved as if the event had never taken place, much to my chagrin. Tonight he was in obvious haste and impatient to be gone. I was so disappointed I was almost angry. I had expected we would at least discuss his plans for the performance tomorrow evening.

"Why are you in such haste tonight?" I demanded, vexation making my voice sharper than intended.

Already holding his dinner and moving toward the stairs, he glanced back at me over his shoulder, startled by the unfamiliar edge in my voice into actually giving me an answer to my abrupt question.

"I have another singing lesson to give this evening – an important one." He explained. "My...*protégée*...will have her first starring performance on stage soon. *Very* soon." I did not miss the way he hesitated over the word, '*protégée*', as well as the proprietary note in his voice. I suppose I knew in my heart that his student and the woman he hoped to marry were one and the same, but I could not bring myself to ask the question that would confirm it. Instead, I asked another, pressing question, the most important one for me, the one all my happiness for the following night depended upon.

"Erik, I wish to thank you for inviting me to the performance tomorrow night. I expect...I mean I hope...shall I see you there?" I tried to keep my tone careless, tried not to reveal how eager I was for him to say yes.

He paused on the verge of starting down the stairs, barely sparing me another glance in his impatience to be gone, not even waiting to see me safely out the window as he normally did.

"See me there? *Non*, that will not be possible. I will be otherwise occupied the entire evening."

My heart plummeted to my feet. "Oh," was all I could manage to say. Could he see the wave of disappointment engulfing me? It felt like it ought to be visible.

Erik must indeed have read something of the dismay I felt on my face, for he hesitated, and took one step back toward me.

144

"Is there something the matter, Sylvie?" But the question sounded perfunctory, barely interested, his thoughts obviously already elsewhere.

I could feel my horrible disappointment rapidly turning into anger. I felt my chin go up and my eyes flash.

"You actually expect me to attend the Opera alone, unescorted, and sit by myself in a private box?" I had to restrain myself from actually stamping my foot on the hard marble floor. "You do comprehend the impropriety of that, don't you? Or perhaps you were telling me the truth when you said you did not think of me as a lady." The words tumbled out unbidden; unshed tears of frustration and resentment burned at the back of my eyes.

Erik stared at me. His cool eyes turned icy. "That is not what I said, as you know perfectly well. You are being absurd. You and your conventions – you spend too much time worrying about the opinion of society. A pack of fools, as far as I am concerned."

Overwhelmed by anger, my response came out in a rush of emotion, accompanied by gratuitous arm-waving. "You say that because you live in a dungeon and do whatever you please!" I cried. "But unlike you, I have to live in *this* world, Erik. You have no idea how difficult it is to always be…oh never mind." Unreasonably furious and frustrated, I flung open the window and began the process of getting through it. But I did not get far. In an instant Erik had crossed the room and his hard fingers seized my arm, freezing me in place.

"To be what?" He demanded, his voice harsh. I turned startled eyes to his face. "What, Sylvie? Go on, say it!" His grip on my arm was just short of painful.

I opened my mouth to speak, but the words died in my throat. As I looked into his face I suddenly felt foolish, and also selfish. To be *alone*, I was going to say, and he knew it. To be *lonely*. My eyes fell.

"I am sorry, Erik," I whispered. Abruptly the anger died out in both of us. He released his hold on my arm and sighed heavily.

"It is forgotten."

I rubbed my arm absently, massaging the place where he had gripped it. Looking up into his face, I said quietly, "You do know, do you not, that you are not the only one who is alone?"

Erik's eyes darted to the tapestry and then back to me. They had that bleak look in them again.

"Yes, but I have been that way for far longer than you, Sylvie." He answered at last. Then he seemed to brighten. "I have to go now

145

or I will be late. I will send a carriage for you tomorrow night. That way, perhaps you will not feel quite so…abandoned." His lips curved just slightly.

"*Merci.* That would be greatly appreciated." I slid through the window and stood looking back at him, clutching the empty dinner tray in front of me. The provision of a carriage was small consolation, but it demonstrated a *little* consideration for me, at least.

Giving me a sardonic look, he made a wry half-smile. "I could not escort you even if I did not have important matters of my own to attend to tomorrow night," he said. "You are forgetting who you are talking to, Sylvie. It would not do for you to be seen with the Phantom in public. I am not exactly popular with those two imbeciles who call themselves managers. You might find yourself under arrest." He looked amused at my startled expression.

Erik turned back to the stairs and prepared to depart, taking his dinner with him. "I will not require anything tomorrow night, by the way." He sounded excited and eager, exactly opposite of how I was feeling at the moment. Then he was gone, and it was time I went as well. Dejected, I went back to my waiting hansom. There was no longer any particular reason to look forward to my evening out. Not even the opportunity to wear a beautiful gown could cheer me now, because there would be no Erik to see me in it. I did ponder, however, what it was that would be occupying him so much the next evening. Whatever it was, he seemed to look forward to it very much.

CHAPTER FOURTEEN

'She was dear…both as daughter and as mistress, and he saw himself reflected in her as in a magic mirror, every passion and every vice.'

A.D.

It is not my nature to be miserable when being optimistic and cheerful will do instead. I decided to make the most of this opportunity for an extremely rare evening out, in spite of my misgivings regarding the lack of an escort. And, to be perfectly honest, also in spite of my extreme disappointment that I had to experience it alone. I intended to brazen it out – the worst that could happen would be some disapproving stares in my direction from other theatre goers. I would be alone in Box Five so at least I would be able to enjoy the performance in its confines, safe from any rude advances I might otherwise have been subjected to as a woman out in public alone. Belatedly it dawned on me that Erik must have set aside Box Five for me for this very reason. He had known all along that I would be there alone.

Alors, I washed my hair and arranged it in a pretty *chignon,* struggled into the blue satin gown, and pulled on a pair of long white kid gloves (also borrowed from Celestine). I dabbed a little violet perfume behind my ears and pressed a bit of tinted balm into my lips. Then I took a twirl in front of my cheval glass, and smiled thoughtfully at my reflection. I thought I looked rather pretty. Tucking my ticket and my note from the 'Opera Ghost' into my little crocheted evening bag, I went downstairs in a flurry of rustling skirts and excitement to wait for my carriage to arrive. I felt like Cinderella going to the ball; the only thing missing was the handsome prince. Not even Celestine would be waiting for me; she expected to be completely occupied behind the curtain.

I had no idea what performance I was going to see. The ticket did not indicate anything but a date and time, with the box information appended in Erik's elegant hand. I was sorry my mother was not here. She would have been thrilled to attend the Opera, she loved music so much. I had inherited her passion for cooking, but not her passion for music or her talent at playing an instrument, alas.

I found I had come downstairs early, so I occupied myself by watching the clock while fidgeting with my neckline and sipping a little *vin blanc* to calm my nerves.   Finally the sound of horses and jingling harnesses outside in the street heralded the arrival of the hansom Erik had ordered for me. Wouldn't it be lovely if I climbed in and saw him sitting there, elegantly attired in faultless evening dress? Perhaps he would offer me a sweet-smelling corsage, and solicitously spread the warm carriage blanket over my lap.

Shaking my head to drive away the tempting fantasy, I donned my black velvet evening cloak, which had once been my mother's, swallowed the last of my wine in a gulp, and went out to meet the coach. It was, *naturellement*, empty.

Having been inside the Opéra Populaire only once, the morning Celestine had invited me to take a tour of it, I was looking forward to seeing it at night, lit up and glowing brightly for a performance and filled with elegantly dressed theatre-goers. Only ten years old, the building was in high baroque style, an extravagant confection both inside and out. Erik so loved the Opera, so lived and breathed it, that I was prepared to love it too.

The hansom clattered down the Avenue de l'Opéra and into the vast, sweeping drive that lay before the building. The forecourt was brilliantly lit, and the drive was filled with carriages pulling up to deposit sophisticated gentlemen and ladies at the entrance. It was just as I had imagined it would be. My hansom took its place in the line. Liveried and bewigged footmen were everywhere. As I took in this spectacular but rather intimidating sight from my window, my anticipatory mood began to evaporate. It was impossible not to notice that all the other carriages were elegant, well-appointed barouches and similar privately owned vehicles. Mine was the only ordinary hansom cab to be seen.

My face burned with shame and embarrassment. I should not have come tonight; this would prove to be an ordeal after all. And I must do it alone! Biting my lip in mortification, I promised myself Erik was going to get a piece of my mind next time I saw him. But then it was our turn to stop at the foot of the long staircase, and a footman was opening the hansom door and putting down the steps. I squared my shoulders and raised my chin.

It was impossible not to notice the quick look of surprise on the footman's face when he saw that I was alone, impossible not to feel my cheeks blooming a little under his curious assessment of me. He was a professional, however, and would be opening many a carriage door this evening, so his expression of mild surprise was almost instantly replaced with blank politeness when he reached up to hand me out. I avoided meeting his eyes while reaching for his white-gloved hand. Shaking out my full skirts, I walked up the staircase and between the enormous entry pillars with my head held high. If nothing else, I told myself, this would make an entertaining story to relate to Father Barbier on Monday.

The foyer certainly lived up to my imagination – how different it looked from my last visit! Multitudes of candelabra and ornate gaslights cast a warm, mellow sparkle over the grand, sweeping twin staircases, and over its vast quantity of marble, gilt and statuary. I was almost overwhelmed by how beautiful it was at night. My attention was caught first by ladies passing by in fine gowns, dripping with jewels (of which I had none, except for the *faux* pearls on my gown), then by the intricate parquet designs in the tiled floors, by the statues, by the gowns yet again. There were quite a few officers swaggering about, attired like peacocks in their formal uniforms. I could feel my face flushing every time someone stared at me, which happened quite a lot, especially after I had left my cloak in the cloakroom. Some of the 'gentlemen' were quite impertinent. I received several disapproving frowns from ladies; I had been expecting that so it came as no surprise. Feeling horribly self-conscious, I tried to pretend I was searching for someone in the crowd.

Finally I found my way to the vast marble counter off to one side where the staff was taking tickets and directing the guests toward their sections. I quickly chose a line and glanced around me surreptitiously. There were, I was relieved to see, ushers waiting to escort everyone to their seats. When my turn came I bravely stepped up to the counter and handed my ticket to the heavyset middle-aged man seated behind it, then waited for him to direct me, but instead his eyes bulged as he stared at the ticket in his beefy hand. Then he looked at me, frowned, and brusquely handed back my ticket.

"Is this some sort of joke?" He asked crossly. "Box Five is always reserved. No one sits there. You may purchase a ticket for another section if you wish. There are a few seats left on the main floor." He looked past me at the next person in line.

This was unexpected, and unpleasant. With an apologetic glance over my shoulder at the man standing in line behind me, I handed the ticket back.

"It is not a joke," I informed him firmly. "This ticket is correct, Monsieur. I am to sit in Box Five."

His thick, bushy brows drew together; he was beginning to be annoyed with me. "No one sits in Box Five, Mademoiselle. I do not

149

think you would care to sit there either. Now, if you please, you are holding up my line."

I saw that I would have to surrender my note. I hated to part with it, but it appeared I had no choice. Part of me wondered how exactly this was going to go over even as I opened my little evening bag and took it out.

"*Voilà*," I said in a low voice. "I have this note for you."

Now looking decidedly angry and impatient, the man behind the counter snatched the note from my gloved hand. He read it, and the transformation in him was rapid and startling. I was shocked to see all the blood drain from his face, leaving him white to the lips. The hand holding my note began to tremble. I hoped he was not going to be ill. He looked up at me with fear in his eyes, and something else: almost a look of wonder or astonishment. However, he rallied quickly.

"*Très bien*, Mademoiselle. Please accept my apologies, I did not understand. I meant no harm, please tell him so...." he added urgently. Then he pointed toward the left hand staircase. "If you will go up the steps to the first floor, the usher will show you to your box. Here, you will need this." He handed me the ticket stub as if it burned his fingers.

"Thank you." I turned away, relieved to get away from the man and all the impatient people waiting behind me in the now rather long line. His strange reaction to my note was puzzling. He had almost appeared terrified. '*Please tell him...*' Was he referring to Erik? What on earth had Erik done, that these people were apparently so in awe of him? As I proceeded toward the grand, sweeping stair on the left side, I saw my aggravating ticket-taker lean toward one of his compatriots and begin whispering to him. Then they both turned as one and stared at me, mouths open. Perhaps it was not Erik at all, I thought anxiously; perhaps it was *me*. I began to wonder if there was something the matter with my *toilette* or my attire. Was the gown too low? Was my lack of jewelry a *faux pas*? Was there something on my nose? I found myself suddenly yearning for the safety and quiet of my apartment, away from all these prying eyes. Invisibility would have been nice.

I was only too glad to reach the first floor and hand my ticket to a waiting usher, an older woman with grey hair wearing a severe black gown that reminded me of the ones Celestine often wore. She took the ticket, gaped at it, and then at me, her eyes round as saucers.

Beginning to feel more than a little irritated, I snapped, "It is correct, Madame. I have permission to sit in Box Five. Please take me there, *tout de suite*." Everyone's peculiar reactions were beginning to get on my nerves. Now I just wanted to get to the dratted box and sit down.

"You have permission from...*him?*" The usher asked, her voice wavering. Good gracious! What was the matter with these people? She made it sound as if *le diable* himself had given me permission to sit in his own box, conveniently located in Hell.

Losing my temper, I replied crisply, "*Oui*, from *him*! If, by 'him', you are referring to the Opera Ghost."

The usher actually blanched; then she gave me a long, measuring look, finally saying ominously, "I do not know who you are, Madame, but I trust you are prepared to accept the consequences." Then she turned and walked away, signaling with her hand that I was to follow. I followed her; eventually she paused before an opening concealed behind a thick, heavy drape, pulled the drape aside, and motioned me into the box. She handed me a program before departing rapidly, without even a backward glance. I thought I saw her hand come up and quickly sketch a cross over her breast. I did not give her any further thought, however; I was thoroughly relieved to be alone at last. I did wonder fleetingly what would happen to someone who sat in Box Five *without* Erik's permission. I would have to ask him next time we met. I could hardly wait to tell him how everyone had acted toward me this evening. What would Erik make of it? He would no doubt be thoroughly pleased at the effect he had on all and sundry.

Now that I was safely ensconced in the box, my previous distress was quickly replaced by curiosity and I looked around me alertly. I could not see that there was anything particularly special about this particular box; it was an exact replica of the box seats I could see on the other side of the theatre, and it was most certainly empty except for myself. It did command an excellent view of the stage below, and of the main floor and orchestra pit. I spent a few minutes allowing my eyes to wander over the vast space before me.

It looked entirely different from the last time I was here, standing on the empty stage with Celestine in early morning light while dust motes floated gently by. I looked up, wide-eyed; the enormous chandelier suspended from the colorful ceiling became stunningly beautiful by night, when all the gaslights were burning. I had never beheld anything so opulent. One thing about the theatre did make me smile: all that gilt, scarlet drapery and opulence reminded me of Erik's home and I remembered he had once told me most of his furniture

151

had been stolen from the Opera. Beggars could not be choosers, he'd said.

I was enjoying people-watching from my plush perch, but I gradually became aware that *I* was being observed closely as well. Opera glasses were being turned on me from the boxes across the way, from the orchestra pit, and from practically every usher in the entire theatre. Dismayed, I hastily retreated as far back as I could to avoid all those prying eyes. It really must be true, I thought, that no one ever sat in Box Five. Except, presumably, Erik. That must explain why I appeared to be such an object of curiosity. I tried to imagine Erik sitting here like a perfectly ordinary theatre-goer and found I could not. While I was huddled back against the wall, I noticed something out of the corner of my eye I had missed on first glance: resting on one of the red velvet seats was a small white box tied up with red ribbon.

Curious, I stepped to the seat and picked up the dainty box. It bore a little tag, and when I examined it, I saw my own first name, written with red ink in a handwriting I knew, and nothing else. No need for a signature to know where it came from. My heart skipped a beat. Eagerly, a little smile on my lips, I pulled off the ribbon and raised the lid. Inside the box a single white orchid nestled delicately on a bed of tissue. It had been fashioned into a corsage. I had to smile, remembering my little fantasy about the carriage. I lifted the corsage carefully from the box and pinned it to the edge of my bodice – a bit of a challenge, since there was not a lot of bodice available. The delicate scent drifted up to me, and suddenly, I did not feel quite so alone. It had been a thoughtful gesture on Erik's part, one I would not have expected from him. I must be sure to thank him later.

The orchestra had by now transitioned from their discordant tuning noises and began to play in earnest, and I remembered my program, realizing I had dropped it when I noticed I was being watched. I retrieved it from the floor and studied it hastily. Tonight's performance was 'Faust' by Charles Gounod. A slip of thin paper affixed inside the program explained there was a replacement from the regular soprano this evening. I was sadly ignorant of the subject of this or any other opera, let alone the names of performers, so I put the program aside and turned my attention to the performance itself. Since this was my first ever opera performance, I was determined to enjoy it, but I must confess it was difficult going. As it turned out by some peculiar coincidence, *le diable* was involved somehow, but the subject matter was definitely *not* one that I would feel comfortable discussing with Father Barbier.

During one of the acts the stage was taken by a very lovely young girl wearing a stunning white gown. According to the program this was Mlle. Christine Daaé, the replacement soprano. She appeared to be eighteen or thereabouts; quite young for such a compelling performance as the doomed Marguerite. With her long, graceful neck and pale oval face framed by masses of dark curls, she looked like a flower blooming on the stage. Smiling confidently, she began to sing and her voice was strong and beautiful, the voice of an angel.

At first I was just as captivated by her singing as everyone else in the audience, but slowly, inexorably, I began to comprehend who I was watching, who she must be. I *knew*. And all the enjoyment and appreciation of the performance drained away. Without the shadow of a doubt, *she* was Erik's student; he was her voice tutor. This surprise performance was what all his lessons had been leading toward, I knew. Not only was Erik her tutor, but he was also in love with her. It was this innocent young *chanteuse d'opéra* who had captured the heart of the Phantom.

The weight of this discovery was too much to bear with equanimity. I no longer wanted to be here, I took no more enjoyment from my opulent surroundings, or all the elegant people in the theatre, and certainly not from the stage. In short, I was miserable. I desired only to be in the solitary comfort of my apartment, and I wished with all my heart that I had remained there. With trembling fingers, I tore the orchid corsage from my bodice and let it drop to the floor, along with the program. Erik's thoughtful gesture to me was meaningless. Why had he even made the effort? I picked up my evening bag and left the performance before the lovely girl finished her song. I could not bear to look at her any longer. By the time I had fetched my evening cloak from the cloakroom and was making my way toward the doors to watch for my hansom, the song was over. It clearly had been well-received, if the applause was any indication. Erik would be pleased.

Home again at last, I unceremoniously pulled off the blue satin gown and replaced it in the bag. Very methodically I went about my evening *toilette*: I donned my nightgown, took the pins out of my hair, shook it out and sat before my mirror to brush it by candlelight. After a moment I reluctantly met my own eyes in the mirror; I set the brush down and leaned forward, gazing glumly at my somber reflection in the glass. In my mind I pictured Mlle. Daaé: tall, willowy, young and fresh as a flower, gems twinkling in her cascades of dark hair. She was my *exact* opposite. And she sang like an angel. It was hardly surprising that Erik had fallen in love with such a girl, even if she was far too young for him. I could not believe that he had a chance with a girl that young, but that did not make his love any less true, and it certainly made sense when one considered his passion for music.

A long sigh escaped me as I pondered the ramifications of such a *folie á deux*. I had to face the truth, even as it gazed back at me in the mirror: there was no hope for me; there never had been any hope. The usher had been correct, I thought to myself rather wryly: there *had* been consequences. With a sigh, I blew out the candles and went to bed.

On Monday, after I finished at St. Giles, I paid a visit to a seamstress who had a small *atelier* a few streets away. It was not a well-known fashion house, certainly not *haute couture*, but she had a reputation for being able to make up stylish gowns in the current *mode* that were much more reasonably priced. I took with me a considerable amount of my savings. She gave me a fitting; I looked over her patterns and her suggestions for fabrics, and placed an order for several new gowns and petticoats. The gown-maker assured me confidently that my figure would suit the new styles perfectly. I had, she told me cheerfully, the type of figure that men loved. Necklines were quite a bit lower than in the past, something that I was going to have to get used to, and bustles were, sadly, now *de rigueur*. I selected mostly blues and pinks, colours that went well with my hair and eyes, but I insisted that the gowns be serviceable daytime muslins, not evening gowns, and not adorned with excessive amounts of lace and trimmings. It would not do for me to be dragging long lacy sleeves through my pots.

I returned home having parted with a sizable amount of money as a deposit, but with the promise of several stylish new gowns and even an *au courant chapeau* in the near future. It was not an imprudent expenditure; after all, I had done without any new clothes for several years and my old ones were showing wear. So I was actually being very practical. And, I reasoned, it could not hurt to try.

CHAPTER FIFTEEN

'Pure love and suspicion cannot dwell together: at the door where the latter enters, the former makes its exit'

A.D.

The shorter, crisper days of autumn arrived at last, sweeping away summer's heat and taking with it all the unpleasant odours that summer brings to the city. The street market stalls overflowed with the bounty of the season: baskets of fluted wild mushrooms, little thin-skinned potatoes with the dirt still clinging to them, bags of shiny brown chestnuts, black figs, and the hard round spheres of celeriac. There is nothing more refreshing for the professional cook than a change of seasons. Perusing my recipes, I was so spoilt for choice it was almost impossible not to want to do everything at one time. I made potato and celeriac soup, celeriac *remoulade*, fig tarts, chestnut soup, and tried to use mushrooms in everything except dessert. I was, in short, in my glory, and the pleasure it gave the recipients of all this bounty only added to my enjoyment of the season. Dr. Gaudet's waistcoat became so tight across his middle that one day a button flew off just as he was reaching for another slice of fig tart, much to his embarrassment.

As for my enigmatic Opera Ghost, Erik unbent so far as to actually invite me to sit down and eat with him one evening. This may have been a result of my bringing too much for one person to manage, and not out of a desire for my company. However, this unusually affable gesture on his part produced unexpected and unpleasant consequences.

The evening began pleasantly enough. We ate by candlelight, a necessity rather than a romantic touch, and he poured us glasses of delicious red wine. Having dinner in this Arabian Nights cavern created a mysteriously romantic *ambiance* I could not help but enjoy. I was wearing one of my new gowns in contrasting shades of dark and light blue and a revealing *décolleté*. I thought I looked rather well in it, but if I hoped Erik might notice (to be perfectly honest, I was hoping just that), I was in for a disappointment, for he made no notice of it whatsoever.

Other than that, the only thing marring my enjoyment of the evening was Erik's insistence on wearing his mask when I was there. I did consider the consequences of asking him to take it off – I would be sitting across from him eating my dinner for one thing. But I asked anyway.

"I do wish you would take off that mask. I cannot see your eyes properly when you have it on." Well, I suppose it was more in the nature of a demand.

Setting down his fork, he gave an exasperated sigh. "You never stop, do you," he said resignedly, but he obeyed my request, removing the mask and placing it on the table next to him. "I cannot believe I am doing this; I am beginning to suspect you of bewitching me, Sylvie."

I took a bite of the chicken with wild *champignons* in a cream sauce I'd made for him that evening, followed by a fortifying sip of my wine. Attempting to appear quite casual about it, I glanced up at him over the rim of my wine glass. He was watching me closely. He need not have worried; although it was only the second time I had seen him without the mask, his was not a face one could soon forget.

"I certainly hope you don't leave that thing on all the time. It cannot be good for your skin." I added thoughtfully, still trying for a casual effect as I daintily speared another morsel of chicken with my fork.

Erik made a gurgling sound that was almost a laugh. "Good for my skin! What an absurd thing for you to say." Applying himself to his dinner, he shook his head. "I do not wear it when I am here alone; there is no need." He glanced around the room. "Why do you think I keep all the mirrors covered?" I followed his glance to the tall, shrouded forms nearby. He could not bear to look at his own poor, disfigured face, I realized with a pang of sadness.

Erik pushed his empty plate away with a satisfied sigh and gave his flat stomach a pat. "You outdid yourself tonight, Sylvie. If I eat any more I will get fat, and no one would be afraid of a fat Phantom." Unable to help myself, I burst out laughing. He looked at me with a puzzled expression.

"Was that amusing?" He asked curiously.

"I was just trying to picture it, but I cannot," I replied, dabbing at my eyes with a napkin.

"That is just as well," he said. Erik seemed to be in a softer mood than usual, so I decided this might be a good time to pursue another subject I had been curious about for some time.

"Tell me what you did before you came to live here, Erik." I asked. "I know so little about you."

157

"And I know how you dislike not having your questions answered." Looking pensive, he poured us each a little more wine. "*Trés bien.* Come. Let us sit in the boat," he said. Humoring him, I followed him down to the water's edge where his skull-prowed boat was moored. Erik stepped in and gave me his hand to help me as I stepped into it after him. The warm touch of his hand set my heart racing; I was quietly thankful that he could not hear it. He untied the boat and pushed it out a little so that we were floating, gently, in the pale green light that sparkled on the water. Here we sat, holding our wine glasses, and it was such a magical, dreamlike moment that I could not speak for fear of breaking the spell.

It was Erik who first broke the silence. "I cannot tell you everything I have done, Sylvie," he said quietly after a few moments. "There are some things about me you would not want to know, and some things that would be too frightening for you to hear." Much later, looking back on this conversation, I understood that he was really saying there were things *he* did not want me to know he had done.

Erik continued, "I *can* tell you that I have always been a masonry contractor – it was the trade I learned from watching my father when I was a child. That is how I happened to find this cavern. I was hired to search for the source of a breach in the foundation and repair it if possible." His arm swept around the vast space in a wide arc. A masonry contractor, this strange, otherworldly man! My mind boggled just thinking about it.

"*Oui,* I remember Madame Giry told me that; you were engaged by the opera to make some repairs underneath, she said." I smiled expectantly, pleased to be getting some information out of him for once.

"Much of what you have seen down here: this cavern, the causeway and storage areas, were here many years before the Opera building was constructed, but they were long forgotten. When I found them, I told no one. I pretended to repair the breach, but as you see, I actually enlarged it."

"But before you came here..." I prompted, studying him interestedly.

Erik sighed as though exasperated, and then went on, "I lived for a time in Persia, where I designed and built a palace for the shah, but I was forced to leave the palace quickly because I knew too much about its secret ways. The shah was planning to have me killed because he thought I had become a danger to him. After that, I went

158

to Constantinople, and did the same for the Sultan." He glanced at me, as I sat listening to him raptly. "And with the same results, unfortunately." He sent me a sardonic glance. "You remember I told you your Moroccan tagine was my favorite of your dishes? It reminds me of those places, of the sun. I have not felt the sun on my face for a long time now." He sounded wistful, his eyes looked almost dreamy.

"Do you miss the sun, Erik?" I asked, wondering how anyone could willingly go from the endless sunshine of Persia to endless night.

Erik was silent for a long time, until I thought he was not going to answer. "*Non.*" He said at last. "I have become a creature of the night. What others fear, I love. *Regardez moi*, Sylvie," he said, spreading his arms in an expansive gesture and smiling a particularly feral smile, "I thrive in darkness, I *rule* the night."

His words wove a spell around me, captivating me even more if that were possible. Never in my life had I ever met anyone like Erik, or even imagined such a man existed, and now my small world and his had somehow collided. I shook my head bemusedly, wishing we could bob peacefully in this little boat forever. His gaze wandered out over the still water, toward the stone portcullis. Lapsing into silence, a soft, thoughtful expression stole over his face. Disgruntlement warred with my pleasure at being here with him. I wished that he would look at me as tenderly as when I knew he was thinking of *her*.

Returning his thoughts to me, Erik suddenly turned back and proceeded to tell me about the ingenious inventions he had created in the two palaces he had built: all sorts of trapdoors, secret passages, rooms full of mirrors and magical spaces, and for the sultan, something he called an automaton. Some of his creations were clearly of an unpleasant sort, for he would stop himself abruptly and then begin telling me of something else. But in the end, it all came down to one man knowing too much about the person who held power, and at least twice he was forced to flee for his life.

When he finished his recital I found myself staring at him in amazement. What a life he had lived before disappearing into the depths of the earth to hide from the world. Frowning, I could not stop myself from blurting out, "How old are you, Erik? It seems as though you have lived enough for ten people, not just one."

The corners of his well-shaped lips turned up in his feral version of a smile. One could see that he was not accustomed to smiling. "I do not know. I have forgotten my year of birth, along with my real name and the names of my parents." Toying with his wine glass, Erik looked at me thoughtfully.

"What about you, Sylvie?" He asked suddenly. I glanced across at him, startled. "You said once that you had been married, but you are not a widow. What happened? Why did the marriage end?"

I was astonished that he was even remotely curious about something in my life. Did he wish to change the subject? Perhaps he had grown weary of his recollections, or more likely, of memories that saddened him. I scowled down into my wine glass, unsure how much I ought to tell him. I disliked dredging up my own unpleasant memories, but I could feel his steady gaze on my face, waiting. He had opened up to *me*, so I drew a breath and answered him, my voice low.

"My marriage was a mistake," I said quietly. "I divorced my husband after only a year of marriage because of his...behavior toward me. I suppose it was as much my fault as it was his. I rushed into it before I really knew him very well. He was an officer, and very dashing. He rather swept me off my feet," I admitted with a flush of embarrassment. "I had cause to repent my hasty actions almost from the first."

Erik leaned forward, toward me, his eyes studying me intently. "What do you mean about his behavior? Was he unkind to you? You don't mean that he... hurt you?"

I shrugged uncomfortably. "It turned out that he was a drunkard and a wastrel. Before we wed, he was able to deceive me, but after..." I shivered, and ran a hand over my arm. I could feel goose bumps. I looked up at Erik, and saw he was still watching me closely. Under that penetrating gaze I finally confessed the shameful truth.

"*Oui*, sometimes he hurt me, when he was drinking, which, it turned out, he did quite a lot. *Alors*, I divorced him within a year of our nuptials, and I do not know what became of him after that." There was a long silence. Erik's face grew hard, his eyes frigidly cold. Afraid I had somehow angered him, I asked anxiously, "What is it?"

"If you say the word, Sylvie, I will hunt him down like the dog that he is and kill him for you. It would give me immense pleasure, I assure you."

My breath caught in my throat. Looking into those icy eyes, that implacable face, I knew he meant every word. He would bring death down upon my unfortunate former spouse like an avenging angel. Hurriedly I sought to reassure him.

"No, Erik, that is not necessary. I expect he has already managed it himself through an excess of drink. But you understand, now, why I do not care to talk about that part of my life. It was years ago and I have put it all behind me."

He sat back again, his eyes gradually losing their frightening chill. I sipped my wine, and we lapsed into a heavy silence.

Finally he said softly, "You did say once, did you not, that we had become friends. It must be true, for somehow I cannot abide the idea of anyone being so abominable that they could purposefully harm you, Sylvie. It would be like kicking a kitten. It makes me feel quite murderous."

A kitten? In an instant my mind flew to the mother cat and her brood in the cemetery the last time I was there. Did Erik see me as something small and helpless like that, in need of protection? I no longer saw myself that way. Independence and adversity had given me strength. I lifted my chin and gazed earnestly into those pale blue eyes.

"*Merci*, Erik. But I would never want you to kill someone because of me. I could never ask such a thing of you, nor wish you to ever harm someone on my behalf. Two wrongs can never make a right, as my mother often said."

"Hmmm," was his only response, but still I felt uneasy. A thick silence fell, each of us busy with our own thoughts.

"Tell me, what is an automaton?" I asked at last, wishing to break the silence and navigate to less difficult topics of conversation. "I have not heard of such a thing. Is it a machine of some sort?"

Almost eagerly, perhaps because he too was desirous of a change of subject, Erik turned to me and explained. "It is something I invented entirely myself. I suppose you might call it a machine. Others make them, mainly as toys, but mine were the best, and far more complex." No false modesty about Erik, I thought with amusement.

"I made the automata for the Sultan when I was in Turkistan — exact replicas of him, and they were so lifelike, no one could tell the difference. They were articulated and could even move in a lifelike way. It was for his safety you see; people were always trying to assassinate him. He could be in a secret place known only to himself, sleeping, while my automaton of him appeared to be sitting somewhere completely different." Erik's eyes shone with pride as he spoke.

Suddenly he sat up straight, rocking the boat, and asked, "Would you like to see one?"

"You have one of the Sultan's automata here?" I asked in surprise, gripping the edges of the boat to keep my balance.

He nodded, and a rare genuine smile lit up his face. "It is not the Sultan. I have a new one here. It is very lifelike, and perhaps my best effort – a true labor of love. Come, I must show it to you." Excited now, he stood in the boat and pushed back to shore, as eager as a little boy to show me what he had made. All moodiness vanquished, his excitement was catching; I found myself smiling indulgently back at him, pleased that I had so successfully steered our conversation to less dangerous topics.

We made our way up the bank and, setting our wine glasses down, I followed him back toward the mirror that hid the secret entrance. Knowing what I now did about his life, a lot of things about those secret entrances here were making sense to me, I mused to myself, thinking of that wooden door painted to look *exactly* like the surrounding brick. Erik stopped before a hanging I had walked past before but simply assumed it concealed yet another mirror. Apparently this was not the case.

Glowing with pride, Erik lifted the fringed hanging aside with a flourish and gestured for me to step closer to take a look. Not knowing what to expect, I did so. If I had known what I was about to see…but there was no warning, so I was taken completely unawares.

"You recognize her?" He asked, his voice reverent as he contemplated the beautiful girl standing before us.

Oh yes, I recognized her. How could I not? And the horrid thing was so lifelike if I had come across it without knowing, I daresay I would have addressed it. Honesty compels me, Reader, to at least attempt to record my feelings at that moment, but they were in such tumult I am not sure I can. Shock, despair, anger, horror and humiliation warred in me, so that I only stared and could not speak. While Erik waited, a little anticipatory smile lighting his features, for the commendations he obviously expected, my tortured thoughts spun around chasing each other.

It took but a second or two for one critical detail to register: the automaton before me had been carefully attired in a wedding ensemble, including a veil. Somehow, knowing that Erik had not only built the thing, but also lovingly dressed it in wedding garments, was enough to make my blood run cold. All my instincts were screaming to me that there was something very wrong about this.

After a long pause, I reached up and dropped the drapery back down, obscuring the uncannily realistic automaton of his young *protégée*, Christine Daaé. I turned my back on it and on Erik, and stalked away. Still standing there, he called after me.

"What is wrong, Sylvie? Don't you like it?"

Incapable of answering, I stopped at the table and began clumsily gathering my things. My cold hands were shaking; my internal turmoil was so great I did not trust my own voice.

"Sylvie?" Erik had bounded down the steps and was suddenly standing next to me, looking concerned. "You are pale; are you well?"

Avoiding his question and those probing eyes, I said, "I must go now, Erik, it is getting late. I have stayed too long. My driver will be tired of waiting." My voice sounded brittle to my own ears.

"I can see you are distressed," he said musingly. "It must be the automaton, perhaps it is *too* lifelike. Christine did not like it, either."

The plate I was holding slipped from my fingers, thudding back to the table. I stared up at him, shocked and disbelieving. "She has been here?" I gasped.

"Yes, I brought her here the night of her triumphant performance, the one I sent you the ticket to see. I told you I was going to bring her here soon, don't you remember?" He looked and sounded mildly puzzled by my reaction.

"Yes...yes, I remember." I muttered crossly. I had managed to avoid the subject of that performance up until now. So Erik had brought that innocent young girl here that night, here to this strange and very isolated place. Now I understood why he was too busy to sit with me in his private box. In addition to the green fire of jealousy I was growing accustomed to feeling, another worry gnawed at me. I frowned; it was an improper thing for him to have done, to bring her here with him, alone. She was so young. But of course, Erik cared nothing for propriety. It was *her* reputation that would suffer, not his, if anyone were to discover it. I only hoped he had behaved like a gentleman. I was too upset with him to ask, however.

He looked troubled now, his eyes slightly unfocussed; he was clearly reliving Christine's visit in his memory.

"Things did not go quite as I'd planned," he said slowly. "I expected we would have more time to get to know one another – for her to get to know me as myself I mean, before..." he stopped. He grimaced; unconsciously his hand went to the disfigured side of his face, covering it.

I sucked in my breath, suddenly understanding. "She *saw* you?" I whispered.

He nodded, squeezing his eyes shut against the painful memory. "She caught me by surprise, and pulled my mask off before I realized what I was going to do. I am afraid I...I lost my temper with her, and I frightened her. I *know* I frightened her. And *this* did nothing to help matters." Taking his hand from his disfigured face, he gestured toward it as he spoke.

"I do not know what she was more afraid of: seeing my face, or my reaction to her seeing it. I thought I would have more time," he muttered as if speaking to himself, his hands curling into fists at his sides, "but now there is a complication, a young, rich and *handsome* complication," his voice became a sneer, and his face abruptly contorted with hate and jealousy.

"It is the Vicomte de Chagny, her old childhood friend. *He* happens to be the new patron of the opera, and obviously wishes to be more than a friend to her now." So, I thought, the green flames licked at him as well. "His appearance on the scene will cause me to force my hand."

I felt no sympathy for Erik's pain, for I was fighting my own, internal battle of jealousy and anger, and suddenly I could not bear to stay there with him another minute.

"This is too much. I am leaving now." Gathering up my warm cloak, I struggled to put it on with shaking hands. I knew Erik did not understand my strange behavior – why should he?

"What is the matter with you tonight, Sylvie? I do not know why you should be so upset. It has nothing to do with you." Erik took the cloak from my fumbling hands and proceeded to arrange it around my shoulders as he had done once before. But this time, the proximity of his handsome face close to mine did nothing to my heart. I was in too much turmoil.

His casual words rankled; it had *everything* to do with me, if he only knew. I felt my temper flaring in response to his callous disregard. I looked at him steadily, our faces only inches apart.

"Has it occurred to you that Mlle. Daaé is becoming an *idée fixe* with you? I do not like it. The way you are behaving is not normal, Erik." His hands froze in place on my shoulders, his blue eyes turned to ice once more.

"*That,*" I gestured toward the place where the automaton stood, "that *thing* is not normal. It is no wonder she did not react well when you showed her that, and in a wedding gown of all things. Any normal girl would be frightened to see such an object. *En plus*, she is too young for you, and...and it was wrong of you to bring her here, unchaperoned." The words tumbled out of their own volition as my temper got the better of me.

His fingers tightened on my shoulders, and I winced in pain. "You are hurting me, Erik." I gasped.

Abruptly he released me, dropping his arms to his sides. He wasn't just vexed with me now, he was furious. "What are you accusing me of – attempting to seduce her? I would never do such a thing! I only wanted...for her to begin to know me."

I glared at him, saying hotly, "I believe you *were* trying to seduce her, Erik, whatever you may say to the contrary. Otherwise, you would not have brought her here alone. If you were not thinking only of yourself, you would have been more careful of *her*. This is not a healthy relationship, Erik, cannot you see? You have created something in your own mind but the reality may turn out completely the opposite! You will end up frightening her with the intensity of your regard for her. Does she know how you feel about her?" I asked. "For I am certain you have not yet declared yourself."

He took a deep breath, his chest expanding. He was quivering with barely controlled wrath. "Don't you understand? I *need* her; she is my voice!" He had not answered my question, but there was no need.

I stared at him uncomprehendingly. "Your voice? You *have* a voice. I do not believe this is about your music any longer, Erik."

"What do you know of it?" He muttered angrily.

My chin came up and my hands made fists at my hips as I glared back at him. "You love her, Erik. But you are selfish to the core, because you will not allow her to make her own choice." Erik flinched as if I had struck him; he took a step away from me, and his face went cold.

"This has nothing to do with love, Sylvie," he spat. "And it has nothing to do with you. I know what I am doing. Do not speak to me about this ever again, or we are *finis*."

Coming from Erik, this was no empty threat. I knew better than to say any more. There could be no reasoning with him when he was this angry. The remains of our pleasant, amicable evening lay in tatters around us, our shared confidences forgotten. Disconsolate and hurt, I gathered my belongings and walked away from him.

"*Bonne nuit*, Erik," I said softly.

Erik made no response. As far as he was concerned, I was already gone. When I glanced back just before passing through the sliding mirror, he was standing where I had left him, head bowed, one hand pressed to the disfigured side of his face. My heart wrenched at his obvious pain, but I turned and went on. Didn't he realize there were other kinds of hurts besides physical ones? Or how very adept he was at administering them, unbeknownst to himself – for he was not thinking of *me* while he was standing there holding that tragic pose, of that I was certain.

The next evening when I delivered his dinner, Erik met me as usual but made it abundantly clear that I was not welcome to accompany him back to his home. Though polite, he was cold, detached. By unspoken mutual agreement, neither of us made any mention of the previous night's argument, but our interactions were cool and formal. I was not forgiven, and as far as I was concerned, he was still in the wrong. I was feeling so cross with him that I was actually tempted to prepare something unpleasant for his dinner, an English dish like boiled beef and cabbage perhaps, but I restrained that unkind urge because the need I felt to nurture him won out over all other concerns.

For some time thereafter we behaved with frigid politeness toward each other. Erik was as helpful as ever, and then I would bid him *bonne nuit* and return home utterly disconsolate. I hated to think of him down there, so alone, his only companion an inanimate object upon which he had projected all his hopes and dreams of love, living in brooding solitude.

However, as the days passed and we carefully avoided that particularly prickly subject, relations between us gradually returned to normal, if that word could be applied to our situation at all. Erik was busy above, fully occupied in theatre business and, I thought resentfully, keeping an eye on his beloved, who was apparently also being courted by another. So our conversations were of necessity short ones. This suited me, because the days were growing shorter and colder. And we were advancing, inexorably as the march of the seasons, toward a greater darkness, and even darker deeds.

CHAPTER SIXTEEN

'My ideas are never so clear as when I have had plenty of wine'
A.D.

Not long after that argument, I made the intriguing discovery that I was *not* after all the only person who was aware of the secret entrance; nor was I the only person with whom Erik had business arrangements. I don't know why this revelation should have surprised me, but I confess that it did. I never gave any thought to how he managed to obtain a suit of clothes, sealing wax for his letters, candles and parchment paper for his music. Or how he managed to obtain a case of expensive wine. But such things did not, in fact, appear by magic.

Having delivered Erik's dinner tray to him, I had slipped through the casement window back on to the alley, closed the window behind me and started to walk toward the street. I had gone only a few steps when I came to an abrupt halt – a dark, sinister figure loomed before me! A man was in the alleyway, approaching me out of the growing shadows, blocking my route to the street, my waiting hansom, and safety. Empty dishes rattled together loudly as I made an involuntary jerk of fear and a great gasp tore down my throat. Even as my heart gave a terrified lurch and my mouth opened to scream, in a little corner of my mind I thought, *"Aha! I told Erik this alley was not safe for me!"*

The scream burst forth at the same time that the tray dropped from my hands, making a terrific clanging on the cobblestones. The sinister figure stopped in his tracks, head jerking up to stare at me in shock. Until that instant, he had not even been aware of me. I found myself staring into a pair of startlingly green eyes. The lower part of his face was covered by a thick black beard and his head by a tall black fur hat. His complexion was swarthy, his nose prominent and hawk-like. He was carrying something in both hands, a box of some sort, like a packing crate. Those sharp emerald eyes now fixed on me wore a decidedly unfriendly expression.

Suddenly the casement window flew open behind me and Erik vaulted through it, landing on both feet as silent as a cat. I felt his hands hard on my shoulders as he pulled me back against the wall, then he was standing in front of me, facing the stranger, his body tensed. He wore a terrifying scowl on his face. Relief flooded through me when I saw that Erik had come to protect me. If the ruffian knew what was good for him, he ought to flee now, while he still could.

Erik seemed about to spring at the menacing stranger, but then his tensed body uncoiled itself and he straightened, his fierce expression smoothing out.

"Oh, it's you, daroga," he said in a conversational tone. "I forgot you were coming tonight. It is a good thing I recognized you." Erik turned back to where I huddled, pressed against the wall. In a soothing voice he said, "Do not be afraid, Sylvie, he means you no harm. He is here to see me." Erik surveyed the cobblestones, his lip curling up in a slight smile. His voice became teasing.

"I see you have dropped your tray again; careless of you, Sylvie."

The strange man, who was apparently *not* a ruffian (although he certainly looked like one), edged forward, keeping a wide berth, looking nervously at me sidelong as though he expected me to scream again. It was clear from the look on his face he thought me a hysterical female, and righteous indignation gave me the will to stand up straight and smooth my hands down over my skirts, surreptitiously wiping down my damp palms as I did so. Lifting my chin, I glared at Erik.

"You cannot blame me for being frightened, Erik. I have never met with anyone here before. You might have warned me this might happen."

The man he had referred to as 'daroga' (a most peculiar name, it seemed to me), turned toward Erik and addressed him in heavily accented French. "Who is this woman? And how is it that she knows your name?" His deep voice sounded almost accusing.

"She is my excellent cook, daroga," Erik answered cheerfully. "She has my permission to be here. Give me the box *tout de suite*." An exchange took place, so swiftly I almost missed it. Erik took the wooden crate and rested it on the window sill, while at the same time handing a little pouch to the man, who pocketed it smoothly.

"You may go now. I will be in touch in the usual fashion next time I require your services." It was a curt dismissal; Erik was obviously eager to be rid of his visitor. The green-eyed man studied Erik's face intently as though searching for something there, then nodded and walked away down the alley without another glance at me. When I looked back toward him, Erik had already picked up my tray and replaced the empty dishes on it. Regrettably, one of my favorite china plates had broken in half on the cobblestones.

"Who was that strange man?" I asked without preamble. "He is certainly not a Frenchman."

Erik shrugged. "Not a Frenchman, *non*. He performs the occasional service for me – in this instance, he was renewing my supply of pyrotechnics." His *what?* Handing me the tray, he lifted the packing case and thrust it through the window, placing it carefully on the floor inside. I saw that the box was marked with several long rows of odd-looking black characters, like hieroglyphs. Peering at the characters, I recognized Chinese writing.

Glancing at me, Erik observed my look of perplexed confusion. "Fireworks ingredients: black powder, sodium, sulphur and so forth." He explained.

"What…but what…"

"Never you mind, Sylvie. I find smoke and mirrors very useful now and then. Let us leave it at that." Giving me a quelling look, he followed the packing case through the window with his usual grace and economy of movement. I could not imagine why Erik, dwelling underground as he did, should require the ingredients for, as he put it, pyrotechnics. He had no intention of telling me, either.

"*Alors,* he is a friend?" I asked, for I was still curious about the stranger who performed services for Erik. Erik had said he had no friends.

Erik paused in the act of grasping the window to close it. I put my own hand out and caught hold of it so that he could not. His face was expressionless as he reluctantly replied.

"Not a friend, exactly. More like a friendly enemy. I knew him in Persia." I could tell by his face and voice I would get no more information from him, so I released my hold on the window. "*Bonne nuit*, Sylvie. Keep a tight hold on that tray." With a smirk, Erik shut the window in my face and vanished. So the man was a Persian; that explained his swarthy complexion and his peculiarly accented French. And 'daroga' was definitely not a French name.

Later, I was to learn that this 'friendly enemy' had in fact saved Erik's life by giving him a warning in time, and by helping to deliver him from danger; thus earning a measure of trust and respect from him. Erik never told me what they were to each other in Persia even though I asked him more than once. He did reveal that they communicated via cryptic ads placed in one of the Paris newspapers.

The Persian brought Erik things that he needed but was unable to obtain for himself, for a price. Thankfully, I never met with him in the alleyway again. It was, however, another little piece of the puzzle that was Erik, and I was pleased to have it.

It was a pleasant Saturday morning not long after my alarming encounter with the Persian, crisp and cold and smelling like roasting nuts when I started out for my weekly constitutional. Paris is justly famous for its many beautiful trees, and the autumnal colours this year were stunning. Wearing sensible walking boots and a navy blue jacket in *le courant* military style, I was planning to walk to the Cimetière de Montmartre to visit my parents' graves and admire the leaves. I stopped before reaching the end of the block, however, my attention caught by the little newspaper boy who always stood at the corner of our street. Just as I was about to pass him, he began shouting in a shrill, carrying voice that made me jump. It was something about a fatal accident the previous evening at the Opéra Populaire.

My pulse quickened with alarm – a death at the Opera? I was instantly groping in my skirt pocket for my change purse. I was not concerned for Erik; he would surely have been safe in his home far below. It was for Celestine and little Meg that I feared, and so sought reassurance neither of them had been involved. I reminded myself that a fatal accident could be anything, even some tipsy audience member at the performance falling down stairs. There were quite a lot of stairs, if my memory served. Or perhaps it could have been an accident involving one of the dancers.

Still, my fingers trembled as I snatched a paper from the boy's outstretched hand.

"*Voilà*, Louis *petit*", I muttered absently, handing him a coin. Anxious to learn what had happened and relieve my suspense, I stepped away and began to read. The story occupied a prominent position on the front page due to its sensational nature.

It was a very disturbing account, and much worse than I could have imagined. According to the article, on the previous evening, during a performance to a packed house, a disruption caused the performers to be in disarray and the performance halted mid-act. The owners were forced to insert an unrehearsed ballet dance in place of the comic opera being performed, something which had never happened before. During this ballet, the chief stagehand, one Joseph Buquet, suddenly dropped from the scaffolding above the stage and dangled by a rope around his neck, dead. The entire building had erupted in pandemonium. The police were summoned, but the managers were insistent that the death was an unfortunate accident: that somehow, this Buquet person must have tripped and fallen after entangling himself in the rope. A propensity to over-imbibe was hinted at.

The article went on to report that shortly before the shocking demise of the stagehand, a weird, sepulchral voice had addressed the House from above in a threatening manner and then abruptly vanished. No one was sure exactly what had been said, but the threats seemed to be directed toward the new owners. The actors on the stage at the time and thus in a position to see who had spoken, all claimed they had seen nothing.

I had a good idea whose was the sepulchral voice. Erik's growing dissatisfaction with the new owners and his theatrical nature made him the obvious candidate. Just a night or two ago he had grumbled to me that the new owners were refusing to pay him his 'salary'.

In a state of perturbation, I handed the paper back to little Louis and hurried away down the street. I walked for some time, not regarding where I was going and occasionally bumping blindly into passersby. Yet somehow, I was not surprised to find my feet had eventually carried me to the Opera building. I came out of my mental fog to find I was standing on the Boulevard des Capucines, looking across at the magnificent baroque façade of that structure, with no recollection of how I had arrived here. A thin layer of last night's snowfall sparkled in the sun and decorated the building like icing on a cake, transforming it into an enormous glittering confection.

I must talk to Celestine. And I was so anxious to do so that I picked up my skirts and ran across both lanes of traffic without a thought or a pause. One hansom cab had to pull up quite short to prevent his horse from running over me, but I carried on without looking back, in spite of the bad language directed at me from the driver. I ran across the large sweeping entrance, up the steps to the closed door. It was locked and unresponsive to my attempts to open it.

Frustrated and out of breath, I finally noticed a sign affixed to the door: the Opéra Populaire was temporarily closed. The management apologized, but for now, all performances were cancelled.

Now that I was actually paying attention, it was obvious that the place was strangely quiet. Some sensible portion of my mind understood that of course, after such an occurrence, they would have no choice but to close, out of respect for the deceased if for no other reason. But the unreasonable portion of my brain refused to accept defeat. I removed my glove and began pounding loudly on the closed door. Celestine had to be in there somewhere, and I must talk to her. If anyone knew the facts of what had occurred here last night, it would be her.

After what seemed like an age, someone finally unlocked the door. It was opened by a large *gendarme*, severely irritated, who looked me up and down before curtly informing me that the Opera building was closed to all but those who lived there, the managers and the police. Couldn't I read the sign? Biting off a retort in response to this insulting remark, I asked instead if a message could be taken to Madame Giry at once. He recognized her name, for an odd, guarded look appeared on his face at the mention of it, but he agreed to dispatch a message to her if I would wait on the steps. Casting a last, suspicious look at me, he departed within, closing the doors smartly in my anxious face.

It was very cold, so as I waited impatiently I hugged myself to stay warm. Many long minutes passed before the door opened once more and I beheld Celestine coming slowly down the steps toward me, draping a shawl about her shoulders as she did so. My heart sank; she looked older, with shadows under her eyes and a haunted expression. Her long braid lay thick as a rope over one shoulder.

"Sylvie, what are you doing here?" She asked, looking into my face searchingly.

Without preamble I demanded, "How can you ask? Were you there last night?"

A wary look came into her tired eyes. "*Oui, certainement*, I had to get the ballerinas ready to go out at the last minute and with no preparation time. But as I have informed the police already, I was back stage and saw nothing."

I stared hard at her. "But it was *he* who addressed the House from above, was it not?" There was no need to say his name. In my agitation I reached out and gripped her by the arms.

Pulling slightly away from me, Celestine turned her head to glance at the closed door. Satisfied we were alone, she reluctantly nodded her head, saying, "Yes, yes it was he. I recognized his voice.

172

He was…displeased because the new owners did not follow his orders about the casting for the performance last night."

I released her arms and resumed hugging myself. The cold seemed to penetrate into my very bones. "So he *was* there." I said grimly. "And he was displeased." I shook my head, trying to rid it of unwanted images.

"They are saying the death was an accident, Sylvie. He was always drunk, that repellant man. His death is no loss."

Slowly I turned to meet her eyes. "Do *you* believe it was an accident, Celestine?" I asked.

Her eyes dropped away from mine. When she looked back up at me, her face was troubled. "*Je ne sais pas.* But I hope so. No one else was seen on the catwalks above except Joseph Buquet himself. So it is possible…" her voice trailed off.

There was only one thing to do, and I ought to have realized it before now. Trying to get the truth of this from Celestine was surely a waste of my time. I squared my shoulders.

"If you do not know, then I will ask him myself." Even as I spoke the words, I was gathering my skirts in my hands.

"No, Sylvie!" Celestine cried, clutching my arm and looking alarmed. "Do not go there now! I cannot answer for the consequences; please don't. Cannot you wait until this evening as you normally would?"

I detached Celestine's cold hand from my arm and stepped away from her. I was on fire to carry my point. "No, this cannot wait. I have to know, it is important. You know why I need to know – how could I continue to work for a…a murderer?" We both flinched when that word came out.

"You will be careful, Sylvie, won't you? Please try not to say anything that might upset him further. He has become so unpredictable of late, even I am a little afraid of him." She shivered, but I noticed she had not defended Erik against the possibility that he might be a murderer. If anything, her panicked reaction rather confirmed it.

"You are catching a chill, Celestine. You came out without a wrap. Do go back inside. Do not worry about me, I am in no danger. *Au revoir.*" I turned, ran heedlessly down the icy steps, and made my way along the boulevard toward my secret entrance to Erik's home. I did not look back, or I might have seen Celestine standing frozen in place, hands clasped together at her throat, watching me as I hurried away from her.

I was not so distraught that I did not take my normal precautions to be sure that my progress went unmarked, or that no one followed me down the quiet alley. I had never made this approach so early in the day, and quite a few people were about. Once safely inside the marble room, I used the oil lamp to light my passage into the underworld of Erik's home. I was telling the truth when I assured Celestine that I did not fear Erik. By now I thought I could trust our strange friendship to protect me from his sudden mood swings and outbursts of temper. I understood that he would not, or could not, manage his emotions. Whatever he was feeling, he simply expressed it fully and immediately, whether it be anger or …well, I could not recall him ever seeming to be happy.

Erik had lived the kind of existence where he was never called upon to regulate his temper. In many ways he was as uncivilized as any savage would be; his excellent manners had been learned by imitating real gentlemen, but he possessed no great understanding of the whys or wherefores of civilized behavior. Nevertheless, I felt sure he would never do anything to harm me now. We were friends.

Was Erik a cold-blooded murderer, though? My blood chilled at the very idea; it was too horrible to contemplate. How well did I really know him? I knew he had lived a strange life, had done bad deeds in his past that he did not want me to know about, but he behaved as though all that was long behind him now. My fingers were feeling for the little catch that would cause the invisible door to rotate inward when another consideration brought me up short, and I sucked in my breath.

What if the worst were true and he *had* committed murder last night, and he confessed it to me? Would he trust me not to tell the police? Would I be allowed to leave here alive? And if he *was* guilty of cold-blooded murder, it was my duty as a citizen to tell the police where they could find him, if I could bring myself to do it. I rubbed my free hand over my forehead – all this was enough to give me a headache.

Perhaps I had been lying to both myself and Celestine when I told her I did not fear Erik. I was always afraid of him, in my heart. The more I came to understand Erik, the more dangerous he seemed. But I had accepted a certain level of trepidation as the price I paid for his company, which I craved like a drug. Standing outside his door in the dim light of the oil lamp, I weighed the consequences of my decision. Finally I made up my mind. It was essential that I know the truth, no matter what might befall me. What I could not tell Celestine,

174

what I could scarcely admit even to myself, was that my love for this fascinating and dangerous man hung in the balance. It was for love that I needed the truth, and needed it now. If he did decide to kill me, all I could hope for was that he would make it quick and painless, for the sake of our friendship. The cold black water of the underground lake lapped continually against the stone of the landing, as though reminding me of the precarious nature of that friendship. I dropped my hand from my throbbing forehead, and straightened.

My decision made, I pressed the catch firmly. Once inside I proceeded slowly and cautiously across the floor of the little storage room. I half-expected to be seized at any moment, for I never came here so early in the day and Erik might mistake me for an intruder. I met with no impediment, however, only an eerie silence.

Sliding the mirror door aside, I lifted the concealing drapery and looked around. "Erik, are you here? It is Sylvie." I called. There was no response to my hail, so I walked further into the cavern. There was no sign of Erik farther below, nor was he at the music bench. There, on the table in the lower region of his home near the water's edge, I saw the dinner tray from last night; it was untouched. Could he still be sleeping? Was he ill? I started up toward the stone steps toward his bedchamber, but had taken only a few steps when I came to a sudden gasping stop, heart pounding.

He was there, slouching limply on that ornate throne-chair, as unmoving as a statue. Only the slow rise and fall of his chest showed he yet breathed. His vacant, unseeing eyes were empty as he sat brooding darkly out across the green water. He was wearing his mask and the dark wig, but he was dressed for home, in a white shirt and black velvet dressing gown. He made no sign that he had heard me calling, or that he was even aware of my presence. I was momentarily taken aback; this was the first time I had ever seen him when his attire was other than immaculate.

I was dismayed to see a glass and an empty wine bottle resting on the floor next to his chair. The sight made my stomach flip and fear knot in my breast; I had seen my former husband in a state of inebriation too many times. But I reminded myself sternly that Erik was nothing like my ex-husband. I had never known Erik to over-imbibe; he preferred to keep his senses as sharp as possible. Something must really be the matter for him to have done so, and this in no way reassured me.

I approached the throne-chair warily, nerves jangling with the strain of appearing outwardly calm. I might as well have been a disembodied spirit for he made no sign he was aware of my close presence. Drawing near him, I put down the lamp and studied his haggard features with concern. A *frisson* of fear ran through me – what was wrong with him? I reached out to touch him, but thought better of it and addressed him instead.

"Erik. Erik, look at me." Concern made my voice sharper than I intended, but it worked because it caught his attention. As though in a trance, he slowly turned his head to look up at me. The eyes that met mine were vacant, as if Erik's body was there but only as an empty shell. There was no spark in their pale blue depths, and it gave me a chill of fear.

"Have you been sitting in this chair all night?" I asked worriedly. "Are you ill? You did not eat your dinner."

He turned his face away from me, resuming his contemplation of the lake below. His mouth turned down at the corners in a grimace.

"No," he said after a long pause, his voice rough from lack of sleep and the wine, "no, I am not ill. And I have not been here all night, not all night. I was up on the roof for a time, standing in the snow."

My mind seemed to absorb what he was saying slowly. I stared at him, nonplussed. *On the roof?* Why on earth would he have gone up there? It was so out of character for him.

"On the roof...of the opera building?" I asked. "What...what were you doing up there?" A little flutter of hope grew inside me. The roof, as I knew having been there once, was as far away from the stage where the accident took place as was possible.

My question brought an unexpected reaction from Erik. His face contorted, his eyes closed tightly as though trying to drive away a terrible vision, and I was shocked to see a tear slide out of the corner of his left eye. Finally he answered me.

"I was eavesdropping." His voice was just a hoarse whisper.

I did not know what to do or say. I wanted to comfort him, but his enigmatic words explained nothing; rather than answering my question, his explanation only confused me further. And I could not permit myself to become distracted and forget the reason I had come here in the first place. Gathering my skirts up, I knelt by the arm of the chair where I could look up into his face.

"Erik, what is the matter? Is it something you can tell me?" I asked cautiously.

He opened his eyes, dragged the sleeve of his dressing gown across his wet face, and glanced down at me. "*Non.* But do not think

176

I am sitting here idly, Sylvie. I have been thinking. I have a great deal to think about, and much to do. My course is set; I am not going back up there again until I am ready." His hands, lying lax on his lap, suddenly tightened into fists.

"And then I will teach them a lesson about consequences." As he spoke a blaze kindled in those cold eyes, replacing the vacant look with a sudden hot flash of anger. I sat back on my heels automatically.

Erik's eyes suddenly focused on me, as if he were seeing me for the first time. His hands slowly unclenched and the flame of anger faded from his eyes.

"What are you doing here so early?" He asked. "Is something the matter?"

"*Oui*, I think so." I got to my feet, straightened my skirts, and gathered up my courage. Heart in my throat, I said, "There was a death at the performance last night, as I am sure you must know. I read about it in the newspaper this morning."

Erik's face instantly closed down, his expression became unreadable, reserved. He looked up at me with tight, wary eyes. He did not speak, only stared at me. Out of the corner of my eye I saw his hands clench convulsively.

I met his inscrutable gaze steadily, with an outward appearance of calm I did not feel. Into the charged silence between us I spoke again.

"You were there, I know you were. And I have to ask you...did you...did you kill that man, Erik?" It was an effort to force the words out. Everything depended on his answer – what would it be?

We seemed to stay frozen like that for an eternity, our eyes locked on each other. As I waited in trepidation for his answer, I saw the icy reserve melt out of his face and he looked suddenly vulnerable and sad. His pale eyes filled with some emotion I could not identify: desolation? I caught my breath at the change in him. His lips parted at last.

"No, Sylvie. It was an accident. I *was* there, but I...was not responsible." He looked straight into my eyes as he spoke, beseeching, and I believed him.

The icy knot of dread and fear that had been building inside me suddenly melted away. I let out my pent breath, felt myself almost sag with relief. Erik must have thought I was about to faint, for he rose from the chair, took me by the arms and put me down on it in his place. It was not very comfortable. Why couldn't he put a cushion in it?

I am not sure what was wrong with me; sitting there on that absurd rock-hard throne chair, I felt so overcome that I started to cry, and once I started, could not stop. Ashamed of my tears, I covered my face with my hands. Erik stood watching helplessly for a moment, then he turned his back on me and stood with shoulders bowed, head cast down.

"Oh, Sylvie," he murmured, his voice filled with anguish, and so low I could barely hear it.

Finally I ran out of tears. I dried my wet face with the hem of my cloak and tried to pull myself together. "Please forgive me; I don't know what is the matter with me." I gasped. He had neither moved nor spoke while I cried myself out.

Now he said, "I do, I think. You know, if you decided you did not want to cook for me any longer, I would understand. Sometimes I think it would be better if you had never been brought into this…this situation. I know I am not…not the man you thought I was. But I don't want you to be afraid of me, Sylvie." He turned his head to gaze at me over his shoulder, a questioning look on his sad, grim face.

I sniffed; finally remembering I carried a handkerchief, I reached into my skirt pocket for it and blew my nose as discreetly as possible before responding to his unspoken question.

"As long as I know you were not responsible for that man's death, I will not be afraid to come here. I…I'd like to keep on with our arrangement if you still want me. I am sorry I doubted you, Erik; I hope you can forgive me for entertaining such terrible thoughts. I ought to have known better." I said earnestly. Indeed I now felt heartily ashamed for the wild idea I had harbored against him.

Erik stared at me, a tortured expression in his eyes. He looked as if *he* were going to start weeping now. Instead, he made a visible effort to pull himself together, his chest expanded with a long indrawn breath, and he said, "I do want you. It is not in *your* best interest, but I do. I am a thoroughly selfish creature as you ought to know by this time. Go home now please, my dear little Sylvie. I am not good company today. It would be best if I were left alone."

It was a command I could not refuse, in spite of that gentle endearment which I had never heard him utter before, so I nodded my head, stood and took up the oil lamp.

"You are not angry with me?" I asked a little tentatively, still feeling guilty that I had for even a moment thought he could be a murderer.

Erik's breath came out in an explosive, exasperated sound of frustration that made me jump. "For God's sake, Sylvie! You are the one person in this entire world I am *not* angry with. Go *now*, or I soon will be!"

I did not understand his answer, but I knew better than to question him further. At least I had received the reassurance I had come for. Thus reassured, I left.

From that day forward, Erik was a driven man. He began composing what he described to me as his greatest work, an opera, the day after I confronted him about the death at the theatre. Never having observed him when he was deep in the process of composing music, I had nothing to compare it with, but never had I seen him so withdrawn, so focused, so absorbed. Although he steadfastly refused to talk to me about it, I was certain that the catalyst was whatever had upset him the previous night and caused him to consume a bottle of wine. Not the accidental death, apparently, but something else which he would not share. The work of composing completely devoured him. His single-minded concentration was almost frightening in its intensity, but as I reminded myself, Erik never did anything by half-measures.

He no longer met me in the marble room to help me through the window; I was left to struggle through alone. I grew accustomed to delivering his dinner in his home instead. I would have left it on the ledge upstairs, but I ceased doing that when I found he was too absorbed in his work to remember to come and retrieve it. And also, of course, I wanted – no, *needed* to see him, even though he seldom spoke more than a few curt words to me. I was an addict, and he was my drug.

I went back to Celestine soon after my conversation with Erik regarding the death at the theatre, as much to reassure her of my own safety as to tell her about his denial of any involvement. This news did not comfort her as much as I expected it would. As the days passed

Celestine continued to worry; she asked me several times what he was doing. Though the theatre had reopened, the Ghost, she said, had not been seen anywhere in the theatre since the night of Joseph Buquet's death, nor had he communicated with her by letter as was usual. He abruptly ceased tutoring Mlle. Daaé, and since that fateful night avoided her entirely.

According to Celestine, Mlle. Daaé's growing relationship with the young Vicomte was very likely to end in an engagement. This was a relief to me, for though he had been the cause of Erik's fierce jealousy, the Vicomte de Chagny was a much more appropriate, and safe, choice for her. I knew better than to allow myself any hope that Erik no longer cared for the lovely young soprano, or that he might instead learn to care for me. For although I was now the only person who ever saw or spoke with him, it gave me little satisfaction. I might as well have been a stick of furniture, an automaton myself perhaps, for all the attention he gave to me now. It was extremely vexing.

Whenever I arrived, Erik was invariably to be found seated on the music bench before the organ, dipping his pen into ink and writing furiously. An unruly lock of hair would have fallen over his forehead, and the sleeves of his white shirt covered with ink spatters. Solidified blobs of candle wax lay everywhere. He had left off wearing his mask and the dark wig. Since I was the only person who saw him, it did not matter to him, and as I preferred him this way, it did not matter to me either. To myself, I took to calling him 'Beethoven' for his evil temper whilst working.

So single-mindedly did he concentrate on his work that he seldom bothered to look up when I entered and approached him. I began to set his dinner tray directly on top of the instrument, sometimes even on top of his sheets of music, because otherwise he would not stop and take the time to eat. Even then, he sometimes ate nothing at all until I would threaten to force-feed him. I wondered how much he was even sleeping. When I inquired about these concerns, my reward was a surly snarl to mind my own business.

Curious about the project that so consumed him, I made attempts to find out what it was about, but he no longer had any interest in conversation. I would sit down and watch him for a while, but even that was unsatisfying, since he behaved as if I were not in the cavern at all. Now and then, he would play a few notes of odd, discordant music, or sing a few words softly to himself. The sheets of parchment piled up. Finally, driven to distraction by my own insatiable curiosity regarding all things Erik, one evening I made the mistake of reaching for one of the pages to turn it over and look at it after setting down his tray.

Even as my hand stretched tentatively toward the crisp sheet of paper, Erik's own hand shot out and closed like a vise on my wrist.

"What do you think you are doing, Sylvie?" he demanded coldly, actually raising his head to look at me for the first time in what felt like days. His expression was not pleasant. He did not release my wrist, and his fingers were so hard on my skin that it hurt. I felt a gasp escape my lips.

"Let me go, Erik. I only wanted to satisfy my curiosity about your opera, since you refuse to tell me anything about it. I meant no harm, as you know perfectly well."

"Can you read music, Sylvie?" he asked in a sneering voice. He knew I could not.

I tried in vain to wrench my wrist out of his cruel grasp. "Erik, you are hurting me," I whispered. We stared at one another, my own eyes large and frightened, and his pale blue ones hard and icy. It was as if I were looking into the eyes of a stranger. He had never deliberately hurt me like this before – punishing me for my transgression. The pain I felt was more than physical; I felt tears of betrayal gathering in my eyes.

"Please, Erik." My voice was pleading now, sounding the way I felt, frightened and confused. "Let me go." Recovering himself, he abruptly released me, and I rubbed my wrist. The marks of his fingers stood out lividly on my skin.

"You did not have to do that," I said resentfully.

Erik leaned back on the bench, put down his pen, and crossed his arms. "Listen carefully, Sylvie, because I am only going to say this once. I do not want to be disturbed when I am working. I've had enough of you hovering over me, asking your endless questions. I am not bound to satisfy your never-ending curiosity. My work is none of your business. No one is going to see my opera, or read it, until it is completely finished and ready to be presented. If you cannot abide by my rules, or respect my privacy, then you should remain upstairs. It is your decision."

The hurt I felt at his cruel words must have registered on my face. It was, he once told me, an open book, especially to him.

"You did not used to be so unkind," I said quietly, then turned away from him and began walking up the steps toward the secret panel, fighting tears. Perhaps I *would* start leaving his dinner upstairs.

181

It would serve him right. And that boiled beef and cabbage dish was beginning to sound even better.

At first there was silence from behind me; then I heard a deep sigh.

"Sylvie," Erik called to me, his voice contrite. Unable to help myself, I paused in the act of lifting the heavy drapery away from the mirror and glanced back over my shoulder. I did not want to; I wanted to keep my back rigid and depart without another word, but it seemed I could refuse him nothing, even when he hurt me. He had risen from the music bench and was approaching me. He looked sad and distraught. Ever true to his mercurial disposition, his mood had made a complete *volte-face* in an instant. I let the drapery fall from my fingers and waited for him, even though my pride demanded that I turn away.

Coming to stand near me, he reached out, took me by the shoulders and turned me around to face him, his fingers gentle now.

"Forgive me, Sylvie. I did not mean to hurt you. This is something I cannot share with you. This is the most important piece of music I will ever write. It means more to me than I can explain, and when it is completed..." he stopped and gave his head a brief shake, as if he had already told me more than he intended. "You cannot understand what it means to me, Sylvie, and even if you could, it is better that you do not."

And then he did something that melted my heart, banished all thoughts about his last enigmatic statement, and reminded me of why I had fallen so in love with him in the first place. He took my wrist in his hand, turned it over, lifted it and very gently pressed his lips to the angry red mark left by his own fingers. It was not a romantic gesture on his part; it was a gesture of apology to a friend. Erik released my wrist, took his other hand from my shoulder, and stepped back from me. He always seemed to be stepping back from me, I thought to myself sadly.

"Go home now," he said, "and let me get back to my work. I have a deadline to meet."

I did not understand what he meant about a deadline, but feeling the warm, moist place his lips had just been, I was thankful yet again that he could not hear the pounding of my heart. What I really wanted was his arms around me, him holding me close to his own heart, but that was not going to happen. Banishing such thoughts, I attempted to muster up a small smile for him.

"It is forgotten," I said gently.

CHAPTER SEVENTEEN

'Now the thing is at work and it will effect its purpose'
A.D.

Three long months passed in this dissatisfying manner. The long autumn gave way at last to winter. In December Alexandre Dumas died, leaving his last novel unfinished. I mourned the passing of my favorite novelist, carried off apparently by an excess of excesses, but the man himself kept a positive attitude as Death approached. He was reported to have said, "I shall tell her a story, and she will be kind to me."

To make matters worse, the beastly Prussians were breathing down our necks, suffering under the delusional impression that they could somehow take over the city of Paris.[2] No cannonballs yet penetrated my *quartier* of the city, so I refused to allow all the upheavals to interrupt my celebration of the holidays. To celebrate *Noël* I invited Celestine and Meg to dinner on *le reveillon;* I served a roast goose and the traditional oysters, *naturellement.* How I was able to obtain these comestibles when the Prussians were blockading the city is best not gone into. Suffice it to say that some of the merchants on the Rue de la Marché had wide-ranging, if not entirely legitimate, connections.

Out of the goodness of my heart I invited Erik to join us for our holiday dinner, even though I knew full well that he would refuse, and he did not disappoint. I had just placed his dinner tray on the table one evening and, pushing back the hood of my cloak, proffered my invitation to him.

Erik's busy pen paused over the piece of parchment, and he looked askance at me. "What did you say?" he asked after a moment.

"Come here and have your dinner while it is still warm, *s'il vous plaît,*" I ordered. "I said, would you like to come for dinner with Celestine and Meg and myself for *Noël* next week?"

"*Noël?* Next week?" He gave me a blank look. Then he made a derisive noise. "Don't be ridiculous, Sylvie. You cannot imagine that I pay the slightest attention to such events. *Ici,* where it is always night, it is easy to forget all the things that Society deems important."

---

[2] *Alas, my confidence in this regard was misplaced, for the Prussians did finally manage to invade Paris, much to the embarrassment of all.*

"But…"

Erik held up a staying hand, the sleeve of his shirt showing splotches of ink. "*Non*," he added, his expression bleak, "I expect my attendance in my present state of mind would cast a pall over your festivities." He would hear no more about it, and further entreaties on my part fell on deaf ears. It was no more than I expected.

He did, however, present me with a very generous gift of a hundred *francs*, refusing to take it back when I tried to decline the gift as being too extravagant. It was, he explained, by way of an apology for his distant behavior. I gave him my own copy of The Three Musketeers. I knew there was no danger that he would see himself in D'Artagnan, as I saw myself in Kitty. There could be no one more unlike D'Artagnan, in fact. I do not believe Erik took the time to even open the book.

Noël at St. Giles was quite a festive affair, with music, singing, prayers in Latin and a great quantity of food, prepared by myself. A few of the patients had invited family members to partake of their holiday dinner, so I wanted to make certain it was a memorable occasion. I always loved *Noël*. When I was growing up my parents made the entire season quite festive. Many of my father's regular patients used to present us with gifts and holiday treats and my mother loved to bake. This was my first holiday season without my mother, and I missed her terribly. Perhaps to compensate, I did rather overdo a bit with the dinner for the Hospital. Robert actually complained out loud about all the heavy pots and pans he was forced to carry for me, but he unbent so far as to mutter something about the meal being acceptable. For Robert, that was praise indeed. As he was preparing to leave that night, I handed him a box containing a traditional *Buche de Noël* I'd made especially for him.

"*Voilà*, Robert. *Pour Noël*," I explained. And then I had the pleasure of watching as he blushed crimson right up to his non-existent hairline.

January 1871, came and went, and Paris was now held in the grip of a long, cold winter. Erik continued to work like a demon on his opera while I tried to take care of him as best I could and as much as he would allow. I was concerned for his health, but in spite of his irregular hours, evil temper and lack of rest, he was a force of nature, strong as a horse and possessed of endless stamina. He continued to ignore me a great deal of the time, and when he did deign to speak to me, it was in a voice as remote and distant as that of a stranger.

On a Saturday evening in mid-February, as I made my cautious way down to Erik's home, I wondered, as I did on a daily basis, what kind of mood he would be in tonight. His frenzied work on his opera had rendered him so surly and distant, it was wearing on me. I was beginning to feel quite cross. This had gone on for *three* months – when would it end? When I lifted the golden drapery back from the secret entrance and stepped inside, I glanced automatically toward the instrument where he usually sat working, but Erik was not there. I stared at the empty bench in consternation.

"*Bonsoir*, Sylvie," said a distant voice from far below, near the water's edge. "You are just in time to tell me what you think of my costume for the *bal masqué* being held at the Opéra Populaire tonight." Startled, my head whipped around as I looked in the direction of that voice, and then I nearly stumbled over my own feet in astonishment. I knew of the masquerade ball, of course, because Celestine and Meg talked of little else for the last few weeks, but it never occurred to me that *Erik* might attend.

He was standing before a tall mirror, usually kept covered, putting the finishing touches on an incredible costume: he was dressed head-to-foot in brilliant scarlet. It made him look even taller than usual. Unable to take my eyes off him from absolute astonishment at his outlandish attire, I made my way slowly and carefully down the steps to join him. As I paused to put my things down on the table, a thickly bound booklet in a leather cover caught my eye: it was the score of his opera.

Stopping to run my fingers over the cover, I asked, "You have finished it?" But when I turned my attention to the bizarre vision in red standing before me, I was so distracted I scarcely listened to his reply.

"Yes, last night. I have worked like a dog in order to finish before this evening. I do not have to tell you, you already know. You have been very patient with me all this time. Hand me that grease pencil on the table."

I picked it up and cautiously approached him, and he looked amused at my stunned expression. "*Bien*, don't you like it?" Not waiting for my response, he took the black grease pencil from my outstretched hand, leaned in close to the mirror and began to completely outline his eye sockets in black. It was the first time I had ever observed Erik to willingly look at his own reflection in a mirror. I watched, fascinated, as he worked.

This task complete, he took a white, full-face mask down from a corner of the mirror and carefully fitted it over his head. He was already wearing one of his dark, smooth wigs. He then turned toward me, spreading out his arms to give me the full effect.

"*Alors*, what do you think, Sylvie? There is a red scarf also but if I put it on now I will ruin it."

I studied him interestedly. He was, as I have said, dressed in scarlet: a snug-fitting red cutaway frock coat, his long legs incased in red trousers so form-fitting, well, hmmm...I shall put such thoughts aside and continue my description...and tucked into tall leather riding boots. An elegant black silk cravat was arranged in an intricate formal knot at his neck. At his waist was buckled the sheath for his sword. I took my time giving him my opinion on his costume because I wanted to be able to ogle him for as long as reasonably possible under the circumstances. Do not say you would not have done the same if you were in my place, Reader, for I would not believe you.

The form-fitting ensemble and calf-hugging boots merited careful examination. I had never seen Erik in such revealing clothes before, and the effect on me was considerable. He looked like a dark angel – Lucifer himself perhaps, about to take up residence in Hell. I felt a flush of warmth overtake me and needed to clear my throat before hazarding to speak.

"Well, all I can say is, you certainly have a flair for the dramatic, Erik." I managed at last, while fanning my face surreptitiously with my hand.

"That goes *without* saying, actually." Erik replied tersely. He turned back to the mirror, studying the effect of the stark white mask and blackened eye sockets. He was clearly on edge, perhaps in anticipation of what was to come.

"I suppose the costume department is now missing a few articles of clothing," I said thoughtfully.

"You suppose correctly."

"What are you meant to be?" I asked curiously.

"The Red Death, of course."

"Oh, well, *naturellement*." I ought to have guessed any costume Erik might invent would have something to do with death. "So that mask..."

"Represents a skull. A clever touch I thought."

Now that I had torn my eyes from his physique to study the *papier-mâché* mask, I could see for myself that it was modeled to resemble a skull. I made a little noise of exasperation.

187

"I have been meaning to ask you about your morbid fascination with skulls. I cannot understand it."

"No one is asking you to," Erik replied shortly. It was the only answer I was going to get from him, so I resolved to try again some other time. He brushed past me toward the table, stopping to glance at his dinner tray. "I will not have time to eat before my dramatic appearance at the masquerade tonight, so this will have to wait until later." He picked up the leather bound opera score.

"Hand me that scarf hanging there, would you, Sylvie?"

"Good heavens," I murmured as I complied with his request. Gathering the red fabric in my hands, I realized it must be over fifteen feet in length. No wonder he didn't want to put it on yet.

He bared his large white teeth in a terrifying feral smile. "It has been several months since I have shown myself to my managers or...or anyone else for that matter. I want to ensure that my entrance will be, as you put it, *dramatic*."

"I am sure it will be," I murmured as I folded the long sheer scarf and handed it to him. "You look...quite frightening, actually." And there was no denying he did: unsmiling now, eyes dark behind the mask, the whites gleaming brightly against the black greasepaint background.

"I wish to frighten them", he replied, sounding incongruously cheerful. "I am going to present those two idiots with my new opera, and if they know what is good for them, they will produce it exactly as written. I do not intend to give them a choice." Picking up his sword, he slid it into the scabbard. I had never seen such a strange figure. I could only imagine the effect he would have on the revelers above. I longed to say out loud what was in my heart – that he was not only frightening – he was magnificent. But so unapproachable, so cold. So I pressed my fingers to my lips in an effort to seal them.

As I watched him prepare to depart, I could not help but wonder what had happened to the Erik that I used to know, the one who played pianoforte for me when I was recovering from my illness, or sat with me in his boat telling me stories. That man had vanished, and I missed him. I could not speak these thoughts out loud to this remote and distracted stranger, who always was on the verge of losing his temper, and who did not seem to care whether or not I was in the room. I could not repress a sigh of melancholy then, which he heard even as he walked to the boat to untie it from its mooring post. His eyes came to rest on my face, but he misinterpreted the reason for my sigh.

"Do not worry, Sylvie," he said. "I am not going to kill anyone tonight. I will not ruin their party, perhaps just disrupt it a little." I caught my breath – what did he mean by that enigmatic remark? Had he already...seeing that his little joke had failed to win a smile, he came back to stand before me. "Sylvie?"

I looked up into that weirdly distorted face that I'd come to love so much. "Erik..." I rested my hand on his arm even though I knew he would not like it. The worry I was feeling must have been easily read on my face. My breath caught again in my throat; I could not finish my sentence; what could I say?

Even behind the mask and black paint, I could see his expression soften. In a gentle yet slightly perplexed voice, he asked, "Are you really worried about me, Sylvie?" I nodded, and my fingers tightened on his arm. Erik shook his head.

"I don't know why you should be. You ought to know better. Nothing is going to happen to *me*. I am the one who usually makes things happen to others, you know that. I promise you, all I am going to do is present my opera to them along with some instructions for the performers. Now run along home, Sylvie. I will see you *demain soir.*" Although meant to reassure, his words, so filled with dangerous implications, had the opposite effect on me. Dressed as he was, how could he not be dangerous? Erik brushed my cheek with his gloved hand, then plucked my hand from his arm and turned away from my upturned face.

I stood at the water's edge as he stepped into the boat. He carefully placed the leather-bound music score and red scarf on the bottom of the boat and poled away toward the portcullis opening. He did not look back. I gazed at his upright, scarlet figure until it vanished far down the canal where the watercourse turned a corner into darkness. Not until the view became blurry did I notice tears were sliding down my cheeks.

I could not shake the feeling that I was having a premonition of imminent danger. Never before had I so wanted to reach out and bind him to me, keep him safe. Or keep others safe from him; perhaps it was the same thing.

Had I but known, this was to be the last amicable conversation I would have with Erik. Disaster was fast approaching, though I knew it not. Perhaps in some inexplicable way I sensed that something was about to happen, for there is no denying I was very uneasy that night.

At last I turned away from the pool and made my way back toward the secret entrance. Erik's surreal home, with its guttering candles that never seemed to be able to illuminate all the dark expanses of the cavern, felt empty and inhospitable now that I was alone there. And the idea of being alone with that very lifelike reproduction of Mlle. Daaé did nothing to put me at my ease; the thing was too much like something out of Edgar Allan Poe. I half expected it to push aside the concealing drapery and step into the room, staring at me with sightless glass eyes. A shiver ran through me, and I made haste to depart.

But as I passed across the raised dais near the organ, something caught my eye: the original hand-written pages of Erik's opera score lay scattered across the surface of the instrument. He had never deigned to share with me what it was about; he'd lost his temper when I tried to find out. I was able to catch only small snippets of the music during all the time he worked on it; he had been so absurdly secretive about it. He had not even told me what the title was.

I decided there was no harm in satisfying my curiosity about his opera at least. He would no doubt be gone for some time. I flung a quick, furtive glance back down the long watercourse to be sure he *was* actually gone (for with Erik one could never be sure). Unable to resist any longer, I sat down at the music bench and gathered up the pages. They contained, I could see, stage directions and song lyrics written in his elegant handwriting as well as his original score. I rearranged the pages to put them in their proper order and began with eager interest to study them.

Standing up abruptly a few minutes later, I dropped the sheets of music as if they had scorched my fingers. I watched numbly as the white pages drifted in disorder to the stone floor at my feet. I heartily regretted having given in to my curiosity on this occasion. My hands felt dirty and I wanted to wash them. I felt a lurch of nausea in my stomach. I had never read anything so debauched, so depraved in my life. It was a tale of the deliberate seduction of an innocent young girl, with malice aforethought. The title of the opera, which had confused me at first glance, suddenly made perfect, if perverted, sense. But what was really horrible, what really sickened me to my soul, as that the person destined to play the innocent girl really *was* one: Christine Daaé.

I was no longer jealous, I was outraged.

As I stood there by the bench, staring out unseeing over the water, in memory I was seeing a lovely young girl in virginal white standing on a stage, wearing a sweet, innocent smile on her face. How could he, how *dare* he expect such a girl to sing these lyrics, be addressed in such a lustful, wicked manner by an older man? I knew with perfect certainty that Erik saw himself as the evil seducer, Don Juan. He'd even written his own name in for those lyrics, confirming my fears. Erik's vile opera was an enactment of his own darkest desires.

Who *was* this man? One thing was an absolute: I did not know him as I thought I had. I hated to think that the Erik *I* knew could be capable of such wickedness. But something would have to be done. This could not be allowed. It was wrong. Feeling a sharp pain in my hands, I glanced down to see that my fingers were curled into such tight fists that my nails were digging into my palms. I forced my hands to open.

Everything was falling into place in my mind: the automaton lovingly garbed in a wedding ensemble, of which he was so proud, the drawings he had made of her face, even the singing lessons. Erik's misplaced love for this girl and his fierce jealousy of her handsome young suitor had veered into the realm of a dangerous obsession. My attempt to warn him of it had no effect. Some kind of madness had taken over the Erik I once knew, and it frightened me.

At least now I had an explanation for his gradual change for the worse, but I was not certain I could do anything to stop it. Nevertheless, I must and would try once more to make him see reason. I determined therefore to return on the morrow, confront Erik and convince him this must stop. He *must* be made to stop, and let some older, more experienced singer be cast in his opera. *Someone* must try and protect Mlle. Daaé, since Erik was unable to see clearly any longer. I knew nothing of her other suitor, the Vicomte, except that Erik was insanely jealous of him; it was difficult to say if he would be an adequate protector or not, but it was to be hoped that he would discourage her from performing this wretched part.

Having settled on a course of action, I took Erik's parting advice to me and went home. I would be back in the morning, however, and beard the lion in his den.

191

CHAPTER EIGHTEEN

'Hatred is blind; rage carries you away; and he who pours out vengeance runs the risk of tasting a bitter draught.'
A.D.

Needless to say, my sleep that night was restless; mental anguish does nothing for a good night's sleep. Finally I acknowledged defeat and rose with the dawn. After preparing my morning *café au lait*, I stood at the balcony doors looking out through the lace panels as the sky slowly lightened to a pearlescent grey. More snow had fallen during the night, leaving the Sunday-quiet street blanketed in white. Holding the cup of hot coffee in my hands was comforting, and I needed comfort that morning.

It was not so much that I did not know what I must do; it was just that I was afraid to do it. Yesterday I'd been full of wrath and righteous indignation, but a night's sleep (or lack of it) brought with it a belated sense of caution. I was not any less determined on my course of action, but I was now more alert to the consequences. The delicate subject of Erik's unhealthy obsession with Christine Daaé was certain to arouse his ire, and there was no way it could be approached subtly. I held very little hope that my pleas would meet with success, but my conscience would not allow me to remain quiet in spite of the potentially dire consequences.

I felt more alone than ever, bereft even, for I saw now that my tenuous friendship with Erik had existed only in my imagination. I could not even turn to Celestine: harboring such *tendresse* for him as she did, she would always faithfully take his part.

My cup drained at last, I returned to my bedchamber to prepare for the dreaded encounter to come. I dressed methodically, feeling a little like a warrior girding for battle as I put on my warmest wool gown, buttoned up my winter boots, braided my hair and coiled it atop my head with care. Ready at last, I plucked my dark blue woolen cloak from its peg by the door. As I went about these tasks, my thoughts were mostly of the negative sort; Erik's mercurial temperament meant he was quick to anger, but just as quick to feel sorry if he realized he had done something hurtful. I could not imagine how he would respond today, but it was sure to be bad. And so I went downstairs, through the kitchen, and out into the snowy street.

I briefly considered taking a hansom, but I felt a walk in the brisk winter air would clear my head and do me good. It also postponed the inevitable confrontation. The streets were quiet; not many people or carriages were out yet – it was too early for churchgoers, though the bells would begin ringing soon. I forged my solitary path through six inches of soft fresh snow until I reached the better-travelled Blvd. Haussmann. From there it was easy walking to the marble room. Once inside, I lit our oil lamp, picked it up and started down the stairs, holding my skirts carefully in my other hand. The hems were now heavy with damp from the snow.

As I proceeded cautiously down into those subterranean depths, I turned over various scenarios for voicing my concerns with Erik, finally settling on a direct approach. I am not an eloquent speaker, but I was going to have to try my best today. Mlle. Daaé's gentle and innocent nature depended on it. No one else seemed to notice how wrong this was, not even Celestine. Perhaps theatre people really *were* as jaded and debauched as one suspected them of being.

I marched across the stone causeway, opened the secret door, slid the mirror back and stepped inside. I did not even bother to announce my arrival. But I knew instantly that Erik's cavern was empty. Only a few candles guttered here and there. Bereft of the strong personality residing there, it *felt* empty and cold, as though its occupant had not been there for some time.

My eyes went at once to the pool of green water: the flat-bottomed boat was resting quietly at its mooring post, and the portcullis gate was closed, so he must have departed the same way I came. This was unusual, for he never went out that way. Some business must have called Erik out early apparently. I wondered what it could be. This was both unexpected and unfortunate. Some of the steam went out of me as I began to wonder how long I might have to wait until he returned.

While I was standing there indecisively a vivid splash of scarlet caught my eye. Draped over the back of a chair was the cutaway coat of the outrageous costume Erik wore to the *bal masqué* on the previous evening. Remembering how he had looked that night, I wondered how the other guests had reacted to his presence among them. It must have been rather like a panther prowling amidst a roomful of housecats.

Approaching the chair, I stopped next to it, lifted up the red coat and held it in my hands for a moment. Following some urge I cannot explain, I raised it to my face and took a long, deep inhalation, breathing in Erik's spicy, manly scent. It smelled wonderful, heartbreakingly wonderful; so delicious it made me want to weep over what had been denied me. After a moment I carefully draped the coat over the chair once more. Glancing around, I noticed there was no sign of sword or scabbard even though he'd worn them last night, but the incredible scarf lay in a loose heap of foamy scarlet on the floor next to the chair. There was a long rent in the delicate fabric.

I bent automatically to retrieve the scarf from the floor, but paused, hand outstretched, as an object on the writing table by the chair caught my eye. It was the exotic little mosaic box where Erik kept his pen nibs and other bits and pieces. It had always intrigued me, particularly the odd design on the lid. Abandoning the red scarf, I lifted up the box instead, and cradled it gently in my hands. The box was fairly heavy, being made of brass, and the interesting and well-executed tile mosaic pattern on it had caught my notice once before.

On one of the many evenings that Erik had been caught up in writing his vile opera, I was lingering after delivering his dinner as I often did, hoping for a scrap of attention from him. Thinking of it now, a flush of humiliation washed over me – what a fool I had been!

He had been writing furiously as usual, and the nib of his pen snapped under the force of his grip. Uttering a low curse in a language I did not understand (but it was clearly a curse), he muttered without looking up,

"Fetch me that brass box on my writing desk, would you, Sylvie?"

Disgustingly happy to be of service to him, I stepped promptly to the desk as Erik had asked. Glancing over the scattered items on its surface, I discovered the little inlaid box he had asked for. Lifting the lid, I saw that it contained pen nibs of various widths as well as bits of sealing wax and other small oddments that men accumulate because they never seem able to throw anything away. Carrying it back to Erik, I studied the unusual design on the lid. I had never seen anything like it before: a circle made of two swirls of black and white, equal in size. Within the black swirl was a small white dot, and within the white swirl was a corresponding black dot. I was certain this must be one of the few artifacts Erik had managed to carry with him when he fled Constantinople for France.

After handing him the box I had retained the lid, turning it toward the light of the candelabra so I could see the design better. "What is this strange symbol, Erik? I have never seen anything like it before." I asked.

Rifling through the contents of the box, Erik selected a nib and began fitting it to his pen. He grunted noncommittally. "It is hardly likely that you would have, Sylvie. It is an ancient Chinese symbol, or so I was told by the Sultan. He gave it to me as a gift – some trifle he had picked up in his travels." He glanced up at me sidelong, seeming amused by my curiosity. I remembered thinking wryly that it was a refreshing change from his usual bad humor.

"It is called the yin-yang symbol."

"What does it represent, do you know?" I asked, carefully placing the heavy little lid back on the box.

Erik had turned back to study the page of music he was working on. "Supposedly the balance of light and dark, or similar opposites," he said rather dismissively. It appeared that his good mood was evaporating.

"Like good and evil, you mean?" I looked at him thoughtfully, thinking to myself that the symbol was rather like his face.

As if he could read my mind, Erik gave his head a firm shake, sending a strand of his light brown hair over his forehead. "I know what you are thinking, Sylvie," he said, "but you are wrong." Before I could reply, he waved a hand dismissively in my direction, indicating it was time I took my leave.

"*Non*. If there were a symbol that represented me, it would surely be all black. Or perhaps red, the color of blood. Do not imagine otherwise."

At the time, I had protested his declaration, for I did not believe he was bad. I knew there were dark places within him, but I thought I comprehended their source. Now, *now*, I knew better. I had been wrong, and Erik right. Perhaps he was only being honest with me that night. Returning to the present, I shook my head regretfully and replaced the little box with its strange symbol back on his desk.

As I turned away, my eyes fell on the music sheets I'd dropped last night, still lying where they had fallen, reminding me of why I was here on this cold morning. My resolve strengthened; I walked down to the edge of the water and began to pace back and forth beside it, to keep warm. Erik could not stay away forever; I vowed I would not leave until I confronted him.

I paced for perhaps half an hour before I heard the sounds I was listening for and half-dreading: rapid footsteps and the sound of the mirror being vigorously shoved aside. Even as I whirled around to face the secret entrance, Erik emerged from it, pushing the heavy gold drapery aside brusquely. My breath caught at the sight of him.

Although he was elegantly attired as usual, in a black coat with a rich brown embroidered waistcoat beneath and his heavy winter cape, everything was in disarray. I saw at once that he was wearing his sword. His trousers were dark with damp; his cravat was in disarray, the back of his dark wig rumpled. His face was flushed and his breathing heavy. He looked as though he had been engaged in some strenuous exercise. But his eyes looked almost wild. One good look at him in this condition was all it took to temporarily banish all other thoughts from my head, to be instantly replaced by concern.

"Erik! What is it?" I asked anxiously. "Have you been hurt?" Without thinking what I did, I gathered my skirts and hurried up the raised area toward him, all the while looking him over closely for any signs of injury.

Not actually looking at me, Erik's face contorted into a harsh mask as some strong emotion swept over him, and his lips curled back in a snarl. I stopped in my tracks and drew back automatically. He was absolutely livid with rage. I did not think I had ever seen him this angry, and that was saying something. Wrenching off his heavy cape, he tossed it aside; the tailcoat followed it to the floor.

"Hurt?" He hissed. "No, I was not hurt. I drew first blood, but the Vicomte is a better swordsman than I. I underestimated him there; he is a trained swordsman and I am not." While he was speaking he paced rapidly back and forth, removing articles of attire as if they were choking him and hurling them to the floor, while I stared at him uncomprehendingly.

"I'm sure he looked quite a dashing *hero* rushing to her rescue. I wasn't expecting him to follow her or I would have been better prepared." His words came out full of sneering bitterness and wrath. He seemed not to be aware of me standing there with an undisguised expression of horrified understanding dawning on my face, as I realized Erik had been *fighting*.

"But what happened?" I managed to gasp.

His waistcoat followed the coat to the floor and he began yanking fiercely at the neck of his shirt, unwinding his damp, disarrayed cravat and sending it after the coat. At first I was afraid he had suffered an injury, but then realized he was simply desperate to rid himself of the stifling articles of clothing. I experienced a moment of concern that he was going to disrobe entirely right in front of me, but he stopped pacing abruptly and whirled to face me, as though finally really seeing me there for the first time. As he did so his hand went to his mask; he tore it off his face and threw it down on the table. He

196

was virtually shaking with fury. I had never seen him so angry, even when he first found me in his home. Perhaps I ought to be afraid of him now, but I was not…yet. I was still too worried about him to be afraid for myself.

Finally Erik answered me. "The Vicomte had me on the ground, without my sword, and would have run me through with pleasure if *Christine*…" he spat her name out like a curse…"if Christine had not intervened."

Suddenly boneless, I sank down on to the music bench, my eyes wide with horror. Even now he could be lying out in the cold, his blood staining the snow as red as that filmy scarf. Erik could have died somewhere out there and I would never have known. I shuddered at the mental picture that formed in my head and glancing down, found I was wringing my hands together like some silly helpless girl in a novel. I forced my hands to still. But Erik was not finished yet.

"Oh yes, Christine saved my life, it was very sweet of her – she *pities* me!" Anger and resentment tinged his voice with acid as he spoke. He turned away and continued as if speaking only to himself. "They would be better off had she let him kill me. I vow they will live to regret this morning, both of them." Staring at his back, a thrill of fear went through me.

"Erik, *what happened?*" I demanded for the third time, more urgently now, my eyes fixed on his rigid back.

He was staring down at the floor, wearing an intense expression. When he spoke, it was in a voice so low I had to strain to understand him.

"We were in the Cimetière du Père-Lachaise, but *he* wasn't supposed to be there! I attacked him – I wanted to kill him, Sylvie!" His voice grew louder as he spoke, until he was almost shouting. "I hate him, I hate him! How *perfect* he is! So young and handsome. *He* need never hide his face; he can go anywhere and always be admired! *Mon Dieu*, how I hate him!"

Never before had I felt the pure, ungoverned force of Erik's fiery emotions. I was utterly breathless as the force of his unfettered rage beat against me like a hot wind. Hatred radiated from him, from every fiber in his body. It poured off him in waves. I felt as if I were standing next to a sulphurous volcano.

"Erik," I asked desperately, "I don't understand. What were you doing there in the first place? Why were *you* at the cemetery?"

There was a very long pause, and an even longer sigh as Erik slowly let out his pent breath. He half-turned so that his eyes met mine.

"I followed Christine," he said slowly, sounding somewhat chagrinned at the admission. "She wanted to visit her father's tomb. I thought she might, she has done so in the past when she was in need of solace, so I was watching for her. But then *he* followed her, too."

Oh no. Not that. Wasn't it bad enough that he had written that depraved opera around her?

"And why were you following Mlle. Daaé?" I asked, a spike of anger sharpening my voice. "Can she not go where she pleases without your interference?"

"I have to take my opportunities where I find them," he replied enigmatically. He turned around to face me, still wearing his sword and with a murderous expression on his face.

"Last night at the ball I learned that they have been secretly engaged, Christine and that...that noble young *jackass*. I followed her this morning so I could get her alone. The cemetery was perfect. She knows I am not what she once believed me to be, but I thought, I hoped, she would still be susceptible to my persuasion." His face suddenly darkened. "I was waiting for her in her father's tomb, but before I had a chance to be very persuasive, *he* came riding to her rescue, on a white horse no less!"

I did not like the sound of this; Erik's idea of persuasiveness often involved some sort of violence. "What do you mean?" I asked him, frowning with consternation. "What do you mean about her being susceptible to your persuasion?"

He had the conscience to look ashamed. "I have always let her believe I was the Angel of Music her father had told her would come to her someday. She knows the truth now, *bien sûr*, but I was not above playing the Angel again if it would bring her to me...if I did not have to do this the hard way..." Suddenly Erik stopped mid-sentence and looked alertly at me.

"What are you doing here so early, Sylvie? Have you come to accuse me of another murder?"

I had been about to ask him what he meant by 'the hard way', and now I was abruptly called back to my original purpose in coming here. I drew myself up and took a deep breath.

Fueled by my indignation, I replied, "No Erik. But I *am* here to accuse you of wickedness. Last night, after you left for the masquerade ball, I...I read your opera." I was surprised at the steady calm of my own voice. It was only much later when I had time to think about it that I realized just how bravely, and how foolishly, I was behaving.

"*Et alors?*" He asked dismissively. I had expected he would be angry with me, but he sounded unconcerned.

I rose from my chair and faced him. "I do not know what you are planning to do, but I know you are planning something *très mauvais* – very wicked. Mlle. Daaé is involved somehow, I know. I came here this morning to ask you, to beg you, to stop this madness, Erik." As I spoke, I extended my hands toward him, beseechingly.

"Please, Erik, please. You must abandon your plans, for I am certain no good can come of this opera performance. Surely it is not too late to stop."

"Stop?" He almost smiled; at least, he showed his teeth in a grimace of a smile. "Oh no, I am afraid it *is* too late. I am about to execute my *coup de maître*, and nothing, no one, is going to stop me. If you think *you* are going to interfere with my plans, you are sadly mistaken, Sylvie."

"What is this about, Erik?" I whispered fearfully. "Why are you doing this?"

A terrifying change came over him then. His eyes narrowed, his lips pulled back in a snarl. "It is about me, getting what I want. It is about me, taking my revenge on all those who have denied me, wronged me!" He took a threatening step toward me as he spat out the angry words. "They have pushed me too far now! Christine *will* be mine, one way or the other. She has no choice."

I felt answering anger boil up in me at his words.

"No *choice*! *Mon Dieu*, Erik!" I cried furiously, "For a man of your intellect, how can you be so *stupid*? The way you have been behaving – tricks, lies, even violence – that is no way to make a sweet, good girl like Mlle. Daaé fall in love with you! You have taken advantage of her innocence, her *naïveté* and her trust in you at every turn! It's despicable! And now this…this opera of yours…"

"I don't *know* how to make a girl fall in love with me!" Erik shouted furiously, interrupting my tirade.

I was brought up short. Beneath the fury his pain was raw. How I wanted to take him by the arms and shake him till his teeth rattled! Did he really believe he could *make* someone love him? Idiot! Blind stupid man!

"Love cannot be forced, Erik," I said angrily. "And trying to kill the man she *does* love, the Vicomte, how can you think that would have any other effect than to make her hate you forever? You are revealing yourself to her as a monster, not a lover! Let me ask you this, Erik, and tell me the truth: if the fight in the cemetery this morning had a different outcome – if it was the Vicomte on the ground and you with the point of your sword at his chest..." I paused, drew a gasping breath and went on, "If she had begged you not to kill him, what would *you* have done?" Was he capable of doing the right thing for love? I soon had my answer.

Erik's face was suddenly and unexpectedly mere inches from mine, his eyes blazing with hatred, a ferocious, terrifying scowl on his face. I flinched away from his wrath, but fear froze my feet to the floor.

"What do *you* think?" He demanded ferociously. With a flash and a ring of steel he drew his sword from its scabbard, and pulling back from me, pointed it directly at me, the point only inches from my chest. Some part of my brain registered that the foil was, inevitably, a silver skull.

"I would have killed him before he could draw another breath. Nothing and no one would stop me. If he were here I would do it now, before your very eyes, being the monster you seem to think that I am!"

Brave fool that *I* was, I carried on despite the fact that he was threatening me with death and was almost at the end of his rope.

"Oh, Erik! Everything bad that has happened to you, all the things you continually blame others for, you have brought on yourself, cannot you see that? You yourself are to blame, and only you! You told me once that you were selfish; I did not believe you then, but I do now." I took a slow, deliberate step toward him, bringing the tip of his sword in contact with my heaving breast. My blood was up, my chin lifted and I glared at him unblinking, even though I knew this could be my last moment on earth.

"If you intend to kill me, Erik, why not get on with it!" I spat it at him like a challenge, recklessly. "You told me once, if you were ever to kill me, it would be in hot blood, remember?"

In an instant the mad fire faded from his eyes, and his expression changed from that of a snarling beast to one of blank horror. His mouth fell open. Without taking his eyes from mine, he lowered the sword and let his arm swing out to his right, away from his body. His fingers released their grip and the sword clattered to the floor with a metallic ringing that echoed through the cavernous room. Still we stared at each other, our faces matching masks of horror. His chest heaved with every heavily drawn breath and I realized I was holding mine, expecting death at any second. I drew air into my lungs in a loud, ragged gasp and placed a hand over my pounding heart.

While I watched, the horror over what he had almost done faded, to be replaced with coldness like arctic ice. He spoke at last in a rough voice, hot with fury.

"Everything bad that has ever happened to me is *my* fault, you say?" He came to stand right in front of me again, his face glaring down into mine. "Was this my fault, Sylvie? Did I bring *this* on myself?" With his right hand he made a harsh gesture toward the disfigured side of his face.

I went toe-to-toe with him, lifting my chin and staring back at him steadily. "Certainly not, Erik. You know I did not mean to imply any such thing. Your disfigurement was and is a terrible tragedy, no one could deny that. But it does not give you the right to abuse your power, to control and manipulate others at will in order to get your way. That is wrong no matter what the cause."

"A tragedy. That is what you call it? My life has been a living hell and you call it a tragedy." Erik stepped back, away from me, putting distance between us. "You have no idea what I've been through, and no right to judge me. We are *finis*, Sylvie. This time you have pushed me too far. Our...association...has come to an end. I do not need you any longer, and I do not want you. Go now, and don't ever come back." A stranger's eyes were looking at me now, completely detached, thoroughly indifferent.

"You...you are sending me away?" I could barely recognize my own voice, suddenly choked with unshed tears.

Erik nodded once, his face stern and forbidding, as it had been when first I met him.

"*Oui*. The only sustenance I crave is blood and revenge; that is the only food I care about now. You..." he gestured toward me roughly, "you do not understand anything about me – you never have. We have come to a parting of ways, Sylvie. Forget about me, and stay out of my life. I never want to set eyes on you again, do you understand?" And with these words he wheeled away, turning his back on me.

I opened my mouth but no words came out. There was nothing more to say. I understood; I understood that I had failed spectacularly in my attempt to break the spell of Erik's incipient madness. I turned blindly and ran away from him and through the curtain into the secret entry without another word or glance backward.

When the sliding panel closed behind me I realized I had no light; I remembered setting my lamp on the table while I paced, waiting for his return. Well, there it would remain, for I was certainly not going back for it. I stumbled several times trying to get up the stone staircase, crawled on my hands and knees once or twice, but finally reached the top and found myself back in that dusty room where I had first laid eyes on the Opera Ghost. *Sans doute*, this was the last time I would ever see him.

I arrived back at my apartment in such a state of despair the journey was a mere blur of motion. My cloak dropped to the floor behind me; I threw myself on my *divan* and gave myself over to a flood of tears. My pathetic part in this sad triangle was over, well and truly over. I had been rendered *hors concours* by events which were already in motion, and no matter the outcome, my role in the story was over. My feelings were in confused turmoil; I was furious with Erik, I was hurt by his rejection, I loved him so much I could scarcely breathe, and yet he terrified me.

And how stupid I felt! How absurdly I had deluded myself! Worst of all, I had failed Mlle. Daaé. There was no one to protect her now. It was too much to bear; I wept myself to sleep right there where I sat, my face resting against the tear-dampened fabric. I believe I spent most of that dreadful day reclining on the *divan*, too dazed and uncaring to rise and go about my business or even to make a cup of tea.

I was visited by the first of many nightmares that night. In the dream I wandered through familiar passageways: the secret way to Erik's underground home. But there was no light, only darkness, and I felt my way through endless night. I was filled with an overpowering sense of dread, the feeling something truly horrible was about to happen and it was up to me to stop it somehow. A desperate sense of urgency pushed me on – I needed to get to Erik, I *had* to find him – something terrible would happen if I did not. The stony corridors and stairs and corners went on and on endlessly as they do in nightmares, and the oppressing darkness weighed on me until I could not breathe. I was going to fail, and Erik would die because of me. I sank, weeping in despair, to the cold stone, trying to crawl when I could no longer walk. Suddenly a circle of light appeared on the stone floor before me, and I beheld a pair of booted feet in its dim glow. Raising my head, I saw black-trousered legs and the swirling hem of a long cape.

"Erik, help me," I whispered, fear and hope warring within me. I reached my hand up, but no helping hand reached down to grasp

202

mine. The cape was flung back over one shoulder and with a swift gesture the dark figure drew his sword against me. I gasped and stared up into his face but it was still in shadow and I could not see it.

"Erik, is it you?" I asked urgently. There was a harsh laugh in answer to my question. The dark figure stepped forward into the light and I saw his face. It was a death's head: a full mask of a grinning, gaping skull.

I woke to the sound of my own full-throated scream ringing in my ears.

The days following that last terrible encounter with Erik in the cavern were dark ones for me. The only thing that kept me from going mad was the hospital, and knowing I was needed there. I could not let them down, so I carried on. But Paris was still held in the iron grip of a very hard, cold winter, making it challenging to get to and from St. Giles or even to do the necessary shopping. I managed somehow, thanks to Robert, who cleverly fitted the wheels of his wagon with metal chains that bit into the ice and snow. Even so, the daily bridge crossing was a nerve-wracking experience. The wagon managed not to slide off the edge into the icy Seine, taking the horse with it. I would have got out and walked across the bridge, but I did not want Robert to think I doubted his ability to manage the crossing.

Evenings, alone in my apartment, were the worst times. I was disappointed in myself, for I did not seem able to stop myself from wallowing in wretchedness. But all my strength of character had somehow abandoned me. Over and over again I replayed the events of our last encounter until my head was spinning. What should I have done differently? What did I leave unsaid, that ought to have been said? I tormented myself with these useless thoughts by the hour. The weather and the ongoing war were perfect counterpoints to my tragic frame of mind: snow and sleet falling in the day and freezing in the night, and all the while the cruel Prussians were tightening their grip on the city.

Because it was both a hospital and under the wing of the Church, St. Giles was not denied food for the patients in spite of the blockade, but I was not given a lot to work with. That dilemma, coupled with my own personal misery, made the burden almost too much to bear at times. Several people at the Hospital, including, *bien sûr*, my dear friends Dr. Gaudet and Father Barbier, commented with concern on the state of my health. My appearance was remarked upon; I was looking haggard and tired – was I well?

Dr. Gaudet suggested a liver tonic, while Father Barbier thought that I was not eating enough. I often found myself making excuses to leave the hospital early to escape their kindly scrutiny. Father Barbier's bright black eyes followed me closely all the while I was there, a little crease of worry between his eyes. Only *I* knew that the dark circles under my eyes were caused by lack of sleep. It was difficult to sleep when each night brought some version of the same ghastly nightmare back to torment me.

Sometimes I fought sleep; sometimes I would have a hot drink before bed, fall asleep, but then lie awake for hours after the nightmare woke me. It wasn't exactly the same dream each time, although I was always on the dark stairs or wandering through endless passageways, sometimes even penetrating as far as the causeway. But I was always driven by a sense of terrible urgency and nameless dread: I had to find Erik, everything depended on that. I would grow more frantic by the minute. Sometimes I would see something glowing white on the steps or on the floor, and when I approached to see what it was, I would see his mask lying there. I would reach out to pick it up, only to see cold, pale, angry eyes staring back at me. I would be propelled into instant wakefulness by my own screams.

I felt like a spectator who had unwittingly walked onto the stage in the middle of a performance. After some confusion, I had been ushered off the stage and the actors continued the play that had begun before my clumsy entrance. The only news of Erik came from Celestine. It was she who kept me informed on the progress of this particular performance.

She came to see me one evening a week after my banishment from the cavern. I was delighted to see her and pathetically eager to learn what I could of what was happening at the Opéra Populaire. She knew I was no longer preparing Erik's meals, for soon after that terrible morning I wrote a note to Celestine telling her I had been relieved of my duties, but sparing her the ugly details.

We sat close to the fire, and I served her a glass of sherry, for she was chilled through, having made the trip to my apartment on foot. Neither of us was looking our best, and we regarded each other with rather grim expressions. Celestine appeared tired, with a haunted look in her eyes. She wore lines on her alabaster forehead that had not been there before. I am certain she was also making note of similar changes in my own haggard appearance. She shook her head sadly as she stared into the fire.

"I am very worried about all this, Sylvie," she said softly. "The owners have agreed to present the Ghost's opera and they are already in rehearsal. Every day brings more instructions and suggestions from him, and I know he is doing something above or below the stage almost every night." She paused to sip from her glass. "I have caught glimpses of him several times, but I cannot tell what he is doing. He will not talk to me."

"*Comprenez-vouz*," she continued, turning her head to look at me, her expression troubled, "the owners are going to have the police at the performance *en masse*. They expect the Ghost to be there since it is his opera being performed, and Christine is to be the star performer. He will not be able to resist watching her, they believe, so they have convinced her she must do it, but I know in her heart she does not want to. That is why they agreed so promptly to present his opera; they want to rid themselves of him once and for all."

I stared at her, wide-eyed. "They intend to try and capture him?" I breathed. Somehow I could not imagine Erik falling into such a trap. He would expect it and take his own precautions.

Celestine frowned, her hand moving over her heart in an unconscious gesture of worry. "Capture him…or kill him. They will be well-armed." A chill swept through me in spite of the warmth from the fire. She was watching me intently.

"What happened between you, Sylvie, if you can tell me?" She asked after a moment. "I do not understand why he ended your agreement with him so abruptly."

It was my turn to gaze into the fire, not seeing the dancing flames but rather, Erik's madly furious face the last time I saw him. Toying with my glass, I spoke slowly, finding I was reluctant to tell her everything that had transpired.

"We argued. I'd already confronted him about his unhealthy obsession with Mlle. Daaé. This time it was much worse; I was angry with him, Celestine. And worried. It was the opera he wrote, that diabolical opera. I read the lyrics; I knew what it was about. I was…I was disgusted and I told him so. We both became very heated, very angry, and it ended with him…ordering me to…to leave and never come back. I have not seen him since." As I spoke I felt a tear slide down my cheek; I turned my face away so she would not see and discreetly wiped it away.

Celestine was silent. When I turned back to her, she was regarding me with a tender expression, her eyes sad and filled with pity. Celestine knew me even better than Erik did. At last she spoke, her voice soft and sad.

"I am so sorry, Sylvie. I never intended, when I first suggested…" Her voice trailed away, for she had seen how my expression hardened at her words.

I stood abruptly, turning away toward the *garde-manger*. "Let me get you another sherry, Celestine." I really did not want to talk about this, nor did I want to be an object of her pity – to be the poor, lovelorn girl, just like Kitty. Celestine understood, and said no more about it, turning the conversation to idle chat about her work, but when she took her leave a little while later, she rested her hand gently on my cheek for a moment and could not repress a sigh.

"I do not know how this will end," she said, "but my heart tells me it cannot end well. I will send you word if…well, if he is caught or…" she could not finish her sentence. I shuddered.

"Send me word no matter what happens." I said firmly. "And Celestine, there is one more thing." I caught her arm and held her back as she started to descend the stairs. "Watch over Mlle. Daaé, watch over her as though she were your own daughter. She is at the center of this storm. If the owners think they will catch Erik somehow, they are underestimating him. *No one* can stand against him, Celestine, and that girl is not safe."

"You don't mean that he would harm her, surely?" She asked, eyes widening in alarm.

"*Je ne sais pas.* I cannot guess what Erik will do any longer, or what he is capable of, if I ever did know. But I *do* know that he is in a very dangerous frame of mind. I am afraid for her, and so should you be." I said, releasing her arm. I prayed Celestine would listen to me. *Someone* needed to take precautions to protect that girl. Erik had set his sights on possessing her, and I suspected that he would stop at nothing to get her. *She has no choice,* he had said.

Looking disturbed and anxious, Celestine took her leave. I watched her hasten away down the snowy street, bundled in a warm coat, her back bent against the cold. Returning to my *salon*, I had an additional *soupçon* of sherry strictly for medicinal purposes and pondered the news she had brought me.

Thanks to Celestine's information I knew the date set for the performance of Erik's wicked travesty of an opera; it would take place a week hence, on a Saturday evening. Everyone looked forward eagerly to a full house, the owners included, because word had spread of its being created by the Phantom himself. The Opéra Populaire now enjoyed the reputation of being haunted thanks to all the mishaps, up to and including the death of the lead stagehand. Now all the elite of Paris society wished to see firsthand if the mysterious Opera Ghost would make another sensational appearance. Perhaps they considered him part of the performance.

The music for Erik's opera was very strange, Celestine had told me, very *avant-garde*, for she was forced to listen while the orchestra practiced it daily. She did not think the audience would care for it. She herself did not care for the dances to be performed on the stage either, but everyone was under orders to do their best and to take the performance seriously.

I tried not to dwell on any of this as the date drew nearer; instead I threw myself into my cooking with a mad intensity, cleaned my larder, polished my copper pans until they gleamed, and went to bed each night exhausted. There I would lie and wait for sleep and the inevitable nightmare. But it was difficult not to picture the theatre swarming with uniformed policemen carrying rifles, so my waking thoughts were not much better than the sleeping ones. In my imagination I kept picturing Erik sprawled face down somewhere in a spreading pool of blood.

CHAPTER NINETEEN

'The tempest was let loose'

A.D.

Far too soon, the week slipped by and it was Saturday. And what a long, restless day! Although it was my day off, I spent it in the kitchen, making a large batch of *boeuf bourguignon* I neither wanted nor ate. It was the ideal way for me to keep my hands and mind busy while the time slowly passed, being an involved and time-consuming dish to prepare. When it was finally finished I gave most of it away to my grateful neighboring shopkeepers as they went home for the night. After nightfall I wandered aimlessly from room to room, turning up the lights, banking the fire against the nighttime chill.

I found myself unable to settle to anything. I was aware of a growing sense of unease as night closed in. Even my usual glass of sherry could not calm the butterflies in my midsection. My thoughts strayed again and again to the Opéra Populaire in spite of all my efforts to think of something else. Frowning as I recalled his distasteful lyrics, I could not help but wonder how Erik's opera was being received, for a glance at my little chiming clock on the mantel showed that the performance would have started by now.

The building must be swarming with armed policemen on the watch for him, but I did not doubt that Erik would easily elude them and carry his point, whatever it may be. There was something wicked behind all this, to be sure, but I could not imagine what terrible things Erik might have planned. He had said he was out for revenge – but what form would it take? And revenge against whom? He was more than capable of outwitting anyone who tried to capture him, I knew. I had done my best to stop this travesty, and failed resoundingly in the attempt. I tried to convince myself that it was no longer my concern. I refused to think about Erik himself: I could not open that door, I would not.

While doing my best not to think about...well...I found I was standing at my tall balcony doors, restlessly pushing the lace curtain aside and gazing out across the intervening rooftops toward the Opera House. It was too dark for me to actually see the building, but I knew it was there, looming large in my imagination. The owners hoped to catch Erik during the performance tonight; they were no doubt correct in their assumption that he would not be able to stay away if Christine was singing. In fact, I was sure of it. Remembering the pages of music I'd seen, I suspected he intended to *be* part of the performance.

According to Celestine, the owners planned to sit in Box Five themselves, eagerly looking forward to putting an end to the troublesome O.G. at long last. They were tired of all his interference and I certainly could not blame them for that, but I doubted they would be successful in capturing him. The rifles, however, were another story. What had Erik done that warranted being shot in cold blood? I knew I should not care what happened to him. He did not care what happened to *me*. I wrapped my arms around myself, feeling suddenly cold, and turned away from the window.

I wished I did not miss him so much, wished I could stop thinking of him, dreaming of him - those tormenting nightmares were added proof of what I longed to forget. After what occurred between us that last dreadful day, I could never go back to the cavern, and it was clear Erik would never come to me. And I was no longer certain I wanted him to. There was nothing left of the man I knew, or thought I knew. I needed to let all this go, let *Erik* go, but it was an uphill battle. Why could I not have fallen in love with someone safe and ordinary?

Tearing myself from the window with a groan of frustration, I went to the bookshelf and tried to interest myself in a novel, but I selected the wrong one. I always thought The Man in the Iron Mask was so sad, and when I found I had turned to the death of Athos, I gave up the attempt and threw the book across the room. Athos was my favorite Musketeer. I would have walked across hot coals for the noble, handsome Athos. Why couldn't I find a man like that?

At that exact moment the smell of smoke drifted to my nose. I glanced automatically at my fireplace, but the fire was crackling gently and no smoke was issuing from it. Looking around alertly, I saw that I had accidentally left my balcony door slightly ajar. There must be a fire somewhere nearby…now I realized I could hear the clang and rattle of horse-drawn fire trucks in the distance. *Alors*, it was a big fire, then. Could it be another attack by those wicked Prussians? The war was not going well for us. Frowning, I rose and went to see where the smoke was coming from, and to make sure it was not anywhere near our street. Fire is a very real and prevalent danger in areas of the city where the buildings are as closely crowded together as ours were.

Looking out, I gasped aloud. The skies were vividly, luridly lit by many flames shooting high into the night sky. I could see at a glance that it was the Opera House; flames and thick smoke were

209

pouring from the upper windows. In the few minutes I had sat reading, the Opéra Populaire had been engulfed in fire!

My mouth fell open in a silent scream of horror as all thoughts of invading Prussians vanished from my mind. My fingers gripped the door frame until pain shot through my hand. Erik, Erik, where was he? Had he escaped the fire, or was he in there? Since it was his opera being performed tonight, it was quite likely he had been watching. He might even have been on the stage. *Mon Dieu*, what if…?

The building was an inferno and Erik was *there*. With no other coherent thought in my mind, I turned and ran to the door, pausing only to snatch my cloak from its peg. I did not even stop to change into my winter boots.

I flew down the stairs, dashed across the darkened kitchen, fumbled with the latch on the door to the street, and at last I was out. The Rue de la Marché was empty – the shops were closed and no one wanted to be out on such a cold night. I flew down the end of the street and turned left, toward Blvd. Haussmann.

When I reached it, the wide boulevard was a madhouse filled with people shouting and running, some toward the fire, some away. Horses pulling water wagons made their clattering way, bells clanging. It was Dante's Inferno come to life, and through it I ran, ducking and dodging all obstacles in my way, the smell of smoke increasing as I progressed. Someone snatched at my arm, trying to stop me, but I shook them off and ran on heedlessly. My chest was tight from fear and distress, my breath coming in little sobs, but I did not stop.

By the time I reached the window of the secret entrance, I was gasping for breath and had a bad stitch in my side. Here the smoke was thick and acrid, billowing like fog between the buildings. I was half-blind and coughing, but the only conscious thought in my mind was that I must find Erik. He was the only thing in the world that mattered to me at that moment.

Driven by that single-minded desperate desire, I flung open the window and slid inside, my feet landing surely on the dusty marble floor. I had not been here in weeks; I never expected to be here again, but here I was. I gave it no thought. Flying across the room, I brushed aside the threadbare tapestry.

The long stone staircase receded into blackness, forcing my headlong rush to come to a sudden halt. No candle – I neglected to bring a candle. Quickly I turned aside to reach for the little pottery lamp that always rested on the ledge, only to discover that it was gone. I stared bemusedly at the stone shelf where the lamp used to sit. The recollection of where I had last seen it pierced my heart like a sword. And now I must make the descent in utter darkness. My head swiveled back toward the gaping opening in the wall. Oh God, it was just like my dream.

I cursed the haste that drove me to come away unprepared, but I was on fire to find Erik, to make sure he was safe underground, where no flame or smoke could reach him. Did I spare any concern for the audience, the performers, the musicians or even my own dear friend who had been inside the building when it caught fire? No, I am ashamed to admit, I did not. Nor did I think of myself, or my own safety.

After a moment's hesitation at the top of the stairs, I started down. Within a few steps, the light from the window behind me faded away. I was alone in blackness, feeling my way down, one hand on the cold wall to my left, the other on the right. One misstep would be the end of me; I would never catch myself if I stumbled. It was fortunate that I had been up and down those stairs so many times; familiarity saved me from what would most certainly have been a deadly plunge.

One stair at a time, feeling my way cautiously, I made my way down. I found myself growing accustomed to not seeing, and my feet found their way. I knew from experience the stones of the stairs were in good repair, Erik had seen to that. And, thank God, I had never observed rats. Perhaps they too were afraid of Erik.

Finally the walls opened out and I could feel the soft brush of cooler air on my face. I had safely arrived at the bottom of the stairs. Sighing in relief, I began to negotiate the intricate but familiar maze of rooms and walls leading to the stone causeway over the black water, homing toward my final destination quickly now, drawn like metal to a magnet. As I stepped out of the last room and looked across the causeway, I became aware of a yellow glow in the dark ahead. My heart leapt hopefully; surely that meant Erik was there, and safe.

I spared no thought for what I would say when I saw him again; all that mattered was to see him, to know he was alive. He could be as angry with me as he liked for disobeying his last command, I did not care. In fact, here in these subterranean depths, he might not even be aware of the raging fire above. He would think me quite mad for rushing here like this.

All at once I became aware that I could hear noise ahead, from the other side of the causeway. I paused, still within the shelter of the passageway, to listen. Straining my ears, I realized I could hear shouting, and male voices raised in anger. Orders were being called.

211

The dancing light I saw must be from torches moving along the walls. There were men in Erik's home!

Mindless, irrational fear gripped me – he had been found, captured. The mob might even now be killing him in anger over his various misdeeds. I expected to hear a rifle report at any second.

"Oh no, no…" A little sob of anguish broke from me as I gathered my skirts for one last plunge across the causeway, utterly heedless of the danger that was lurking in the dark, right behind me.

I had no warning, heard no sound, but I was abruptly seized from behind. An arm clamped around my body at the same time a large, cold hand closed over my mouth. My arms, in the act of catching up my skirts, were pinned firmly to my sides. Complete, paralyzing terror engulfed me, but I could neither move nor call out. Rendered helpless, I could offer no resistance as I felt myself being pulled, not ungently, back against a damp, cold male body. I heard myself make a little moan of fear, a muffled whimper against the pressure of the hand over my mouth. I felt warm breath against the side of my face and then a voice, a familiar, welcome voice, whispered in my ear.

"Shhh…don't make a sound, Sylvie. They must not find me here."

At the sound of Erik's soft whisper a wash of intense relief swept over me. If he were not holding me so tightly against him, I would have fallen to the floor. His hand left my mouth and went under my arm, lifting me and holding me steady.

"I didn't mean to frighten you, Sylvie," he murmured quietly into my ear. "But one cry from you is all it would take…." His voice trailed off, and I realized something was wrong with it; he sounded hoarse and thick. But he was alive!

"I am…I am not frightened, Erik," I whispered raspily, forcing my legs to hold me. I took a long, deep breath and my pounding heart began to slow. *Sans doute* he assumed fear had caused me to give way, rather than utter thankfulness that I had found him alive and presumably unharmed. I turned eagerly to look at him, and his supporting arms dropped away from me. His back against a smooth brick wall, and he placed his hands against the wall as though in need of support. I could see him reasonably well by the distant glow of light.

As my eyes roved over him searching for any wounds or burns, it was immediately apparent that something was wrong, terribly wrong. Erik was wearing only a ruffled white dress shirt of a rather old-fashioned *mode*, gaping open almost to the waist, and dark trousers. No waistcoat, no cravat. For some reason, his clothes, especially his trousers, were soaked through with water. I wondered if he'd fallen into the lake. God forgive me, even at that moment I had to fight to drag my eyes away from the sight of his exposed chest. It was the most beautiful thing I'd seen in a lifetime.

Ashamed of myself for ogling him at a time like this, I tore my eyes away from that splendid expanse of muscle and forced myself to look up into his face instead.

Erik's usual disguises were nowhere to be seen. His hair was disheveled and falling over his forehead, and he appeared exhausted and drained. His face was wet, and I realized with shock, it was wet with tears. Erik had been crying. And his eyes! Even in that dim light I could see something in his eyes I had never seen there before: defeat. Defeat and heartbreaking sadness.

It was only a matter of a few seconds that I stood looking at him, and then I could not help but turn and glance back toward the cavern. The fire, the searching men, his wild disarray: a dark thought began to shape itself in my mind, even as I looked quickly back at him. I went cold with dread. By accident or design, in my heart I knew Erik was responsible for the catastrophic fire above. Was this what he had been planning to do – destroy the Opera House?

Unaware of the change in my demeanor, Erik dragged a sleeve across his wet face and gave a shuddering sigh. He seemed so *vulnerable*, so lost.

I had never seen him like this; it was as if I were regarding a pathetic stranger. I reached up and pushed back the damp hair that fell in straggling strands over his forehead. I laid my palm against his cheek, and then touched his hand. Both were ice cold. He was in shock, I realized suddenly. His innate sense of self-preservation had got him this far, but shock was immobilizing him now. It would be up to me to get us away from here, or he would be captured, and I with him. Any moment now the secret entrance would be discovered, sending searchers pouring over the causeway with their torches and rifles. They would not stop there.

A sense of calm purpose came over me, and I took Erik's cold hand firmly in mine. "We have to get away from here at once. Come, Erik, you must come with me." I tugged at him encouragingly, pulling him away from the wall. He nodded mutely at me and followed without resistance, his sad eyes like those of a lost child. He did not look back.

Still grasping his hand, I took the lead as we started back, but it soon became prudent for Erik to forge ahead and pull me along in his wake. It was fortunate that he could see so well in the dark – it enabled us to proceed fairly rapidly. Only once did Erik break his silence with a question.

"Why did you come here tonight, Sylvie?" He asked, catching me off guard. Was he remembering, as I was, the last thing he had said to me? I wished he would not ask me that particular question; I wasn't sure of the answer myself. Out of breath from hurrying up the stairs, I kept my response brief.

"I saw the fire from my window." I replied breathlessly. *And I was so afraid for you, I could not stay away.*

He said no more the rest of the way. I was thankful, for I had much to think about, and I was listening for the dreaded signs of pursuit behind us. *En plus*, I needed to save my breath for the breakneck climb.

As quietly as possible, we retraced my steps until at last we arrived at the open window. The thick smoke was almost overpowering and I stifled a cough. Releasing his fierce grip on my now somewhat numb hand, Erik moved past me and slipped through the casement window, then reached back to assist me out. As soon as I was standing safely on the pavement beside him, he pulled the window closed. His eyes rested for a brief moment on the painted skull on the glass and his lips quirked as though with amusement, but there was no humor in his bleak expression. He must have known it was the last time he would ever see it.

Impatient to make our escape before we were followed, I took his hand again and hastened down the alleyway, tugging him along behind me. We made our cautious way to the corner and, huddled close together, peered into the boulevard.

Utter chaos awaited us there. The broad street was filled with people, horses and fire wagons. There was still a great deal of shouting and running going on. A large crowd of people in evening dress stood across the street on the next block, obviously audience members watching the fire. The orange glow played across their rapt faces – they looked exactly as if they were engrossed in watching a performance. Fortunately they were so fascinated by the sight of the magnificent building being destroyed so dramatically that they spared no glance for us. I was relieved, for there was now no way to hide Erik's face and one look would seal his fate and mine. Here was the man responsible for this disaster, and I was helping him to escape

214

justice. Drawing back into the relative safety of the dark alleyway, I turned to him and put my hands on his shoulders. Through the thin fabric of his shirt his skin was icy, and I felt a stab of anxious worry. He needed to be somewhere warm and safe.

Looking up into his sad eyes, I asked, "Are you ready, Erik?"

Instead of answering my question he shook his head grimly. "Sylvie, you should not have come here tonight. You ought to go home and leave me to make my own way. It would be safer for you, believe me."

"No. I am not going without you." I was not about to abandon him after getting him this far. Erik glowered down at me, almost looking like his old imperious self for a brief moment.

"I am dangerous, Sylvie, do not you understand?"

Frustrated, I gave his shoulders a shake. "I am going home, and you are coming with me. This instant. There is no point in arguing."

Erik closed his eyes briefly, and then he whispered, "Shrew."

That single word brought an absurd bubble of laughter to my lips. It felt somehow like the old Erik, *my* Erik, was back with me at last.

"*Allons.*" Taking his arm in a tight grip, I led him around the corner and down the boulevard, keeping to the shadows. He followed unresisting, making no further protest; though he had said we ought to part, I did not think he really meant it.

We encountered less smoke in the air as we progressed and I was able to breathe without coughing. Nevertheless, that return trip to the sanctuary of my apartment was a much slower, more cautious affair. Reader, I cannot tell you all my feelings then, but inside me was a peculiar mixture of numbness, determination and absolute terror. At last we made the final turn on to Rue de la Marché. Thankfully it was still empty and quiet, and I was so relieved I could have fallen to the pavement and kissed it, had it not been covered in a thin layer of dirty snow.

Erik was on the verge of collapse. He was moving like a sleepwalker now, only continuing to stumble on behind me because I held his arm and pulled him like a mother towing an exhausted child. After reassuring myself the street was empty, I turned back just in time to see him bend over and rest his hands on his legs like a runner who has reached his limit and can go no farther. My relief turned to panic in an instant – we were so close to safety!

"Erik, *allons*, we are almost there." His only reply was a slight shake of his head; he did not even look up. Gently I placed one arm around his bowed shoulders, wondering again what on earth had brought him down to such a dreadful state. It must be regret, I thought. Perhaps the fire was an accident after all. I could not imagine Erik deliberately destroying the place that he loved, or putting so many innocent lives in danger. With my free hand, I stroked his hair back off his face tenderly and leaned close to his ear.

"Erik," I whispered, "please...*please*, dearest. It's only a little farther. You have to do this. *Pour moi*. Oh please come." Desperation made my voice unsteady, and a little sob rose in my throat.

He raised his head, slowly turning that beautiful, ravaged face toward mine. We stared intently at one another while I kept on stroking his hair soothingly. Finally he gave me a nod, drew a deep breath and with an effort, straightened. I can only imagine what it cost him to summon the strength to go on. Sighing in relief, I took his hand once more and we hurried down the block to my door. It was slightly ajar; in my haste to get to him I had not even stopped to close it.

Drawing Erik inside, I quickly closed and locked the door behind us. I pulled him across the room and up the stairs to my apartment. I did not feel we were truly safe until that moment.

How extraordinary to step across the threshold of my *salon* after such a harrowing night! I gazed around me in some confusion. Everything was exactly as I had left it, contributing to the dreamlike quality. The book I had so precipitously discarded lay open on the floor. The fire in my fireplace was dying. Only the panting, bedraggled man next to me and the lingering smell of smoke, acrid on the night air, gave evidence that our nightmare journey was not a strange dream.

After hanging up my cloak, I hastened across the room to close the tall doors and shut out the icy cold air, smoke and distant noise. There was still a bright orange glow in the night sky. I paused in the act of closing the door and stood staring, transfixed by the sight, and felt Erik come up behind me. He stood watching the glowing sky over my shoulder, so close we were almost touching.

"Erik," I murmured almost to myself, "What have you done?"

The man next to me drew a long, shuddering breath, held it, and then slowly released it in a sigh.

"Oh, Sylvie," he whispered raggedly. "My wickedness and infamy knew no bounds this night. But it's over now, it's all over!"

Suddenly overwhelmed, he turned and sank onto a chair. Bowing his head, he covered his face with both hands, and began to weep freely. He wept for several minutes, silently, hiding his face in his hands as if ashamed of his tears. After closing the balcony doors and drawing shut the curtains, I lowered myself onto my *divan* and watched him helplessly, dreading to think what horrors must have brought him to this pathetic condition. Finally he seemed to master himself, and slowly lowered his hands to his lap and spoke, his voice so weakened by agony and regret that it was scarcely more than a whisper.

"I've lost everything, Sylvie – every hope, every dream, even my own home. There is nothing left."

I suppose I thought he must be referring to the Opera House even now being ravaged by flames. The need to comfort him overwhelmed me. "Oh, Erik…" I began, and I rose to go to him, but he held up one hand palm out in a commanding gesture that I could not but obey. Slowly I lowered myself back down and stared at him, waiting for him to speak.

"You do not understand, Sylvie, though you will, once I have told you everything. I do not deserve your sympathy, or your kindness, or any consideration from you whatsoever. You will be sorry you ever came back for me, you will see." His face was filled with misery.

I found I was beginning to feel a little frightened. I wasn't entirely certain I wanted to hear what Erik had to tell me. My throat felt dry and I had to clear it to speak.

"What, then, Erik? Tell me."

He cast his eyes down to the floor, and kept them there. A shiver ran through him; finally he spoke. His lips trembled a little. "Do you remember the day you came to see me and I told you I had been on the roof of the building, eavesdropping?" I murmured my assent and he went on in a low voice, still not looking at me, while the occasional tear trickled down his face and dropped off his chin.

"I was eavesdropping on Christine and…the Vicomte. I overheard them pledge their love to each other that night, and I heard her tell him…tell him what she really thought of me. I could not bear it, Sylvie; I was so…hurt, and then oh, so unreasonably angry. It seemed a complete betrayal to me. All I wanted was revenge. That was the night I conceived of writing my opera. It was all part of my great *coup de maître*."

He paused then and finally looked at me. "You were right about me, Sylvie, but it was even worse than you could have imagined.

217

You accused me of being a monster, remember? I was not only that, but I began to think of myself as a kind of avenging god, not a mere man any longer. I became inhuman. You see, I believed that the entire world had been set against me because of my face; everyone but you." I could not look away from him; I was trapped by his tortured memories and by his eyes holding mine in his wet blue gaze. Without looking away from me, Erik continued matter-of-factly.

"I conceived the idea of dropping the chandelier as a distraction so I could disappear through the trapdoor with Christine; I knew it would start a fire and I was glad. I wanted to destroy the opera and everyone in it. My plan worked perfectly except that *he* saw us go. I dragged her back down to…to the cavern. I suppose it was Madame Giry who showed him how to follow us," he did not sound angry but I confess to a little worry on that account. She would have been the only person who knew enough to guide someone down to Erik's home.

"But…but…you mean you *intended* to burn down the opera, with all those people inside?" I asked, incredulous.

"Oh yes. It was all part of taking revenge on them, those insufferable new owners who had had the nerve to defy me. By then I was so angry with everyone that it seemed to me quite fitting, even…" he paused, drew a ragged breath, and went on, "even strangling that fat old bore, Piangi…I did not give it a thought, you know. I had always thought of him as a ridiculous, absurd figure and his voice was mediocre. You see, Sylvie? Completely inhuman."

I stared at him in utter, disbelieving revulsion, while dreadful images swam before my eyes. "You…you *killed* him?" I gasped. Poor man, his only crime had been that he did not meet Erik's exacting standards.

Erik nodded grimly. "So I could take his place on the stage." His face darkened, he looked down at the floor again. "That is bad enough, but there is worse to come, I fear. I do not suppose you really want to hear all this, Sylvie, but somehow, I need to say it; I need to tell you. You saved my life tonight; I owe you the truth for once."

In the fraught silence that followed this ominous statement, a burned-out piece of coal in the grate settled with a little hissing sound. I wondered what could be worse than killing a man in cold blood, kidnapping an innocent girl, and burning down the opera house. A terrible possibility occurred to me then, of such a wicked deed, an unforgivable deed. Could he have…? I felt the blood drain from my face. I sprang to my feet, hands clenched, and interrupted his confession in my agitation.

"Erik, for god's sake, you did not…please tell me you did not…" but I could not bring myself to say the words out loud. Could he have been guilty of such a despicable act, when he had her alone and in his power? I would never, ever have entertained such an idea but for all the monstrous things he'd already done. What more was he capable of?

Erik stared up at me, a blank look on his face, his eyes uncomprehending. Then the blood rushed into his face as understanding came.

"*Non*, Sylvie, *non*. I swear I did not touch her, except taking her by the arms. But…" his face contorted with pain. "I forced her to put on that wedding gown, the one you saw, remember? And I gave her back the ring I took from her before." Seeing my blank look, he added, "I never told you about that. It is not important now. But if the Vicomte had not come when he did…" his voice sank to a whisper. "I might have hurt her, Sylvie. I wanted to hurt her, because she hurt me so badly."

"Sylvie, she…she exposed me, Sylvie…exposed my face to the entire theatre, so everyone could see what I really looked like. I could not believe she would do that to me, but she did." He grimaced at the memory of Christine's betrayal.

The rest of the story was quickly told. Even as I was tearing madly through the snowy streets of Paris in a blind rush to find him, he was trying to force Christine into a terrible choice. Either stay with Erik, or he would murder her fiancé right before her eyes. Noble girl that she was, she made the choice, put on the ring, and kissed him. How she could do so with such utter tenderness under the circumstances was surely a testament to her excellent character. I was not at all sure that I would have behaved so kindly to Erik at such a moment.

He wore a look of wonder in his eyes as he told me this. "I've never been kissed before, Sylvie, never kissed a woman before, not in my entire life. My own mother could not bear to look at me, let alone to kiss me." I thought of my own sweet, loving mother and silently cursed Erik's mother to the depths of Hell for her cold, unfeeling treatment of her son, her own flesh and blood. She must have possessed a heart of stone.

"I had no idea, no idea at all that it could be like that. So…so powerful. From that point," he continued in a voice tremulous with

219

pent emotion, "I was only a poor dog ready to die for her. In that moment everything altered for me...I saw it all then, what I had become, what I had done, what a beast I had been to her, and how much better she was than I. It was as if I had been on fire and then all at once I was cold. All the hate and anger seemed to drain out of me. I let them both go then, and I left it all behind me. That was when you found me."

But alas! His appalling revelations had not yet come to an end.

"I have to tell you something, Sylvie; something more, I mean. You deserve to know. I lied to you once. It was the only time I ever told you a lie, I swear." He was watching me, his eyes sad, and his voice wistful. I didn't want to hear any more – what more could there be? I gazed at him helplessly, unable to speak. I lowered myself back down on the *divan*, and we were again sitting across from each other.

"Do you remember that morning you came and asked me about Buquet, the stagehand, when I told you I had been up on the roof?" He prompted softly.

My eyes widened. Of course I remembered; we were just speaking of that morning. And then realization quickly followed. "Oh. *Oh.* You lied to me?" I whispered, horror-struck. "You...you did..."

"*Oui.* I know you, Sylvie. I knew you would leave and never come back if I told you the truth. You would finally see me for what I was." He was staring down at the floor now, a grim set to his mouth.

"But I believed you, Erik!" I cried furiously. "I *wanted* to believe you. And you surmised correctly; I would have left and never come back. You know me that well, at least. Why did you kill him, Erik?" I asked angrily. "What had he done to you?"

His mouth twisted as though he tasted something bitter. "He was following me that night, trying to catch me I suppose. As if he could! Joseph Buquet was a disgusting, dirty, lecherous drunk who would not be missed by his own mother. I assure you, the dancers were glad to be rid of him. I can't really find it in me to regret killing him; I just did not want you to know. I'm being completely honest with you, Sylvie."

"I only hope you do not have anything else you feel compelled to confess – I do not believe I can stand much more." He shook his head, not looking at me, not wanting to meet my eyes, to see the disgust in them that he heard in my voice. I felt sick in my very soul. I had saved this man; I was now an accomplice to murder on top of everything else. Perhaps Erik was right when he said I would regret helping him tonight.

"When was the last time you had something to eat?" I asked after a moment's tense silence. Even now, I could not suppress my innate instinct to nurture, but I hoped Erik would want food because I could not bear to sit there another minute.

He answered tonelessly, without bothering to raise his head.

"Days. I don't remember."

"I will make you something." Relieved, I instantly rose to my feet. I needed to get away from him, to put space between us. Listening to his monstrous revelations had almost been too much for me.

Leaving Erik still sitting staring at the floor, I went into the *garde-manger* and took three eggs and some *crème fraîche* from the cold box. My hands shook as I lit the gas on the cooking ring, warmed a copper *sauté* pan, melted butter into it and cooked eggs for Erik. It felt strangely unreal to engage in such a homely, domestic act after listening to that horrendous litany of crimes, but nonetheless, it was a relief to have something simple to do with my hands. When the eggs were formed into soft little curds, I plated them, added a fork, and took them to Erik. I rested the plate on his lap, carefully not touching him. He appeared to be comatose.

"Eat this. You need food; I am sure you must be hungry." I prayed I would not have to actually physically feed him. At this moment the very thought of having to touch him made me cringe. But the warm eggs smelled good and he responded: picking up the fork he took a bite. With the first forkful his eyes closed briefly; after that the eggs disappeared quickly. When he finished the last bite I took the plate away. Back in the pantry, I busied myself making him a hot drink with honey and a large dollop of cognac in it. My father had often recommended a hot drink with spirits in it to anyone who had been exposed to the cold. It warmed them from the inside out, he always said.

When I brought in the steaming hot cup, Erik had not moved.

"Here, Erik." I held the cup out to him. Automatically he reached for it and as I placed it carefully in his graceful, merciless murderer's hands, his cold fingers brushed against mine. I jerked my hand away as if it had been shocked, then stepped back from him and sank down on my *divan*. Erik noticed my reaction; he comprehended the cause. He gave a wry, twisted sort of smile.

221

"You hate me now too, don't you, Sylvie? I expected nothing else. I can't blame you, but I hate myself even more – even more than usual I mean." His voice was sad and wistful.

I stared at my hands folded in my lap. I could not bring myself to look at him. Did I hate him? I wasn't sure: could hate and love coexist simultaneously? I realized that I was exhausted; it was like a weight pressing on my body, dragging me down, preventing me from thinking clearly. Perhaps I should have made a warm drink for myself as well. Here he was, the man I had loved with all my heart and soul, here he sat on my chair drinking his toddy quietly like a normal person. Not like the demented, heartless creature he had become. The descent from love into obsession and madness had been rapid, unstoppable. Certainly I had been unable to stop it. I had tried, but I would always wonder if I could have tried harder, found some way to break the spell that held him in thrall. But it was far too late for that now.

When, lost in my own thoughts, I did not reply to his question, Erik began speaking again, in a soft, appealing voice.

"Even after all this, there is one thing that has been preying on my conscience, something I have regretted for days, and I have not been able to forget it." I looked up to see him watching me, his eyes gentle and remorseful. It had been a long time since I had seen such a tender expression on his face.

"Sylvie, I can't tell you how sorry, how truly sorry I am for drawing my sword on you that...that last day. You didn't deserve that. You were trying to help me, I know. It's just...I was beyond anyone's help by then, even yours." His blue eyes glittered with the intensity of his remorse. "I actually sat down to write you a letter of apology before I...before I went up to the theatre tonight, but I wasn't in any frame of mind for such a pursuit, so I put it aside. I don't know what happened to it, probably trampled underfoot by the mob. But please believe me, my inexcusable behavior has preyed on my mind ever since. I am thankful that you came looking for me tonight so that I could tell you. Forgive me for that, if you can forgive nothing else I have done. I never meant to hurt you, Sylvie, you were always so good to me, but I did anyway, I know."

I was moved in spite of myself. His remorse over this at least was completely sincere. I nodded, and my eyes fell back to my hands in my lap.

"*Oui*, I forgive you for that. I know you did not mean it." I looked up at him again quickly. There was something else I needed to say. "You know," I continued, "you would never have...I do not believe you would have hurt Mlle. Daaé, Erik. You could never have done such a dreadful thing to her."

A black look came into his eyes. "I might have, though. I was like a man possessed tonight. You have more faith in me than I have in myself, Sylvie."

"No, Erik," I said gently, shaking my head. "Had you behaved in such a dishonorable way, you would have hanged yourself by one of your own ropes. You would never be able to live with yourself. You are not that kind of man." I was glad to be able to reassure him about this one thing; a cold-blooded murderer Erik might be, but he was no ravisher of innocent young women.

He seemed to be staring at emptiness across the room, his eyes focused on the painting above my head but not really seeing it.

"I would like to think you are right about me, that I am not *that* much of a monster. But I don't know..." the last emerged as a half-sobbed whisper. The empty cup slipped from his hands and landed with a soft thud on the rug. I realized that exhaustion, his wild emotions and the frenzied actions of the night were catching up to him. I shook my head sadly.

Now was not the time to tell him, but I was absolutely certain that if Erik had gone about it the right way instead of an insanely *wrongheaded* way, he would have had no trouble in winning Mlle. Daaé's love and regard, as well as her hand, in spite of the difference in their ages. Her heart would not have been swayed away from him if a thousand Vicomtes de Chagny waving diamond rings stood in the way. I should know. If his poor disfigured face did not prevent *me* from loving him, why should it prevent her? But he had never given her the opportunity to really know him, as somehow, he had given me.

"I don't know what to do now," I heard Erik murmur plaintively, as if to himself. I felt a stab of pity at his words, for I knew that he had just single-handedly ruined his own life and lost his only home. Not to mention what he had done to the others.

Motivated by the pity I felt, I went to him and touched his arm. He raised his head and looked at me, his eyes slightly unfocused.

"I'll take care of you, Erik," I said calmly. "Stay with me *ce soir*. We can talk more in the morning." He nodded without speaking, rose and followed me into the bedroom. I led him to the side of the bed and drew back my mother's rose-covered quilt. He sat on the edge of the bed utterly dazed, the strong dose of *cognac* I put in the hot drink was making him sleepy, as I'd hoped it would. I knelt at his feet and tugged his wet boots off. His clothes felt dry now at least.

"Lie down now, it's all right. You are safe here."

He looked down at me as I knelt at his feet, and then he reached for one of my hands, held it in both of his, and whispered,

"Thank you, Sylvie." Releasing my hand, he rolled onto his side without another word, threw one arm over his face, and closed his eyes. Rising, I pulled the quilt over him and tucked it gently around his shoulders. By the time I finished he was asleep. I stood watching him for a few moments, my heart a welter of conflicting emotions. Finally I turned down the gaslight and slipped out of the room, half-closing the door.

Feeling the need of something for the soul, I made myself that warm drink with a generous splash of *cognac* in it. I am not actually fond of *cognac*, but extra honey and nutmeg helped. By that time, the drink was purely medicinal, I assure you. I built up the fire and sat in the rocking chair in front of the fireplace, drank my toddy and forced my exhausted mind to work.

There was much to think about. For one thing, how long would I be able to conceal Erik here? His only clothes were those he was wearing, and they were dirty and smelt of smoke. I was also desperately worried about Celestine and Meg: had they been able to get out in time? I felt horribly guilty that I had rescued Erik from the flames without giving my dear friend a second thought. What did that say about me? I rubbed my aching temples, one worrisome thought after another crowding into my head.

Now and then I could not resist a primal urge to go and peek at Erik. I assured myself it was just to check that he was still sleeping soundly, not because I needed to see him. The irony of the situation was not lost on me: had I not wanted him in my bed, had I not even dreamed of that? Now he was here, a fugitive, a cold-blooded criminal, a heartbroken shell of his former self. Not to mention possibly quite mad, sleeping peacefully under my mother's quilt.

In spite of everything I was no longer afraid of Erik, for I knew in my heart he would never hurt me. I am not certain how I knew, but I knew to a certainty. I would not have said as much before, but all things had changed. Erik owed me his very life, and we both knew it.

224

I fought a war with myself while sitting there, a war over doing the right thing. What was the right thing to do? Here was the Phantom, at my mercy, completely trusting that he was safe in my rooms; completely trusting *me*. How easy it would be to slip away to the street below and flag down the *gendarmes* who even now must be swarming through Paris searching for him.

I saw it all in my mind: how they would creep upstairs behind me, silently enter the bedroom to find him asleep and defenseless. They would seize the murderer and drag him away to face justice. He would resist, and they would beat him into submission. I could even see the look in his eyes when he understood that it was I who betrayed him. I saw it all, and so vividly that tears streamed down my face. It was right that Erik should be brought to justice, I knew that perfectly well; nothing could excuse the terrible things he had done in the name of unrequited love and fanatical jealousy.

The question I had to grapple with that night was: how far do you go for love? Love that was in your heart alone, without hope of ever being returned – what did that matter, really? Whether the object of one's love could return it or not, one still loved, did not one? Well, I did. It scorched my heart; it made me complicit in every bad thing Erik had done since the day I met him, or very nearly. Did I plumb the depths of my own conscience that night? I did, though it gave me little satisfaction.

Et alors, I made my choice, and wondered if I had forever severed myself from the rest of the human race by so doing. I learned what evil I was capable of, for all I wanted was to protect him. I had never ceased to love Erik, although I had tried. As I sat quietly there, a ferocious flame ignited inside me, as I had never felt before, as if I were a lioness ready to launch herself at an enemy to protect her cub. I saw with surprise my hands were knotted into fists in my lap. I forced myself to unclench them, and to face some very uncomfortable facts about myself: *my* love was unrequited, too. Perhaps all that prevented me from being *exactly* like Erik was the fact that I was civilized, and he was not.

And here was the ugly truth I faced that night: I wanted him to love *me* as he loved Christine, with that same passion, that same determination, that *surety* that this was right. And that to be deprived of this love meant one's life had no meaning. For that was how I loved him. How much did I really care about her, that poor girl who had not asked for such a terrifying lover nor deserved such treatment from him, except that I had compared myself to her and came up

225

wanting? This night was one for painful truths, and they were almost too much for me to bear.

I finished my drink, wiped away a few stray tears and was just beginning to think about making up a bed for myself on the *divan* when I heard a noise coming from the balcony. It sounded like hail clicking against the glass in a storm. But it wasn't stormy tonight. Even as I glanced up, frowning, something struck the glass with a ping. Reluctantly and a little afraid of what I would see, I approached the doors, opened one, and stepped out onto the balcony. Peering cautiously over the railing, I beheld a form bundled in a dark cloak on the street below. Upon seeing me, hands pushed back the hood and a pale face looked up. Relief swept over me. It was the person I most wanted to see: Celestine.

I hastened downstairs to admit her, locking up behind us after a quick glance showed the street still dark and empty. Neither of us spoke; once the door was locked we made for my *salon*. Celestine did not have to ask if the fugitive was here. She must have known I would get to him somehow. Upstairs again, I took her cloak and hung it on a peg. I flung my arms around her, embracing her in my relief to see that she was safe. There was a pervasive odor of smoke about her black silk gown.

"Are you all right? And Meg?" I asked anxiously.

"We are both fine, c*hérie*, do not worry. We were safe on the lower levels."

"Celestine, the fire…were…were many people hurt?" I dreaded what her answer might be, but I had to know.

Celestine shook her head in wonder. "By some miracle, no one was hit by the chandelier when it fell – it landed against the stage. That is how the fire started: the footlights were broken over. I believe everyone was able to escape although several people were injured in the rush to get out. But the theatre, it was completely demolished."

"I'm so thankful everyone escaped, that no more blood was shed…" I averted my face and bit my lip, finding I was unable to finish my sentence. She put her hand on my arm in a firm, comforting grip. I spoke again without meeting her eyes.

"You know Erik killed that stagehand, Celestine, he told me so tonight. He lied to me before, when he told me it was an accident." My voice was bleak.

Celestine nodded. "I realized it must have been so, later, when I saw that he…he was no longer able to control his actions. Now he is a murderer twice over. I am so sorry, Sylvie." I turned into her arms then and she held me gently, stroking my hair like a mother would do, and let me cry some more.

Presently she released me and said, "I have brought something, Sylvie. Meg, that fearless child, ventured as far as...the other side of the lake, and she brought this back. I thought it might be needed." She reached into a pocket in the folds of her skirt and drew out an object, placing it on my open palm. It was Erik's white mask. I turned it over in trembling hands, staring at it almost fearfully. It was the first time I had ever actually touched one of Erik's masks. I had never noticed before that they were formed from supple leather.

"Where is he?" She asked. We were both conversing almost in whispers.

With the hand that held the mask, I gestured toward the bedroom door. "He is there. Sleeping. He was completely exhausted by the time I got him back here. I was afraid we would not manage it."

I knew she would want to see him, and see for herself that he was safe, it was written all over her face. I led her to the bedroom, placing a finger over my lips to ensure she would be silent. We entered quietly and stood together looking down on the recumbent form. Erik's breathing was slow and regular; he lay on his back, and his arm had fallen away from his face, leaving it exposed to our view. Sleep had smoothed away the lines of stress and pain; he looked as sweet and innocent as a boy. Dark lashes lay upon his pale cheek, and his lips, so often twisted in anger, were relaxed into a beguiling softness. I could not help but glance obliquely at Celestine, curious as to how she would react to seeing Erik's ravaged visage at such close range for the first time.

She sighed softly, and her hand reached out and very gently smoothed in a motherly gesture over the quilt where it covered his shoulder.

"Poor Erik," she breathed softly, "poor unhappy Erik". She shook her head sadly before turning slowly away from the bed. We left him then, and went back to the *salon* to confer over a glass of sherry about what was to be done.

Celestine spoke first, toying with the stem of her small glass and staring into the embers of the dying fire.

"It was such a shock to see his face tonight – I had no idea how badly disfigured he was. He always took such pains to hide it. What a terrible sight! *Le pauvre homme.*" She sighed again. Then she turned to look at me appraisingly. "But you already knew what he looked like, didn't you, Sylvie?"

227

"*Oui*, I am accustomed to his face."

"Poor Christine! She was forced to expose him in front of the entire theatre. I think it nearly broke her heart."

I was not interested in talking about Mlle. Daaé, so I brushed aside her sympathetic remark rather more brusquely than was polite.

"She has seen his face before as well, Celestine. Never mind that now. It is Erik I am concerned about at the moment. He needs to stay here quietly and rest. He was in a terrible state when I found him. I was afraid every moment he would collapse in the street and I could not move him. Will he be safe here, do you think?"

I did not have to ask to know we were of like mind in this. Celestine considered a moment before replying. "Yes, I should say so. I am sure I am the only person who knows of your connection. No one would guess he was here, as long as he remains unseen. There is Meg, of course, but no one will question her about this. But Sylvie, he will have to leave Paris and leave soon. They will comb the entire city until they find him."

"Yes," I whispered. "I know. But, a few days…he could stay a few days…then he ought to have strength enough to flee the city." I could hear the pathetic desperation in my own voice as I spoke those words: Flee the city, disappear into darkness, never to return. I didn't want to think that far ahead. It made me feel too despondent.

Suddenly I thought of something else, a more pressing and immediate concern. It was wrong of me, but I could not help myself.

"Celestine, I…I hate to ask it of you after all you have been through, but do you think you could somehow get to Erik's…rooms…and get something for him to wear? He has only the clothes on his back, just what he was wearing when I found him, and they need cleaning."

Undaunted by my request, she thought for a moment, then replied,

"*Oui,* I will try. But that place was thoroughly searched; I can't say what may be left. The Chief Inspector of the Sûreté himself was in charge of the search, and I can tell you he would have left no stone unturned. I will go tomorrow. If I can bring anything, I will come to you in the afternoon, as if I were coming for tea." Finishing her sherry, she stood up and we embraced once more.

"Be careful," I said, pulling her cloak from the peg. She smiled that rather chilling little smile of hers. Unlike myself, Celestine possessed nerves of steel. Her *sang-froid* was indestructible. She put on her cloak and we went down. I watched her walk briskly away down the street and then I shut and locked the door one last time. How tired I was! I could barely drag myself back upstairs. By my mantel clock it was now a little after one in the morning.

I took an extra duvet and a pillow from my linen chest and made up a bed for myself on the *divan*. Slowly I moved from room to room, turning down the gaslights. Finally after one last trip into the bedroom to retrieve my nightgown and make certain Erik still slept, I made my way to my own couch. I brought with me the mask and for some unaccountable reason, placed it under a cushion beneath my head. Somehow I derived comfort just knowing it was there. I expected I would have difficulty falling asleep in spite of my exhaustion, but I drifted off almost at once.

It was not restful sleep; I was plagued by frightening dream images drawn from my experiences of the night – flames shooting up, people screaming, and then finding myself wandering on the dark stairs yet again. And then all the frightening images coalesced into a genuine nightmare. Somehow I knew it was a dream but I was trapped inside it, unable to awaken or shake it off.

I became aware that I was part of a great mob of shouting and pushing people. The sun was shining brightly on me, on the people, and on a raised wooden platform in front of me. The lumber of the platform looked freshly cut. The excitement of the crowd around me was palpable. They were all watching the platform expectantly, so I looked that way too. Then I saw the scaffolding, the thick rope noose hanging, the executioner standing next to it in his black hood. I realized with a lurch of horror that someone was about to be hanged, and the crowd was eager and excited, full of bloodlust, impatient for what was to come.

Catching sight of something I could not yet see, the mob surged forward, electrified, shouting even louder, pulling me along as though I were caught in a wave. Finally I saw what the crowd had seen: a tall, broad-shouldered man with a rough brown hood covering his head, being led up the steps of the platform by two large guards on either side of him. His hands were bound behind his back. When the man stumbled blindly on one of the steps, he was pulled up roughly, and the mob shouted their approval.

There was something familiar about the shape of the condemned man, even though I could not see his face. A sense of dread and horrified helplessness took root inside me. My hands came up and covered my mouth as if to stifle a scream.

"*No*", I whispered, but no one heeded me.

229

Upon climbing to the platform, the prisoner was roughly jerked around to face the teeming mob below. One of the guards flashed a broad smile toward his excited audience, and with a theatrical flourish, plucked away the hood covering the prisoner's head. The crowd seemed to gasp in unison, and then went wild, sending jeers and catcalls and hurling crude insults at the man who stood there unmoving, expressionless, still as a stone, with head held high. The prisoner's pale blue eyes disdained to survey the faces of the crowd before him as they cursed him and demanded his death.

"Erik!" I screamed, "Erik!" As if he could somehow hear my desperate cry over the shouts of the mob, Erik's eyes sought unerringly for mine, and as we stared at each other warmth kindled in their pale depths. He gave me a little nod, almost a smile. Tears flowed hotly down my cheeks. The press of people held me trapped and unable to move, forced to watch helplessly as he was walked to the scaffold, and the thick rope noose was placed around his neck, even as he had done to others. He was about to die right before my eyes. This, I knew, was the justice I had told myself he deserved to face. Watching as the rope settled around Erik's neck, a terrible scream burst from my lips, a wordless cry of anguish and despair.

Just then someone took hold of me, sending a wave of fresh terror through me. Feeling myself being grasped, I struggled against my unknown attacker, crying, "No!" But then I understood this was no longer my nightmare, I was not being held by the mob in my dream, and my struggles subsided. I was awake, and Erik's arms were holding me close; he was soothing me gently, murmuring my name, pulling me into consciousness and away from the horrible nightmare.

He wasn't about to die, he was *here*, alive and well. *Dieu Merci!* Without a thought or an instant's hesitation, I threw myself against his chest, sobbing.

Erik spoke soothingly into my hair. "It's all right Sylvie, you are awake now, and everything is all right. You are safe, don't be afraid."

"I'm sorry," I gasped, "I didn't mean to wake you – oh, I was having such a terrible nightmare!" I realized one of my hands was fiercely gripping the ruffled front of his shirt. I relaxed my hand hastily and tried to sit up, but his strong arm held me firmly against him. It felt amazingly good to cry, so I went on doing that while he stroked my hair gently with his free hand. That felt good, too.

After a moment he said wryly, "After everything I told you last night, it's no surprise you had a nightmare. I featured prominently in it, *sans doute*."

I *really* did not want to tell him I had just dreamed of his impending death and my reaction to it.

"*Non, non*, Erik. It...it wasn't about you," I murmured against his warm chest, the lie coming easily to my lips. I could feel his steady breath come and go. I thought idly that I could happily spend the rest of my life right here.

"Do you want to tell me about it?" He persisted patiently.

I shook my head emphatically. "I'd rather not. I just want to put it out of my mind. It was only a dream after all." One I was eager to forget.

We sat in silence for a minute, and then I felt his chest expand with a deep breath.

"*Do* you hate me, Sylvie? You can tell me the truth," he asked anxiously. And I could tell from the tone of his voice that it really mattered to him. I burrowed my head closer against him and bit my lip hard so I would not blurt out the humiliating truth, and confuse him even more. But he was waiting for my answer; he was holding his breath now I could tell.

"No Erik. I don't hate you." I whispered. He sighed, releasing his pent breath, and briefly tightened his hold, as if he were embracing me.

"I'm relieved, very relieved to hear that. Sylvie...you must understand by now that I don't know how to be a friend. All my life I've been no one's friend and no one has been my friend. I always felt I was outside of humanity you see, never a part of it. I ruin everything when I try to be part of...of humanity. You and I tried to be friends, Sylvie, but see what has come of that, look what I have done to you." Erik's voice was low and bitter.

I tried again to sit up and push away from him, and this time he released me. I wiped my wet face with the sleeve of my nightdress, and took his hand in mine.

"We *are* friends, Erik." I said firmly. And I meant it, in spite of all that he had done.

Erik gazed down at our two hands clasped together. He did not seem to notice that he was holding on to my hand as tightly as I was gripping his. Not long ago, he would never have allowed it.

"I think that is the reason I lied to you before," he said quietly. "I did not want to lose your friendship and company. It was the one good thing left. I missed you, Sylvie, after I sent you away…even all the things about you that used to drive me to distraction." I managed a little smile at that. "Perhaps especially those," he added wryly.

"That would have been just about everything I did, *n'est-ce pas?*" I asked, to tease him a little and lighten the mood. Now fully awake, I glanced toward the lace-covered French doors and saw that dawn was not far off; from the window a pale glow was showing. Without his warm arms around my shoulders, the room felt cold. I shivered.

Seeing my shiver, Erik immediately stood up.

"You should be in your own bed, Sylvie, not out here," he said firmly. "You should have given me the *divan*, or perhaps the floor, which is all I deserve." He reached down and grasped a handful of the duvet and pulled it off me, letting it fall to the floor. Before I knew what he was going to do, he gathered me up into his arms, just as he had when I was ill. I started to protest – I could walk perfectly well – but my flesh was weak, and so I let him. He carried me into the bedroom and carefully deposited me on my bed, in the warm place just left by his body. My mother's quilt, which he had tossed aside when my screams woke him, was now tenderly tucked up over me.

Perhaps it was his gentle care of me, so reminiscent of how tenderly he had watched over me during my illness all those months ago, but all at once I felt fresh tears welling up and I reached for him and caught his hand in mine.

"Please don't leave me. Please. Stay with me here. I don't want to be alone." The memory of that ghastly nightmare was still too fresh; somehow I was certain I would have another nightmare if Erik was not here with me. Desperation made me bold.

Erik stared at me, clearly shocked by my unexpected (even to me) request. He hesitated next to the bed, frowning.

"Sylvie, you can't mean you want me this close to you, not after…not after…" He held his hands out to me, palms up, as if showing me they were covered in blood, the hands of a murderer.

Ignoring his tragic expression and gesture, I said, "Erik, I am not afraid of you. You are no ravisher and I know you would not harm me. I am asking you to stay here for what is left of the night, so I don't have to be alone. Please." The shimmering tears tipped and ran down my cheeks and I brushed them away with consternation.

He shook his head, still frowning down at me.

"I will never understand you, Sylvie. You never fail to behave completely differently than what I would expect. After how I have behaved toward you, and what I told you tonight, how can you bear to… you should be disgusted by me, as so many others are. I still do not comprehend how it is that you can bear to look at my face!"

I replied truthfully. "I think it is because I have learned to look at what is inside people, not just at what is on the outside." It was not the full truth; if I had told him I *liked* looking at his face, he would have been incredulous at the very idea.

Erik gazed down at me sadly. He shook his head.

"But I am as bad inside as I am on the outside, you know that, Sylvie. If you didn't know it before, my deeds last night must convince you." He spoke softly, full of anguish that tugged at my heart.

"No," I replied firmly. "I refuse to believe you are beyond redemption. I don't believe you are bad, Erik. I refuse to believe it."

"Then you are the only one," he said, very quietly. "*Bien*, I know better than to argue with you, Sylvie. You will always get your way." I said no more, only watched him. Slowly and carefully, as if trying not to startle a deer, Erik moved to the other side of the bed, pulled the quilt away and lay beside me, being careful not to touch me.

"*Merci*," I whispered gratefully. Strangely, I felt that all was right with my world, at least in this moment. I nestled down into my pillow and lay on my side so I could see him, but my eyes were heavy and they drifted closed. I stifled a yawn.

"Let me sing you to sleep now, Sylvie." Propped up on one arm, facing me, Erik began to sing a sweet song in his beautiful voice, a gentle song like a child's lullaby, but in a language I had never heard before. I felt myself relaxing and the dreadful nightmare began to fade away.

But the dream had only reaffirmed what I already knew – no matter what he had done, it would never be possible for me to deliver him to justice. I knew now that if I had to watch him suffer and die, I would die myself from the pain of it.

I drifted off to a peaceful, dreamless sleep with his voice coaxing me along, and the last thing I was aware of was his hand gently lifting a strand of hair off my face.

CHAPTER TWENTY

*'Moral wounds have this peculiarity – they may be hidden, but
they never close; always painful, always ready to bleed when
touched, they remain fresh and open in the heart'*

A.D.

I opened my eyes to the pale, silvery light of morning
gleaming through my bedroom window. The sky was flat
grey and a mist was falling outside. *Good*, I thought, *it will melt away the
snow.* Perplexingly, I felt quite tired in spite of sleeping soundly.
Why...*oh.* I sat up so abruptly it almost made me dizzy as the memory
of last night's events came rushing back. What a night! Could it have
been real? I rubbed my eyes and looked at the other side of the bed; it
was empty, but there was a depression in the pillow where Erik's head
had rested. Hesitantly, I leaned over and touched the pillow with the
flat of my hand. It was cold, and I felt a bubble of panic rising in me.

My eyes turned toward the half-open door, and then I heard
the cheerful crackling of a fire in the fireplace. A sense of wonder
replaced the fear that Erik would have vanished like a mirage. He was
still here! He had made a fire in the fireplace to chase away the
morning chill – such a domestic, homely act. Unable to resist, I leaned
over and pressed my nose to his pillow, inhaling the familiar scent of
him, faintly tinged with smoke. How I had missed that wonderful
smell!

Lifting my head on a long inhalation, my nose twitched; I could
smell coffee brewing. I shook my head a little and smiled; I always
associated Erik with the fantastic, the extraordinary and mysterious,
larger than life somehow. How incongruous this domesticity seemed!

Shaking my head in disbelief over the previous night's events, I
rose from my bed, hastily slipped into my ruffled *robe de chambre* and sat
before my mirror. I pulled the ribbon off my night braid and began
combing through my hair and smoothing it down. As I did so, I stared
with rueful amazement at my reflection in the glass. What possessed
me last night, to have begged Erik to share a bed with me? Hectic
colour bloomed in my cheeks when I thought of it. What would my
mother have said? It did not bear contemplating, but one thing was
certain: since meeting Erik, I had become another person altogether.
It had been such a comfort to know he was there, only an arm's reach
away from me. What did that say about me?

After several weeks of pain, heartbreak and futile attempts to forget Erik, he had returned to my life with a vengeance. Now I could think of nothing *but* Erik. But what was I to make of that mercurial, brilliant and dangerous man? It was impossible to reconcile the two vastly opposite images of Erik that presented themselves to me: the gentle, tender man singing me to sleep versus the inhuman monster of the previous night. At times his ravaged face appeared to present a mirror of these opposites: the 'good' side and the 'bad' side of Erik. However much he had once denied it, he reminded me of the yin-yang symbol on his little mosaic box.

Celestine once told me that he could not comprehend right from wrong. The man himself had assured me once he was quite selfish. In my opinion it was high time he was set straight on that account, and the sooner the better. I had several ideas about how to begin to affect his redemption. The man who had hand-carved a toy camel to please a child could not be all bad; his impulses needed redirection was all.

A sound of rattling china interrupted my reverie and the object of my musings appeared in the doorway carrying my silver tea tray in his hands. On it I saw two steaming white cups. Shirt tucked in and hair combed, he undoubtedly looked more presentable than I did, and the sight of his handsome form made my heart thump with pleasure. He crossed the room, set the tray down on a side table and handed me a cup with a little flourish, as though he were performing a magic trick for my benefit. Once glance told me it was my favorite, *café au lait*. I looked at him curiously.

"How did you know…"

"The cups, of course. I am not a mind-reader, whatever else I may be." Ah - the big white cups for *café au lait*, they were the ones I always used and I always left them out near the coffee-making apparatus. Appearing perfectly at ease, Erik climbed back into the warm bed, pulled the quilt up to his waist and took the other cup. Casually I rose from my vanity table and joined him on the bed, sitting on top of the quilt. We sat sipping our coffee in an extraordinarily comfortable silence, as if we had done this together for years. As if it were quite normal for me to have a man who was not my husband sharing my bed. Not to mention a man who was possibly quite mad and who had been busily terrorizing and murdering people the night before. Oh well; best not to dwell on that. I do think, in some way, we were both so glad to be back in each other's company, it was such an indescribable relief. It certainly felt that way to me.

235

The coffee was perfectly made. "Where did you learn to make *café au lait?*" I asked him wonderingly.

He slanted me a look accompanied by a raised eyebrow.

"Sylvie, I was not raised by wolves, you know." He said, his voice gently chiding me. I flushed and looked away, concentrating on my coffee. For that was *exactly* how I had come to think of him.

Composing myself, I glanced up sidelong through my lashes at said madman. "Thank you for staying with me last night. I didn't have any more bad dreams." I said at last, feeling absurdly shy. Frowning, I plucked at the quilt with my fingers.

"I can't think what came over me, asking you to…" a blush of heat washed over my face as I spoke. "Please believe me; I've never done anything like that before."

Erik shrugged, unconcerned and oblivious to my discomfiture.

"To be perfectly honest, I did not mind. It was an interesting experience. I've never shared bed with a woman, chastely or otherwise, so this was a first for me," he said matter-of-factly.

I had not thought of that…that he would never have…embarrassment and remorse instantly seized me. How selfish, how thoughtless I had been! "I'm so sorry Erik. I should have realized, I didn't think…well, I hope you were able to sleep too." I finished lamely, blushing even harder and unable to meet his eyes. Of course, the fact that he did not find me even remotely attractive would certainly have made it easier for him.

"You will be pleased to know that you do not snore, Sylvie," he said sardonically, his lovely lips curving into a brief smile that did not reach his eyes. They were the same as the night before, pale blue pools of sadness and pain. "I sleep lightly and briefly always. Don't worry about me, Sylvie. Being here with you was comfort for me as well."

Erik studied me for a moment, and then said, "I have never seen you with your hair down like that. You have beautiful hair, Sylvie." And of course I blushed furiously and decided that since our cups were empty it must be time for more *café*.

I rose from the bed, wrapping my dressing gown more securely around me. We had shared a peaceful interlude, but it was time to face memories which were not so pleasant. I stopped in the doorway and looked back at him, meeting his eyes with an expression I hoped conveyed the seriousness I felt.

"I will make us another *café*, and then I want you to tell me what happened – everything that happened, from the beginning." And I left the room before he could reply.

I propped myself up against my pillow again, cradled my cup of *café* and looked intently at him. "Now," I said briskly, "tell me everything, Erik."

He looked away from me, out the window at the grey misting sky. He was now perched on the edge of the bed, as far away from me as possible without actually sitting on the floor. Studying the back of his head, I remembered with a little start that his mask was still hidden away behind a cushion on the *divan*. I wondered if I should give it to him, if he would feel better wearing it, but as I preferred him without it, I decided against telling him.

Finally Erik sighed softly, resigning himself. "It all began about ten years ago, not long after I..." he began, but I interrupted him quickly.

"*Non, non*, I mean *everything*, from the beginning. *Your* beginning, your life." I clarified. I needed to know these things, how else could I understand what had brought him to commit such atrocities? I felt certain Erik's past would shed light on his present circumstances.

"I want you to tell me your life story, Erik," I continued firmly. "Right up to and including last night. I want to know, I *need* to know, what brought you to this."

His head swiveled around sharply; he stared at me, shocked. I met his gaze with a level one of my own, unyielding. He bent and set his cup down on the floor and then covered his face with his hands.

"Please do not make me do this, Sylvie. I have tried so hard to forget...many things." The last came out as a ragged whisper.

I drew my legs up under me and tucked the ends of my dressing gown neatly around them. Outside, it continued to drizzle, but here in my apartment we were warm and safe, in our own little world. Uncurling one leg, I dared to extend it and nudge him with my foot.

"If you tell me what I want to know, I will make you breakfast," I murmured.

His hands dropped away. "Extortion? I had no idea you could be so hard and cold. I am seeing a new side of you, Sylvie." A pause. "But now that you mention it, I *am* hungry..."

"I thought you might be."

His tense face softened as we gazed at each other. "I did miss your cooking," he said at last. I knew he was saying that he missed *me*. And then he squared his shoulders, drew a deep breath, and began to talk.

Erik's life story was more hair raising and harrowing than I could ever have imagined, but the hardest part for me was his tragically heartbreaking childhood in a small village near Rouen. Listening to him recount the brutal treatment he received at the callous hands of his mother and the father who refused ever to look at him made me cold with fury inside. His mother would never look at him unless he wore a mask, and she avoided touching him or ever showing him any affection. Very likely, she felt none. I really could not blame him for escaping that life of neglect and abuse at a very early age.

Erik decamped with a band of gypsies that were passing through his village when he was only about six years old. They were happy to have him, for with his exceptional ugliness he could be displayed for coins at *faires* and fetes. But if he had hoped for any kindness from that quarter, he received none.

As he spoke of this terrible time, his feelings, always close to the surface and hard for him to govern at the best of times, could not be hidden and he wept. So did I, for that pathetic, love-starved little boy. How I longed to be able to sweep down the years and gather him up in my arms!

Erik was always precocious, already a budding genius, and he had inherited his father's abilities in architecture and building. During his travels with the gypsies he learned to play several musical instruments quite well without any formal training whatsoever, and possessed a naturally gifted voice. He put himself on display to earn money, and performed magic tricks for those who came to look upon his hideous visage. Everywhere he went, traveling with a circus or living with the gypsies, and finally building those incredible palaces for sultans in Persia, he learned everything there was to learn, and excelled at all of it, including death. He was remorseless, conscienceless, and utterly fearless; he admitted as much to me. He had to be that way, he explained, or be killed himself.

He confessed to me that there were many times when despair over his lot in life had caused him to contemplate suicide, but his will to live proved strong enough to overcome such dark thoughts. Self-preservation and self-hatred warred always together in his breast.

Although while he talked he could not bring himself to meet my eyes, Erik now told me many of the things that he had concealed from me before when telling me about his life before the Opera. He'd never spoken of these things to anyone before, and it seemed to be a relief for him to do so now. I listened quietly, trying to avoid any movements or noise that would betray my shock and distress at what I was hearing – tried, even, to become invisible. I was afraid if he saw the horror reflected in my eyes, he would stop talking. As, for example, when he told me this:

"I have killed many times, Sylvie," he said quietly, his pale blue eyes still focused on the window, "too many times to count, but never for pleasure, I assure you. When I was passing through India I became an expert with the Punjab lasso, and this became my weapon of choice. I was better at it than anyone else. I had no choice." It was good he did not glance behind him just then, where I sat, rigid and round-eyed. I had no idea what a Punjab lasso was, but for certain it must be deadly.

While staying in the Sultan's palace in Persia (which he had designed and caused to be built), Erik became a pet of the Sultan's favorite, a beautiful young concubine. Erik devoted many hours to her amusements, most of which were cruel and perverse. Erik was young as well, and fancied himself in love with her; he allowed himself to hope that she might return his feelings because she had absolutely no qualms about seeing him without a mask. In fact, she seemed to like him very much, but not in the way that he hoped.

To her, Erik was but a plaything. His very ugliness was a source of entertainment in its way. One of her favorite entertainments at the palace was to place two combatants together in an enclosed courtyard from which there was no escape, while she and the ladies of her court looked on from an upper balcony. The combatants must fight to the death; that was her only rule. One of them would be a warrior captured in some battle or other, armed with whatever weapon he chose – a scimitar, a sword, or long knife. The other would be Erik, armed with nothing but a length of light rope. Each of these mortal combats ended the same: eventually, the rope would whistle through the air, the noose would unfailingly find its target; Erik would drag his dead foe by the end of the rope and leave his body beneath the Sultana's balcony, an offering to her bloodlust.

After a time, Erik's infatuation with this beautiful but wicked concubine evaporated like water under the desert sun, and he departed that place before he could be discarded, his usefulness at an end. It was, in fact, the Persian known as 'daroga' and none other than the man I once encountered outside the secret entrance who delivered the warning that enabled Erik to escape Constantinople in time. For some unaccountable reason, this man, a high-ranking officer of the Persian military, believed Erik's life was worth saving, in a barbaric land where life was cheap indeed. Hearing this story made my hair stand on end.

Eventually growing tired of the nomadic and dangerous existence that was his life so far, he returned to France to take up his father's profession of masonry construction. He soon found himself with a contract to work on the just-completed Opéra Populaire, helping to repair and expand the foundations of that enormous edifice. During work on the many underground levels, a worker had accidentally made a breach deep under the cellars of the building, causing a flood and creating the underground lake. When Erik saw it he realized at once its potential to be a safe haven where he could live at peace from everyone, alone as he thought he wanted to be, away from prying eyes and cruelty.

Using all the knowledge he had accumulated thus far, he built a magical, whimsical and above all secret home on the other side of that accidental lake. And so he went from the hot deserts of Persia and the Middle East, to dwell in a cold, sunless cavern far under the earth. No one but Erik even knew of its existence or how it was reached, with the exception of the Persian, who had also found his way to France. Anyone attempting to find the cavern would fall into one of Erik's many ingenious traps, never to be seen above the ground again. Here, with a pipe organ stolen from one of the Opera storage rooms, he would spend his days and nights composing and playing music, which had by now become his ruling passion. He was sure his days of killing were behind him, and he was thankful for that. He had no use for people, but he was sick of dealing out death.

Erik spent the rest of his time exploring every inch of that many-leveled structure, creating secret routes for himself that were unknown to all others, writing music, and taking a real interest in the fortunes of the Opéra Populaire. So much so that he began to feel proprietary, even possessive, toward it. The then-manager, M. Poligny, had good business sense but no real idea of how to organize performances, operas or musical events and the newly-opened Opera suffered as a result. Concerned that the opera would fail, Erik began giving him 'hints', actually orders, and demanding payment in return for his 'help'.

A few unfortunate occurrences when payment was not forthcoming assured M. Poligny that the Opera Ghost was real. He not only was faithful in providing the 20,000 *francs* a month, but in following Erik's instructions with care. He frequently wrote back, so that they were in regular communication for years. Under Erik's guidance, the opera flourished. Erik worked tirelessly during those years to create and nurture his reputation as a phantom or a ghost, a powerful, all-seeing, all-knowing supernatural being who inspired terror in the denizens of the Opéra Populaire. Reminding me of the day I saw him receiving a delivery of fireworks, he explained that all he ever used were simple magician's tricks to accomplish his reign of terror over the superstitious residents of the Opera.

Erik befriended Celestine early in the theatre's existence, and that touching story has been recounted elsewhere in these pages. His kindness to her and Meg assured him of her loyalty and willingness to assist him in his various endeavors, and as no particular harm was ever done, she was happy to comply with his every request. He needed a helper and an extra pair of ears and eyes, and Celestine needed a friend. She admired him, respected him, and grew to care for him. His concerns became her concerns. Celestine's respect for his need for privacy was of paramount importance to him. Not once did she ever betray his secrets.

Eventually the Persian who had saved Erik's life arrived in Paris and somehow their paths crossed. An uneasy alliance was formed; Erik had money, and the Persian the means to obtain just about anything Erik desired, including the Imperial Tokay of which he was fond. By means of advertisements placed in the newspaper in a kind of nonsense code known only to them, the Persian would furnish Erik with whatever he required, except for food. This arrangement continued for years to the satisfaction of both men.

It was through Celestine that Erik first became aware of Christine Daaé, only about ten years of age at the time and recently orphaned. She had just won a place at the Conservatory and come to live there under Celestine's protective wing.

"Madame Giry happened to mention what a naturally gifted voice she possessed, even at such a young age. Although she was training to be a dancer, Madame Giry thought her voice was where her real potential lay," Erik explained.

By this time in his story, we were dressed and quite properly seated on my *divan* in the *salon* rather than in my bedroom with me *en dishabille*. I had made a simple *petit dejuneur* for us, just some croissants, soft cheese, jam and more coffee, and we enjoyed this repast in front of the fire while I listened, fascinated, to his life story. But we were approaching the difficult part, and I could tell he was reluctant to speak of it even now.

"Is that when you began tutoring her?" I prompted, popping a last morsel of flaky croissant in my mouth.

Erik shook his head. "No, that did not start until she was older, when her voice was more mature. No, to begin with, I just listened and talked to her. She was only a child and lonely, she missed her father. She was the only orphan living there. She needed a friend, and so did I. I knew well what it is like to be alone, adrift in the world. She could never see me, *bien entendu*, which was a good thing all considered, but because of that she came to believe I was her Guardian Angel, not a real person at all. She called me her Angel of Music. I let her believe it because I did feel protective of her, and she would never expect to be able to see me. We went on like this for years.

"I started giving her singing lessons in secret when she was about fifteen I think – I can't remember exactly. Under my tutelage her voice progressed quite remarkably. I had plans for her career: I wanted her to sing the music I wrote. Her voice was exactly what I was looking for. Only Madame Giry knew what I was doing. Her assistance in keeping the lessons a secret was invaluable." *Of course*, I thought ruefully. Celestine, eager to help Erik, was always complicit in all his schemes and plans. He sighed sadly, gazing into the fire. He had got up to sit apart from me, and now was seated on the floor, his long legs extended toward the fireplace. He seemed to be talking to himself; perhaps that made it easier for him to revisit these painful memories.

"She was such a good-natured, sweet girl. I had never been around anyone with such innocent good-heartedness. She was so willing and eager to please, and she loved the lessons I gave her. And how good her voice was! Christine trusted me completely. As she grew into young womanhood, she grew very beautiful as well."

Erik glanced at me before returned his gaze to the fire. "You saw her once, remember? Is she not an exquisite creature?"

It took me a moment to find my voice. I found myself glancing down at the front of my gown, half expecting to see blood running there. All unknowing, it was so easy for him to twist the knife into my heart.

"Yes," I said quietly after collecting myself. "Yes, she is a lovely girl. But she was too young for you, Erik."

He colored slightly, but did not dispute that unpalatable fact, as he would once have done.

"It was wrong, I know," he admitted after a moment. "But she seemed somehow to be mature beyond her years, so it was easy for me to forget how innocent she really was. I did not even realize I had fallen in love with her until it was too late." He glanced up at me, his expression bleak.

"Alas for me and for her! I tried to take a girl who was born to live in light and turn her toward darkness."

I regarded Erik solemnly. "You are speaking of yourself, are you not? You believe yourself to be, not an angel, but a creature of darkness."

"Without a doubt." He answered firmly. I opened my mouth to argue the point but he spoke before I was able. "Even Lucifer was an angel, *vous savez*." He added softly. I closed my mouth, not knowing how to respond. In the silence Erik continued. "And you already know what a controlling nature I have, Sylvie. I tried to control Christine as well; hers was a pliant nature, so it was a very bad combination."

"And, do not forget, you were an uncivilized, if highly intelligent, recluse. I do not believe anyone ever taught you the proper way to behave." I said disapprovingly.

This brought a small, rueful smile to his lips.

"No, I do not suppose living with gypsies or blood-thirsty Turks could teach one the proper way to behave. I was damned on all accounts."

Attempting to interject a touch of humor, I said pertly, "You certainly failed to control *me*. Perhaps you are not as mesmerizing as you seem to think you are, *M. le Fantôme*!" I felt a little shiver when I said that name; I had not called him by that *sobriquet* for a long time. My ploy succeeded; he tilted his head in my direction with a wry expression.

"Now that is true, I cannot recall one time when you did anything I asked of you, but I believe that is due more to your obstinate nature than to my own powers of persuasion, Sylvie. Somehow or other, you seem to have been quite immune to them."

I sighed, looking away. "Not totally immune," I murmured softly, perhaps so softly that he did not hear.

Gracefully rising to his feet, Erik walked to the French windows and stood looking out through the lace panels into the wet street.

"Well, you know the rest, more or less. At around the same time I had decided it was time to reveal to Christine that I was a real, live man who was in love with her, and a hideous one at that, not an angel or a ghost, her old childhood friend the Vicomte also arrived on the scene. The timing could not have been worse. That was the beginning of the end." His voice sounded tired.

He looked so tall, upright and handsome standing there with his back to me. I thought again, as I had many times before, how different his life would have been if he were not so visibly disfigured. Unable to prevent myself, I rose and crossed the room to stand next to him. I felt some intangible bridge had at last been spanned between us, so I did not hesitate to rest my hand lightly on his shoulder in a comforting gesture, and he allowed it to remain.

"It must have been rather alarming for her," I murmured gently, "to discover that not only were you no angel, you were instead the Phantom of the Opera, at whose feet all manner of misdeeds had already been laid."

He gave his head a shake. "I have no one to blame for all these things but myself, just as you told me, Sylvie. I wish I could take it all back, but I cannot. All I really wanted was for Christine to love me as I loved her. But I can see now, those two loves were not evenly matched."

I sighed. So much damage had been done, all in the name of love.

"She did care for you, of that I am certain," I said, forcing the words out reluctantly. I felt small; it was small of me to still resent that poor girl after all she had been through. Nonetheless, I did resent her, for she had been given what I wanted most in the world, and she wanted it not.

"You may be right," said Erik thoughtfully. "She gave me her engagement ring before she left me – a parting gift, and her way of saying goodbye. I never told you this, but I stole it from her the night of the masquerade ball, out of jealousy and spite. I behaved like a beast to her that night." As he spoke, he reached into his pocket and then opened his hand to show me what he held. The ring Christine had given him lay on his open palm, where it sparkled like a captured star.

"She probably thought I would need to sell it for money to live on, since I had to leave in haste."

I gazed at the ring; it was enormous, and the stones were obviously of the highest quality.

"I do not care for diamonds myself, and it seems a bit gaudy," I said with a sniff. "What will you do with it?"

"I shall keep it for a memento; it is all I have left." He looked down bemusedly at the glittering gem in his hand and gave his head a little shake. "I expect the Vicomte can afford to buy her another." Erik glanced at me, his expression earnest. "I want you to know that I never intended to dishonor her, Sylvie. I wanted to marry her. It was a dream, a fantasy, but I allowed my imagination to run away with me." His hand closed over the ring, putting out its bright light. Slowly, he returned the precious object to his pocket.

Smiling sardonically, he added, "There was never a chance of that happening, as I should have known."

I felt the green flame flicker to life in my breast as he talked of his romantic fantasy, but I fought it back.

"I think..." I hesitated briefly before forcing myself to continue. "I think there might have been a possibility that Mlle. Daaé would have eventually learned to love you, Erik, if you had approached her in an appropriate manner." How it pained me to utter those comforting words!

Slanting a wry glance down at me, he gave a little snort of derisive laughter.

"You mean, instead of lying to her, tricking her, misleading her, stalking her and frightening her out of her wits?" He asked.

"Well...yes. I suppose that is what I mean, but I would not have put it quite like that."

Erik's brief smile faded. "No, no. I do not believe that ever would have happened, no matter how I approached her. You see, that night when I overheard Christine talking to the Vicomte De Chagny on the roof of the theatre, I heard her tell him...ahhh..." he paused on a sighing breath, his eyes closing briefly.

"She told him she could never forget the horrible sight of my face."

"Oh," I murmured with dismay. My heart ached for him. "You know," I said gently, "you are not as alone now as you think. You still have me, Erik."

His sad eyes contemplating the view outside my window, he replied,

"Words, just words. Last night Christine said something very like that to me, just before she left, never to return. No, Sylvie, this loneliness I have lived with all my life, I am cursed with it."

"Erik, listen to me: you are here, safe for now, because of me. Because I am your friend." I gave his shoulder a comforting squeeze.

"One thing I am extremely thankful for is that you did not come looking for me last night any earlier than you did. If you had seen me like that, if you had witnessed my barbaric behavior firsthand, I fear you would never wish to be my friend, now or ever." His voice was bleak.

"Then I am thankful for that as well." I glanced up at him ruefully. I had already seen a terrifying side of him, but now I knew there had been much worse. I suppressed a shudder when I thought of it.

Erik's story was at an end, and what a story it was. I could not have imagined such a life, and if I had read of it in a book, I would have tossed the book aside as being incredibly unbelievable. I had never, I saw now, stopped to consider just how isolated, how lonely and empty his life had been. He always seemed so self-sufficient and strong, needing no one. But in fact, his need to be loved was great indeed. And he had so much love to give, but he had spent it on the wrong person. It pained me to think of how he had been forced into this isolation through no fault of his own. I wondered if there had ever been a single moment in his life when he had been happy.

"Thank you for telling me all this, Erik. It helps me to understand you better."

Erik reached up and placed his hand over mine where it still rested on his shoulder.

"I am glad I did. I feel better – I did not think I would but I do." He turned his head to look down at me quizzically. "You, Sylvie, *my cook*, you know more about me than any other man or woman on this planet. It seems very odd that you can be standing here next to me so calmly after everything you have heard last night and this morning. If it were not for you, *I* would not be standing here this morning, and we both know it. Sometimes I think my life is just one long nightmare, a living hell, but I am not ready to leave it yet, and so I thank you. You have been much kinder to me than I deserve, and I cannot fathom the reason for it."

The reason was one I could not say out loud, so I said nothing. There was an awkward pause, during which we heard the distant chime of my clock in the kitchen downstairs, below our feet. I was astonished to hear the clock strike two; how did so much time pass so quickly? It felt as though we had just finished our breakfast.

Almost the instant the clock ceased to chime the hours, someone rang the door bell urgently. We both started at its demanding notes. Removing my hand from his shoulder, Erik moved swiftly to the French doors. As he opened one to slip around the lace panel and look over the balcony, a cold draught of misty air entered the room. He was back almost at once, his expression unreadable.

"It is Madame Giry, bringing you a parcel of some sort." He said quietly. I could see that he was feeling uncomfortable, guilty even, at the thought of meeting her again so soon after what had happened. He did not, I knew, harbor any resentment toward Celestine because she had been compelled to help Raoul rescue Christine. He knew it was the right thing, and necessary thing, to be done. So that was not a worry at least.

I put a hand to the side of my head. *"Bien sûr!* I asked Celestine when she came by last night..."

Erik interrupted me, his face a study in surprise.

"She came here last night? When? Why?"

"Allons, I do not want to leave her waiting in the damp air outside. Let us go down and I will explain as we go. She came here in secret after you were asleep – she wanted to make sure you were safe." We were hurrying down the stairs to the kitchen now.

Erik caught my arm, stopping me mid-step. "But, how did she know I was here? How did she know to look for me at your apartment? I do not understand that."

I made a helpless little gesture with my free hand, buying myself a few seconds while I tried to think what to say. Inspiration came.

"Celestine knows that we are friends, Erik, and that I...I care for you. She cares for you, too. We both do." Pulling my arm free, I proceeded down the stairs and over to the front door before he could ask me any further awkward questions. He followed behind me more slowly.

I flung open the door and drew Celestine into my kitchen. Her nose was pink with cold. It was cold in the room, since Sunday was not a cooking day and I had not even been downstairs yet, but at least it was dry.

"I cannot stay long," she said breathlessly. "The police are not finished questioning me. I slipped away just long enough to bring you the clothes. I was not followed." She pushed her bundle into my arms and turned, almost reluctantly, to look at Erik.

I turned toward him as well and explained, "I was just about to tell you, I asked Celestine to try and fetch some articles of clothing from the cavern if she was able, since you had nothing with you when you came away last night." Erik did not appear to hear one word of my explanation. His eyes were riveted to Celestine's pale face.

They regarded one another in silence across a void of perhaps six or seven feet. The silence stretched out. I knew Erik was thinking of just how much he owed this small but fiercely determined woman. Celestine wore a worried, yet yearning expression on her face, and Erik looked…well, ashamed. I waited, saying nothing, for I knew there was no need. Finally, as if pulled by magnets, they began to walk cautiously toward each other until they met in the middle. He may have feared to see revulsion on her face, but there was none to be seen. After a brief pause, Erik suddenly enveloped Celestine in a warm embrace, which she returned with interest. It was a moving moment, and one I will not soon forget. They held each other for a few seconds, and when they pulled apart, Celestine's eyes were shining with tears. My own eyes were suspiciously wet.

"You and Meg are all right?" He asked her worriedly.

She dabbed her eyes discreetly with her handkerchief, sniffed, and returned to her usual composed self.

"*Oui*, we are fine. But the police, especially that Chief-Inspector, they will not allow us to leave yet, not until they have finished their investigation." She turned toward Erik. "They have torn apart your living place; they have been over every inch of it, even dredging the lake. I was able to slip down there from the secret entrance and pick up a few articles of clothing without being seen, but you *must* stay away from there."

"I have no reason to go back," he said quietly.

"Why are they questioning you so much, Celestine?" I asked. "Do they suspect you of complicity?"

She shook her head. "They suspect me of something, *certainement*. I think, I am almost certain in fact, that the owners told the Chief-Inspector (he is in charge of the investigation) that I was always apparently in communication with the Opera Ghost. They thought I knew too much to be completely innocent, which, of course, is quite true. But they did not trust me. He does not trust me, either, but he cannot prove any connection and so will have to release me to go soon." She paused and glanced at Erik.

"I have cooperated with them fully, *vous comprenez;* I have told them everything except I did not tell them anything about Sylvie. I knew nothing of your plans, since we had not been in communication for some time. And it was in my favor that I helped the Vicomte to find Christine. I could not risk being taken into police custody...what would happen to Meg?"

"It is all right, Madame Giry, I do not blame you in the least." Erik assured her.

She gave him a warm smile in return. "If all goes well, I will be free to come and go as I please very soon. And I hope it will be soon, for I must find another place for us to live."

Erik frowned in consternation, being fully aware of his part in her misfortunes.

"I am sorry, Madame Giry. More sorry than I can say."

"I know, dear boy, I know." She patted his arm kindly. I was surprised, but pleased, at how well she was handling being in such close proximity to Erik's unmasked face. She had only seen it for the first time last night. But it did not appear to bother her at all. Her affection for him overrode all other concerns, I was sure.

"I must go now, before I am missed." She embraced me hurriedly, and there was a mischievous little twinkle in her eyes as she did so. Then she pulled back, all business again. "If I learn anything of interest, I will send word or come myself if I can. But you ought not to stay in the city much longer. You run the risk of being seen by someone the longer you remain." This last was addressed to Erik.

After Celestine had cautiously taken her leave, I turned back to him apprehensively. "You can stay a few days more, can't you?" I asked, hoping I did not sound as desperate as I felt at the thought of his going.

He regarded me gravely. "Every day that I remain here puts you at risk too, Sylvie. But I think it would be safe for me to remain a few days perhaps. As long as no one learns that I am here. And if you still want me."

If I wanted him? Now that he was here, I could scarcely bear the thought of being parted from him. If it were not for the fact that he was in love with another, and would always be in love with her, I might have told him how I felt about him. But it was too soon, and there

249

was also the fact that I was *his cook*. He would feel sorry for me, indeed he would.

My face, always so revealing to him, gave away some of the turmoil of my secret thoughts.

"What is it, Sylvie?" Erik asked, looking stricken. "Do you wish me to go, is that it? You can tell me, I will understand." But even as he said the words, he looked hurt.

Seeking to reassure him, I spoke quickly.

"Of course I want you to stay, Erik. How could you think otherwise? For as long as you wish." *Stay forever. I will always want you.*

I breathed again when I saw the look of hurt vanish from his face.

CHAPTER TWENTY-ONE

'For all evils there are two remedies – time and silence.'
A.D.

*A*man had just arrived in the vast underground cavern that was until recently the secret lair of the most-wanted criminal in France. *Every inch of the cavernous space was brilliantly lit by torches that flickered all around, illuminating every dark corner, revealing every secret to his rapt gaze.*

He was a tall man, dressed in an elegant and expensive riding habit. *His tan breeches were tucked into knee high brown leather riding boots, and he wore a perfectly-tailored jacket. He hadn't been riding; he simply knew the form-fitting garments looked good on him. His russet-brown hair, touched with silver at the temples, was a little windblown. He was momentarily alone in the cavern, standing at the edge of the still pool of water. He looked about him with alert interest, fascination even. He flicked the end of a riding crop against his thigh absently as he did so.*

He thought of himself as a hunter, a predator-extraordinaire, *and he was here to study his prey.*

The Hunter walked from place to place, taking everything in. *He studied the intricately constructed model of the theatre stage far above, his arrested gaze taking in the fact that the little replica had been deliberately set on fire. Although partially burned, enough of the model was left to reveal its delicate beauty. His emotionless eyes rested briefly on several charcoal sketches of a young woman's face. He frowned slightly, puzzling over them, and then moved on. He ran his ungloved fingers across the dusty surface of the pipe organ, examined several sheets of music, removed the cork from a bottle of red wine and sniffed it thoughtfully. He observed that all the mirrors were lying in shattered shards. He took in the elaborate fabrics, and the baroque furniture, filing every detail away in his mind.*

Slowly he made his way to what he had been told was a bedroom, and he *entered it and looked about him interestedly. He picked up a peculiar music box, wound it and set it back down, listening as it played. The tune, though simple, was melancholy. While he listened, he lifted up a small brass dish and held it to his nose, inhaling the fragrance of incense. Moving further into the room, he discovered a tall wardrobe cabinet of the sort that costumes are shipped in and opened it expectantly, his fingers riffling over the clothing hanging inside. He noted that all*

251

the articles in the wardrobe were immaculate and well cared-for. Removing a charcoal grey tailcoat, he gave a cursory glance over the dark silk lining and saw what he expected to see: nothing. No label, nothing to identify the tailor who made it.

Replacing the coat, he examined the other garments carefully. They were all well-made, of excellent material, and something about them, their old-fashioned elegance perhaps, made him think they were from England rather than France. Bond Street, most likely. Resting his riding crop against the wardrobe, he extracted a cloth tape measure from his pocket and measured the breadth of the shoulders on the coat, and the length of a pair of black trousers. He measured the waist of a richly embroidered waistcoat, and the soles of a pair of black leather formal shoes resting on the floor of the wardrobe. The clothing belonged to a big man, probably as tall as himself, with wide shoulders and large feet.

Leaving the bedroom, the Hunter walked back down to a table near the water's edge and stood perusing its contents. There was not much to see: a sterling silver inkwell and a fountain pen, a piece of blotting paper, and a box containing the Phantom's particular style of correspondence paper: heavy, expensive, with a black border such as was often used when announcing a death. The ink in the well was red. He lifted the mosaic lid of a small brass box and peered inside; it contained only some pen nibs and a wad of sealing wax.

Then he saw the seal. He was particularly fascinated by it. Something about it amused him. He slipped it into his pocket, for he thought it would make a perfect souvenir once he had cracked the case. He liked to collect souvenirs.

The Hunter started to move away from the table, but suddenly he froze where he stood and looked down. His boot had crackled on something underfoot; there was a sheet of the heavy writing paper on the floor under the table. He bent and carefully picked it up between thumb and forefinger. He saw that it had been muddied and stepped on several times, but fortunately, the writing had been face-down and was still fairly legible. His cold eyes narrowed; someone would pay dearly for overlooking this note, he would see to that. It was a shame he had not been here when the Phantom's Lair was first breached, but at the time he was still above, trying to control the exodus of the terrified audience as they fled the fire in mad haste. But he was here now.

Holding the paper carefully by its corners, he read the few lines on the wrinkled page, absently stroking his neatly trimmed goatee with the other hand. The note was unfinished, but that was of no matter. His eyes glittered with satisfaction and he folded the paper carefully and placed it in the inside pocket of his jacket. A picture of his prey was beginning to form in his mind; he sensed he was beginning to understand the strange creature that had created this space, and set those ingenious traps along the way. A complicated being, with a multitude of interests and abilities; and, if he was not mistaken, an unexpected Achilles heel.

252

He would not make the mistake of underestimating this ugly, tormented beast again, indeed he would not.

Suddenly his attention was caught by the sound of oars in the water, and he glanced expectantly toward the portcullis opening. A boat was approaching with three men in it, and he watched as it landed gently at the water's edge and the men stepped out. Two of them were his own men, hand-picked and trained by him personally. The other, now looking around warily, was a middle-aged ticket-taker who had worked at the Opera House for about seven years. He seemed to think that the Phantom might still be lurking somewhere nearby. He was stout, with bushy eyebrows like furry caterpillars, and possessing the commoner's mistrust of authority and of policemen in general. Thus far he had been a decidedly unhelpful witness. But that was about to change.

One of his men steered the ticket-taker up to him by a firm hand on his shoulder. The Hunter's lips curled up, but the smile did not reach his eyes.

"Monsieur Dupuis, isn't it?" He asked pleasantly. His voice was soft, gentle, and unexpectedly warm.

"Oui, Monsieur." Replied the ticket-taker rather reluctantly.

"You may recollect that we met during my last investigation." In fact, when this beefy opera employee had been routinely questioned about events the night of the murder of Joseph Buquet, there had been something about him – a sixth sense told the Hunter that M. Dupuis was concealing something from him, and today he had been proved right. It was delightful how well pieces of the puzzle were beginning to fall into place. Now M. Dupuis was staring at him sullenly, determined not to cooperate in the slightest, due to his ingrained mistrust of the police. Ah well. Time to prove him correct about that. The Hunter exchanged a quick glance with his man, the one who still gripped M. Dupuis by the arm.

"You perhaps are not aware that today we conducted a very thorough search of your ticket counter, Monsieur. You will not be surprised to hear that we now know you have been keeping something from us." With a flourish, the Hunter pulled something from his pocket: a note, creased and worn, written in red ink. The ticket-taker blanched, and began to tremble. All his sullenness and bravado seemed to leach away.

"You recognize this, I see. Très bien. Now, M. Dupuis, I suggest you do your best to cooperate with me. I want a description of the lady who gave you this note."

The unfortunate M. Dupuis was caught between two evils, and after a moment's consideration, made the wrong choice.

"I cannot, Monsieur. Many ladies pass my counter before every performance. Hundreds, at least. I do not recall this particular one – it would be impossible, what you ask of me."

"But you know who wrote this note, don't you?" The Hunter inquired softly.

M. Dupuis licked his lips nervously. "The...the Ghost wrote it, Monsieur. It is his writing. I only kept it because of that. I didn't think it had anything to do with the murder, is why I never mentioned it."

It was the answer his questioner was expecting.

"I see. But you say you cannot remember anything about the young lady who gave it to you — how odd. I would have thought, under such unusual circumstances...perhaps we can think of a way to refresh your memory, Monsieur." He nodded to his men. *Instantly the ticket-taker was seized, and his hands tied behind his back.*

"What are you doing?" M. Dupuis exclaimed fearfully. *"I have done nothing wrong!"*

"That remains to be seen," was the suave reply. *Struggling uselessly, M. Dupuis was dragged to the edge of the still, green water. The Hunter watched impassively as he was forced to his knees.*

"Refresh him." He said, sounding slightly bored. *By a hard hand gripping the back of his neck, the unfortunate ticket-taker's head was pushed under the water and held there. Bubbles rose and broke the water's surface. Watching, the Hunter smiled, for in fact, he wasn't bored at all.*

Erik and I whiled away the rest of the afternoon perusing the day's newspapers, hoping to glean any information we could about the investigation of the fire and the murder. All the Paris papers were full of nothing but the events at the Opéra Populaire complete with luridly drawn sketches of the building with flames and smoke pouring out its windows. There was even an artist's rendition of Erik's home. It was obvious the artist had not been there. Corinthian columns would have been a bit much even for Erik. In a typical example of journalistic purple prose, the newspapers were referring to it as his 'lair'. The shocking kidnapping of Mlle. Daaé from the stage in front of a packed audience and under the very noses of the police, as well as her daring rescue by the dashing young Vicomte, was recounted in high dramatic style.

Although Erik had singlehandedly committed those dreadful crimes only the night before, reading about them in print caused him great (and well-deserved, I might add) discomfort. I felt certain that he could not have been in his right mind when he did those things, being maddened by jealousy and hate, but they were terrible crimes, nonetheless. Reading about them did not prove particularly helpful, however. Very little was revealed about the Prefecture's investigations, but at least no one appeared to have any idea where the mysterious Phantom might have gone when he fled. Later, we burned the papers ceremoniously in the fireplace.

That night, we ate dinner on trays before the fire: steaming bowls filled with the last of the *boeuf Bourguignon* I had made to distract myself the day before. It was clear from his obvious enjoyment of the meal that Erik had missed my cooking, if nothing else. We spent a quiet hour talking about Celestine and Meg, music and books, scrupulously avoiding references to anything more serious. We both felt need of a respite from the still too-recent horrors. I slept that night in my own bed and Erik in the *salon*, after I exacted a promise from him that he would still be there in the morning. For the first time since Erik had banished me from his life, my sleep was restful and untroubled by dreams.

Monday morning found the sky washed clean by the rain; it was a beautiful, cloudless blue, cold and clear. I was up early as usual, working in the kitchen, and so was Erik, at my insistence. I deemed it wise that he be kept occupied. And besides, while pondering our predicament the night before, I had an interesting idea.

While I browned small chunks of lamb, I put him to work helping me chop onions, potatoes and carrots for a hearty stew. Once I demonstrated the proper way to chop and how to hold his fingers so as not to cut himself, he proved to be a deft hand with a knife. I found myself trying not to look at those hands, because it was hard for me not to view them as metaphorically stained with the blood of innocents. I did not want to think of that now; rather, I was devoting myself to Erik's redemption, and how to achieve it. As I pondered the ramifications of my idea, it occurred to me that it might be just the thing.

As we worked together in easy companionship, Erik asked me about the hospital, what it was like, how long I had been working there. This was a perfect opening for me to broach my clever idea.

"You will be able to see for yourself, Erik. I am taking you with me today." I said matter-of-factly.

His hands froze mid-chop. "Sylvie, you know that would be impossible! How would I disguise my appearance?" He looked shocked that I even proposed such a scheme. "They would realize who I was." He added meaningfully.

As I stirred the pieces of lamb in the pan, I shot him a reassuring smile. "The fact is, you cannot remain here today. On Mondays my *domestique* comes in to clean while I am at the hospital. We will have to remove both you and anything that might indicate you have been here, at least for today. *En plus,*" pausing, I began lifting the lamb pieces into a large pot. Erik waited, resuming his chopping in silence.

"St. Giles is a very insulated place," I continued once all the lamb had been safely transferred. "They take no newspapers, nor do they take much interest in the outside world. They live much as you did, in a way: unknown to the outside world, and not wanting to know it." To this remark Erik made a sound which can only be reproduced as 'hmph'.

I splashed some red wine into the pan to deglaze it, saying as I did so,

"I am certain that no one at the hospital will even be aware that the Opera House burned two nights ago, and they certainly will not have heard of the Phantom of the Opera. I thought I would introduce you as my cousin from Rouen, visiting me for a while." Gesturing toward the pile of vegetables on the chopping board in front of Erik, I asked casually,

"Are you finished with those?"

Expressionlessly Erik helped me add the vegetables to the pot. It was impossible to tell what he was thinking. He set down the knife carefully and turned so he was facing me.

"Sylvie, look at me," he commanded, his voice bleak. Slowly I turned from my stirring to look up at him. With his right hand, he pointed at the lividly scarred side of his face.

"How do you plan to explain *this*?" He hissed, sounding vexed.

Gazing into those beautiful, soulful eyes momentarily took my breath away. It seemed to me that Erik's face was different somehow, since the fire – more open, less cold and reserved. The alteration, though subtle, was irresistible to me. I had to look away, back to the stove, in order to speak coherently. Naturally I had already thought of a reasonable explanation.

"Well," I said carefully, "I was thinking about that. You, my cousin, were badly burned in a fire when you were a child." Warming to my subject, I went on more confidently, "it was a terrible tragedy.

Possibly a pan of hot grease caught fire and tipped over on you. It was a miracle that you survived. We will say it was your mother's fault; it will serve her right." *The witch.* I looked up at him and smiled.

Erik, standing next to me, did something I had never seen him do before. He actually threw his head back and laughed out loud. Had I ever actually seen him laugh so freely? It was almost a little frightening. Suddenly he picked up the knife, thrust it point down into the chopping block so deeply I would never be able to pull it out, and gasped,

"The audacity! You are beyond belief!" But he was smiling back at me as he said it.

"Why? I think it is a good plan; you can help me. You will like it there, I believe. I certainly do."

"You think I will enjoy spending time among your lepers, do you?" To my relief, he sounded amused rather than annoyed.

"*Oui*, I do." I replied earnestly. It would be good for him to see and meet others who were carrying their own physical burdens, and doing so with grace and dignity. If he were to step onto the road to redemption, this was as good a place as any to take that first step.

"And you are certain they will not have heard that I am a wanted man, a fugitive?"

"*Oui, naturellement.* I would never think of suggesting it otherwise. Besides, I have always found the hospital to be, well, a kind of sanctuary really." I paused, considering thoughtfully. "It seems to me like a place not of this world. I find it very comforting, and I believe you will, too."

"Perhaps," Erik muttered, sounding unconvinced. "But are they not contagious, Sylvie?" He asked, arching an eyebrow at me.

This was a topic that I had some understanding of. I had, after all, heard this from Dr. Gaudet more than once.

"It was once thought that leprosy was very contagious, but it is not as bad as once thought, at least that is what Dr. Gaudet believes. By taking precautions, such as limiting contact, one can prevent contagion. Lepers are kept in enforced isolation mainly because so-called normal people do not like to look at them. It makes them uncomfortable." I spoke matter-of-factly, my eyes on the pot I was slowly stirring.

Erik was silent; my statement about the lepers was a shot across the bow, which was my intention. Then he shook his head in wonder.

"I suppose I should not be surprised by anything you do or say, but Sylvie, you take my breath away sometimes. *Très bien*, I will come with you today, but if I end up being caught and hanged just remember it will be your fault." He stood there looking down on me, hands on his hips, unconsciously handsome, full of confidence and looking slightly amused.

I had to keep my eyes on my work, for it was he who took *my* breath away.

"Excellent. I look forward to introducing you to Father Barbier."

"Who is this Dr. Gaudet?" He asked, frowning.

"He is in charge of the Hospital, and I can assure you, he spends a lot of time studying leprosy. You will meet him today. I think you will like him," I added, smiling.

Two hours later, everything was ready, and we were climbing into the wagon with Robert. We had scoured the apartment making sure no evidence remained of Erik's presence for my housekeeper to find, and made him reasonably presentable in the clean attire Celestine had delivered on the previous afternoon. Fortunately, she had had the foresight to include a black cloak with a hood. I could have kissed her for that. I was also going to have to procure him the means to shave very soon, for he was getting quite bristly. I decided that when we returned to the apartment I would visit the shops for a razor.

The taciturn Robert looked the unexpected guest up and down while I awkwardly performed the necessary introductions, then he gave an abbreviated nod of greeting and went on loading the wagon. He said not another word on the way to the hospital; in other words, he behaved exactly as he always did. Sitting behind Robert, the hood of the borrowed cloak throwing his face into shadow, Erik gave me a questioning look, and I responded with a shrug and a reassuring smile. Later I would have to explain about Robert and his general unfriendliness. I did not want Erik to take it personally, as I had done at first.

The trip to St. Giles seemed to take forever to me, but for Erik, it probably went by too quickly. As we crossed over the Pont

Royal Bridge and drew closer to our destination, I could see that he was growing increasingly apprehensive. He was not as confident as he preferred to appear, and he did not like it. Tension radiated from him. His hand, holding on to the side of the wagon, gripped it so hard the knuckles were white.

I knew he was dreading the encounters he was about to face. What thoughts must be swirling through his mind? I could imagine some of them — for this would be the first time in many years he had allowed strangers to look upon his face. He was accustomed to people turning from him in disgust or even fear. To hide had seemed the best, most natural course; it was self-preservation.

He was no longer in control of his life and destiny, no longer really in control of anything, this man who desperately needed to be always in control, of himself and of others. And he so disliked being dependent on anyone, for anything, even me. I reached for his free hand and took it in mine. After a second or two, his fingers tightened and his warm hand held mine firmly. He took a deep breath and squared his shoulders. Erik was brave, and he had placed himself in my care and protection. He *was* depending on me now, for good or ill, and I would not let him down.

"We are here," I said unnecessarily, for we had turned into the gates as I spoke. Erik released my hand and pushed back the hood of the cloak. He gave me a wry little smile, and my heart filled to bursting with pride. He had courage to spare.

Robert drove the wagon to the side entrance leading to the refectory and clambered out, groaning as though he were a hundred years old. I ignored his performance as I always did, and he began to unload the pots of lamb stew.

When I readied myself to jump down from the wagon, I was taken aback to find Erik already reaching up to catch me around the waist and lift me down. Once my feet were on the ground, I was even more surprised when he did not release me, but instead leaned in toward me, his eyes bright, his hands resting lightly on my waist. My heart sped up, my breath caught. Was he going to...? No, alas, he was not. His lips moved close to my ear, his warm breath fanned my neck, and he whispered,

"There is one thing we neglected to discuss. What is my name, *ma Cousine*?"

Collecting my scattered thoughts, I muttered,

"That is a very good question." I frowned worriedly; why hadn't we had thought of this before? There was no time to discuss it now. The refectory doors were thrown open; several nuns could be seen bustling about within, laying the long table for *déjeuner*. Robert disappeared inside, bearing a pot of lamb stew to the kitchen. Erik was still watching me and waiting for my answer. My boggled mind flew over the possibilities – no one knew the Phantom actually had a name except myself and Celestine. Even Erik claimed not to remember his own family name, so we would need to make one up.

"Erik. Your name is Erik…and since you are my cousin, hmmm, let me see. I have it! Erik Bessette!" I was whispering as well; we had only a few seconds alone now.

"Not brilliant, but at least it will be easy to remember," he said sarcastically. Releasing me, he turned to the wagon, picked up a basket of bread and followed Robert inside. I stared after him for a moment, my face hot with embarrassment. How could I possibly think he was going to…to kiss me? As much as I longed for Erik to have such feelings, he was never going to feel that way toward me; it was high time I pushed such romantic thoughts aside. It was difficult enough to be in such close proximity to him without indulging in hopeless fantasies that would only serve to make me feel worse. Giving myself a little mental shake, I followed Erik through the refectory doors.

Once inside, I immediately sought out Dr. Gaudet, who could always be found making sure all his charges were in their places at the long table for their noon meal. He gave me his usual warm, welcoming smile, oblivious to the fact that I was feeling decidedly nervous and guilty. Erik's words of this morning came back to haunt me: 'if I end up being hanged, it will be your fault.' I gave a slight shudder of apprehension. I wished he hadn't said that; it was too much like my nightmare for comfort.

Putting such negative thoughts out of my mind, I forced myself to give Dr. Gaudet an answering smile as he greeted me cheerfully.

"Good day, Mlle. Bessette."

"Hello, Doctor," I murmured, stepping close to him so that no one else could hear. "Er, I need to speak to you for a moment in private if you don't mind. I brought someone with me I would like you to meet." This was the worrisome part – introducing a complete stranger to St. Giles Leprosarium without any warning. The doctor would be within his rights to be very unhappy with me. It would go without saying that I was violating my oath of secrecy today, I thought guiltily. Dr. Gaudet's eyebrows shot up and his welcoming expression became a frown of consternation.

Before he could reply, I saw Erik coming out of the kitchen; his eyes swept the room until they found me, then he quickly strode to my side. There was no more time for my explanations now. One of the nuns who served the meal came to stand in the kitchen door, staring after him with a wide-eyed look of shock on her face.

Taking a deep breath, I took Erik by the arm and presented him.

"Doctor, this is my cousin, Erik Bessette. Erik, allow me to introduce you to Dr. Gaudet. He runs the hospital." I held my breath, watching the doctor's face. Surreptitiously, I gave Erik's arm a little squeeze and felt his muscles contract under my fingers.

Dr. Gaudet's sharp, well-trained eye scrutinized Erik for only the briefest of moments, then he turned his gaze back to me. Was it just my imagination, or was there a look of reproach in his eyes when he looked at me?

"*Bien sûr*, Mlle. Bessette. Let us step into my clinic. We can talk there." He turned at once and led the way across the refectory and out into the main corridor. We followed obediently, and I was conscious of nine pairs of eyes following us out of the room. I avoided meeting the patients' eyes, for I knew they all wore matching expressions of perplexity. There was no opportunity to greet Father Barbier, but he was watching us along with the others, his dark eyebrows drawn together. I hoped he would not be disappointed in me, too. As we passed out into the corridor, Erik looked down at me and raised his eyebrows inquiringly. I shrugged helplessly. I could only pray that my impetuous idea would not end in disaster.

But we were both in for a surprise. I was expecting to be reproached but once inside his clinic, Dr. Gaudet closed the door behind us, turned up the light and proceeded to scrutinize Erik's scarred face with rapt attention.

"Hmmm," he murmured. He did not ask permission to examine him, and I hoped Erik would not be offended.

Jumping into the silence, I said nervously,

"My cousin is here visiting from Rouen for a few days. He is staying with me, so, I hope you do not mind – he would like to help me while he is here. I have told him what I do and given him the oath of secrecy." I finished in a breathless rush.

"Yes, yes, of course," the doctor murmured abstractedly, still studying Erik's face as though it were some sort of treasure map.

Erik spoke for the first time. "No one will learn of the existence of your hospital from me, I can assure you." He must have

261

been uncomfortable under such intense regard, but he gave no indication of it. He held patiently still until Dr. Gaudet straightened at last.

Extracting his pince-nez from his nose, he stuffed them into a pocket and asked,

"What happened to your face, young man? I have never seen anything like it in all my years of practicing medicine."

Erik and I exchanged looks. It seemed that Dr. Gaudet's professional curiosity had won out over any concerns regarding my violation of the secrecy oath, but would our hastily contrived story convince him? We both started to speak at once.

"I was…"

"He was…" I stopped myself and, with a gracious gesture, allowed Erik to speak instead. After all, it was his face.

Erik looked Dr. Gaudet firmly in the eye. "I was injured in a cooking fire as a child. I received a bad burn on my face and almost died as a result of it." The lie was delivered so casually, so convincingly, I almost believed it myself. I ought to have expected that; after all, he had lied quite convincingly to me at least once.

"Ah, I see. It must have been extremely painful. What a tragedy for you. Well, well," Dr. Gaudet turned away, his impromptu examination finished. Now that he knew no strange, exotic disease was involved (as far as he knew at least!), his interest in Erik's face waned. I breathed a quiet sigh of relief. We were past the biggest hurdle.

A few minutes later, we were back in the kitchen, helping the nuns finish serving lamb stew and salad. The nuns cast a few nervous glances at Erik, for his strange appearance had startled them. They were not, thankfully, frightened of him, for they were long accustomed to viewing disfigured features.

Dr. Gaudet introduced Erik to everyone in the refectory as my cousin from Rouen, and explained that he would be accompanying me to the hospital during his stay. At first the patients did not seem to know where to look; they cast their gazes to the windows, the table, the ceiling. But gradually they found themselves looking at Erik, for they were drawn to him in spite of themselves. They were curious, and probably a little fascinated to see this disfigured stranger in their midst. But the nine leprosy patients did exactly as I had hoped they would: they looked beneath his ravaged visage to find the man beneath. Soon they regarded him with polite interest, showing no more concern than if his face had been perfectly normal.

Erik gradually relaxed under their acceptance of him, although I knew he had been expecting the worst. St. Giles had come through for me, and him, as I knew it would. It was most gratifying, for I intended he should come and help me every day as long as he was staying at my apartment, because it would do him good.

When the serving was finished and we had all partaken of the lamb stew, I helped myself a small glass of sweet wine from the kitchen and went to sit with Father Barbier, as I usually did once the mid-day meal was finished. It was still too cold to sit in the courtyard, so he was sitting by himself at one of the tables, reading. He seemed subdued today, not himself for some reason. He had taken no part in the conversation around the table, only watched and looked thoughtful. As I approached him, he folded up a piece of paper and tucked it into his book to mark his place. It was a collection of sermons, *naturellement.*

"How are you today, Father? Are you feeling all right?" I smiled at him as I seated myself next to him and adjusted my skirts around me, but I gave him a careful visual examination. He seemed well enough.

"I am fine, *ma chère*," he replied, setting his book aside. His kind eyes were thoughtful and a little sad. He was looking, not at me, but at Erik, who was at that moment listening to one of the missionaries engaged in telling him a story about his days in India, something to do with a large snake. Still not taking his eyes from Erik, he continued,

"But you must tell me about this cousin of yours. His visit was unexpected, was it not? I do not recall you mentioning it before."

Of course I had not mentioned it before, since it was a complete fabrication. More fabrications were necessary, apparently. I tried to keep my expression bland as I replied carefully to his probing question.

"It must have slipped my mind, Father. I hadn't thought of bringing him with me to the hospital but he was very interested and wanted to help. It is good for him to see others who have...physical afflictions...besides himself." This last part was true; thankfully I did not have to lie about everything.

Father Barbier continued to study Erik. His intent regard was beginning to make me uneasy. He turned at last to look at me with those bright, bird-like eyes.

"Did I understand correctly, that he was burned in a fire as a child?" I nodded. "What a grievous injury. Yet he seems to have borne it well."

I looked away from the old priest, back to Erik. His face was serene, kind even, as he listened, his eyes never leaving the ugly, pitted, leprous visage in front of him. I could barely repress a shudder of remembrance as I watched him; he had *not* borne it at all well, but falling in love had been the ruin of him, his complete undoing, the final injustice that robbed him of reason and sense. And yet there was such a sweet and good side to him. What might he have been like under other, kinder circumstances?

"Yes," I said firmly.

"Are you and your cousin very close, Sylvie?" Father Barbier asked, watching my face. I thought I knew why he was asking me all these questions – perhaps he felt a little paternal interest in my affairs.

I sighed, pondering that last question. *Not as close as I would like*, I thought. As I opened my mouth to answer with another lie, Erik suddenly turned and looked at me, just checking to see where I was. In the brief second that our eyes met, my heart seemed to jolt to a stop, my breath halted. It was like being hit with a bolt of lightning. Erik gave me a little smile and looked back to the missionary.

Dazed, eyes unfocused, my thoughts completely jumbled, I turned back to Father Barbier. "W- what did you say, Father?"

He gave me a melancholy little smile, but his eyes remained grave.

"Never mind, my dear. It was not important."

"Are you quite certain you are feeling well, Father?" I asked, worried. "You do not seem yourself today."

"Oh, *très bien, certainement*. Thank you for asking." Father Barbier seemed to make an effort to shake off his melancholy mood; he folded his hands together in his lap and regarded me with his usual cheerful expression. "Oh, by the way, did I tell you that Sister Chantal plans to dig up part of the courtyard for a new herb garden this spring? I believe she intends to consult you on the best varieties to plant." After that, our conversation turned to general things, and presently it was time to go.

After assuring Dr. Gaudet we would both return on the morrow, we assisted Robert to load his wagon with the empty pots and baskets and climbed in behind him. Robert complained liberally about his arthritis and was mercifully silent thereafter. As we drove out the iron gates Erik slipped the hood over his head and drew the folds close to shadow his face.

"That went well," I ventured presently, mindful that Robert, though a man of few words, could hear perfectly well.

"Yes. Thank you. I did not have the opportunity to speak with your Father Barbier though."

"Well, there is always *demain*. He seemed a little tired today."

We said no more until we arrived in the Rue de la Marché and saw Robert on his way. I made tea for us then and we sat quietly at my little kitchen table. (Later I was to learn that Erik disliked tea. His favorite beverage was the thick, sweet Turkish coffee he had been accustomed to drink when living in the east). I became aware that Erik was studying me intently. Coloring under his steady regard, I focused on carefully stirring a lump of sugar in my cup.

"It was an interesting day," he said finally. "For one thing, I learned that you have more compassion and goodness about you than anyone else in the city of Paris. It explains a great deal."

I was embarrassed by his compliment. "What do you mean, 'it explains a great deal'?" I glanced at him obliquely through my lashes, afraid to look him full in the face after what happened to me the last time.

Erik tilted his head to one side, regarding me thoughtfully.

"I was referring to the way you seemed to accept me so easily when I first unmasked for you. I cannot recall anyone else who did not mind looking at my face. It is the same with the lepers at the hospital. You behave as if they were perfectly normal-looking people. You have a very good heart, Sylvie, but of course I knew that already."

I was too flustered (and pleased) to speak. Presently he went on, unaware of my discomfiture.

"I enjoyed today much more than I had expected I would; in fact, I did not expect to enjoy it at all. I begin to understand why the hospital means so much to you. I would like to go back with you tomorrow, if I may."

"*Naturellement.* I intended that you should." I said pleasantly.

"Oh you did, did you? Have I no say in my own life any longer?" He was only pretending to be offended, I could tell because his eyes were warm. When he was really angry, they were like twin shards of ice.

I shrugged, and, giving him a determined look, said, "Well, I obviously couldn't drag you along with me if you refused to come, but it would certainly be better than staying here alone all day. You have had too much of that if you ask me."

"I did not ask you, but that never matters where you are concerned." He said, not sounding a bit cross, as he might have done at one time.

Finishing my tea, I rose and reached for my jacket and cloak, preparing to go out again. Erik eyed me curiously.

"Where are you off to now, Sylvie?"

"I am going down the street to the *apothicaire* to purchase a razor and some shaving soap for you. You cannot show yourself at the hospital again until you look a little more presentable."

He rubbed his bristly chin, producing a rasping noise.

"Is it really that bad? I have not looked in a mirror."

I regarded him gravely for a moment. "Yes, it really is that bad." And with that, I departed for the *apothicaire*, leaving Erik staring after me in consternation.

CHAPTER TWENTY-TWO

'Know you not that you are my sun by day, and my star by night?'

A.D.

What followed was a week I will never forget…five days that, in spite of the fact that danger lurked around every corner, were the happiest days I had spent in a very long time. During those halcyon days we talked of simple things: of the Hospital, of my childhood memories, of cooking, of music. It seemed we neither of us wanted to drag a dark cloud over this peaceful, safe haven. I clung to every precious moment we had together, mindful that everything could change in an instant. Only a few days after the fire, in fact, Erik talked of leaving, but he was easily dissuaded.

"I should go," he muttered one morning, staring balefully out the window. "The longer I remain here, the harder it will be for me to leave."

I had been gathering my cloak and gloves in preparation for our trip to the hospital, but I paused to stare at him, filled with dread.

"Do you *want* to go, Erik?" I asked, my voice scarcely a whisper.

Erik had turned to look at me, and his eyes were full of confusion and yearning.

"No, I do not. And that is the problem. I feel safe here, I feel almost…" he turned away abruptly and shook his head as though to clear it. My breath caught as I watched him. He was about to say *'happy'*, I knew. And it was a feeling he was not accustomed to. He must feel like a wolf in a trap.

Horrified at the thought of him leaving, I said anxiously,

"You are safe here. What harm can there be for you to remain a few days longer?" It was hard to keep a pleading sound out of my voice. How I wanted him to stay! I could have gone on like this forever if allowed to do so.

His shoulders relaxed, and he regarded me with a small smile. He seemed relieved by my request. It had not taken much to persuade him.

"*Trés bien*, I will stay a little longer. But we must be careful, Sylvie." And so he stayed, and together we played a little game of domesticity that was as fragile as a butterfly's wing, and soon to shatter.

Five days after the fire at the Opera House, a peaceful evening was unfolding in my apartment; calm before a storm, as we were soon to discover. Erik was seated at the pianoforte, engrossed in practicing on a composition of his own. The piece was a bit too *avant-garde* for my taste although I would never have admitted it to him. Meanwhile I worked doggedly on my embroidery, content to listen as he ran through various combinations of seemingly discordant notes. The footstool cover was almost finished, a good thing because I was getting well and truly sick of it.

Since his confession, and his recent experiences helping me at the Leprosarium, it seemed to me that Erik had begun to mend, to heal a little. He was growing more like the Erik I used to know: kinder, gentler. And now, his innate arrogance was tempered by a newly learned humility. He appeared calmer, more at peace with himself, even though sometimes I caught a haunted, sad expression cross his face, when I knew he must be thinking of those terrible events only recently passed. And, *bien entendu*, he would be thinking of *her*, his lost love, whose ring was always in his pocket, and whose lovely face would be enshrined in his heart forever.

During the past week we had fallen into a routine; it is amazing how only a few repetitions of the same activities can take on the comforting aspects of a routine. Comfort was something Erik was desperately in need of, and I was happy to give it to him. Each morning Erik, sleeping on the *divan*, would have already risen by the time I awoke and made a fire to warm the apartment. He was a light sleeper and did not seem to require as much sleep as ordinary people do.

The cup of *café au lait* without which I could not function would be steaming and ready when I emerged from my bed chamber, pulled irresistibly by the delicious aroma. I confess I enjoyed this helpful domestic assistance very much, being accustomed to always having to do everything for myself. And there was no denying that I enjoyed his company, far more than I should have. Since Erik no longer had any dark secrets to keep from me, he was much more open and willing to talk. He was quite unaccustomed to talking, however, and had no concept of idle chatter. When Erik said something, it was always from his heart.

After a light breakfast and our morning ablutions, taking turns in my small bath chamber, we could be found downstairs, cooking for the hospital. Well, I cooked, while he was my very efficient *sous chef*. We kept the curtains pulled closely so that passersby could not catch a glimpse into the kitchen and see two people working there. Thus far, none of my neighbors had any idea Erik was hiding in my apartment – we were always very careful coming and going with Robert, to make it appear as though Erik joined us from a different direction and was never seen entering or leaving my door. We dared not take a chance of arousing someone's suspicions about my mysterious lodger. It was fortunate that my closest neighbors were shopkeepers who did not reside over their shops the way I did. But there were times when Erik was forced to wait until the dark of night and then climb the plane tree to access my balcony, especially on Market Day Wednesday.

Mid-day and a good part of the afternoon were spent at St. Giles. Erik, while in the chapel admiring the stained glass windows one afternoon, discovered an old piano against one of the walls in the chapel. It was kept in tune because one of the nuns played it on Sundays and for some of the other services that were conducted there. Of course he could not resist it, and once the patients learned that Erik played so beautifully, he was called upon to play for them in the afternoons.

But I digress; to return to the events of my story, it was on this quiet, unremarkable evening five days on that doom fell upon us, in the form of the downstairs bell.

Erik ceased playing at the sound of its jangling, his head came up and our eyes met. A bubble of panic rose up inside me, making it suddenly hard to breathe. After a moment of wordless communication he arose from the bench, crossed the room and very quietly eased open the balcony door. Needless to say, I followed close behind him, heart pounding.

"Who…" I whispered, agitation making my voice raspy. Silently he slipped out onto the balcony, peered over the railing, and returned.

"It is only a foot messenger. I saw no one else." He murmured, gently closing the door.

"Who would be sending me a message at this hour of the night?" Dread descended over me, for surely it could not be good news delivered so urgently. Such things never happen.

"I'll go down and fetch it before he goes away." I said reluctantly, collecting a shawl and my coin purse as I spoke.

"I will come with you," said Erik, "in case it is a trap." That idea had not occurred to me; a trap hardly seemed likely, considering our efforts to keep his presence here a secret. But, I reminded myself, Celestine knew. We had not seen nor spoken to her since her visit to bring Erik his clothing, for we had all agreed it was best she stay away, and not bring attention upon us here. But, what if somehow...? Agitated now, I hastened down the stairs to open the door. Erik faded silently into shadow behind me.

But it was only a letter after all, not a trap. Relieved on this point at least, I sent the messenger on his way after dropping the requisite coin into his palm, and we hurried back to the *salon*. Pretending not to be curious, Erik returned to the pianoforte, but he was watching me out of the corner of his eye. The letter carried no return address. I tore it open, both reluctant and anxious to see what message it contained.

"Oh, it is from Celestine," I said, recognizing her familiar handwriting. Now I really was worried, for it seemed to confirm my fears. But such was not the case, and I ought not to have doubted my friend.

Erik looked up, watching me as I read, and so saw the blood drain from my face. He stood at once and came to me.

"What is it? What is wrong, Sylvie?" He asked worriedly. "You are as white as snow, do sit down."

Having achieved a state of full-blown panic in mere seconds, I could only stare at him in wild-eyed alarm.

"Sh-she writes to warn us. The police have somehow found me out. They will come looking for me soon – *Mon Dieu*, Erik, you must leave here at once! You are no longer safe!" My trembling hand plucked at his sleeve as I spoke.

"Found you out...what do you mean? *Comment*...let me see her letter." He pulled it carefully out of my frozen fingers. "Sit down this instant, Sylvie." He took me by the shoulder and pressed me firmly into a chair without taking his eyes off the letter. I sat, though I hardly knew what I did; my mind was in such tumult. Erik began reading while I watched his face.

"Box Five!" He exclaimed contritely. "So the ticket-taker remembered you, and described you to the police. Ah, that is my fault! When I sent you that note so there would be no difficulty, I never guessed that fool Dupuis would keep it! *Sacré*! Now she says the police are going to run an article in all the Paris newspapers, asking for information regarding a Mademoiselle Bessette." He lifted his head from the letter and looked down at me, a deep frown creasing between his eyes.

"I thought it odd, that night, the way people stared at me. The ushers kept looking at me and pointing, whispering to each other. I could not understand why." I said, remembering. "I thought there was something wrong with my dress or my *toilette*."

Erik shook his head. "No, I am sure there was nothing wanting in your person. It was a grievous error on my part, thanks to my own infernal sense of infallibility. I thought I could get away with anything, but of course it would be remarked on, since it was the first time I ever sent someone a ticket or permitted anyone to sit in my private box. And to include your name! The audacity! This is entirely my fault." He repeated with real remorse. "I owe Madame Giry a debt of gratitude. That she should still be watching out for me, after I could have been the cause of her or her daughter's demise!" He sank on to the *divan*, dropped the letter, and passed his hand over his face. Despair and self-hatred rang in every word.

I crossed to sit next to him and placed my hand gently on his shoulder.

"Celestine loves you very much, Erik. I believe she thinks of you as a younger brother, someone to be watched over indeed. She is a true friend. She has forgiven you, and someday you will make it all up to her, I know."

"I certainly can do nothing for her *tout de suite*," he said bitterly. "I am a wanted fugitive with a net closing around me. I must make sure it does not close around you as well, Sylvie. I need to think what to do." As he spoke he stood and began pacing across the small room, his expression troubled, like a wolf trapped in a too-small cage. I kept silent, leaving him to think. It was obvious to me what needed to happen, there was only one conclusion: he must leave, and soon.

Suddenly Erik's troubled expression cleared. He stopped in front of me, pulled me up to stand before him and looked down at me tenderly; I could scarcely breathe. Reaching up with one hand he gently brushed it across my cheek, and then dropped his arm back

271

down. My cheek seemed to sparkle, so alive did my skin feel from his warm touch.

"It is you I must think of now, Sylvie," he said, his voice low and contrite. "It was selfish of me to stay at all, endangering you every moment I have been here. I am very adept at selfishness, but now I need to learn how to put someone else's needs before my own." He reached for my cold hands and took them in his warm ones, gazing earnestly down at me.

"I have to leave here this very night, almost this instant, and you must take care that no trace of my presence remains anywhere in your apartment or in the kitchen. That should be a simple matter since I have almost nothing to my name now. Once your whereabouts are discovered, this place will be searched, I have no doubt."

Wretchedness washed over me until I scarcely comprehended the words coming from his lips. All that I could think of just then was this: the moment I had dreaded and pushed aside for five days was here at last. Tears sparkled in my eyes. I averted my face so I could blink them away. I had derived such quiet, peaceful joy from these five days, and such happiness from our time together. But I had always known his departure was inevitable, it had only been a matter of time. How was I to bear it?

Erik cupped his hand under my chin and turned me back to him, claiming my attention with his blazing blue gaze.

"Listen to me, Sylvie," he said urgently. "This is important. Tomorrow you will go to the Préfecture de Police and tell them you are the person they are searching for, the person who was in Box Five that night. Do not wait. You *must* do this tomorrow; if you do not, when they eventually find you it will appear as though you were hiding something."

"But I do have something to hide!" I wailed, unable to stop tears this time. But now I was crying out of fear.

Exasperation crossed his face. "Not as far as the police are concerned. I do not believe they will suspect you of any involvement with me if you go to them of your own free will. As it stands, the police *must* suspect a connection between us or they would not be looking for you, and you have to convince them otherwise. They may be grasping at straws, but we cannot take a chance. Being forthright may divert their suspicions away from you. Pay attention now." His fingers tightened on my chin, his eyes bored into mine.

"When they ask how you came by a ticket and a note from the Phantom to attend the Opera that night in Box Five, you will answer that you found it outside your door one morning. You might tell them it came with a flower attached. I suppose you will have to say it was a red rose, although…" he paused, grimacing slightly, then continued, "you have never heard of the Phantom, never seen him in your life. You cannot imagine why he favored you with the gift. However, lately you have felt as if you were being watched, perhaps followed. Do you see what I am getting at, Sylvie?" He released my chin and took me by the shoulders. His voice was urgent, willing me to comprehend.

When I did not immediately reply he went on in a frustrated voice, "I am trying, belatedly to be sure, to protect you. I owe you my life, and this is no way to repay you. I hate to leave like this, abandoning you to the mercies of the Paris *gendarmes*, but if you proclaim your innocence and that you have no knowledge of me, they can have no proof that we ever knew each other so everything should be well."

Struggling to understand, I said, "So you want me to make them think you…that you may have been…" but I could not continue.

"Stalking you, yes, exactly," he said, finishing my sentence for me. "They will think that I was hunting for another innocent girl to brutalize. It would be easy for them to believe." His voice was rough with self-loathing.

"But Erik, wh-where will you go? What will you do?" I asked, hearing the note of despair rising in my voice but unable to control it.

Almost angrily, Erik gave my shoulders a shake, hard enough to loosen my hair.

"Leave Paris, hide somewhere in the country – it doesn't matter – you must think of yourself now, not me! I am more worried about you than anything else at this moment. According to Madame Giry the newspaper article will appear in the morning editions. Promise me you will follow my instructions and go to the police tomorrow, without delay. *Promise*, Sylvie. Please, do as I ask this once, for my own peace of mind if nothing else."

How could I refuse his heartfelt plea, or resist his efforts to protect me?

"I will, Erik. I promise." I whispered.

"Thank you," he said fervently, releasing me from his grip. "I'm going to trust your word; do not let me down this time. *Mon Dieu*, I have to go." He ran his hand through his soft brown hair, tumbling a few locks over his forehead in his agitation. "If anything happens to you because of me, I will never forgive myself. I would take you with me if I had any idea where I was going or how I was going to get there, but it is too dangerous." He hastened into the bedroom, returning in the process of buttoning up his waistcoat, and tossed his tail coat over a chair. He handed me something; taking it automatically, I saw that it was the razor I had bought for him. I stared at it dumbly.

"Get rid of this somehow – I cannot take it with me." I could not respond; everything was happening so fast, my thoughts were in a whirl. I was thinking of so many things I yearned to say, I had to bite my lip to hold them inside.

"I'm going to have a look at the street before I go," he muttered, slipping out to the balcony. I watched him with a desperate intensity as he cautiously peered up and down the street, which was dark now except for golden circles of light where the lampposts stood. After a moment he came back inside and closed the doors, pulling the drapery closed. I was still staring at him; I could not seem to take my eyes away from him.

Turning to me, he said, "I don't know when or how or if we will see each other again, Sylvie, but I hope someday I will be able to thank you for everything you have done for me. I cannot believe I am repaying your friendship in such a way." He again ran a hand through his hair, as he did whenever he was upset about something. "There is nothing else of mine here, is there?" He asked, glancing around the room. Indeed there was, but only I knew of it. And it was high time I gave it up.

Silently, I went to the *divan* and sat down. He watched me, looking puzzled.

I reached behind a cushion, pushed my hand down behind the seat, and my fingers gripped Erik's mask, hidden there these five days. I had almost forgotten about it.

"Don't be angry with me, Erik." I said.

"Why on earth would I be angry with you, after all you have done for me?" Erik asked, sounding perplexed.

I tugged the white mask from its hiding place, holding it out to him.

"Because...I withheld this from you."

He gave a slight start at the sight of it. His lips parted, he drew a long breath but said nothing. Slowly he reached out and took the mask from my trembling hand. He stared at the stark white mask as though seeing it for the first time. Finally he spoke, almost in a whisper.

"How did you come by this, Sylvie?" He asked, sounding perplexed.

Reluctantly, I told him how Celestine had brought it when she came to my apartment the night of the fire, while he slept.

Erik turned his eyes from contemplation of his mask to my face. I could feel myself coloring.

"I am glad to have it back, it will probably prove useful now, but I do not understand why you never told me it was in your possession." He looked at me questioningly.

"Why were you concealing it from me, Sylvie? I could have worn it when I went to the hospital."

This was in all likelihood the last time I would ever see him; I knew I owed him complete honesty now as never before. I owed it to Erik, and to myself, to speak, to say the words I'd kept close to my heart and secret all this time. This was not the time to be a coward. I stood up, squared my shoulders and faced him.

"I have always preferred you without a mask, I thought you knew that," I said quietly. My voice shook only a little. "You never need to hide your face with me, you know. You never did need to. Both sides of your face are part of the same man; both sides are so very dear to me. And...and I love that man, Erik, with all my heart. I love *you*."

At last, at long last, the words were said; there could be no taking them back. If my heart were a compass, he would always be my north. There could be only one Erik. He was a man like no other (which was probably a good thing). As long as I lived, there would never be another man for me.

Upon hearing my sudden and completely unexpected confession, Erik froze in place, a look of profound shock and even distress crossing his face. His mouth fell open. I had seldom ever seen him so discomposed.

"What...what are you saying, Sylvie?" He asked at last, his voice low and ragged.

Sighing, I lifted his coat from the chair, stepped behind him and held it out by the collar so that he could slip his arms into it. He shrugged the coat on automatically before turning to look down at me, clearly still shocked, not quite comprehending. I grasped his lapels in my hands, looking up into his beautiful pale eyes. My own eyes sought to memorize every detail of that face – both sides of that face: those eyes, the cleft in his chin, his strong jaw, those soft, full lips. I lifted my hand to his cheek gently.

275

"Oh, Erik! You were not the only one in love with someone who did not love you in return. I know as well as you what that feels like. I cannot allow you to leave here tonight without knowing this, without knowing how I feel about you, how dear you are to me. If there is a chance we may never see each other again, I would regret it forever if I kept silent."

Erik put his hand over mine and pulled it away from his cheek. He did not seem to know what he was doing. "But...but..." he stuttered to a stop, a deep frown creasing between his eyes.

"*C'est vrai*, Erik," I murmured gently. "I do love you, in spite of all that I know of you, and your deeds. Ever since I first laid eyes upon you, you have haunted my dreams and all my waking thoughts." I raised my eyes to his again.

"*She* may not want you, but I do. I always have, and I always will. I told you I do not believe you are beyond redemption, and I still believe that. I could not love someone I believed was truly bad, you know. 'Whenever we find each other, in whatever place it may be, you will find me loving you as I love you today.'" Kitty's parting words to D'Artagnan, which I had committed to memory, could not be more appropriate now.

Unable to resist the urge to touch Erik again, I reached up a trembling hand to lift and push back the unruly lock of hair from his forehead. I would be in tears soon, I could tell, but I had one last thing to say.

"I know you cannot return my affection, and I do not expect it. But if you would do one thing for me, as a friend, for I hope we will always be friends, I would ask of you this one thing: that you do no more harm in this world. I want you to be a good man from this day forward, Erik, for my sake."

I rose up on tiptoe and kissed him on both cheeks, and then, as I'd dreamed of doing so many times, I kissed him, just once, very lightly, on the lips. I owed myself that at least, so I would have something to remember should I never see him again. Erik did not respond; it was like kissing someone who was asleep. He appeared to be in shock, incapable of speaking or acting. I released his lapels and stood back.

"Go now, Erik, *please*." I could feel myself coming undone. My throat burned with the effort to hold back tears.

Poor Erik looked positively dazed, as well he might, having just received my declaration of undying love for him. The love of a cook, I well knew, could carry little weight in comparison to the misguided

276

love he had fought like a demon for and lost. I pushed him toward the door. He slipped the mask into his coat pocket and reached for the knob. Pulling the door open, he paused on the threshold, turning to look back at me with a sad, lost look in his eyes.

"Why did you not tell me this before?" he asked softly.

I shook my head. "You would not have listened, we both know that. It would have made no difference to you before."

He acknowledged the truth of my words by briefly closing his eyes as though trying to shut out painful memories. We both knew what he was thinking of just then. All at once he stepped back toward me and quickly embraced me in a one-armed hug, holding my face pressed against his hard shoulder. I inhaled his wonderful spicy scent for the last time.

"I do not deserve someone as good as you, Sylvie, but you little deserve to love for naught. I am sorry. But I swear to you, I will do no more harm in this world. I can give you that much, though you deserve so much more. *Je suis votre ami à jamais.*" Words whispered in a voice tremulous with emotion, close to my ear. Then he released me so abruptly that I swayed and caught the doorframe for balance.

Clattering down the stairs without pause, he called back over his shoulder, "Do not forget your promise, and I will not forget mine!" And then he was gone. Dimly, I heard the slam of the door below.

I was alone, my body still feeling the warmth of that impetuous embrace. We had not, it suddenly occurred to me, actually said *adieu* to each other – was that an omen, for good or ill? For we French, '*adieu*' has a ring of finality to it, as though you will never meet again. I ran to the balcony doors and threw them open, flew out to the railing and peered down in to the darkened street. I felt myself leaning over it as if I would fly after him. Erik was already moving like a swift shadow on the sidewalk, away from me. Somehow he must have felt my presence: he paused and looked back, his face a pale oval in the darkness. His arm came up in a wave, and then he turned to vanish like smoke into the shadows.

"*Bonne chance*, Erik," I murmured, gazing at the empty place where he had just been. I stood transfixed, staring down at the street until I realized I was shivering from the cold. On a sigh, I sent a quiet plea into the night.

"Please," I whispered, "don't let this be the last time."

CHAPTER TWENTY-THREE

'I will do more than I promise.'

A.D.

I arose at dawn the next morning with my thoughts clear, my plans made, and the determination to carry them out. Last night I had wept until no tears were left. My grief was spent, my resolve firm. Today was for action.

For the first time in a week I made my own *café au lait* and stood watching as the sky grew pink with approaching dawn. When I glanced at myself in the mirror, my face was almost unrecognizable: my eyes were red and swollen, my complexion pale. Grimly, I turned away from my reflection and found myself wandering slowly from room to room, searching for someone who was no longer there.

My apartment felt so empty, and it seemed strange to be drinking my morning coffee alone, strange to find the grate cold, no cheery morning fire chasing the chill from the room. Strange what a difference five days can make in one's life. I had never felt lonely here before.

Morosely I made up the fire myself, and then went over each room in my apartment with meticulous care, reluctantly eradicating all evidence of Erik's presence. There was precious little, to be sure. I pulled open the top drawer of my nightstand and carefully lifted out a small box. It was an old cigar box of my father's I had kept for years as a trinket box. You could still smell, ever so faintly, the hint of fine tobacco lingering in the box even after all these years.

Now it contained all the notes I had received from Erik, starting with the very first one. Picking up that first letter Celestine had brought me, a reluctant smile tugged at my lips when I remembered how cold, businesslike and subtly threatening it had been. There were but a few notes in the box, and no time to sit and read them. I took the little box downstairs to the kitchen, wrapped it in a dish towel and nestled it deep in the midst of a large bag of flour in the larder. If by some unlikely chance the police actually searched my rooms, I doubted they would decide to grope through a bag of flour.

Returning to my bedroom, I pulled a wadded up bit of linen from the bottom drawer of my chest of drawers. When I felt the thin fabric in my hands, I did give way, but only briefly. I sank down on my bed and wept a little into Erik's white shirt – that dirty, sweat-and-

279

smoke-scented shirt he was wearing when I found him after the fire. After Celestine brought him a change of attire, I put that shirt away, thinking at the time I would wash it and give it back to him, then forgot all about it. This shirt, I thought as I held it tenderly in my hands, was the one he was wearing when he killed a man, almost killed another, kidnapped Christine Daaé and burned down the Opera House. And there was no way on earth I was going to part with it, for it was all I had left of him. I knew I was behaving idiotically, but I couldn't seem to help myself.

I dried my tears with the sleeve of the shirt, stood up and looked around me. I was not going to part with it, but it would be the end of me if that shirt were found here should my rooms be searched, as Erik seemed to think would happen. I had my doubts about that, I thought the possibility was rather farfetched, but it would not do to take a chance. And Erik had been so concerned about it. In the end, I wrapped the shirt up carefully into a small bundle and thrust it deep inside the pianoforte. As I did so, a picture formed in my mind of Erik seated there only the night before, but I shook off the memory briskly.

An inspection of the rest of the rooms took only a few moments, and I was satisfied no other incriminating evidence of him could be found here, not even an unwashed teacup. I dressed, went downstairs, slipped into my pinafore apron and began to cook. I have absolutely no recollection of what I made for the patients that day. I slipped the safety razor into my jacket pocket and, choosing a moment when Robert was looking the other way, tossed it into the Seine as we rattled across the Pont Royal Bridge. As we parted at the refectory door, I told him I would not require a return trip home today. I thought he would be pleased, but such was not the case. He asked no questions, merely stalked off looking offended.

Everyone at the Hospital probably wondered what was wrong with me. Several people inquired about Erik: why was he not accompanying me today? Had he returned to his home in Rouen? I explained rather perfunctorily to all who inquired that yes, my cousin had indeed been called back home unexpectedly on urgent business, but he did enjoy his visit to Paris very much.

Father Barbier was particularly curious, asking me several questions I was hard pressed to answer. Why did Erik abandon me on such short notice? Would he come back? Had he not found his visit to Paris and his fair cousin (me) to his liking? I am sorry to say I was rather short with my dear friend that day. On the other hand, it was gratifying to see that everyone at the hospital had taken to Erik so well, and that they missed him. I hoped to have the opportunity to tell him about it one day.

I did not lose sight of my mission and my duty, however, and I finished helping serve the meal as soon as I possibly could. Going to the police filled me with apprehension. I dreaded the task of fulfilling my promise to Erik, but I knew it would be better to get it over with. But as I slipped quietly out the refectory door, I felt someone touch my cloak, tugging at it a bit. I turned, and was dismayed but somehow not surprised to see Father Barbier. He had stuck close by me all afternoon.

"I am sorry, Father, but I must go. I…I have an appointment that cannot be delayed." I reached for the door handle as I spoke, to pull it closed behind me, but Father Barbier put his thickly bandaged hand out and pressed it against the door. I was so taken aback that I stopped and stared at him.

"I do not mean to detain you, *ma chère*, but I could not help but notice something was amiss with you today. Is something wrong?" He sounded apologetic, but his kind eyes were anxious. He was worried about me.

I felt hysterical laughter bubbling up in my throat, but I forced it back. Everything was wrong! Where would I start? But I could not give way now. Unable to speak, I shook my head. It took everything I had in me not to simply burst into tears.

Father Barbier's face grew perceptibly serious.

"Something is the matter, I can tell. Is it anything to do with…your cousin? Has he done anything…caused you any harm?" The question took me by surprise. Why would he ask such a thing? Gripping my baskets firmly, I spoke in Erik's defense from my heart and with considerable heat.

"Of course not! How could you think that? Father, please believe me, Erik is not…not a bad man. He is my cousin and I trust him…I love him, Father. I do not know what you are thinking but whatever it is, you are wrong, completely wrong!" I regretted my vehement tone instantly, and felt a flush of shame come to my cheeks.

The old priest dropped his hand from the door and stepped back. His face took on the sweet, kind expression I was accustomed to, and he smiled, I thought, rather sadly.

"That is all I needed to know, my dear. If you ever need someone to talk to, please remember I am here. *À demain*, and God bless you, my child."

For a few seconds, I thought I would surely give way, but I mastered my emotions somehow. I had to.

"*Merci*, Father," I whispered. "Good day to you." I wrenched open the refectory door and passed out of that peaceful, safe haven into the frosty air.

My destination, the offices of the Préfecture de Police, was also located on the Île de la Cité. However, it was too far to go on foot so once I had walked as far as the Boulevard des Invalides I flagged down a passing hansom. My hand went nervously to my skirt pocket, my fingers closed over the folded piece of paper inside cut from this morning's newspaper. The article had appeared just as Celestine warned us it would. The police were trying to find me. I was the only lead on the Phantom that they had thus far. Thank heavens I knew so few people, and that the Hospital received no newspapers. Otherwise, both Erik and I might have found ourselves in police custody by now.

The hansom driver left me off on the street before a newly constructed, modern and imposing sandstone building. It was several stories tall, with a very business-like façade. Bright flags and banners flapped in the afternoon breeze off the Seine. Uniformed policemen bustled in and out the doors. Beyond the ugly modern façade of the Préfecture building, the graceful gothic spires of Notre Dame Cathedral rose up in glory.

I stood for a long moment on the sidewalk looking up at the building, trying to muster my nerve for the performance I was about to give. It went against all my principles to lie, most especially knowing that my lie would serve to put the man I loved in an even worse light, if that were possible. But having given Erik my promise, I could not renege now. He wanted to protect me, and I wanted to protect him. This was the only way. Taking a deep breath, ignoring the hammering of my heart, I marched bravely up the steps and through the door of the Préfecture.

I found myself in a large foyer of darkly paneled wood. I introduced myself to a policeman sitting far above me; I could just barely see his head over the top of the very tall desk he sat behind. Mindful of my role, I kept my chin up, my face calm, and hopefully the correct amount of slightly perplexed curiosity showing on my open countenance. Producing the article from my pocket, I handed it to him through the iron grille across the front of his desk and explained my purpose in coming. Raised eyebrows and a piercing stare were the only indication the policeman gave that he was surprised to see me standing before him, but he recovered himself quickly and, after collecting some information about me, ushered me into a chilly waiting room. I declined his perfunctory but polite offer to fetch me a *café*, my stomach being too full of butterflies to allow any space for a beverage.

Looking around the long, wood-paneled room, I saw there was not only no source of heat, but only the meanest, most uncomfortable wooden benches to sit upon. There were a few recruiting posters on the walls, and framed lithographs of notorious criminals from days past. There was no one else in the room except myself, for which I was immensely grateful.

I was kept waiting for almost half an hour in that chilly antechamber, and the wait only served to increase my nervousness. Finally I was approached by a different uniformed policeman, younger than the first and as handsome as Adonis. He bid me follow and escorted me down several corridors, coming at last to a short, carpeted hallway. He stopped before a door at its end, and paused to straighten his uniform.

An elegant brass name plate on the door caught my eye immediately.

Victor Gaston, Principal-Inspecteur
La Sûreté Nationale

My fragile composure slipped a bit when I read that name. I was to be interviewed by the Chief-Inspector of the Sûreté, I realized with a sinking feeling. I had expected I would be giving my report to another policeman, someone in the Prefecture's Office. The Sûreté was another matter altogether – its reputation was shady at best. Separate from the ordinary police and operating independently, it was known to be an organization that achieved its goals by fair means or foul. Even as the policeman escorting me raised his hand to knock discreetly on the door, Celestine's voice came unbidden into my head. *'The Chief Inspector of the Sûreté himself was in charge of the search,'* she had said on the night of the fire.

Responding to a softly murmured reply from within, the handsome policeman opened the door, stepped aside, and motioned for me to enter. When our eyes met briefly I saw that his were completely expressionless, flat and almost reptilian. I took a deep breath and walked forward into the room, aware that my heart was beating faster than normal.

The door shut behind me with the gentle yet sinister snap of a trap closing, and I found myself alone with a man seated at a desk

283

made of dark, rich wood. The gleaming polished surface of the desk was empty except for a large flat envelope, of the sort documents were kept in, and a short plaited leather riding crop resting on the corner nearest its occupant. On the wall behind the desk was a large framed painting of a cheerful-looking, rather rotund man wearing the mutton-chop sideburns of a bygone era. It seemed incongruous in that sterile, businesslike setting.

But it was the man seated behind the desk who quickly claimed all my attention. He was in middle age, with reddish brown hair going grey at the temples and worn a little longer than was currently *en vogue*. A distinguished-looking, close-cropped goatee and mustache adorned his long face. There were deep lines running from nose to mouth; his lips were full and sensual. He might have been considered handsome. But it was his eyes that riveted my own to his face.

Under heavy, dark brows, a pair of cold, calculating grey eyes took me in, roving over me slowly, head to foot and back again, almost insolently. I felt chilled to my very core, frozen, unable to move or look away, rather like a bird being hypnotized by a snake.

He stared at me in this bold manner for a long moment, and then the corners of his full mouth turned up in a sly, secret little smile. His eyes released me at last, and, glancing toward an uncomfortable-looking wooden chair placed before his desk, he inclined his head slightly toward it. I was relieved to be free of that unnerving, insolent gaze, and drew my first breath since entering his office.

"Please sit down, Mademoiselle *Sylvie* Bessette." His voice was silky, almost seductive in its softness, yet carrying an undercurrent of menace. He placed an odd emphasis to my first name, and his teeth closed with a snap on my last. I stumbled forward to the chair and collapsed more than lowered myself into it; my knees were weak with a numbing fear. And I wasn't merely afraid; I was terrified. This man was no fool, and he radiated power and intelligence. My planned lie felt feeble and pathetic; he would never believe me. But I was trapped now and had no choice. There was no way on earth I was going to tell him the truth.

"Are you familiar with *la Sûreté Nationale*, Mademoiselle?" The Chief-Inspector asked, his silky voice sounding thoughtful, almost bored. But his eyes held mine again, and they were cold and watchful. I did not trust my voice, so I only nodded my head in assent. In fact I knew very little about *la Sûreté*, except what I'd occasionally read in the newspaper. I recollected that they were often criticized for their somewhat unconventional detecting methods.

284

"The word, loosely translated, means 'safety'. We toil in secret to ensure the continued safety of the citizens of Paris." He swiveled slightly in his high-backed chair and directed my attention to the rotund man in the painting behind him. "That is our founder, M. Vidocq. It is his principles we follow, and as you may have heard about us already..." he turned back to me and his voice suddenly changed, pitched lower and intense, his eyes boring into mine, "we are not afraid to use any means necessary to track down the criminals we want, and those whose actions place them *outside* society. Our methods are not always approved of, *certainement*, but we pride ourselves on our effectiveness. We always get our man," he paused, watching the effect his words had on me, "or, in this case, our...Phantom." He pronounced the last word slowly, almost caressingly.

I was waiting for this, expecting it even, and I held myself perfectly still, forced myself to gaze calmly back at him, not blinking, not blanching; in other words, trying my best not to look as if I possessed a guilty secret. I *must* convince M. Gaston that the Phantom meant nothing to me.

"*Oui*, Monsieur." I murmured. "That is also my understanding, and why I came here today." To my relief my voice, though lacking strength, at least held conviction and did not break or waver. I reminded myself sternly that there was no reason for him to doubt me or my story. I need only tell it to him and then I could go. And how I longed to be away from that room, and that penetrating stare!

M. Gaston regarded me thoughtfully for a few seconds, saying nothing. Then his long fingers picked up the envelope on his desk, opened it and removed a piece of paper, which he made a show of studying interestedly. I could see perfectly well that it was a copy of the newspaper article asking for information about me, the same article folded in the pocket of my skirt. I caught a brief glimpse of several other papers in the envelope before the flap fell shut: the one on top looked like a piece of Erik's own stationery, for I recognized the black edging.

I waited, saying nothing. Finally, he raised his eyes to my face.

"*Alors*," he said in his velvet-smooth voice, "you have come in response to this article, I understand. How very...*forthright* of you, Mlle. Bessette."

"Thank you," I murmured quietly. It was a supreme effort for me to keep my neatly gloved hands folded calmly in my lap, but I managed it somehow.

"Proceed, then," he said dismissively, with a languid wave of his hand. Picking up the riding crop, he turned slightly away from me in his chair and gazed into space, slapping the end of the crop gently in the palm of his hand.

"Monsieur?" I asked, frowning in sudden confusion. M. Gaston sighed, as though he were a teacher talking to a slow pupil.

"Proceed with your story, Mlle. Bessette, if you would be so kind."

I gaped at him, rendered momentarily speechless. He was behaving as if he did not really care. There was something very odd about his behavior. But then I thought of Erik, alone again, hiding who knew where, bereft and miserable, and my spine stiffened. I could do this – I *would* do this. I sat up straighter in the hard wooden chair and proceeded to tell him the story, *our* story. I embellished my narrative a little, since it was a bare-bones tale to begin with: walking home from my regular evening meal delivery to a shut-in (never mind who), it began to seem as if I were being followed, but whenever I glanced behind me, all I could see was a shadowy outline that quickly vanished into the night. This happened several times. And after that, I thought I saw someone peering through the lace curtains into my balcony windows, but when I investigated (M. Gaston here remarked how very brave I was), no one was there.

And finally, I told him about finding the ticket to the Opera, my presence in Box Five, and the corsage. I was able to tell him that tale in its entirety, omitting, of course, the part where Erik had sent me a note along with the ticket. The ticket, I explained, had simply appeared outside my door one morning. I took Erik's suggestion about mentioning the red rose, thinking it might add a touch of verisimilitude to my story, even though I did not comprehend its significance.

"I assumed," I lied earnestly, "that some anonymous benefactor was attempting to do me a kindness; I certainly did not connect the gift of an opera ticket with the person who may have been following me." And why should I not attend the Opera? There could be no danger to me in such a public place.

"After that," I explained, "no more strange occurrences took place, and I forgot all about them." If it really was this so-called Phantom who had been stalking me, after reading about the events at the Opera House in the newspapers, it could only be concluded that he had given up on me and turned his evil intentions on another (I really hated this part, it was such a betrayal, but it had to be said). Busy with my work, I spared no further thought to it until I saw the article in today's newspaper asking for information about me. And that was all. I spread my hands wide as I concluded my tale.

"I cannot imagine how it was that the police were able to obtain my name." I added with what I hoped was an air of innocent curiosity.

Just because my story was told, I dared not let down my guard, because M. Gaston would surely have questions for me; sharp, subtle questions designed to winnow information out of me that I did not want to impart. Imagine my surprise, therefore, when he simply closed up the envelope on his desk and shot me a wry little smile.

"*Merci*, Mlle. Bessette. That was very well-told. I think I understand everything now. You have confirmed my own deductions quite nicely."

While I sat staring blankly at him, he put down the riding crop and stood up, signaling that it was time for me to leave. I saw that he was a tall, well-built man. Gathering my scattered wits, I rose as well, and held out my hand to him.

"Thank you, Monsieur. I am glad to have been of help. I am only sorry I could tell you so little." I lied sincerely.

M. Gaston reached across his desk and enveloped my outstretched hand in his long-fingered one. But instead of shaking my hand as I had expected, he turned my hand palm up and, bending over it, pressed his full lips to the inside of my wrist, just above the edge of my white kid glove. He let his moist mouth linger there a second too long, branding my wrist with its heat, while his mocking eyes met mine over my hand. A thrill of pure terror flew up my spine. I dragged my hand out of his, staring at him in shock. He gave a soft chuckle; his cold grey eyes, suddenly predatory, sparkled brightly with enjoyment at my discomfiture.

"Good afternoon, Mlle. Bessette. It really has been a pleasure to meet you. We shall meet again, I expect. Someone will be waiting to show you out." I waited until the door closed behind me before wiping my damp wrist on my skirt with a shudder of disgust.

Night was falling by the time I finally returned to the Rue de la Marché. My kitchen still awaited its afternoon cleaning, and the rooms were cold and gloomy. Yet what a tremendous relief it was to bolt my door against the street and the outside world! Leaning against it, I let out a long, heartfelt sigh. It was over, and I was safe. My promise to Erik was fulfilled.

Glancing down, I saw that a letter had been dropped through the mail slot and was lying on the floor at my feet. Without much interest, I picked it up. It was a very business-like envelope, and I saw that it was from M. Blanc, our old family *notaire*. I could not imagine what he might be contacting me about, as our business was long concluded. As I made my way upstairs I hoped it was not a repeat of his addresses of the previous winter. Only think of what my life might now be like if I had accepted his proposal! I would never have met Erik, never had any knowledge of his existence far below the streets of Paris. The thought was insupportable.

As I perused the letter M. Blanc had written me, my astonishment grew. After a few perfunctory and polite inquiries about my health, he got directly to the point.

"Imagine my shock, Madame Bessette, upon seeing your name in today's newspaper in connection to a police inquiry into the tragic events at the Opéra Populaire. I waste no time, therefore, in writing to inform you of my intention to contact the police to assist them in their inquiry, as is my duty to the law. If you have already done so, please disregard. Additionally, I cannot but feel some *relief* that matters resolved themselves as they did last year, as I would not wish to be associated with someone about whom I was so badly mistaken as to their character. Yours, etc. etc."

Stifling a peculiar urge to laugh, I tore up the letter and tossed it on the grate.

Bringing with me a fresh candle and a box of matches, I unlocked the balcony doors and stepped outside. All along the street the gaslights were being lit, creating pools of warm light on the cobblestones. I kept a glass hurricane lamp on my little wrought iron table next to a pot of bright pink cyclamen that bloomed despite cold and snow. I went to it and lifted the tall glass chimney of the lamp, placed a candle on the dish and lit it, then replaced the chimney. I took one last look up and down the empty street before I stepped back inside and shut the doors against the nighttime chill, pulling the lace panels closed.

Anyone who happened to pass by on the street would be able to see the candlelight, but there was only one person in the world who would know what it meant. I knew the chances of it being seen by that individual were less than slim, but I did not care; a candle would burn on my balcony every night from this night forward, letting Erik know he was remembered, loved and anxiously awaited.

It was only when I slipped back into my *salon*, closed the doors and twitched the lace panels back into place that I noticed something was amiss.

There could be no mistaking it: my rooms had indeed been searched. All my things were in their places, but not *exactly* as they had been. The painting hung slightly askew, a little pillow on the *divan* was placed differently now. The hair on the back of my neck stood up. I found the same thing in my bedroom when I flew in there to check. The bed was just a little bit disheveled-looking, and when I looked in the top drawer of my dresser, my lingerie was not in the same order I had left it. Slowly I sank on to my bed, feeling sick and a little dizzy. While I had been detained so long at the Préfecture, while that dreadful M. Gaston had been listening to me tell him my story, someone was in my apartment conducting a very careful, very professional search of the premises. They had wasted no time. How had they got in? My door had been locked just as I had left it that morning. Erik had been right after all.

Suddenly I gave a great gasp and jumped to my feet. Dashing into the *salon* again, I went at once to the pianoforte. The little miniature of my mother rested in exactly the same place; the sheet music lay scattered across the instrument exactly as before. Moving everything aside, I hastily lifted the top of the pianoforte and looked inside, holding my breath until I saw the bundle was still there, tucked away right where I had left it. My pent breath came out in a long sigh of relief. If the thorough searcher were to have found Erik's shirt hidden there, my story would have unraveled completely.

Celestine and I met the next day for a *tête-à-tête* over afternoon coffee at a nearby *café*. It was a different one than the Opera House Café where we used to meet, because that establishment had been forced to close its doors when the Opera building burned down. I wanted to thank Celestine for her warning which had arrived just in time, and also to bring her *au courant* on events thus far. I was just apprehensive and suspicious enough since my rooms had been searched that I did not dare to confide anything to her in a written note. We sat inside the large baroque-style *café* since it was too cold to be outside, tucking ourselves away in a corner banquette behind a convenient potted palm.

"How are you and Meg settling in to your new rooms, Celestine?" I asked her after we gave our orders to the waiter and he had departed. She and her daughter had finally been given permission by the Police to leave the Opera House and find another place to live. A good thing, for the lower levels smelled of smoke and it was difficult to come and go. Many of the workers, students and dancers who had resided in the lower level dormitories were forced to relocate in haste. It was a difficult time for all concerned.

Celestine removed her hat and carefully patted her hair, which was braided and coiled into a neat bun atop her head. She shrugged.

"Well enough, I suppose. We actually have a little more space than we did before. I am only worried about how I am to pay for it. What with one thing and another, there has not been time to begin searching for another position. I have a little money saved, thanks to…but never mind that. Tell me what has happened, for I can see by your face something is wrong."

I glanced cautiously about us before I leaned across the table toward her.

"Celestine, I cannot thank you enough for sending me that note. I am convinced that Erik had a very narrow escape. But yesterday was a very strange day…" without further ado, I launched into my tale, pausing only when the waiter arrived to place two steaming cups of *café au lait* in front of us. Celestine, nibbling on a crisp *palmier*, listened raptly. When I had told her everything, she frowned at me in consternation.

"I do not trust that Chief-Inspector, Sylvie. There is something very sly about him. He has spent many hours investigating the opera house, he has been on every level, looked into every cupboard and box room. He was in the gho…I mean, Erik's Lair, for a very long time, and he also questioned me for a long time. He was very suspicious of me, and if it were not for the fact that I helped in the rescue of Mlle. Daaé, I think I would have been placed in police custody. I hope you will not need to have anything more to do with him." Her slight hesitation over Erik's name did not escape my notice – she still found it natural to refer to him as 'the Ghost', but she was trying to overcome it.

"I know what you mean; I did not like him at all. He made me feel very uncomfortable, although I cannot say exactly why. There was something decidedly odd about the way he looked at me." I repressed a slight shudder at the memory of my encounter with M. Gaston.

"But there is no reason why our paths should cross again. He seemed satisfied with my story; *en fait*, he appeared rather bored by it."

"I am relieved they were unable to find anything when they searched your rooms", she said feelingly. "Such a thing ought to be a violation of Parisian law, if you ask me. But I would not put anything past that horrid man, especially in these lawless times." I nodded my agreement with her. He had himself said the Sûreté would use any means necessary to capture their quarry: the Phantom. A few broken laws would mean little to a man like Gaston as long as his efforts were successful. Why could he not put his time to good use fighting the wicked Prussians rather than harassing helpless females?

Celestine took a sip of her coffee and then looked at me searchingly.

"Do you expect to hear from him at all, Sylvie? I can't help but wonder where he has gone..." her voice trailed off, and she looked pensive. I understood that the 'he' she was now referring to was not the Chief-Inspector.

I could not keep a note of sadness out of my voice when I answered her, for I felt so bereft with Erik gone.

"No, Celestine, I do not really expect it. He said, before he left...that he did not know when or if he would be in touch with me again. But I wanted to tell you...he was truly grateful for your help and loyalty. He comprehends, I believe, the enormity of what he has done, and how his actions have impacted you and all the others." Her face softened a little. She was transparently pleased that Erik expressed concern over her and Meg. It had meant so much to her when he apologized the day they met again in my kitchen.

"Celestine, what will happen to the Opera building, do you know?" I looked at her curiously. Although I had not actually seen it since the night of the fire, I knew it to be but a gutted ruin. "I wonder if they will tear it down."

Celestine shook her head dispiritedly. "It is a sad ending to such a fine place, Sylvie, and the building only ten years old. The main patron was the Vicomte de Chagny, and he has requested it be boarded up and fenced off for now to keep curiosity-seekers away. I do not know what will happen to it in the end." Glancing at me wryly, she added, "he certainly wants no more to do with it, and I cannot blame him, the poor boy. It is filled with bad memories for both him and Christine."

And others as well, I thought privately. Thinking it only polite to inquire, I asked, "and what of Mlle. Daaé and the Vicomte? Are they...are they well?" Although I knew everything regarding the ordeal they had gone through while they were being held by Erik in the cavern, I did not want to speak of it to Celestine. She did not know the details of that terrifying night, and I thought it best to maintain silence. Mlle. Daaé had apparently felt the same.

Celestine looked a little wistful. "Oh yes, the last I saw of Christine, she seemed fine. The young are very resilient, after all. She came to say *adieu* to me and Meg just two days ago – they were given permission by the Préfecture de Police to depart the city, and have gone to his estate in the north to be married. I expect they are married already. She will be happy with Monsieur Raoul, I daresay. He is very much in love with her."

I sipped my coffee and made no immediate reply. I had always suspected that Celestine harbored hopes that Christine would choose Erik. Celestine, loyal to him as she was, wished him to have whatever he desired, whether it was for the best or not. She was rather biased in that respect.

"Well," I said finally, "I am glad to hear they are all right after everything that has happened. I wish them happiness together."

Celestine looked at me shrewdly. "I am sure you do," she murmured.

I looked down quickly, so that she would not see the haunted expression in my own eyes. "It does not signify, Celestine. It is time we all moved on, and put the past behind us. If there is anything I can do to help you and Meg, I want you to tell me at once. You can start by having dinner with me tonight – my apartment feels so empty now." To my embarrassment, my voice caught as I spoke the last words.

"*Certainement, chèrie.* We would love that." She rested her hand over mine, her face full of maternal sympathy. Gently I disengaged my hand from hers and changed the subject. I did not want sympathy; it would only serve to make me wallow in my despair.

CHAPTER TWENTY-FOUR

'All human wisdom is summed up in two words – wait and hope'
A.D.

A week crawled by, and then part of another. Although I went about my duties as conscientiously as ever, time seemed to drag along hopelessly. I tried to keep busy at the hospital, though even that place of peace could not comfort me as it always had before. Now I kept envisioning Erik there, too. He had enjoyed it so much, been so patient and kind to everyone. I would not have guessed he had such kindness in him, considering the life he had led.

True to the vow I made for myself, every night I placed a fresh candle in the glass on my balcony and lit it. The last thing I did before I went to my bed was to check and make sure it still burned; by morning nothing remained of it but a dead stub and a puddle of hardened beeswax. As the days passed, I found that the ritual of the candle lighting brought me comfort. I would stand on the balcony and cast my eyes along the darkening street, where the shopkeepers, bundled against the cold, were hurrying home to warm hearths and their loved ones. Several times I thought I caught a glimpse of a vaguely familiar figure disappearing down the Rue de la Marché: a tall, wide figure in a long coat and wearing a black fur hat. But I could not place him, and never managed to catch a glimpse of his face.

I heard no more from the police or *la Sûreté*, so I allowed myself to relax on that account. I followed the investigation in the newspapers, scouring the pages daily for any news, but as day followed day and there was no new information, no suspect apprehended, the papers and the public gradually lost interest in the fire at the Opéra Populaire. There were many more important things happening on the world stage and the tragedy at the Opera House was quickly eclipsed. I had been worried for nothing; the police accepted my story – why shouldn't they? No doubt by now they had forgotten all about me.

But all the while, a net was drawing ever closer around me, and finally, without warning, I found myself caught in it.

One afternoon almost two weeks after my interview at the Préfecture de Police, when Robert delivered me back to the Rue de la Marché after the dinner service, I was surprised to find my kitchen door unlocked.

"How odd," I murmured, more to myself than to the taciturn Robert. "I must have forgotten to lock it when we left." I shook my head ruefully; it would not be the first time in recent days that I had forgotten to do something. Robert looked at me sidelong but said nothing; he brought the large pots in for me as usual while I carried in the baskets and platters, and then took his leave with a touch of his ancient plaid cap – his way of saying goodbye.

I was relieved to be alone again; it was exhausting to pretend that everything was fine while I was around the patients and Dr. Gaudet. I leaned against the closed door, allowed my face to relax into its normal, gloomy expression and slowly mounted the stairs to my *salon* to make a cup of tea. But when I reached the top of the stairs, I was taken aback to see the door standing wide open. I was absolutely certain I hadn't left it that way. What on earth...?

There was a tall man dressed in black standing on the carpet with his back to the doorway, holding an envelope casually in one hand. For one brief, thrilling instant, I thought Erik had come back. But then the figure turned to face me - my heart stopped and my breath came in a shocked gasp - it was M. Gaston, the Chief-Inspector!

Suddenly I felt myself roughly grasped from behind, my arms pulled behind my back with brutal force. Someone was trying to bind my hands together, I realized in a burst of terror. M. Gaston watched impassively, strangely making no move to stop what was happening. I shrieked and struggled automatically against my attacker, and the unseen man holding my arms wrenched them tighter. The pain caused me to cry out loud. The Chief-Inspector looked mildly exasperated. What was wrong with him? Why was he not helping me? Staring desperately at him, I opened my mouth intending to demand his assistance, but before I could speak his cold eyes flicked above and behind me. He was looking at the man who held me.

"Shut her up," he said, sounding bored.

I felt a sudden, blindingly sharp pain on my temple, saw a brilliant flash of light, and then I descended into black nothingness.

Sometime later, I awoke to find myself in utter darkness. I recalled everything that had just happened to me between one heartbeat and the next. It was the profound darkness that was so disorienting. I had to blink several times to assure myself that my eyes were open. It was as if I had been struck blind, and perhaps, I thought in mounting panic, I really had been.

I immediately tried to sit up and bring my hands to my eyes when this terrifying thought came to me, but found that I could not move. Pain knifed through my arms and shoulders and I realized in rising panic that my arms were bound tightly at the wrists above my head – but to what? Where was I? Forcing myself to concentrate on my surroundings, I determined that I was lying on my back on a rough surface; a bed perhaps, or more likely a cot. It was very hard and uncomfortable. My hands were tied with some sort of cloth to the bed frame, but my legs, *Dieu merci*, had been left free.

I forced myself to lie quietly in the blackness, tried to calm my breathing and swallow the dreadful panic that kept bubbling up inside me, making me want to scream. Slowly I became aware of feeling pain in places I had never felt pain before: my temple and one side of my forehead hurt and throbbed; my head ached fiercely. My arms, shoulders, wrists, even my back and neck ached. I surmised I must have been handled like a sack of potatoes during the time I was unconscious. I was also terribly thirsty; my mouth felt dry and dusty.

I wondered how long I had been gone from my apartment, for this most certainly was *not* my apartment. One thing was absolutely certain: I was here because of the Chief-Inspector. He was the last thing I could remember seeing before I was struck unconscious. I knew to a certainty that I was now at the mercy of the one man in all of Paris that I was most afraid of. My insides churned with cold, sickening fear. Why? Why was I here? There was only one conclusion to be reached, and I reached it fairly rapidly under the circumstances: I was here because of Erik. The only connection between myself and Chief-Inspector Gaston *was* Erik.

Having no other senses available to me, I listened, trying to identify my surroundings in this way. It was also a way to help myself stay calm. It felt damp in this place, although not particularly cold, and so dark – like a dungeon, I thought fearfully. It smelled of old, mildewed stone. I hoped and prayed it did not contain any rats. All was perfectly silent; the only sound was the rustling of the lumpy mattress when I struggled or moved.

It would have been so easy to become hysterical. It was really tempting to give myself over to a bout of terrified tears, but I forced myself to remain calm. The thought of tears running down the sides of my face and being unable to wipe them away was almost as bad as the sickening fear rising up in my throat. Swallowing hard, taking deep breaths, I tried to think of a way to keep my mind off my desperate situation, so I passed the time by counting. I had reached three thousand and six when I heard the first sound; it seemed quite loud after the interminable silence. It was the metallic clang of a bolt being pulled back. I froze, trying to determine where the sound came from.

Suddenly, a long rectangle of light appeared high up in the wall on the far right side of the room. The light seemed as brilliant as sunshine after so long in darkness. It illuminated an ancient-looking, worn flight of stone steps down into the room where I was being held. There was no handrail of any kind, just the mean steps against a rough stone wall. A figure abruptly filled the doorway with shadow. He held an oil lamp in one hand. It was, of course, M. Gaston, the Chief-Inspector. The sight of him filled me with dread.

After lying in complete darkness for so long, the light cast by the oil lamp he carried almost blinded me. I blinked rapidly, trying to see. It was a relief to know I wasn't blind, but fear made the reassurance I felt less than it might otherwise have been. I saw M. Gaston's head turn toward where I was lying, and his eyes found mine. A slow, satisfied smile spread across his face. Descending the steps with loose, easy grace, he came to stand near my cot. Holding the lamp up, he studied me for a moment in an unemotional way, as if I were a specimen under a microscope. Finally he turned and rested the lamp as well as another object I was unable to make out, on a small table next to my cot. Coming to sit next to me on the cot, M. Gaston smiled his chilling, sly smile. It was a smile I would soon come to detest with all my heart.

"We meet again, Sylvie." He said softly. "I told you we would, *vous savez*. I hope you do not mind me calling you Sylvie, it is such a pretty name and I feel that I know you quite well already." His voice was as suave and silky as I remembered, only now, without even a veneer of civilization to it, it sounded like pure evil to me. I had never been more terrified in my life. I wanted desperately to move away from him, but I could not. Even though I knew pulling at the bindings on my wrists would do no good, I could not stop myself from doing it anyway, to no avail. He watched my efforts, looking amused. I tried to speak, but my mouth was so dry with thirst and terror, no sound came out.

"I apologize for leaving you in such uncomfortable surroundings, but I am here to make you…more comfortable." He then proceeded to leer at me, taking his time, looking me up and down even more insolently than he had when I first stood in his office. But this was so much worse: I was at his mercy here, completely in his power.

"I must say, you do possess an exquisite figure, Sylvie, and I am certain I have not been the *first* to admire it." Something about the way he said this sent warning bells ringing in my head, but I had other things to worry about right now.

Gaston lifted his hand and reached toward me; I cringed back against the bed, gasping. I had never felt so helpless in my entire life. He smiled, looking thoroughly pleased by my reaction. Placing his hand flat on my stomach, he very slowly let it glide up my body, between my breasts. His hand paused; a tremor ran through me and I stopped breathing.

"Mmmm," he murmured, and then his hand continued on above my head and took hold of the cloth strip that was wrapped around my wrists, securing me to the bed frame. A small, wicked-looking knife flashed in his other hand, and suddenly my hands were free.

Instantly I rolled away and sat up, my back against the rough stone of the wall behind me, my body curled in on itself. My numb hands and fingers began to tingle ferociously as blood flowed back in to them. Bits of dirty cloth were still wrapped around my wrists, and I began peeling them away, while staring at Gaston like a frightened rabbit might watch the wolf circling around it.

The knife vanished as quickly as it had appeared. Reaching over to the table, he picked up the object he had placed there. It was a clear glass bottle and the water inside sparkled like topaz and diamonds in the lamplight, reminding me of how thirsty I was. My eyes left Gaston to fasten themselves eagerly on the bottle, but I did not move.
He held the water bottle out to me, waggling it a bit as though handing a treat to a dog.

"This will make you feel much better, Sylvie." He said coaxingly.

As desperately as I wanted that water, I was afraid to take it. I shook my head, my dry lips closed tight.

"It is not drugged, if that is what you are afraid of," said Gaston, sounding slightly exasperated. "I have had ample opportunity to ravish you, my dear, drugged or not, if I wished. When you get to know me better, you will understand that when I decide to ravish you, I want you to be fully awake and aware of everything that is happening to you." He paused, studying my face, waiting for a reaction. My eyes felt as big as dinner plates, my heart was thumping like a drum in my chest, but aside from that, I had still said not one word. The silence dragged on. Finally he shrugged carelessly.

"It is tempting, very tempting, but I think I will save that treat for another time and surprise you. Anticipation extends the pleasure." He set the bottle down next to my huddled form.

Fluidly, he rose and stood next to the cot, his tall frame looming over me. Picking up the oil lamp, he held it out for a moment so that it illuminated the room. It was small, scarcely larger than a root cellar, with a beaten earth floor and ancient-looking stone walls that were dark and damp. One corner contained a set of porcelain bathroom essentials, ugly, old and stained, with not even a curtain to divide them from the rest of the room. Gaston curled his lip slightly when he looked at them.

"I apologize for the lack of amenities, Sylvie my dear, but I am not accustomed to detaining ladies here. I will of course see that you are furnished with the means of ablution."

Unable to contain myself any longer, I snatched up the water bottle, took out the stopper and allowed myself a small sip, just enough to wet my dry, dusty mouth. When I spoke, my voice sounded cracked and old.

"Wh-where am I?" I asked unoriginally.

He answered readily enough. "Somewhere known only to myself, a place where no one will ever look for you. You may as well resign yourself to being my guest for a while." He looked at me and gave me another of those wicked smiles. "By the way, do not waste your energy in calling for help, because no one can hear you. But do not worry, I will be back soon. Then we can have another little chat. *À bientôt.*" I felt a shiver run through me at the threat implicit in his voice. Taking the lamp, and the light, with him, he mounted the stone steps to the door standing open at the top.

I wanted to beg him not to leave me in the suffocating dark again, but I hated to beg him for anything – he would enjoy that, I was certain. He was already revealing a nasty sadistic streak and I suspected it would only get worse if I showed fear or weakness. Gaston stepped through the door and closed it behind him, leaving me in absolute blackness. I heard the sound of a bolt being shot home, the metallic snick of a lock closing.

I realized my hands were still clenched around the water bottle. Lifting it to my lips, I drank deeply, not stopping until the bottle was empty. I sincerely hoped the water was not drugged, but by now I was too thirsty to care. Once my thirst was satisfied, I spent a few minutes reassuring myself that I had *not* yet been 'ravished', as he had put it. Other than the aching lump on my temple and very sore arms, nothing else seemed to be the matter. Relieved on that score, I rolled to the edge of the cot, swung my feet to the floor, and stood up.

My temple throbbed ferociously, but my legs held, and I did not swoon. I'd glimpsed enough of my prison by the light of the oil lamp to know roughly where everything was, so in the darkness I began to pace the space. Eight steps brought me to the stone stair; I crawled up the rough surface on hands and knees, pulled myself carefully to my feet at the top and ran my hands over the door. The wood was smooth; there was no knob or handle on the inside, nothing I could take hold of. The door fit snugly into the frame, allowing no light to seep under it. It opened to the inside, and on those narrow stairs, there was no possibility of concealing myself behind the door when it opened again. I gathered from what Gaston had said that I was not the first person to be imprisoned in this dank, horrid place. Even though I knew it was an exercise in futility, I pulled and pushed against the door with all my strength. After a few fruitless attempts I stopped and listened with my ear pressed to the door. Not a sound could be heard from the other side. Slowly, I dropped back to hands and knees and crawled down to the bottom step, where I sat quietly in the dark, filled with despair.

And where was I? Where was this place? I wondered if it could be located under the Préfecture de Police building. It did not seem like that kind of building, being quite modern, but a cellar like this might have existed on the site long before the Préfecture was constructed. There were many ancient structures hidden away beneath modern buildings in the city of Paris. The catacombs, for example. Unpleasant thoughts drifted through my head, of piles of skulls and rats scuttling in dark, damp places, and the fact that a secret room like this one, where no one could hear you scream, would make a perfect torture chamber.

I was not even aware that I was crying until my hand came up automatically to wipe the tears off my cheeks. I wondered where Erik was now. Wherever he might be at this moment, he was my only hope. If he would only come back to my apartment, he surely would see that something was amiss with me. Would he search for me? Slowly, I folded my arms across my knees and rested my head on them. A wretched little sob escaped me. How on earth would Erik even begin to know where to look, since he would have absolutely no idea what had happened or who had taken me? I could scarcely even hope he *would* come back. My hopes for rescue, such as they were, hung on a very thin thread indeed – so many questions, so many 'ifs'.

I was still sitting on the bottom step when the sound of the lock releasing and the bolt shooting back startled me and I leapt to my feet, turning to look up at the door as it swung open. Warm light filled the rectangle, outlining Gaston's tall frame as he stood once again in the doorway, holding the lamp. Instinctively, I backed away.

He glided down the stairs into the room, followed by another man, whose subservient posture clearly identified him as a servant. He was older, short and stout, and one of his eyes was all white, giving him an eerie appearance. He carried a washbowl and jug, and a towel over one arm. Under Gaston's watchful eye, his servant deposited these things on the table next to my cot, and immediately departed without so much as a glance at me, even though I was standing only a few feet away from him. The door closed behind him with a solid thud, leaving me alone with my enemy. He was watching me, his grey eyes gleaming in the light of his lamp.

Gaston set down the lamp and walked purposefully toward me, eyes bright with anticipation. I backed away from him until my legs hit the cot. They gave way under me and I sat down abruptly. My breathing was coming shallow and fast, and he laughed softly, pleased at the effect he was having. I never in my life had ever felt hate toward anyone – it simply is not in my nature – but I felt hate surge through me now, like a searing, boiling flame that swept away fear. My own words, spoken in another context entirely, came back to me unbidden: *I would never want you to kill someone because of me. I could never ask such a thing of you, nor wish you to ever harm someone on my behalf.* I knew in my heart that if Erik were suddenly to be here, I would rejoice to see him kill Gaston for me.

Coming to stand next to me, Gaston's hand shot out and caught my chin in a hard grip, causing me to gasp; he forced my head slightly to the side, toward him, and he made a show of studying the bump on my temple by the light of his lamp.

"Hmmm," he purred softly in a voice like warm honey. "That bruise does not become you, Sylvie my dear. I do regret the necessity for that, but we could not be seen carrying a struggling young woman out of her apartment, now could we? People might talk." He squeezed my chin in his hand until tears of pain filled my eyes before finally releasing me. I was certain my chin bore the red marks of his

300

hard fingers. I wanted to rub it, but I put my hands together in my lap instead. I would not give him the satisfaction.

Forcing myself to meet his amused grey eyes, I asked, "Why am I being held here? What is this about?"

Gaston seated himself casually on the cot next to me; I scooted myself as far away from him as possible, which was not far enough. He half-turned toward me, extended his hand out and began slowly to stroke up and down the length of my arm as he spoke. His eyes were lingering on my chest, and I struggled mightily to keep from breathing too hard.

"Such a charming figure...." he murmured. "But you were asking me why I am holding you prisoner, weren't you?" To my enormous relief, he abruptly ceased ogling me, crossed one leg over the other in a relaxed manner, and dropped his hand away from my arm.

"I find your company very pleasant, *bien sûr*, but your primary usefulness to me is as bait. I am hoping to catch a very big fish, and you are my lovely lure."

I stared at him, worried and wary. I knew the fish he was after, but how could he imagine that I was valuable enough to Erik to furnish the bait to catch him with? It seemed to me Gaston would have been better served by kidnapping Mlle. Daaé, not me. I would have told him so, but I could not afford to stop playing my role; to do otherwise would be tantamount to admitting I had lied to him. All this flashed across my mind in a brief instant; hopefully he did not notice my hesitation.

"I have not the pleasure of understanding you, Monsieur." I said as haughtily as I could manage under the circumstances.

Gaston laughed rather heartily at this. "*Au contraire*, my dear, I think you do. I think you understand me perfectly well. As it's highly unlikely that you will survive our pleasant little interlude here, I don't mind telling you of my plans."

I was shocked, I confess, when he so casually mentioned my impending demise. But what other outcome could there be? If I lived, I would inform the police about him and his nefarious deeds, and he could not risk being found out. No matter if he succeeded in capturing Erik or not, I was doomed.

"When your lover learns that I hold you in my power, he will act to save you, I am sure. If he does not do exactly as I instruct him, I will leave him a little reminder that I really do mean business. As an incentive for him to cooperate with me, you understand." As he spoke, Gaston grasped my hand in his and lifted it up to his face. I tried to pull it away, but I could not break his grip. Helplessly I watched with mounting disgust as he kissed my palm, and then each finger in turn, his full, moist lips lingering on each. Then with his other hand, he circled his fingers around my little finger and held it tightly.

"This one, I think. He will recognize it, *certainement*, for it has a little scar just so. The eyes of love miss nothing."

Gasping in horrified understanding, I found the strength to yank my hand out of his grasp, wiping it on my skirt.

"Let me go! I have no lover. That is the truth."

Gaston gave a wicked little smile, exactly like the one he had given me when I first walked into his office at the Préfecture de Police. A sly, knowing smile.

"I am not telling you a lie!" I said vehemently. "It is impossible, believe me." My voice rang with the truth of my words, and it *was* true, painfully true. Erik did not love *me*.

Gaston shrugged, unmoved. "Ah well, we shall see, shan't we, Sylvie. But these things take time. We shall have ample opportunity to enjoy each other's company in the meanwhile." He made the words sound like a whispered caress. I shuddered, praying he would not touch me again.

Standing, Gaston looked down at me. "I will see that my servant brings you food later. Do not attempt to talk to him or impede him in any way. He won't respond in any case, but if you disobey me, I *will* punish you, in a way that I will enjoy, but you most certainly would not." He moved to the little table, took something from his pocket and set it down, then picked up the lamp.

Indicating the table he said, "You will find I am not altogether unkind, my dear. Here is a candle to light the darkness. Use it well." With that, he departed, trotting briskly up the stone steps and leaving me in darkness once more.

I did not light the candle. Instead, too frightened and desperate to do anything else, I curled up into a tight ball on my side on the hard cot and wept in the darkness. Eventually, unbelievably, I cried myself out and fell asleep. The weight of all that had happened to me had become, perhaps, too much to bear, and my mind sought refuge in sleep. And I dreamed of Erik.

It was only a brief dream, and in it I was a disembodied spirit floating through the night, observing him without his knowledge. He was standing in a dark street somewhere in the city. He was wearing his mask, and he had a hat pulled low over that side of his face, casting it in shadow. As I floated along, watching him, he moved cautiously, gliding along the pavement, keeping to the shadows, looking around him. It seemed as though he was searching for something; he stopped once or twice to study the walls of the old stone buildings carefully. I wondered what he was looking for there. After a moment he stepped into the glow cast by a streetlamp and when his face turned toward the light, I saw it clearly. He looked exhausted and desperately worried. Longing to comfort him and ask him what he was searching for so urgently, I drifted closer and called his name. My voice came out as barely a whisper, but as if he could hear me, his head whipped around and he looked about him alertly. Emboldened by his reaction, I summoned the strength to speak again.

"Help me, Erik, please help me," my dream voice whispered.

Miraculously, he heard my heartfelt plea. "I am trying, Sylvie," he answered, his voice catching on the words. "Where in hell are you?" I was attempting to float closer to Erik when I woke with a start and the dream dissolved.

Uncurling myself stiffly from my sleeping position, I sat up in the blackness and pressed my hand to my wildly pounding heart. It was bursting with joy and hope – it was me he was searching for! He *had* come back and my heart told me it was true. The dream was real - Erik was here, in Paris. If I could only hold on long enough, he was going to find me. If only he could somehow manage it before Gaston decided it was time to cut off my little finger. And before he decided to dispose of me altogether. How much time did I have?

Rising from my uncomfortable cot, I stumbled to the little table and groped blindly for the candle and matches Gaston had left there. After several tries, I finally managed to light it. I fixed it to the table with a drop of hot wax, finished the last drop of water, and began pacing.

Back and forth, back and forth across the hard earth floor, from one wall to the other, I paced. I was aware of being very hungry, and my temple throbbed where I had been struck, but it was impossible to sit still. As I walked, I studied my prison carefully, trying to memorize everything for when I would be in the dark again. My idea of it being a perfect torture chamber was not, I observed with dismay, far off the mark: on one wall, rusted metal manacles hung from the stone, just at the height where a man might stand. I was thankful I had only been tied to the cot – probably due to the fact that my stature was too short to reach the manacles.

Slowly, as I paced, I forced myself to empty my mind of all thoughts except one: Erik. I concentrated on conjuring up the image of his face the last time I looked at him, the night he fled my apartment. I remembered what it felt like to kiss his warm, unresponsive lips, remembered his brief, hard embrace in the doorway. I bent all my thought toward him, willing him to find me. I had somehow formed the idea that by concentrating my thoughts on him, I could draw him to me, and then he would save my life. Although it seemed an impossible task, I reminded myself that Erik was no ordinary man, he was an extraordinary one. Who knew that fact better than I?

I lost track of how long I paced back and forth across my dark prison; perhaps an hour, perhaps longer. I stopped in my tracks when I heard the door being unlocked, and stared at it, my heart filled with dread. But it was not Gaston returning to torment me further, it was the silent servant framed in the door when it was pushed open. He simply stepped through, came down the stairs a short way, set down a small tray, and left again without a word or a glance in my direction. Remembering Gaston's threat, I refrained from addressing his servant. I did not want to even consider of what his idea of a suitable punishment would be.

As soon as the door closed, I flew up the steps to see what they had given me to eat, for by now I was quite hungry. I didn't get my hopes up; Gaston would take diabolical pleasure in watching me slowly starve to death, *sans doute*. But on the tray I found a piece of bread torn from the end of a loaf, some cheese, and a rather withered-looking apple. A little bubble of hysterical laughter forced itself from my lips as a sudden vision appeared in my mind of the many trays of warm, delicious, fragrant meals I had delivered to Erik. But I was so hungry now that I didn't care; I sat on the step and devoured everything ravenously. It was not chicken tagine, but at least it was sustenance. Afterward, I availed myself of the wash water, soap and towel to bathe my face, neck and hands, and then I resumed my pacing.

Even after the candle burned down and went out, leaving me in the dark again, I carried on pacing. It was fourteen steps from one wall to the other; I counted each one and then turned. It was a meditative act, as well as a way to keep up my stamina. I whiled away the lonely hours trying to recall every single detail of every meal I had ever prepared for Erik. Even though it only served to increase my hunger, it did help the time pass and seemed to bring him closer to me somehow. Sometimes I slept, fitfully, but dreamed no more. I measured time by the number of trays of food I received. The food was all variations on a theme: plain bread, cold meat or cheese, tired fruit. How I longed for a comforting cup of tea! I would have cut out my own tongue before asking Gaston to give me tea, or anything for that matter.

It was three trays of food before Gaston honored me with another visit – perhaps another day (or another night?). When he came down the stairs he seemed amused about something.

"Ah, Sylvie, how are you this evening? I am sorry to have been away so long, but it is necessary for me to keep up appearances, *vous savez*. I've been working today. I've missed our little chats, as I am sure you have."

While he was speaking, he walked right up to where I stood, rigid and wary, next to my cot. The light from his lamp was so bright I had to shield my eyes, for I had been in the dark, having used up all but a stub of my last candle. As he approached me I briefly debated with myself about trying to knock him over the head with the water jug, but without the element of surprise I decided it would serve only to anger him, so I refrained. Gaston stopped uncomfortably close to me, but I stood my ground.

"I was thinking today," he continued in a conversational tone, "that I would like to see you with your hair down." He raised his hands to my hair and began searching with his long fingers for the pins holding my bedraggled chignon in place. I had been trying my best to keep it tidy but without a mirror or comb, it was a hopeless task. He let each pin drop to the floor. I tried to move away from him, but he caught my forearm in a grip of iron and, holding me in place next to him, went on removing pins with his free hand. Then he ran his hand through my hair, pulling it out of the chignon and arranging it down my back. Slowly he stroked over my hair as though he were petting a cat. My skin crawled at his every touch.

"Your hair is like silk, and so lovely, a river of gold. You know, I really cannot wait for your Phantom to turn himself in to me. I so look forward to the opportunity to tell him all about your stay here with me, in exquisite detail. But I confess I hope he will not do it too soon, because it would spoil my entertainment. There are so many pleasures left untasted...."

He abruptly seized the nape of my neck with the hand that had been stroking my hair, so that I was unable to move my head. I gasped in shock; slowly he inclined his head toward me. I felt his hot breath and then his lips crawl across my cheek, moving toward my mouth. I could not stand it if he actually kissed me; to have those lips touch mine was more than I could bear. I could not help myself: I sucked in a great gasp of air and screamed at the top of my lungs! At the same time, my free hand came up and I sank my nails into the hand that gripped my arm.

Uttering a foul oath, Gaston released me instantly and shoved me away from him. I fell hard against the little table, caught myself, and sank down into a sitting position between cot and table, my back to the wall, utterly terrified. He loomed over me, cursing furiously, while holding one hand over his ear. My piercing shriek had, apparently, hurt. I did not know if I should be happy or sorry that I hurt him. I curled myself up tightly, my arms wrapped around my knees, and stared at him, panting. Eventually he calmed down, but not before calling me a variety of ugly, unrepeatable names and kicking me once.

Finally, running out of invective and breath, he sank down on the cot and looked at me, breathing agitatedly. Huddled on the floor, my back against the wall, my breath coming in little terrified gasps, I waited in some trepidation for the punishment that was surely about to come. I did not think I could bear it if he actually made good on his threat to...*no*, it was too horrible to contemplate.

But Gaston straightened his cravat, ran a hand over his hair to smooth it, and said,

"You distracted me from what I wanted to tell you, you stupid girl. You will never guess who came to the Préfecture today to report you missing." He gave me a sly, secretly-amused look. My thoughts flew to Celestine – could it have been she?

"I cannot imagine," I said, my fear-weakened voice barely above a whisper.

"No guesses? How dull you are, my dear. Oh very well. It was your employer, one Dr. Philippe Gaudet. He was quite concerned about you. It was touching."

I could feel my eyes go round as saucers as I stared at Gaston. Had Dr. Gaudet said anything about my 'cousin from Rouen'? I sincerely hoped not. Erik had, as far as the hospital was concerned, gone back home almost two weeks ago.

"Oh," was all I said in reply. I realized with some shock that since my capture and imprisonment I had not thought even once about the hospital, but of course they would have been the first ones to discover my absence and attempt to find out why I was not in my kitchen, preparing their meals.

Gaston shifted position on the cot, crossing one leg over the other. "*Oui*," he went on cheerfully. His brief but terrifying burst of temper had subsided completely and now he was enjoying his story.

"And it was rather amusing really, that he came to report you missing, I mean. Because you are not actually missing at all, just...misplaced. The police took the report and passed it along to me since they know you are connected with my investigation. I was pleased to assure Dr. Gaudet that every means at my disposal would be used to locate you." He looked at me smugly. So this was the source of his amusement: Dr. Gaudet's innocent concern over my disappearance.

I regarded him steadily. "But there *is* no connection. And I assure you, there is no reason why you should expect the...the person you are searching for to come back to look for *me*. I...I was nothing to him. I wish I could make you believe me; I cannot understand why you should think such a thing."

Gaston gave me a patronizing little smile and shook his head, as though I were a sulky, disagreeable child.

"Only time will tell if I am right, but I have not arrived where I am today without being willing to exhaust every means to achieve my goals. Sacrifices have to be made sometimes for the greater good. If this ploy fails, I shall devise another." He rose from the cot and I automatically stiffened, but he merely picked up his lamp and moved away toward the stone steps.

Pausing, he added, "Only a few more days now, I think. You must be patient, Sylvie. If nothing has transpired by that time, well then, I will have to see about detaching that little reminder for your Phantom."

It was some time after he left before I was able to get up from the floor and sit down on the cot. I was thinking about what Gaston had said, especially the part about sacrifices having to be made. My life was the sacrifice; I would lose my life whether or not his little gambit succeeded. But not, I was sure, before he took as much enjoyment as possible in tormenting me.

Somehow or other, his plan was apparently to communicate with Erik – by what means I could not imagine – an ad placed in *Le Monde*, perhaps? Besides, he could not know whether or not Erik was in Paris, or even still in France. How could he think otherwise? It was a mystery to me, but he seemed quite certain on that count. My vehement denials of any connection between us made no difference to him whatsoever. Did Gaston really think that Erik was going to march into the Préfecture de Police and turn himself in just because I was being held somewhere? I would be sadly disappointed in him if he were to do such a thing. And even if he did, it would not be enough to save me.

I tried not to lose my courage, but there were times during those long, dark hours that I was filled with such despair! Gaston came nearly every day for one of his 'little chats' with me, but, to my enormous relief, he made no more attempts to touch me. I began to suspect that it had never been his intention to 'ravish' me, as he put it. Like the sadist he was, he took pleasure in the effect of his threats on me, up until the point when I had screamed loudly in his ear.

However, he continued to take great enjoyment in relaxing on my cot and telling me lurid tales of his past exploits, usually after enjoying a few glasses of liquor somewhere above my cellar, apparently a *salon* of some sort, for I could smell liquor on his breath sometimes. Tales of torture, of beatings, of unfortunate 'accidents', all in the name of *la Sûreté Nationale* – for Gaston always got his man. Horrible stories that I will not attempt to recount here. As he talked, his eyes would glow and sparkle; his face would flush with pride. The more disgusted I became, the more he seemed to enjoy relating his exploits to me. Erik's tales of his past deeds paled in comparison to Gaston's wickedness.

It was the stuff of nightmares, and I had my share of those. The rest of the time I was left alone, and when I was not sleeping, I paced my small cell and bent all my thought toward Erik. If I died here, I wanted my last thought to be of him. I did not want to die in this damp, dark dungeon, but it was beginning to seem inevitable.

Then one day (I say 'day' but of course I do not really know), Gaston arrived for his daily visit in a state of perturbation. He seemed displeased about something; a frown creased his forehead and his grey eyes were distant. He did not linger as he usually did, and made no move to approach me, but instead addressed me in a brisk, businesslike manner from the bottom of the steps.

"I came to let you know that I have set our deadline. In two days time I will be attending to that little matter of your finger. I will see to it personally, *naturellement*. I am rather looking forward to it. I wanted to tell you right away so that you would have ample time to anticipate it as well." I was resting on the cot, but I had sat up abruptly when he entered. So his plan had not borne fruit yet; he was preparing

308

to send Erik that little incentive. I shuddered. Knowing Gaston as I now knew him, he would do his best to ensure I suffered as much pain as possible in the process. Already mounting the steps toward the door, he looked back down at me, his grey eyes hardening.

"If that does not suffice to bring him to his knees before me, I regret to inform you, Sylvie, that it will be necessary for us to part company at last. You know what I mean."

Staring at him wide-eyed with fear, I heard myself whisper, "You are a monster."

Gaston pulled his lips back in an ugly smile that did not reach his eyes. "You brought this on yourself when you chose to consort with a wanted criminal," he said coldly. Then, giving me a mocking little salute, he opened the door, slipped through, and pulled it closed behind him, leaving me in the dark once more. I heard the bolt slide into place, and my breath released in a long sigh.

Hands shaking, I lit the stub of a candle I had been hoarding and sat studying my hands by its light. They were work-worn hands, with little knife scars here and there. It is difficult to have soft, pretty hands when one works with them every day. I never gave much thought to my hands or my fingers before. How many heavy pots of water had I lifted up to the stove, how much time had I spent scrubbing cooking residue from that same stove? How many knife cuts had I accidentally given myself? These were not the hands of a pretty, spoiled lady, but they were dependable hands, nevertheless. Hands that I had always taken for granted. Two days, and I would lose a finger; a few more days and I would lose my life.

Thinking about that harsh reality as I sat on the side of my hard cot, I wondered if, when I was dead, I would be able to see my mother again. Was there truly a heaven, as Father Barbier believed?

If such a place existed, my mother would surely be there, but I could no longer be confident of my own admission to that hallowed place. Gaston was right, if he but knew. I had, after all, willingly and knowingly aided and abetted a criminal, not once, but several times. And if I had to do it all over again, I would do the same.

CHAPTER TWENTY-FIVE

'What a terrible noise he made with his sword! One might have said that twenty men, or rather twenty mad devils, were fighting'
A.D.

I lost any sense of the passing days. Since no glimmer of daylight or starlight could pierce my hellish prison, time had ceased to have any meaning for me. I could not even be sure how long I had been held prisoner here, for I had given up trying to keep track. At least a week, I guessed, but it could have been longer. And by now I wasn't sure how much it mattered. My entire existence was reduced to those moments when the door at the top of the steps would open, a rectangle of light would appear, and that evil silken voice would return to torture me again. And time was running out for me. I knew it would not be long before Gaston would make good on all his threats.

Mounting terror made it difficult for me to sleep, but even so my every waking moment passed in the same way: I paced from one side of the cellar to the other by the faint glow of my one candle or in the blackness. I never ceased to think of Erik, willing him to find me, praying more and more desperately that he was out there somewhere, looking for me. Would he find me before it was too late?

Gaston had explained with great relish that if Erik did not find me before one more day passed, he would enact my punishment. Gaston was not bluffing, of this I was certain. Having put his plan into motion, he would see it through. And I could not bear to think of Erik actually turning himself in, putting himself at the mercy of that horrible man. At least if I had to die, I could do it knowing Erik still lived, and was free. I prayed he would never learn what had become of me because of him.

As I paced I listened with considerable trepidation for any sounds to indicate my tormenter was returning. I did not put it past him to decide not to wait another day to cut off my little finger; he was looking forward to it so. I never would have believed, before meeting Victor Gaston, that such a wicked man could possibly exist, much less be placed in charge of anything as important as *la Sûreté Nationale*. And I never could have imagined how sharp one's hearing grows when it is the only sense one has left.

I ceased my endless pacing when I heard the sound of a door opening somewhere above, a signal that Gaston was returning to his *salon*. It must be evening. With my sharpened sense of hearing I easily caught the murmur of his low, silky voice, the guttural sound of the one-eyed servant responding, and presently the pleasant smell of smoke drifted down to me. The fire was lit in the *salon* above. I thought of the warm fire longingly, picturing the cheery flames dancing, the snap and crackle. I was certain Gaston had the fire lit there every evening just to add an extra element to my torture. A door closed, which meant the servant had departed and Gaston was alone in his *salon*.

I knew what would soon come: after a glass or two of liquor he would be ready to pay me his nightly visit. I wished yet again that I had some way of hiding behind the door so I could bash Gaston's head in with the water jug. In my imagination I must have seen myself doing so at least a thousand times. But there was no hiding place on that narrow stair. Hate and fear left an acrid taste in my mouth. But at least, I told myself, he was not going to cut off my finger tonight. He was apparently going to save that treat for tomorrow after all.

Suddenly I froze in place, startled by a muffled banging noise from the *salon* above that I could not identify. I was afraid, I suppose, that the noise must herald some new evil directed at me. It was followed almost instantly by the sound of a chair being abruptly pushed back, scraping across the floor and then falling over with a thud. I held my breath, straining to hear what was happening above me. Gaston stuttered out an oath which I could not hear, then, louder, began,

"You! *Mon Dieu*! How did you..." His furious shout was abruptly cut off by a ferocious, feral snarl.

"Where is she? What have you done with her?"

I recognized that voice, as I stood frozen on the dirt floor of my prison; oh yes, I recognized that voice, even when it was distorted and thick with rage. It made my heart sing and beat until I thought it must burst from my chest. My pulse beat so hard I could feel it in my hands. Intense relief made me almost faint for a moment; I closed my eyes and drew a deep, steadying breath. And then, though I was in complete darkness, I ran sure-footed up the worn stone steps and flung myself against the locked door, pounding on it with my fists.

"Erik, I'm here!" I cried, my voice breaking into a sob. "I'm in here!"

311

"Sylvie!" His answering cry sounded almost weak with relief. "Thank God I found you!"

I heard the ring of steel as a sword was drawn – whose? I pounded on the door again in frustration; I needed to see!

"Get back, you bastard, or I'll have your liver for supper!" Erik growled, sounding closer now. And then I heard him try the door. Oh, he was *there*, right on the other side of the door!

"Give me the key!"

"You don't imagine I have it on me, do you?" Gaston replied suavely. Liar! Of course he had the key! But before I could say as much, he continued, "I admit I did not expect you to make an appearance here, but you will not find me unprepared for your company. I have been looking forward to meeting you, *Monsieur le Fantôme*."

"Oh, believe me, I have been looking forward to coming face-to-face with you as well." He did sound quite pleased, enthusiastic even. Then Erik called a command through the door to me. "Get away from the door, Sylvie."

"*Oui*, Erik." I hastened to comply, flying back down the stairs. Erik had no need of a key. The ancient wooden door quivered with the force of a resounding kick from his booted foot; a second kick caused the door to give way with a loud rending sound, then it slammed against the wall. I was glad I had not been standing there. Erik was not in the doorway as I had expected; he had already spun swiftly back to face his enemy.

On fire with the urgent need to *see* him, to know he was really there, I climbed the stairs again until I reached the doorway, my hand gripping the doorframe to steady myself. Blinking in the glow of gaslight, I stumbled at last from my prison. My eyes sought for Erik. He was standing with his back to me, facing Gaston, sword drawn, and I saw that Gaston held a sword as well. One of a matched set on the wall near the fireplace was missing.

Erik threw a quick glance over his shoulder to me, unable and unwilling to take his eyes off his opponent, and gestured brusquely with his free hand toward the wall.

"Stay back against the wall," he commanded in a take-no-prisoners voice. I nodded; I found it was impossible to speak just then. My mouth felt dry as dust. *À propos*, I noticed Erik was wearing his mask, just as he had been in my dream.

Our eyes met, and then he focused on me harder. I knew he was taking in my disheveled appearance, my streaming hair and dirty

312

gown. His eyes rose to my temple, where I knew I still had a lump and very likely a bruise. His face suffused with dark blood, he was suddenly livid with fury. If I thought he had been angry before…he whirled back to Gaston.

"She has been struck! Damn you, you bastard, you struck her!" Erik shouted furiously. His opponent was circling him delicately, a sneer curling his lip.

"It was necessary to subdue her. She insisted on struggling and I couldn't have that. Such an inconvenience, you know." He managed to sound just slightly amused at the memory.

Erik spoke to me in a low, quivering voice that was only barely under control.

"Sylvie, has he harmed you other than that blow?" He did not turn to look at me when he spoke, but his back was rigid.

"No, Erik, I am unharmed. All my torments have been of a different kind." I raised my chin and glared directly into Gaston's eyes, sending him all the hate I could muster in that fierce look. I found I was looking forward to watching Erik deal with Gaston as he so richly deserved. Gaston understood my thoughts perfectly well; he gave me a brief sardonic smile, his cold grey eyes flicking back to Erik almost at once.

"I must confess," he said to Erik conversationally, "I am a little disappointed not to have an opportunity to cut off Sylvie's finger tomorrow. I was rather looking forward to that, and all the other things I was planning to do to her. It is such a shame you found this place so soon." He was baiting Erik, trying to throw off his concentration, but Erik's only reaction was a tightening of his eyes.

They continued to feint from side to side, eyes locked, taking one another's measure, each searching for an opening to strike. Erik was not a trained swordsman, he had told me so himself, but he had the advantage of his size, strength and agility, as well as being younger than his opponent. But Gaston possessed both skill *and* training, it was obvious from the way he carried himself: he moved with the easy grace of a much younger man. They would be fairly evenly matched, I thought worriedly. An idea for improving the odds came to me and I called out to Erik.

"Take off your mask, Erik – it might help you to see." To be honest, I wasn't sure if it would or not, but I thought it might throw Gaston off a bit. And I was right. I saw Gaston's eyes flash to me, his expression slightly shocked. Erik complied with my suggestion unhesitatingly; pulling off the mask with his free hand, he tossed it to

313

me. Then his lips drew back into a snarling smile, baring his teeth, his eyes brilliant with anticipation. Gaston's face contorted in a grimace of disgust at the sight of that scarred and hideous visage smiling at him. He could not resist hurling another taunt at his opponent.

"I knew you must be ugly, Phantom, but I had no idea you were this ugly. I cannot fathom what she sees in you. *C'est vrai*, love is blind." Erik paid no attention, but anger boiled inside me at Gaston's cruel words, even as I registered the implications behind them. Gaston persisted in believing Erik and I had a bond of romantic love between us; why, I could not imagine. But *I* knew it was a bond of friendship, and our friendship had held true; his return just in time to save me from a hideous fate was proof of that, and it warmed my heart.

Having caught Erik's mask in both my hands, I pressed myself against the wall, knowing I must avoid doing or saying anything that would break his concentration. Erik had shrugged out of his coat in order to move freely, and I gazed admiringly at his upright, manly form, marveling that anyone could think him ugly. His body was leaner than when I had last seen him, and several days' unshaven beard darkened his cheek and chin, but he was still magnificent.

Before he engaged his foe, Erik had one last thing to say to me. He tilted his head toward me without taking his eyes off Gaston and spoke in a low, intense voice.

"I have to kill him, Sylvie; you know that, don't you? I have no choice. Even if he had not struck you, I would still have to kill him." He was remembering his promise to me, never to kill again.

"*D'accord.*" I answered without hesitation. "If anyone deserves death, it is this fiend. And I should know."

Gaston divided a smirk between us. "How sweet," he murmured, his voice dripping with sarcasm. "I am so happy to have witnessed this reunion of lovers parted. Only it is I who will kill *you*, Phantom, while she watches, and when you are dead, she will be next, but much, much more slowly. You should know this: I have never yet failed and I do not intend to fail now." No longer smirking, Gaston's face was set in grim determination.

"But I am a Phantom no longer, as you shall soon learn." Erik answered calmly, and then he abruptly lunged toward the other man. The two swords crossed near their hilts. At the first ring of steel on steel I shrank back against the wall, gripping the mask in both my hands. Its fading warmth comforted me as I watched the two men engaged in mortal combat. My heart seemed to be lodged in my throat.

314

In spite of having been married to a military officer, I had never before witnessed a sword fight. This was a duel to the death, and the most terrifying thing I had ever seen, *vraiment*. Erik, perhaps in compensation for his lack of formal fencing expertise, fought like a tiger against his opponent, never giving an inch, and as they lunged, parried and sometimes came up against each other with a ringing clash of steel, furniture was overturned, lamps broken. I prayed they would not start a fire.

Aside from their panting breath and occasional grunts of effort, the two men fought in fierce silence. Several times Gaston feinted, drove Erik back and then attempted to circle closer to me, but each time Erik forced him away again. The difference between the two combatants was great, even to my inexperienced eyes. Gaston was all controlled grace and form, Erik brute force and strength. Face contorted, teeth bared, eyes blazing, he looked as if he intended to rip his opponent to shreds with his bare hands if he could. Gaston, on the other hand, never changed his cool, focused expression at all – no fire lit his eyes.

Though both men were breathing heavily now, it was clear that Erik was gradually wearing the older man down with his ferocious onslaught. Gaston was a fierce and determined fighter, however. He was not accustomed to losing, and not to be underestimated. With a blindingly fast slash he caught Erik off his guard. Unable to bring his sword up to parry in time, Gaston's blade bit across his left forearm. Erik leapt back cursing while the white sleeve of his shirt blossomed red with blood. I clapped my hand over my mouth to stifle a shriek.

Gaston laughed, lunging again, pressing his advantage against his wounded opponent. I found myself looking around for something I could use as a weapon – a heavy silver candlestick would do very well. I vowed that if he struck Erik down I would bash in his head and kill him myself. It was unbearable and unthinkable that Erik should perish on my behalf. The idea had never entered my mind until Gaston drew his blood, but now I was beside myself. It was as if I were looking through a filmy red scarf, my own blood lust at that moment was every bit as strong as theirs.

But the fight was almost over. Erik rebounded ever more fiercely, attacking without pause. The wound to his arm had only served to infuriate him further. He was not following any rules of engagement. I do not think he knew any. Just watching him fighting for his life and mine was the most exhilarating and terrifying experience I had ever known. I do not believe I drew breath for a full five minutes. But finally he found the opportunity he needed; he caught Gaston's sword handle with the point of his own and ripped it from his hand, sending it flying across the room where it hit the wall and fell clattering to the floor.

"Don't look, Sylvie," he said in a low voice. He did not hesitate in delivering the *coup de grâce*. And why would he? He *was* Erik, after all. I saw his sword arm pull back; I closed my eyes as instructed and turned my face away as the mortal blow fell. But I heard Gaston gasp out a foul curse, heard the dreadful sucking sound of Erik's sword pulling out, then, after a brief pause, a thud, and a soft sort of sigh. And then all I could hear was Erik's gasping breath. Turning back, I opened my eyes.

The first thing I saw was Gaston was lying on his back on the carpet, one leg bent at the knee, one hand on his chest where the front of his waistcoat was rapidly staining with bright red blood. He was already dead; his empty eyes glared at the ceiling, his lips were frozen in a snarl. For Gaston I spared only a passing glance before my eyes flew to Erik; he was standing over Gaston's body, breathing heavily, blood soaking through the sleeve of his shirt. He raised his sword arm and used the clean sleeve to wipe his sweating brow. I was breathing rather heavily myself, and my heart was thumping like a drum. I wanted to weep and throw myself on Erik in gratitude and relief, but I knew I must keep a level head on my shoulders, for he needed me and my medical expertise.

By the time he replaced his sword in its scabbard and turned back to look for me, I had shoved his mask into my skirt pocket, pulled up my hem and began tearing off the bottom ruffle of my dusty petticoat. I felt a dreamlike sense of unreality, as if I were a character in some romantic novel instead of Sylvie Bessette, Cook. I was a heroine, sacrificing a petticoat to bind the wound of her lover. How could this be real?

But though he was not my lover, Erik's blood was real, and so was another noise that now became insistent – the sound of shouting and battering on the barred door. Several of Gaston's loyal servants, having heard the altercation, were desperately trying to get in. There would be no escape for us that way. There might not be any escape for us at all, but I pushed that thought away and ran to Erik.

Still breathing hard from his exertions, wordlessly he held out his bloody arm for me. He watched my hasty ministrations with a strange expression on his face as I wrapped the strip of cloth around the wound over his bloody shirtsleeve. I had never seen Erik look at

316

me like that before: almost as though he were trying to see through me. I could not look directly into those intense blue eyes; it would be too unsettling. I had to concentrate on binding his wounded arm as tightly as I could to stem the flow of blood.

I had watched my father do this once, when a neighbor's servant appeared at our door, bleeding badly from a sword wound. An affair of the heart, my father had explained at the time. But the medical lesson had stayed with me, thankfully. Since I could not see the wound in Erik's arm, I could only guess at how deep it went. Unbelievably, my hands were steady.

I had just finished tying the last strip when there was a reverberating crash on the door, causing it to shudder. They were ramming it with something large and heavy. We both turned our heads toward the sound, and then looked back at each other.

"What are we going to do?" I asked, staring wildly up at him after the second crashing blow on the door. Suddenly his eyes seemed to catch fire; they blazed with strong emotion. A wordless gasp tore from his throat and he caught me up and pulled me against him, seizing me in a hard embrace that took my breath away.

"Sylvie," he whispered urgently into my disarrayed hair, his voice full of contrition. "Oh, Sylvie, I am so *sorry*." His hand went to the back of my neck, holding my head against his chest. He was trembling.

"*Dieu*," he whispered. "How good you feel."

And we just stood like that, everything else momentarily forgotten. Pressed firmly against him, feeling his heart hammering beneath my cheek, my fears faded and I felt safe and happy for the first time in weeks, in spite of the fact that escape appeared to be highly unlikely. All that mattered, in this moment, was that heart beating, those arms holding me close. My own arms stole around his narrow waist, and I whispered his name over and over.

Then his hands changed their position. I felt one wrap around a fistful of the hair that was streaming down my back and then the other cupped under my chin. He lifted my face up toward his, and before I knew what was going to happen, his lips came down on mine with crushing intensity.

The kiss did not last long. It could not, for the door was on the verge of being breached and could no longer be ignored. When Erik released me I staggered, head spinning, and I had to hold on to him to avoid falling. With one scorching look that stopped my heart, he seized my hand and tugged me, still in a state of shocked surprise, toward the open window on the far side of the room. I had not seen anything of Gaston's *salon*, being unconscious when I was carried through it, but now I saw there was no balcony, only a decorative iron *grille* that stood out perhaps a foot from the side of the building. We were not, as I assumed all this time, on the ground floor of the house. I tried to pull back against his hand.

"We cannot escape this way!" I cried.

"Oh yes we can," he said, brimming with arrogant masculine confidence. "Remember, Sylvie, I am far better with rope than I am with a sword." He gave me a sidelong look to make sure I understood his little joke. I groaned. I could guess what was coming, and did not look forward to it at all. Suddenly Erik's face brightened, his eyes glittering with mischief.

"Do you still have my mask, Sylvie? Yes? *Bien*, give it to me, love."

Bewildered as much by his request as by the unexpected endearment, I pulled the mask out of my skirt pocket obediently and held it out to him. Appearing oblivious to the rending sounds of wood emanating from that end of the room, Erik grasped his mask and strode back to Gaston. His smile was triumphantly feral as he stood over the sprawled body. Reaching down, he arranged the white mask precisely on the blood-soaked chest of his vanquished foe. Watching him, I could not but be reminded of all those unfortunate combatants he had methodically dispatched for the Sultana's pleasure. Still smiling like a schoolboy who has just pulled a particularly naughty prank, he returned to me, exclaiming,

"*Dieu!* That felt wonderful." I could not help myself; I smiled back at him.

Erik stepped lithely to the top of the iron balustrade and reached out for a rope which I could see hanging down from somewhere above. So that was how he had managed to get in – dropping down from the roof above. Gaston, for all his cunning, had apparently not been aware of Erik's skill with a rope. Erik could very easily have dispatched him with one of those ropes, but I think I understood why he chose to fight tonight with his sword instead. Now my hero took me by the arm, pulling me up to stand next to him.

"Lean against the wall for a moment," he instructed, while his hands, swift and sure, were efficiently tying a large loop and a complicated knot in the rope. "Don't look down." But of course I did look. The street seemed far, far below us, and the cobblestones looked very hard. Behind us, the beleaguered door at last gave way. Gaston's servants rushed into the room, where they promptly stumbled over his prostrate body. One of them fell across it with a horrified yelp. I wasn't certain, but I thought it might be the little one-eyed fellow.

There was not a moment to lose now. I took a deep steadying breath.

Erik reached for me. Reading the panic in my eyes, he said,

"Trust me, Sylvie, we will be fine. I did this same thing at the Opera." I *did* trust him, but what we were about to do seemed insane.

"Couldn't we go up instead?" I asked fearfully, my voice scratchy.

Smiling, Erik pulled me close so that we stood firmly pressed against each other, and passed the looped end over both our heads. By some contrivance I could not see, he secured it so that it wrapped tightly around us but left our arms free.

"Put your arms around my neck and hold on for your life," he said.

Following his instructions, I locked my arms around his neck and buried my face in the front of his shirt so I would not be able to see what was coming. I felt rather than saw him look up and test the rope hanging from above us.

"When we land, bend your knees. *Allons!*" Without further ado, he pushed off from the railing, propelling us out into empty air. We plunged downward toward the sidewalk, and it rose to meet us with alarming swiftness.

By some miracle, I did not scream, probably because I was too terrified to draw enough air into my lungs. Cold wind whipped my face, and my insides felt as though they had decided to remain on the balcony. I was certain we were both going to die, but at the last second I felt his hands do something with the rope. We were abruptly jerked up short, and our feet hit the pavement, hard. Folding at the knees as instructed, still tightly bound to him, my legs gave way. Actually, if I am being completely honest, all of me gave way. I toppled over on my side, drawing Erik over with me. Loud voices could be heard above us, shouting and calling. We had been seen, pursuit was eminent. Swiftly Erik whipped off the rope, leapt to his feet, and caught me under my arms, pulling me to my feet as well.

"Are you all right?" He asked breathlessly, still supporting me by the arms because my knees felt like *crème brûlée*. In spite of his wound, his blood was hot, his eyes glowing; he was enjoying himself immensely.

"Grrr," I replied, giving him a speaking glance.

Erik laughed, sounding almost light-hearted. "*Allons,* we must get away from here." Grasping my hand firmly in his, we set off at a run down the street, me a little shakily. As we rounded a corner, I beheld standing in a circle of gaslight a sporty-looking Phaeton with two horses harnessed to it. I was not surprised when Erik made straight for the Phaeton.

Unceremoniously he boosted me up on to the tall seat and followed rapidly; I slid over to make room for him. Catching the reins, he whipped up the surprised and snorting horses and we set off at a furious pace. I swiveled on the seat to look behind. Several of Gaston's servants were shouting and pelting after us, but they were no match for the Phaeton, a vehicle currently very popular for its speed, and our two swift steeds. This was, *sans doute,* why Erik had selected it. Pursuit soon faded away.

"You stole this, didn't you?" I asked him after I had got my breath back. I was fairly certain I already knew the answer.

He gave me a wary sidelong look. "Possibly."

"And the owner…"

Erik smirked a little. "He will have a headache when he wakes, but he is otherwise unharmed."

"Where are we going?" I could not think of very many options available to us. The police would look for us in my apartment and his old home before they looked anywhere else.

"To your apartment, but we will not go inside just yet. We will wait and watch for a while." Erik turned his head to look at me. When I met his eyes I was startled and confused; he was looking at me as if he were dying of thirst and I was a glass of water. I could feel myself going hot all over in spite of the cool night air. He had never looked at me like that before, of that I was certain. I could not resist sliding across the seat so that I could lean against his uninjured right arm. With a swift movement he passed the reins to his left hand, and with his right he picked up my hand, held it to his lips and pressed a warm kiss into my palm. Just as quickly, he released me. His inexplicable behavior toward me tonight must, I thought, be due to his relief at our successful escape. It would not do to think otherwise, so I searched for something to distract me from such tempting thoughts. Ideas were not long in coming: there were many things I wanted to ask him about.

"I am confused; I thought that room where I was being held was a cellar of some sort, but we were on the second floor." I looked at Erik, perplexed.

Erik responded promptly. "It was not a cellar, Sylvie," he said, shaking his head. "Once I traced Gaston to that particular building, which took some time, I was able to explore its surroundings. I suspected I would find such a place as that when I got inside. His rooms are built right up against a very ancient structure, and quite often, such older structures fall below the current street-level. All the bastard had to do was create an opening in the wall from his *salon*, add some steps and he had access to what amounted to a secret dungeon." As he spoke, I reminded myself that Erik was a masonry contractor among other far less mundane things.

"It really *was* a dungeon," I told him. "There were several sets of old manacles attached to the wall, as a matter of fact." I tried to keep my voice from betraying how that place affected me, but Erik noticed the slight waver. He put his arm around me and gave my shoulder a comforting squeeze before continuing.

"The *pied-à-terre* Gaston kept there was secret to all but his most trusted men. He has a legitimate house on the Île de la Cité, near the Préfecture building. I went there first of course, and searched it thoroughly, but that was a complete waste of my time. It took me several more days to trace him back to the rooms where I found you tonight. He did not appear to go there every night, and he was extremely cautious when he did, the bastard. He used different approaches, different transport – he was not an easy man to follow. But once I finally found the place, I knew it was where he was holding you, if only because of the secrecy surrounding it." Erik explained.

It was several miles from Gaston's secret *pied-à-terre* to my apartment. Erik kept to the lesser-used side streets, causing our journey to be longer than it otherwise would have been. But I did not mind. Breathing deeply, I reveled in the cold, crisp air on my face, and the clean, pure light of stars. I also reveled in the fact that I was alive and free, possessed of all my fingers, and Erik was sitting next to me. Part of me still could not believe he was real, that this sudden freedom was real; I was afraid I might find I was only dreaming my dramatic rescue.

We traveled speedily along in our purloined Phaeton. The horses were wonderfully responsive, apparently not minding in the least having a strange driver at the reins. Bizarrely, we drove down one of the boulevards close to the burned out Opera House on our way to my neighborhood. Both of us turned our heads to stare silently at that ghastly blackened ruin, visible in the distance. It was the first time I had seen it since the blaze. According to the Vicomte's wishes, the

321

building had been boarded up and a fence placed around it. It would remain in that abandoned state for many years to come, and its reputation of being haunted never left it.

The fire seemed very long ago to me now, like something from another lifetime. I wondered what thoughts passed through Erik's mind as we drove by, but I said nothing and neither did he. I saw his hand make an almost unconscious gesture; raising it to his chest he touched something briefly through his shirt, but I could not see what it was.

We left the Phaeton two blocks away from the Rue de la Marché, and approached my apartment cautiously, on foot. Erik led us on a circuitous route, threading carefully in the dark through an alley filled with refuse, along a little-used mews between two buildings, across someone's back garden, and finally emerging across the street and down a little from my apartment. There was my little wrought iron balcony plainly visible under the arching canopy of the leafless plane tree. The tree's pale bark glimmered faintly in the starlight. All was dark and quiet, except for the warm circles of light where the occasional gaslight stood. I looked up at Erik in amazement. How did he know his way here so well? I could not have found my way through the maze we just traversed, and I lived here.

Erik looked down at me with a small, almost apologetic smile. We were standing in the shadow of a recessed doorway, and he wrapped his arms around my shoulders from behind and pulled me against him, my back to his front. I felt his chest expand and release a long sigh. I assure you, Reader, I would have been happy to stand like that forever.

Putting his mouth close to my ear, he spoke in a low murmur. "I came back to Paris two weeks ago, Sylvie. I could not stay away any longer. I was worried about you and I needed to know you were safe. And...I needed to see you. Every night I stood in this doorway and watched you come out onto your balcony and light your candle. I was standing right here each time you came out before you went to bed." Shock must have registered on my face, but he could not see it in the dark, thankfully.

"You were here? Why, why didn't you..." I stopped, unable to finish. I tried to turn to look at him, but he held me firmly in place.

"Why didn't I come to you? I wanted to, believe me. You have no idea how much. I knew that candle on your balcony was burning for me." As he spoke his lips left my ear for a moment, sliding down to my neck where he pressed a soft kiss. My breath hitched, my heart struck up a quicker rhythm. Why was he kissing me like that? It felt so…so…like the kiss of a lover. He must know what he was doing to me.

"But I was trying, for once in my life, to do the right thing. I owed you that much, Sylvie. It seemed to me you deserved better, much better than this monster I had become. I could not bring myself to come back to you, but I couldn't leave you, either. It was torture for me, but at least I was watching over you, or so I believed." And this was sweet torture for me, feeling his warm breath on my neck while he was whispering to me.

I couldn't believe it – he had been here, all that time. If I had only known! I must have glanced across into this dark doorway every night, completely unaware of his presence. It made me want to weep with frustration. But now his voice changed, became rougher. His hands on my shoulders tightened.

"When I couldn't be here, daroga, the Persian, was. I asked him to watch over you when I left. You remember him, don't you? You met him once." Was there a thread of amusement in his voice just then? I sighed ruefully; I did remember. Now I realized who it was I had seen in the street one night, but only from behind.

"I hadn't slept in a bed in days," he said, sounding rueful, "or I would not have left it to him, but I was worn out from sleeping in such uncomfortable places. It was he who told me something was amiss with you. He came here one night to check on you for me, but there were no lights on in your apartment, it was dark. He watched for some time but you never came out. Realizing that something was amiss, he came back and told me. I was frantic, and really angry with him because he did not see what had happened to you. I waited outside, in this doorway in fact, fearing a trap, but finally when it was fully dark I climbed the plane tree and entered your apartment. You had taken my advice about locking that door, so I had to break in." His breath was warm and moist in my ear.

"No one was there, I could tell." He went on. "So I took a chance and lit a lamp, and I saw…signs of a struggle. And blood…there was dried blood on the floor just inside your room. I was so afraid for a moment…I was about to run downstairs when I saw an envelope lying on the floor. I almost overlooked it, I was so worried. I picked it up, and saw it was addressed to *me*, to the Phantom." He was rigid and tense with remembered anger.

As he spoke, a picture formed in my mind: Gaston standing on my carpet, an envelope held casually in his hand. I was unable to repress a shudder, and Erik, thinking I was cold, held me closer. I did not mind.

"The cunning bastard, he gave nothing away, left me nothing I could use to find him or you. I thought I would go mad, not knowing where you were or how to even begin to look for you. All the time knowing you were in his power, thinking of what he might be doing to you…." he stopped abruptly, too overcome to go on. He rested his head gently on top of mine, breathing hard.

"His letter hinted at all sorts of horrors. Sylvie, I cannot tell you how relieved I was to hear your voice tonight."

I thought now that I understood the source of Erik's behavior toward me tonight. Desperate to reassure him, I swiveled my head so I could look up at him.

"I knew you would find me, Erik. I never doubted it for a moment."

"I *had* to find you; it was because of me that you were in such danger in the first place. You saved *me*, Sylvie; Indeed I will never forget the sight of you when you came running headlong to my rescue. How could I not save you in turn?"

"You did not do any harm to the Persian, did you?" I asked worriedly. "It was not his fault Gaston kidnapped me before he got here in time to see them carry me off."

I felt Erik smile into my hair. "*Bien sûr que non*, Sylvie. What do you take me for, a violent criminal?" I clucked my tongue at his poor joke. "No, but after assisting me in acquiring the rope I needed and that estimable Phaeton and pair, he bid me *bonne nuit* and went home. He cannot understand all this worry and effort over a mere woman and does not want to have anything more to do with me unless I can be sensible. He would not welcome us tonight, unfortunately."

I smiled, as Erik plainly wanted me to do, but I was growing increasingly worried about our predicament. How long were we going to stand here and watch my dark apartment, and what were we watching for? Erik's arm needed to be disinfected and bandaged properly and I was impatient to take care of it. There had been no time to retrieve his coat when we made our abrupt departure from Gaston's house, so it was plain to see that the sword wound was bleeding again. The sleeve of his shirt was glossy and I knew it was fresh blood. I twisted around to look at Erik.

"Why…" I began, but stopped when he looked up sharply, then pressed us back into the darkness of the doorway as far as we could go.

He placed his fingers gently over my lips and whispered, "Shhh."

We were silent, invisible shadows in the blackness, the only witnesses as several *gendarmes* wearing the uniforms of the Paris police, moving quietly down the street, arrived at the door of my kitchen. It was not locked – no one was there to lock it, so the dark shapes soon swarmed inside, closing the door behind them. We watched as the lights were lit first downstairs, then up. Room after room sprang vividly to life. One of the searchers came out on the balcony and peered all around, even into the branches of the tree. We could clearly see them tossing things about, throwing clothes out of the armoire, looking inside my trunk.

Minutes passed while we stood silently in the dark doorway, Erik holding me tightly, my hands gripping his hard forearm for support. Finally the policemen issued out of the door, slammed it behind them, and then clustered briefly in the street arguing irately over what their next move should be. We could hear every word.

"I told you they would not come here. He must have taken her to his underground lair. We should have gone there in the first place."

Another voice broke in. "The blood we saw back there on the Chief-Inspector's window sill…he must have succeeded in wounding that beast, and he may need a doctor. We could…" Here the speaker was interrupted sharply by his superior.

"A doctor! Idiot! He could not show that face before any doctor in this city. No, he has gone to ground, and taken the girl with him." His voice was angry and impatient.

One of the other policemen spoke up. "But how did the girl come to be there? This is passing strange."

"She came with the Phantom, there is no other explanation. He has some hold over her, apparently. Let us try his Lair next. It is not far." I hated the way everyone insisted on referring to Erik's cavern as a *lair*, as if he were a wild beast in a cave. I could not think of it as anything but his home.

The policeman in charge turned toward the one he had called an idiot. "You: remain here on guard. I'll send someone to relieve you in the morning." Addressing the others, he explained, "he will expect us to set a watch for him here so it's probably the last place he would try to bring the girl; it's unlikely but we can't take chances. If we've learned anything it's not to underestimate what he's capable of. The rest of you, *allons-y*." In a moment, they had slipped quietly away, leaving the lone policeman on guard. He stood watching them disappear down the street, then turned and went back inside the kitchen, presumably to spend his watch in relative comfort. The gaslight went out, plunging the kitchen into darkness once more.

I turned my head to look inquiringly up at Erik. He smiled down at me, shaking his head a little.

"What is it?" I asked, puzzled by the bemused expression on his face.

"Did you hear what he said? They think I have some hold over you. *Vraiment*, it is the other way around." While I was still pondering this quizzical remark, he again whispered softly in my ear, causing goose flesh to rise along my neck.

"Wait here until I call you." He gave my shoulder a quick squeeze, then drifted, dark and silent as the ghost he had once pretended to be, across the street toward the door. Without the warmth of Erik's large body I shivered in the cold spring night. Hugging myself, hardly daring to breathe, I strained my eyes to see but could discern nothing except the dark window and door.

I had scarcely stood there alone for thirty seconds when the door opened and Erik's voice came to me as a low murmur:

"Sylvie." Not anywhere nearly as quiet as he, I flew from my hiding place to where he stood in the door. He pulled me inside and I looked around the dark room. I could just make out the hapless guard lying unconscious on the floor. He appeared to have been overtaken in the act of raiding my larder: a partial loaf of stale bread lay on the floor next to him. He obviously had not been expecting any interruptions.

"I will need some more of your petticoat, Sylvie. I have no more rope to tie him with. We'll leave him here in the larder – he will be sleeping for a while." I hastened to oblige him. This one was already ruined in any case.

After Erik had attended to the guard, we went upstairs. My apartment was in a state of disarray thanks to the rough attentions of the *gendarmes*, but at least nothing was broken. Erik crossed the room, drew the draperies closed, and busied himself building a small fire in the fireplace. I went straight to the *garde-manger*, anxious to attend to Erik's arm.

"I am going to heat some water so I can clean your wound. It must be very painful after everything you have done tonight."

"*Oui*, it burns like fire," he replied simply. Sinking to his knees on the rug in front of the fireplace, he struck a match to start the coal burning.

"How long do you think we will be able to remain here?" I called from the adjoining room as I lit the gas ring and put my copper kettle on to boil. "I am longing for a hot bath and a change of clothing." I was acutely aware of not looking my best; unsurprising after having been imprisoned in a dark, dirty cellar for several days and nights without the means to wash effectively or a clean frock to put on. I dared not look in a mirror to see the state of my hair. A bath! I could scarcely wait. Immersion in hot water would be heaven. And it was more than just physical dirt I needed to rid myself of: it was the overall sense of contamination from having been so long at the mercy of that wicked, depraved man.

Erik considered my question for a moment before answering.

"We should be safe here for a few hours. So far all has proceeded exactly as I hoped; we know the police won't return until morning. There is enough time for you to bathe and for me to get some sleep. I have not slept more than two or three hours a night since you were taken. It isn't easy for a fugitive to find a safe place to sleep in this city. If it were not for my old friend the Persian allowing me to hide at his house for a few days, I would have had no rest at all. I confess I am dead on my feet." He did sound tired, I thought anxiously. He had not rested, day or night, until he found me. No matter what miseries he had put me through before, the debt was more than cancelled now. I owed Erik my very life.

When the kettle sang I busied myself collecting hot water in a bowl, soap, a clean cloth and some alcohol from my first aid kit. When I returned to the *salon* Erik was still kneeling in front of the now-blazing fire. By unspoken understanding we did not light the gaslights or a candle; the firelight would have to be enough. We dare not take a chance on alerting anyone to our presence here tonight.

Erik looked up at me and smiled as I approached him. He looked exhausted, but also happy, relaxed even. Noting the new leanness of his face, I wondered how long it had been since he had anything to eat. Regrettably, there would be nothing edible in my apartment except stale bread. And our prisoner had helped himself to that already. These Parisian *gendarmes* were as bad as mice, I reflected irritably.

Setting the bowl of hot water down, I knelt next to Erik and reached for my makeshift bandage, struggling to undo the knot I had

327

tied around his arm. The strip of petticoat was soaked with his blood and refused to cooperate. Before I had got very far, Erik stopped me, catching hold of my hand in midair. He was gazing at me with concern, demanding my full attention with his eyes.

"Sylvie, are you certain that you are all right?" He asked gravely. "You really were not harmed, were you?" He could not keep the edge of dread from his voice, or out of his expression. I knew what he was asking, what he could not ask out loud.

"*Vraiment*, I am fine, Erik." I assured him firmly. Looking relieved, he released my hand so I could continue prying at the bandage.

"How did you manage to find me?" I asked. It was a question that had been nagging at me for some time. I also hoped that answering my question would distract him a little from the painful procedures that were about to take place. The bandage was untied at last and I cast the bloody strip into the fire.

"You will have to take off that shirt, it is ruined in any case," I added.

Absently, gazing at the dancing firelight, he began with his good hand to untuck his shirt and pull it open. "It was the second letter," he answered.

I stared at him alertly. "Second letter?"

He glanced at me wryly. "*Oui*, there was a second letter. Our friend Gaston was quite the correspondent. It was waiting for me when I took a chance on slipping back into the cavern. I needed to retrieve several things from there; my sword, for one. I was afraid it would not be there, but it was. I am rather attached to my sword, and even more so now. Gaston left the letter resting on my miniature of the theatre, right on the stage, where I could not miss it. I do not know how he knew I would return, but he did." Erik's voice hardened as he spoke; I knew he believed he had been out-maneuvered by Gaston then, and perhaps he had. But it little mattered now, for Erik had won, as he always did.

"What did the letter say?" I asked while assisting him to draw his bloody shirt over his head and toss it aside. As the hideous garment lifted from his chest I gasped. But it was not the sight of that bared chest that caused my sharp intake of breath. Something else had instantly caught my eye.

The dancing flames from the fire sent brilliant shooting prisms of light from an object hanging suspended from a thin gold chain around his neck – I instantly recognized Christine's engagement ring.

So that was what his hand reflexively clutched at when we drove past the Opera House! I stared at it, unable to look away from its cruel, cold sparkle. The second letter and its contents were momentarily forgotten. My heart sank; a sad despair washed over me at the sight of the ring, a glittering symbol of his enduring love for another. It served as a sharp reminder of my place in the triangle: I was Kitty, the servant girl who loved D'Artagnan for naught.

Erik saw at once the change in my expression; he followed my gaze downward to the ring, but his eyes came darting quickly back up to my face, reading there the pain I could not conceal. Ashamed and furious with myself, I averted my face, dipping the cloth into hot water and wringing it out. Concentrating fiercely on my task, I began as gently as possible to wash the dried and fresh blood away from the gash in his forearm.

"Sylvie," he said, his voice a low, urgent growl. "Please listen to me. I owe Christine a debt I can never repay. If it were not for her, showing me compassion and tenderness I did not deserve, I would not be sitting here with you tonight. You saved me, Sylvie, but so did Christine. It was she who helped me to become a little more human, to stop the monster in his tracks."

My hands shook as I worked, I could not help it. Nothing had changed; I ought to have known it would not; but I realized that I had foolishly begun to allow myself to hope. Those kisses, those scorching looks tonight had deceived me. I felt tears burning in my eyes but I fought them back, forcing myself to concentrate on the task at hand.

As I had feared, the wound was deep, but the edges looked clean and the bleeding had stopped once more. It should really be stitched to ensure proper healing, but I had not the ability or the necessary supplies to sew up a wound, in spite of being a physician's daughter. We would have to settle for cleaning it well and binding it properly. I reached for the bottle of alcohol and poured some on to a clean cloth. The smell rose up strong between us.

"I am sorry, Erik, but this is going to burn," I warned him, my voice low but steady.

I placed the cloth firmly over the gash and held it there. He gave a quick intake of breath, but did not flinch even though the alcohol must sting like *le diable*. He turned his head to look at me. Refusing to meet his eyes, I focused on his wound, dabbing at it carefully. It was Erik who spoke.

"I will always love her, Sylvie. You know what she meant to me, what she was to me. She woke my heart to love, but unfortunately, it awoke in darkness." He shook his head sadly, and I felt a tear, unbidden, slide down my cheek. I bit my lip hard to keep it from trembling.

Erik touched the ring resting against his chest tenderly as he spoke.

"This is all I have of hers, all that is left to remind me of that love. She was so much better than I, so much more kind and compassionate. So good and innocent. I on the other hand was a hateful, jealous, conniving monster. Everything you told me I was, and more. But I am not like that any longer. That chapter is closed."

Still staring steadily at the cloth I held pressed to his wound, I wondered miserably how much more of this torture I could stand. After all I had been through in Gaston's dungeon, this felt just as awful in its own way. Why had I ever confessed to Erik that I loved him? How I wished now that I had kept that secret.

Erik covered my hand with his and pulled it from his arm, interrupting my tragic train of thought. The wet cloth dropped to the floor. He took me by the shoulders, turning me to face him. I tried to look away, but he caught my chin in his hand and held it, forcing me to meet his intense blue gaze.

"I am not saying these things to hurt you, Sylvie. You've been hurt enough, and I never want to hurt you again. I am just trying to explain how I feel. *Dieu*, don't cry." I realized more tears had escaped and were flowing down my cheeks.

"I am better now, because of *you*. Christine could give me compassion and understanding, but she could not give me the one thing I wanted more than anything else in the world: she could not give me *love*." As I stared into those pale blue eyes, a great tenderness could be seen there. I wanted to respond to it, but I was afraid. Hope was a luxury I could not afford.

Erik's lips quirked into a brief, wry smile. "It was you, Sylvie, who gave me the love I so badly needed. You were there for me all along, but I couldn't see it. I understand so many things you did for me, now that I can see. You risked everything to save me, because you loved me." He sounded mildly surprised that this should be the case. Releasing my chin, he gently wiped a tear off my cheek with his fingers. I stared at him, hypnotized by his words and by his gentle touch.

"You were right about me, Sylvie: I am not a bad man, not really. To be good, all I ever needed was to be loved." There was such wistful sadness in his voice as he spoke these words, a reminder of all the years of lonely isolation he had endured. I suddenly wanted to touch him – *needed* to touch him so badly that my hand came up of its own volition and rested gently against his cheek. Covering my hand with his, he turned his face into my palm and kissed it softly.

Looking back at me with a piercing gaze, he asked, "*Do* you still love me, Sylvie? Please don't be afraid to tell me the truth."

Staring into those mesmerizing eyes, I thought recklessly, *why not?* He had just saved my life, *après tout.*

"Yes, I do. Of course I do." I whispered. "Nothing has changed. I love you with all my heart. I always will. I told you that." I let my hand fall away from his face and into my lap. A sigh escaped me; as usual, I could deny him nothing. Erik studied my face intently for a moment.

"While I was in hiding, I had quite a lot of time to think. There is something I want to ask you. Tell me, Sylvie...how long have you loved me?"

I felt a blush spread across my cheeks. I hoped he would think it was from the glow of the fire. I looked down as I spoke, unable to meet his eyes.

"Since that evening when I tripped and bumped my head and you helped me." I murmured, feeling unaccountably shy; absurdly, hopelessly romantic. Like some silly novel heroine.

Erik sighed softly. "All that time..." he murmured wistfully. "Most people who meet me are afraid of me, and with good reason. But not you."

I raised my eyes back to his and allowed myself a small, tremulous smile.

"Oh, I was afraid of you, do not doubt it. But that did not stop me from seeing all your good qualities as well. I noticed the first time I ever saw you that you were handsome, but I also saw that you could be kind, gentle, and ... and *good*."

His face was a study in disbelief. "Really, Sylvie. No one has ever thought me *handsome*." I reached my hand up again and gently, deliberately, stroked the rough, red skin of his disfigured cheek.

"Well, I think so." He closed his eyes, enjoying the touch. "You know," I added thoughtfully, "if it were not for this face of yours, I would never have met you. Our paths could never have crossed. So you see, it *is* beautiful to me." Erik caught my hand in his and pulled it away from his face, holding it carefully in his lap. He was not finished yet.

"You loved me that long ago, and you love me still. Did you ever stop loving me, Sylvie?"

331

"*Non*," I said simply.

"That is why you came looking for me the night of the fire." It was a statement; he already knew it was true. "I wondered why you did that, for I felt sure you must hate me after the way I treated you." Erik turned his face toward the fireplace and stared into the dancing flames for a few seconds before he spoke.

"What a fool I have been." His voice was low and sad. He was still holding my hand in his lap, his fingers twined with mine. Then he turned back to me and his eyes were filled with such warm affection that I felt my insides begin to melt like chocolate over a *bain-marie*.

"I will always be good, gentle and kind to you, Sylvie, I promise." He said earnestly. "Not like before. I will try my best to make you forget what I was like before. I may have your love, but I want to earn it, too."

My mouth fell open. I stared at him blankly. What was he talking about? Erik laughed a little at my incredulous expression, and squeezed my fingers gently.

"Why do you think I did not rest day or night until I found you? Not only because it was the right thing to do, but also because I realized I could not go on without you. That bastard Gaston was right, you know. He understood about us, what we meant to each other, and that is why he knew he could use you against me. Warm, wonderful Sylvie, I am going to marry you just as soon as we can get safely away from here. If you will have me, that is."

I was stunned, and you cannot blame me, Reader. "You...you want to marry *me*, Erik?" I stammered witlessly. "But..." I longed with all my heart to believe him but my eyes darted down to the ring hanging from his neck, then back again to his face. He understood my glance.

"Oh, Sylvie. Yes, I have come to care very much for you. I must convince you I am telling the truth." Erik frowned at me for a moment, and then he continued.

"I believe this has been coming on for a long time, rather like a disease..." here he gave me a pointed glance, so I produced the scowl he so clearly wanted. Smiling, he continued, "...probably ever since you first managed to worm your sweet, stubborn way past my defenses, something I had never allowed anyone to do before. I couldn't seem to say no to you. I ought to have realized what was happening the night I found you lying on your stone floor downstairs – you have no idea how thankful I was when I saw you were alive. I probably would have comprehended my feelings for you much sooner if it were not for...for Christine. I will always love Christine, but now it is different, no longer an *idée fixe*. There is a place for her in my heart, and there always will be, but the rest of it, and all of me, are yours." *All of him!* Oh, I wanted that! My heart leapt at the thought, and I forgot all about his reference to his love for me being like a disease.

Caught completely off guard by the unexpected turn our conversation had taken, I became aware that I was gaping at him, mouth hanging open, eyes wide. I closed my mouth, but my head still spun deliriously.

"I seem to have rendered you speechless," Erik said tenderly. "There is just one more thing before you finish with my arm and have your bath," he continued. I looked at him questioningly. What now? I had just swung from heartbreak to joy in a matter of a few moments and was not certain I could manage further revelations. It soon became clear, however, that further speech was not his intention.

Erik put his hand under my chin and lifted my face up toward his. At his gentle touch I felt my skin turn hot; it felt as though I were about to go up in flames. He inclined his head toward me, just as he had done once before, only this time he wasn't doing it so he could whisper in my ear. Gently and deliberately he brought his warm lips to mine. Who would have thought the fearsome Phantom had it in him to be so tender?

Soft and sweet to begin with, then growing more passionate as we gave ourselves over to it, this was really our first kiss. Not the one I gave him as he was leaving me, nor the hard kiss he gave me when he found me again. *This* kiss was a shared exploration. For someone who had not a lot of practice, Erik was quite proficient at kissing. *He was a natural*, I thought, before all rational thoughts were wiped from my head.

My arms twined around his neck and my fingers went into his soft hair, holding him to me. I seemed to transfer some of the heat that engulfed me over to Erik; how warm his skin felt through the fabric of my gown. Somewhere in the back of my mind, I was vaguely aware that I was doing something incredibly improper: embracing a man who was not wearing a shirt, but I could not be bothered to feel even the slightest bit guilty. In fact, I was reveling in it. Definitely not the same Sylvie I had once been. What would M. Blanc say if he could see me now?

After a few moments, during which our breathing became fast and heavy, we pulled apart and stared at each other, panting. His eyes were hungry and smoldering.

"It is good to know what I have been missing," he said breathlessly. Then, seeming unable to stop himself, Erik pulled me close again, and tenderly cradled my head against his shoulder. Holding me in a tight embrace, he sighed softly.

"Sylvie," he whispered. "You cannot imagine what hell I went through this week. My every waking moment was utter torture. Trying desperately to find you before..." he paused to press a hot kiss to my forehead. "I wanted to kick myself a thousand times over for being such a selfish, thoughtless brute."

I put my hand on his cheek soothingly. "What do you mean?" I asked, puzzled.

"What if I hadn't been in time? What if Gaston had killed you before I got there? How could I live with myself knowing I had stupidly thrown away your love in hopeless pursuit of someone who could never care for me the way you do?" His arms tightened until I could scarcely breathe. "I can't bear to think about it." He muttered ferociously.

I forced my hands between us and pushed firmly until he released me. Staring into his flushed face, it was all I could do not to smile ridiculously at him, his tormented words gave me so much pleasure. Instead I gave his broad shoulders a little shake.

"Then do not think about it." I admonished firmly. "We have enough problems without your worrying about things that did not happen."

Erik sighed. "*Oui*, you are right, as usual. Come then, hurry up and finish with my arm. We will have the rest of our lives to sort things out between us, but only if we get out of here safely." Reluctantly, I had to admit he was right. My hands none too steady, I finished disinfecting the wound and wrapped it in clean bandages.

A belated sense of guilt was coming to me. Walking through my downstairs kitchen tonight had brought the Hospital to the forefront of my mind. I was filled with chagrin when I thought of how they must have thought themselves abandoned without a word. That it was not my fault did not matter.

"What must they think of me at St. Giles?" I said woefully to Erik as I rose from the floor cradling the bowl of red-tinged water.

"What do you mean?" He asked, looking up at me questioningly.

"All those days I was imprisoned, unable to get word to them – Dr. Gaudet even reported me to the police as a missing person."

Erik looked smug. "They know that you have not abandoned them. I sent Dr. Gaudet a note after I learned you were missing, telling them you were called away suddenly and they would need to make alternate arrangements until further notice."

"You thought of that?" I asked, surprise and admiration in my voice.

He opened his mouth to reply, but was overtaken by an enormous yawn which he was unable to completely stifle. *Pauvre homme*, he was exhausted.

"You ought to sleep now. I have probably slept more than you have. After I bathe, I will stand watch so you can rest." I rose and reached down for him. He followed without protest as I led him into my bedroom and once again, found myself tucking him under my mother's quilt. A queer sense of *déjà vu* came over me as I pulled the edge of the quilt up over his shoulder.

"Be careful," was the last coherent thing he said to me before falling soundly asleep. It was good advice. But I wasn't certain how to follow it.

CHAPTER TWENTY-SIX

'Everyone knows that drunkards and lovers have a protecting deity'

A.D.

Words cannot describe how incredibly good it felt to empty the last can of hot water into my bath and immerse myself in warm lavender-scented water. I had the misfortune of catching a glimpse of myself in my cheval glass on my way to the bath chamber, making my need for hot water all the more urgent. My tangled hair hung limply around my head and shoulders; my face was ghostly pale and streaked with dried tears. Even worse was the ugly, yellow-green bruise spread over my right temple. No amount of hot water would wash *that* away. How on earth Erik could have found me kissable in such a state was beyond my comprehension. I won't even mention the state of my poor gown; suffice it to say, that gown was going straight into the rubbish bin. I never wanted to see it again.

I lay back in the warm scented water with a sigh of pleasure, and tried somewhat reluctantly to come to grips with everything that had happened, and all that still needed to happen. So much had occurred in such a short period of time, I was having difficulty taking it all in. I refused to dwell any further on my ordeal at Gaston's hands; it was over, and we had more urgent matters to think about. Getting away from my apartment before someone came back to relieve the guard, for instance. We could not be sure exactly what hour of the morning that might occur. And then there was the small matter of where we could go. I had a little nest egg of money tucked away in an old teapot in my *garde-manger*; the police search had left it undisturbed. I must remember to collect it before we left.

There would be no safe haven for us, and I could not imagine even Erik finding a way to get us both out of the city undetected. Erik had nothing but the clothes on his back, and he certainly could not go far wearing a torn and bloody shirt without attracting undue attention. And he had willfully left his mask behind! I wished he had not done that. Sighing, I dipped my hair under the water so I could wash it.

Perhaps, I thought, Erik intended to appeal to his mysterious friend the Persian for additional help. Hmmm. There was definitely more to that story than I had any idea, and eventually I intended to find out more about the man Erik called 'daroga'. I harbored a bit of resentment toward him for his flat refusal to shelter us when we most needed it.

I turned my attention while washing my hair to the much more interesting fact that the former Phantom had just proposed to me. It was a rather unorthodox proposal, in that he had not exactly given me a choice, but he could be in no doubt of my answer. How like Erik that was! He still retained his forceful, controlling personality, and probably always would.

How odd this was – when I had given up all hope of winning his affections, Erik was bestowing them on me freely. Did he mean it? I sincerely hoped so, but I knew it mattered not a whit because of course I would accept him. He was everything I had ever wanted. But how could we possibly marry under such difficult circumstances as we now faced? There were so many obstacles to overcome.

A little frown creased my forehead. We would be two fugitives, both of us hunted across Paris, and the death of Gaston, although richly deserved, would only make pursuit that much stronger. It was far more likely that we would both hang than have the chance to wed. Even Erik could not alter those unpalatable facts.

I rinsed my hair with a fresh pitcher of water, and began sponging myself idly while my thoughts wandered and the water gradually cooled. All obstacles aside, if we actually *could* marry, I knew that I wanted Father Barbier to perform the ceremony. Over time he had become like a true father to me, the closest thing to family I had. A happy picture formed in my mind: I saw Erik and me standing before the old priest, right there in the chapel at St. Giles. Under those beautiful stained glass windows.

And then it struck me. My hand froze in mid-air, squeezing the dripping sponge. Why hadn't I thought of it before? There *was* a safe haven waiting for us! I sat up so rapidly water splashed over the edge of the bath. Erik's friend the Persian might be unwilling to give us shelter, but we would always be welcome at St. Giles Hospital. We would be safer there than anywhere. No one save Gaston knew of my connection to that place, thanks to my vow of secrecy. And Gaston was in no condition to tell anyone. All we needed to do was get there undetected, a journey of only a few miles. Then we could rest in complete safety, we could wed in safety, and plan our next steps. It could be done – the Phaeton and pair were still at our disposal assuming they had not been discovered yet.

I hastily finished bathing, toweled myself off, and selected a gown from the *armoire*: one of the pretty new ones recently made for

337

me. After a luxurious dusting of scented talcum powder I slipped into it. It was wonderful to feel clean and fresh again.

When I returned to the *salon* to dry my hair before the embers of the dying fire, Erik was still sweetly sleeping. I hated to wake him, but I knew I would have to do so before much more time passed. I was anxious to be off. Any sense of safety here was ephemeral at best.

Looking around my little room, disheveled as it was, I felt a pang of loss. It was mine, and I had been happy here. I would never see it again, never run my hand over the keys of the pianoforte ever again. It broke my heart to part with my mother's beloved instrument. But then the warm glow of the fire triggered other, more recent memories, reminding me of the promise of future delights, helping to drive away my melancholy thoughts. Having Erik belong to me for the rest of my life was certainly adequate compensation for the loss of some material objects.

When my hair was almost dry I twisted it into a neat coil at the back of my head, secured it with a few pins, and descended the stairs to check on our prisoner. We had left him as comfortable as was possible under the circumstances, as comfortable as one can be when trussed up like a turkey with a strip of my petticoat tied around his mouth. I found him asleep and snoring softly, as yet blissfully unaware of his current situation. I hoped he would not be in trouble when someone came to relieve him: poor man, it was not his fault. He was, I thought ruefully, fortunate indeed to still be alive.

Leaving the guard to his forced nap, I peered cautiously out the window. All was quiet on the street outside. Checking the time by my clock on the wall, I was surprised to see it was not very late, only a little after 10:00 p.m. So much had happened, and my sense of time was so confused, I assumed it to be much later. This was all to the good; there would be plenty of other carriages and cabriolets plying the streets of Paris at this hour, so hopefully we could blend in.

I hated to do it, but it was time to awaken Erik. Back upstairs again, I slipped quietly into the bed chamber and sat down carefully on the edge of the bed, next to my soon-to-be-husband. My eyes drank him in eagerly.

He was deeply asleep, his breathing soft, regular. I was sorry I could not let him rest any longer, for his face looked tired and drawn. He lay on his right side, his wounded left arm held close to his body. I reached out and very gently lifted back the lock of soft brown hair that always fell forward onto his face when he exerted himself. He had been absolutely magnificent tonight, and although the ring he wore

338

against his breast testified to his undying love for another, he was here, with me. He had risked capture and death to save me. Such a fierce feeling of love came over me as I sat there quietly watching him sleep – no, more than love, a sense of triumph even. My hands clenched in my lap. He was *mine,* my wonderful *homme fatal.* After all this time, after everything that had happened, he belonged to me, and I was never going to let him go. But first I must get him to sanctuary. If we were apprehended at this juncture, without a doubt we would both hang.

Releasing my breath in a little sigh, I forced myself to reach out and place my hand gently on his shoulder. "Wake up, *mon amour,* it is time to go," I murmured.

Without opening his eyes, he gave a low but heartfelt groan. Rolling over to his back, he brushed his hand across his face. There was a rasping sound as he did so, for he badly needed to shave. Finally he opened his eyes and regarded me with a mutinously grumpy expression.

"I thought you were going to let me sleep," he muttered accusingly.

"I am sorry, Erik, but we really must leave here." Being quite pleased with my idea, I allowed a little note of smugness enter my voice. "I have thought of a place we can go, and once we get there, you can sleep all you wish in perfect safety. And there will also be something to eat." I was by now conscious of being quite hungry.

He was already two steps ahead of me, *naturellement.* "We are going to the hospital." He said matter-of-factly.

I sat back, disappointed. "You already thought of it?"

Erik shrugged. "It was our only option. We could not hope to escape from Paris tonight – all roads out of the city will be watched, if not barricaded against us. *Après tout,* I did just kill the Chief-Inspector of the *Sûreté.*" He sat up as he spoke, running his hands through his unruly hair.

"In self defense!" I cried, bristling with indignation. "What injustice!"

Erik smiled. "Yes, my little Firebrand, but they cannot know that. No one knows the truth except us. And then of course I threw out that little taunt by leaving my mask on his body. I don't suppose anyone but Gaston and his hired thugs even knew he held you prisoner, Sylvie. He would have been careful about that, the swine." He reached out and gently caressed the bump on my forehead.

"I wish he were still alive, so I could kill him slowly and at my leisure." He meant it, I knew. He was still Erik, I reminded myself with a slight shiver. Still capable of frightening me now and then.

"Never mind that now." I said rising from the bed. I pulled the quilt away and took his hand. "I'm afraid you have nothing to wear except that horrid blood-stained shirt and your waistcoat does nothing to hide the stains."

Erik rolled out of bed and stood up with a heartfelt groan. He stretched deeply, and heat kindled inside me when I saw the way his chest muscles contracted with the movement. I looked away, momentarily flustered. Erik did not notice.

While Erik splashed water on his face and put on his hideously stained shirt and waistcoat, I went on with my own hasty preparations for departure. I gathered a few necessary articles of clothing and toiletries into a valise, and fished inside the old cracked teapot for the few hundred francs hidden away there. I would have to leave every other thing, and what would become of it all I had no idea.

I paused to pick up the miniature portrait of my mother, wrapping it carefully in a handkerchief. My mother's beloved pianoforte! To think that I was now forced to abandon it. I felt tears well up in my eyes but I blinked them back fiercely. This was no time to grieve over my lost possessions. It was far better to lose one's possessions than ones' life, after all.

I wrapped myself in my cloak; standing by the door, I looked about the little room one last time. The fire was dying in the grate; shadows were growing long in the room. Erik, emerging from the bedroom, saw my distress and came to me at once. Taking my hand, he squeezed it sympathetically before pulling me out the door and down the stairs.

As we passed through the kitchen, I ran my hand over the gleaming black surface of my *Godin* stove. It had been my pride and joy.

"I paid a small fortune for this," I murmured sadly.

"*Allons-y*," said Erik urgently, leading me toward the door. "Do not think of it now. I will buy you a hundred stoves once we are safe." Out on the cold, dark street, Erik began pulling me along in his rapid wake.

"We might as well see if the Phaeton and pair are still where we left them," he said. "I would rather ride than walk all the way to St. Giles." I could but agree.

We retraced our earlier steps, coming out at last in the mews where we had abandoned the Phaeton. To my relief it was still there, the horses stamping patiently and steaming a little in the cold. Erik stroked their beautiful soft muzzles and fed them each a sugar lump he had somehow purloined from my kitchen. They appeared ready to do his bidding, as though he had known them for years.

Soon we were on our way, the horses eager to be moving again. We decided to proceed directly to one of the main boulevards so that we could mingle with many other people, carriages and broughams and hopefully pass unnoticed to our destination. Although I could pull the hood of my cloak over my head and cast my face into shadow, Erik had no such article of clothing, nor had he a hat, so there was no disguising that distinctive face. All he could do was keep the right side of his face turned inward, toward me, and keep to the darker portions of the streets, away from the lamps.

Frowning at him worriedly, I asked, "Could you and your friend not have stolen a *closed* carriage, Erik?"

Raising an eyebrow sardonically, he replied gently,

"It was speed I was in need of at the time, Sylvie."

I could not but acknowledge the truth of that. The Phaeton was a famously nimble vehicle and we had needed the speed to outrun Gaston's servants. But still....

I kept a sharp eye on the busy streets we were threading through. Fortunately, no one seemed to give us more than a cursory glance. Unsurprisingly, there were quite a number of *gendarmes* out tonight, and each time we passed one I held my breath.

"A closed carriage would be much safer, Erik," I said, gritting my teeth.

Erik laughed. "Amazing," he said cheerfully. "I feel married already." He glanced at me, looking both amused and happy.

"Shrew," he murmured tenderly, his eyes warm.

I could not resist an answering smile and felt myself relax a bit. But after a few minutes I remembered something else I wanted to ask him. I turned to Erik once more.

"You never actually told me about the second letter Gaston left for you. What was in it?"

He did not respond right away; a slight grimace passed across his face before he spoke.

"A small lock of your hair, for one thing," he answered slowly. "I still have it, here in my pocket." He patted the pocket of his waistcoat. "I was hoping it would bring me good fortune in my search for you." We were passing through the Tuileries now, heading for the Pont Royal Bridge. In my imagination I saw the bridge held against us by countless *gendarmes*, fear multiplying them into an army. I pushed the vision away and tried to concentrate on our conversation instead.

"A lock of my hair? I do not remember...I suppose it must have been taken while I was still unconscious." I mused. Erik made a sound in his throat like a low growl. His hands clenched on the reins. "Well, it must have worked, for you did find me," I added.

"Gaston wanted me to be absolutely certain you were his prisoner. He knew I would recognize your hair. He told me you were hidden away where I would never find you, and I had until tomorrow morning to turn myself in at the Préfecture de Police, or...or a part of your anatomy would be found somewhere, and to watch the newspapers so I could read about it. An *incentive* for me, he called it." So my idea of Gaston placing an advertisement in *Le Monde* was, in fact, perfectly accurate, I thought wryly to myself.

"One of my fingers," I explained. "He made sure to tell me about that on a regular basis. I believe he was hoping you would not come back in time."

"He also said, if I still did not turn myself in after *that* reminder, your body would be found floating in the Seine. He assured me you would be...tortured first." His voice grew bleak and chill with remembered horror. "If I took any other action besides the one specified in his letter, he swore he would kill you at once." His voice sank to almost a whisper.

Giving himself a little shake, he added, "But the bastard made the mistake of providing me with a little too much information about where he was holding you – he was only too happy to gloat over what the place was like, how difficult it would be to find, and on and on. That was how I knew what I was searching for, and then I was lucky enough to observe one of his servants on the street." Erik gave me a dark look.

"I knew I would have only one chance to save you, Sylvie," he said.

I could not repress a shudder. I did not want to think about what might have happened to me if Erik had not come back to look for me. If he had not bothered; if he did not care enough. I wanted, in fact, to forget that entire, terrifying ordeal. But there was still the perplexing question of how Gaston knew he could use me against Erik. Perhaps he had told Erik something of this in one of his taunting letters.

I said, "But what I do not understand is how Gaston could be so certain you would come back and find the notes he left for you. I cannot fathom how he even knew of our connection to each other. I thought, I *believed*, he had accepted my explanation for how the ticket you gave me came into my possession. He never told me, even though it was obvious that he knew more than he was letting on." How he had bragged in that suave, silky voice of my being the lure, the bait to bring Erik to his knees. My vehement denials had meant nothing to Gaston.

Before Erik could respond we reached the bridge, we were crossing it – it was not being held against us. I released my pent breath in a long sigh. Perhaps they did not expect we would take that way, closer to the Préfecture de Police rather than away from it. Once across and making our way down the Avenue des Invalides, we both breathed easier.

Erik shook his head grimly. He glanced at me, his expression pained as he continued his story. "Gaston was withholding evidence from you the entire time, Sylvie. The bastard knew you were lying to him from the first."

"What?" I stared at him, shocked. "How could he have known? What evidence?" I asked, mystified.

"My fault again, unsurprisingly. You remember the letter of apology I started to write you that night, the one I could not finish?"

I cast my mind back, trying to recollect him telling me about a letter. Then it came to me: we had been sitting in my apartment after the fire. His apology for drawing his sword against me. So long ago! I nodded.

"*Oui*, I remember. You said you thought it must have been trampled underfoot."

"Would that that had been the case, but it was not, unfortunately. Gaston himself found it when he searched the place. He was a skilled detective, remember. He would overlook nothing. I addressed you by your first name in the salutation, and before abandoning the attempt I wrote enough for him to guess, clever as he was, not only that we knew each other, but that I cared for you. He was now in possession of two pieces of evidence involving you and me: my note for you to have my box, and that unfinished letter. He kept the letter and pretended to go along with your story, but all the while, he was plotting how to use his knowledge against me. He thought of you as fair game, I believe, because you had no one to protect you." He finished on a bitter note.

343

We turned off the main avenue onto a quiet tree-lined side street. We would soon be at our destination. Here traffic was much lighter, most of the houses and buildings dark and shuttered. The sound of the horses' hooves on the cobblestones seemed to ring loudly in the relative silence. The hour was late.

"But I did have someone to protect me: I had you." I said, slipping my arm through Erik's and giving it a squeeze. "It was very fortunate for me that you came back to Paris in time to find the first note the same day it was left. Gaston could not have expected you to be on his trail so quickly."

"*Non*, he did not, for he had not yet taken precautions to guard his *pied-à-terre* against me. As it was, I was almost too late. Not that there was any hope of his keeping me out once I found where he was holding you." He added matter-of-factly.

"*Nous voici*." He slowed the horses to a walk as we approached the forbidding iron fence surrounding the hospital.

My heart sank as we drew alongside the wrought iron gates — they were closed and barred for the night. The courtyard was empty. The cloister stood far back from the road, the warm inviting glow of lamp light visible from several of the upper windows. No one was to be seen anywhere about. How were we to get in?

"Oh dear," I said, feeling horribly discouraged. Perhaps my brilliant idea was not so brilliant after all. "I forgot the gates would be locked by now. They have all gone to bed."

Erik turned on the seat to look askance at me. "Sylvie, are you forgetting who you are with? There is no wall or fence that can hold against *me* if I want to get through it." His eyes burned into mine. "After all, I found you, didn't I?" I suppose I must have stared back at him like a moonstruck calf, for he smiled a little and said,

"I love it when you look at me like that. It makes me feel…makes me feel…" but here he stopped, unable to go on. I understood, though, what he could not say.

"Like what you are." I finished for him, my voice a gentle whisper. My magnificent hero.

We gazed at each other for a long moment, while a blue flame seemed to kindle in his eyes. I felt as though I were melting into their depths. Unexpectedly, he grasped me by the shoulders, pulled me to him and kissed me so thoroughly that it was several seconds before I realized he had released me and leapt to the ground. Opening my tightly closed eyes, I drew a ragged breath and looked wildly around for him. There was a soft laugh from somewhere near the flank of the horse on the left, then he tossed me the reins.

"Wait here, Sylvie." I heard him give the wide flank a pat, and then, moving silent as a shadow he was gone. I watched him glide along the tall iron fence, looking for a way over.

While I waited, keeping a watchful eye on the few other carriages, carts or horses passing by, I found myself musing upon the many shortcomings of my former spouse. I could not help but compare him to Erik, or more correctly, Erik to him, for other than Erik I had never kissed any man except my husband. I realized now that my ex-husband was as inadequate in that area as he had been in others.

I was interrupted from these cogitations by the sound of metal scraping against metal. Looking up, I saw Erik lifting the heavy iron bar from across the gates. In another moment he had pushed the gates wide and climbed up next to me on the seat. Taking the reins, he drove the horses inside, and then stopped to close the gates and bar them again. A few seconds later we were drawing up to the cloister doors.

"Well, are you ready for this?" He asked.

"Of course. We need have no fear of discovery here; I assure you they know nothing of what has happened." I was confident in my declaration, for I had yet to see anything from the outside world penetrate this private place. They would certainly be *very* surprised to see us, however. As far as the hospital was aware, I had callously abandoned them.

"'What has happened'?" Erik made me jump as he echoed my words brusquely. "You make it sound as if all your troubles just fell from the sky, instead of being entirely due to my actions. Thanks to me, you were almost killed by that…that…" unable to think of a word bad enough that could still be uttered in my presence, he stuttered to a halt, grinding his teeth.

"Thanks to you, I am free and safe." I answered firmly. "Now stop recriminating and let us knock on the door. I do hope someone will still be awake; I am very cold." I said briskly, putting an end to his guilty rant. I could see he was starting to become upset, but I knew it was only nerves and exhaustion.

"I am sorry, Sylvie," Erik replied contritely. "I am so used to cold that I no longer feel it the way others do. Let us go in." He assisted me to climb down from the high seat of the Phaeton and together we mounted the steps to the cloister door. As we stood side by side, his hand slipped into mine and grasped it firmly. With the other, he lifted the knocker and rapped it soundly several times. We could hear the muffled reverberations echo through the open space of the chapel.

I confess to a little uneasiness at that moment. Belatedly, I realized that I had given no thought whatsoever about what I was going to say to Dr. Gaudet. How was I to account for my abrupt and mysterious departure, and now my sudden reappearance, along with my 'cousin' demanding to be allowed to stay at the hospital? I had thought only of reaching a safe haven, not what I would say when we reached it. I was just about to say as much to Erik when footsteps could be heard approaching the door.

Visitors after nightfall were unheard of; I wondered who would open the door. Bolts were drawn back; finally one of the great doors drew inward and a face appeared. It was the grizzled visage of Robert, holding an oil lamp in one hand and frowning at us suspiciously. To my surprise, I found I was glad to see him again. I moved forward, into the circle of lamplight, and addressed him.

"Good evening, Robert; it is I, Sylvie Bessette. I apologize for arriving at such a late hour, but may we come in, please?"

Robert's face assumed an expression of utter astonishment when he saw me. It took him several seconds to form a reply.

"Mademoiselle Bessette? What are you doing here? We were told you were gone." His voice was accusing, as though he had taken my desertion personally.

"Robert, I must speak to Dr. Gaudet at once, it is very important. Can you take us to him?" My voice sounded sharp to my own ears; I was running low on patience. All I wanted at that moment was to be inside, where lay safety. I felt Erik's grip tighten on my hand. At the word 'us', Robert became aware that I was not alone; he transferred his astonished gaze to Erik. Robert regarded him in silence, his obstinate face not altering its stubborn lines in the slightest.

"You have come back too?" He asked at last. It was clear from his unfriendly tone that Robert was not particularly pleased to see Erik with me. Erik moved forward a step to stand next to me, placing his arm around my shoulder.

"Robert, Mademoiselle Bessette is cold." He said firmly. "She needs to come inside now." Robert gave one of his Gallic shrugs that are so much more eloquent than mere words, and stepped back, holding the door wider to admit us. When we stepped over that venerable threshold and heard the sound of the heavy door bolted

346

behind us I breathed a long sigh of relief – we had reached our sanctuary. Here we would be safe.

"*Merci*, Robert. Do you know if Dr. Gaudet still awake?" I asked anxiously while tugging at my gloves. I hoped he was not already in bed, but the hour was late.

Robert left us warming our hands in front of the great fireplace in the refectory, where a few welcome embers still glowed, while he went to fetch Dr. Gaudet, who was fortunately still puttering about in his clinic. Reluctantly Robert agreed to Erik's request that he go out and put the horses in the medieval stable at the back of the property even though, he grumbled, the cold would be very hard on his arthritis.

"Well, he hasn't changed a bit," Erik muttered sourly as he watched Robert's retreating form. As soon as we were alone, I turned to Erik, my fingers gripping the front of his waistcoat in agitation.

"Erik, what are we going to say to Dr. Gaudet? I confess I cannot think of anything sensible, and I know he must be very upset with me." Erik reached up and gently untied the ribbon that held my cloak around my neck, saying as he did so,

"It is no wonder, Sylvie, after what you have been through. I am not thinking very clearly myself." He removed the heavy cloak, tossed it over a nearby chair, and then drew me very tenderly into his arms, cradling my head against his shoulder.

"Everything will be fine," he said. "Dr. Gaudet is a good man; he will listen, whatever we tell him." I relaxed against him, a sigh escaping my lips. I could feel all the terror and fear from my nightmare ordeal of the past week melting away. It was thus that Dr. Gaudet found us a moment later when he came hastening into the room, pulling a rather elaborately embroidered silk dressing gown over his wide girth.

"*Alors, c'est vrai*! I could not believe what Robert told me, but I see with my own eyes it is true. Mademoiselle and Monsieur Bessette! How glad I am to see you both!" He crossed the room quickly and took my hand in both of his, obviously pleased to see us, but also looking perplexed. I was momentarily caught off guard myself, for I had forgotten that we had given Erik my last name when I first introduced him to the hospital.

"*Bonsoir*, Doctor," I said. "It is very good to see you again, too. I hope it is true, what Robert said, that we did not get you out of bed; the hour is late, I know, and our visit unexpected."

He gave a dismissive little wave of his hand. "Ah, bah, I always spend a little time in my clinic before retiring. It is the best chance for me to conduct my research of the disease…" he paused, for his eyes were finally really taking us in: the ugly yellow bruise on my forehead, Erik standing close to me, one arm around my waist, the other revealing my bandaging efforts through the rent sleeve, the dried blood. Dr. Gaudet's eyes widened in alarm.

"But what has happened? *Mon Dieu,* you are both injured; do you require medical attention?" It was probably a good idea. If one has an actual medical doctor at one's disposal, one might as well take advantage of the opportunity. Erik apparently agreed;

"If it would not be too much trouble, Doctor," he said.

"I believe the wound may need to be stitched, Doctor," I murmured. Erik gave me an annoyed look.

Dr. Gaudet turned at once and began to stride away, talking as he did so. *"Mais oui!* Come to my clinic, then. This is all very strange, we thought you were gone away for good, Mlle. Bessette; at first we were afraid you had met with foul play, but then we received a note but it was not signed…" muttering to himself, he led the way to the clinic and we followed in his stout, stolid wake.

Settled in the neat, clean little clinic room, smelling of antiseptic, the gaslights turned up brightly, Dr. Gaudet proceeded to carefully unwind the fresh bandages I had dressed Erik's arm with. I held my breath as he inspected the wound. There was a little more fresh blood, from Erik's having to keep using his arm so much, *sans doute,* but it looked clean otherwise, and the skin was not red or unduly warm, both signs of infection.

"Mon Dieu!" Dr. Gaudet exclaimed again. "This is a sword wound!" He frowned in concern. "Were you attacked, young man?" Dr. Gaudet began to rummage about in a drawer for what he would need. As he did so, he peered at us inquiringly.

Erik's immediate welfare was of paramount concern to me; he was exhausted, suffering from loss of blood, and very likely hungry. I decided it was time to put an end to questions, so I spoke up before Erik could even open his mouth to answer.

"No, Doctor, it was I who was attacked, and my…my cousin…came to my rescue and fought off my assailant, but he was wounded as you see. We came here because, well, because we need a safe place to stay for a little while. And Erik needed medical attention." Hastening through my explanation, I thought it sounded preposterous to my own ears. Erik must have thought so too, for he very studiously avoided looking at me while I stumbled through my contrived and necessarily expurgated story. Dr. Gaudet paused in the act of sterilizing a very sharp-looking needle and stared at Erik, a shocked expression on his face.

"Someone set upon Mlle. Bessette? But that is terrible! Did the assailant get away? Should we not notify the police?"

Erik very deliberately raised his head and looked the doctor in the eye. "There is no need," he said levelly.

Dr. Gaudet's eyes widened slightly; they dropped from Erik's face to the sword still at his side, and then he returned to what he was doing. He had never seen Erik wear a sword, let alone one with a silver skull for a foil. I wondered what was passing through his mind.

"Is that how you received that blow to your head, Mademoiselle?" He asked after a moment's thoughtful silence. He must know otherwise – it was clearly an old bruise.

"*Oui*," I answered promptly. Erik was enduring Dr. Gaudet's ministrations with stoic silence, but glancing at his pale face, I continued, "Dr. Gaudet, I promise we will explain everything clearly in the morning, but for tonight, I really think that Erik…that my cousin needs to be in bed. He has lost a great deal of blood and he is worn out. We were hoping…you see, I have lost my apartment and…and Sister Chantal told me once there were a few empty rooms on the third floor, that were the nuns quarters…could not we have two of those for the night?" I asked hopefully.

Dr. Gaudet finished stitching the wound closed, disinfected it and began to bandage it again. Then he sat back and regarded me through his pince-nez thoughtfully. Finally, he rose, rested his hand on Erik's shoulder for a moment in an almost fatherly gesture, and smiled.

"*Certainement*, Mademoiselle. It is as you say: there are several sleeping rooms on the third floor. They have been unused for a long time but they are at your disposal. If you will give me a few minutes, I will see to it. Robert has gone out to tend to your horses."

Approximately twenty minutes later, I was making up a small bed with fresh linens in a small, snug room on the third floor. The patients were prohibited from that floor due to concerns of possible contamination; it was kept exclusively for the nuns who lived and worked at the hospital. There were a number of vacant sleeping chambers because there were fewer patients now than when the hospital was first opened. The room was a bit musty from being long closed up, but at least the linens were fresh and clean.

Erik was sitting nearby at an old wood table, watching me while he devoured bread, cheese and ham which I had located in the cold room off the hospital kitchen. Tucking in the last corner, I twitched the duvet into place and came to sit at the table across from him. Breaking off a morsel of cheese, I began nibbling on it rather reluctantly.

"This reminds me too much of the fare I have had for the last week; I cannot summon any enthusiasm for it I'm afraid." I said ruefully. "I have been dreaming of all the meals I made for you, Erik. And a cup of tea! You have no idea how much I longed for a cup of tea."

Mouth full of ham and cheese, Erik made a sympathetic noise. Swallowing, he replied, "Don't worry, Sylvie. You can have all the tea you can possibly hold in the morning."

Brushing a few crumbs from my skirt, I murmured, "This has surely been one of the most unusual nights of my life."

"*Vraiment?*" Erik looked at me askance. "This sort of thing happens to me all the time." Then, seeing my startled expression, he laughed. "Don't look at me like that; I am teasing you, Sylvie. But I do not think I can remain upright for another minute. That bed looks extremely welcome." I had completely forgotten where we were and that we would not be sharing a room. I blushed to the roots of my hair and hastily rose to leave.

"I need to make up my own bed anyway. I am in the room next to yours. I will go so that you can sleep." Erik, too exhausted to take notice of my suddenly crimson face, sat on the edge of the bed and pulled off his boots.

"I must say, Dr. Gaudet is a man of hidden depths," he mused. "He surprises me almost as much as you do, Sylvie. He had to know we were telling him a string of lies, and yet he went right along with them. I must think of a way to thank him for taking a chance on us." He gave his head a shake, and looked up at me with a wry smile.

"I know! It was certainly not what I was expecting. And he did not seem angry with me in the slightest." I sighed, wrapping the end of the loaf in a clean dish cloth. "I rather hate to break the news to him that I cannot resume my former duties."

"You are never happy unless you have something or other to worry about, are you, Sylvie?" He said with a touch of his former sardonic teasing. I was glad to hear it. Sitting on his bed looking tired, rumpled and outrageously handsome, he asked,

"Aren't you going to kiss me goodnight? After all, I am your *fiancé* now."

I needed no further encouragement to sit next to him on the bed.

"To be perfectly honest, I am reluctant to leave you at all – I am afraid you will vanish into thin air when my back is turned." It still felt like a miracle that he was here with me.

Erik smiled at me gently. "I will be here in the morning, I promise, Sylvie. I am never leaving you again." Bending his head, he kissed me softly on the lips, and then his face split into an enormous yawn. Laughing, I rose, stroked his hair gently and bade him goodnight.

Alone in my own room next to his, I stripped away the dusty bedding and remade the little iron bed with clean sheets and a duvet. I peeled myself out of my gown and chemise, took off my stockings, pulled my nightgown from my valise, shook it out and quickly assumed it, the room being chill. I stood before a small, foxed mirror to brush out my hair and braid it for the night. The green and yellow bruise on my temple was already fading. Dr. Gaudet had given me arnica salve for it, and soon it would be gone.

After performing my ablutions I was tremendously happy to slide between the cold linen sheets. Curling on my side under the duvet, I lay still and let heat gather, and wondered if I had been dreaming all the events of the past few weeks. It hardly seemed possible that such things could all have happened to one person. If this was what it felt like to be a heroine in a novel, I thought bemusedly, I was certain I never cared to be one. From now on, when I daydreamed, it was going to be about really mundane, boring things, I was sure.

Then there was the small matter of what we were going to tell everyone at the hospital on the morrow. I turned over on the rather hard little bed, fluffed my pillow, and deliberately put that worry out of my head.

Just as sleep was about to pull me under, I smiled a little: I had a *fiancé*!

CHAPTER TWENTY-SEVEN

'Leave me then, to act, and have no fears of the result'
A.D.

I awoke in the morning from a heavy, drugging sleep. I had dreamed I was making *tarte tatin* with my mother and smothering it with thick fresh cream. She was scolding me for using so much cream. But the dream quickly vanished, to be followed almost instantly by heart-pounding panic. Would I open my eyes and find myself still trapped in Gaston's secret torture chamber? When I forced my reluctant eyes to open, the first thing I saw was sunlight sparkling off ancient leaded glass panels in the narrow cloister window.

Panic instantly changed to joy; I threw back the duvet, slid out of bed and went to look out at the morning light. Words cannot express my feelings at that moment, so I will not attempt it. But I will attest this; after my imprisonment in windowless darkness I would never again take sunshine, moonlight, or the stars for granted ever again.

Presently I remembered Erik sleeping in the next room. Anxious to check on him (and perhaps also anxious to assure myself that he was, indeed, there), I drew on my dressing gown and slipped out into the chilly corridor. Carefully, quietly, I opened his door and peeped in. He was there! Wild joy suffused me in the few seconds that followed, while I hovered in the doorway peeking in at Erik. Unsurprisingly he was still deep in slumber, flat on his back, one arm flung out over the edge of the small bed. He looked so young and sleep-sweetened, I battled an almost irresistible urge to sit next to him and stroke his tumbled hair. It would have been cruel of me to wake him, however. Reluctantly, I retreated and closed the door.

Returning to my own room, I performed my ablutions in a basin of cold water, assumed my blue gown, and put up my hair, all the while pondering what lay before us. The day would, I knew, be filled with complications and little pitfalls we must find a way to avoid if possible.

Fortunately for us, the patients spent time in the mornings taking a cautious amount of exercise. Great care was necessary at all times in order to prevent injuries to their numb extremities, but Dr. Gaudet was a proponent of exercise, believing good circulation would delay the progress of the disease. After taking their exercise, each of the priests spent a few minutes in the clinic for an exam, medications, and fresh wrappings on hands and feet. I was glad they would be thus occupied, for it gave us some time alone to consider what we ought to tell everyone. How to account for my sudden reappearance with my erstwhile 'cousin' in tow, like two lost souls in the night?

Feeling unequal to the task of facing the patients alone, I waited in my room until Erik arose an hour later, looking well-rested and healthy. We went down to the refectory together, but when I attempted to broach the subject of my worries, he was strangely quiet.

'Not now, Sylvie," was all he would say. Although I wished to contradict him, because *now* seemed the best time, his quelling expression bade me keep silent.

The previous spring, when I first obtained my contract with St. Giles, I'd made arrangements for a nearby *boulangerie* to deliver soft rolls and fresh butter to the hospital each day, to make a simple but nourishing *petit déjeuner*. Erik and I now hungrily availed ourselves of this repast while sitting at the refectory table. Never had fresh rolls, jam and butter tasted so good! Biting eagerly into a warm buttered roll, I licked a bit of jam off my lip and closed my eyes, savoring the taste of real, delicious food. When I opened my eyes, however, I saw that Erik was watching me, his expression bleak.

"Don't look at me like that,' I said firmly. "Eat your breakfast."

Exasperation replaced guilt on his face, and he shook his head. 'Shrew,' he murmured, biting into his own roll. Pleased, I went back to my own repast.

Once our appetites had been satisfied, I again brought forth the subject foremost on my mind – our explanations – but for some unaccountable reason this morning there was an awkward, almost uncomfortable void between us. We made little eye contact and there was an air of awkwardness surrounding us.

Erik was preoccupied and quiet; he wore a grave and thoughtful expression on his face. For my part, I worried inwardly that it was because he regretted saying certain things to me the previous night. Perhaps he had only been carried away by the success of his daring rescue, and now repented his declaration and proposal of marriage. Or, even worse, he had decided he still loved Mlle. Daaé much more than he did me. These chilling thoughts kept me silent and downcast.

Presently the patients began arriving to have their morning coffee and rolls, and each one stared in disbelief at finding us there.

The last to arrive was the one I most wanted to see: Father Barbier. Upon observing us, he gave a start of surprise and came to a full stop, his black eyes round, moving swiftly from me to Erik and back again.

"Sylvie!" He exclaimed at last. He started toward me, but Erik rose swiftly and intercepted him.

"Father," he murmured in a low voice, "Will you come with me for a moment? I must speak with Dr. Gaudet about several pressing matters, and one of them concerns you."

Father Barbier looked at him searchingly for a few seconds, then nodded his assent, and turned to retrace his steps. Starting away with him toward the clinic, Erik paused to look back at me. He saw me watching him anxiously with a question in my eyes. He sent me a reassuring smile; his eyes alight with tenderness. Some of my distress lessened, but still I watched them go with trepidation.

Meanwhile I was left on my own to face the others, who promptly took their places at the table near me, full of questions and all very pleased to see me again so unexpectedly. Was I going to cook for them again? It was to be hoped so, for, although they did not want to complain, the fare since my abrupt departure over a week ago had been sadly lacking. Where had I been? How had I acquired that bruise on my forehead? And so on, ad infinitum. I was scarcely required to speak a word, only to smile and nod and listen to their speculations. I kept one eye on the door, though, anxious for the return of the man who was my hero and my heart's desire.

They were gone some thirty minutes. Erik came first, looking smug and self-satisfied, like a cat with cream on his whiskers. It was a look that inspired the direst forebodings in me. Dr. Gaudet and Father Barbier followed. Dr. Gaudet smiled warmly at me.

"*Bon matin*, Mlle. Bessette. I trust you slept well. I cannot linger – I am entrusted with an important errand that will not keep, so I am off this very moment." He pulled on his old fashioned frock coat as he was speaking, picked up a roll from the basket on the table, and bustled out the door, eyes alight with poorly suppressed excitement.

I turned my inquiring gaze upon Erik, but that vexing individual instead turned to Father Barbier, and spoke to him in a voice too low to carry. Father Barbier nodded, and led the way to the fireplace on the opposite wall. He picked up a bible and the two of them began poring over it, talking quietly. After a moment, Father Barbier marked a place in his bible with a bit of ribbon and closed the book. Erik was not the slightest bit religious, as I well knew.

I was now beginning to feel quite cross, and had just made up my mind to go to Erik and demand to know why he was keeping secrets from me. But just as I was about to stalk across the room, Father Barbier looked up and made a gesture for me to approach. I was happy to do so, since Erik was sitting next to him. As I crossed the room to join them, however, Erik rose, gave me a reassuring nod, and walked away. Perplexed, I watched him depart into the chapel; after a few seconds I could hear him running his fingers over the keys of the piano. I took his empty seat next to the fire, looking expectantly toward Father Barbier. I did not speak, for fear my voice would give away my inner turmoil. Father Barbier regarded me with a serious expression.

"That young man seems very accustomed to getting his own way," he said at last, shaking his head disapprovingly. If he but knew!

"He has just informed me that you and he are to be married *demain*, and I am to perform the ceremony." His stubby bandaged hand touched the Bible in his lap, and he fixed me with his bright black eyes. *Oh.*

"Are you certain this is the right thing, *ma petite*? I do not mind telling you I have misgivings about this. I would hate for you to make such a grave mistake."

It took me a moment to gather my wits sufficiently to respond to his question; my breath caught at the word 'tomorrow', and I had not got much farther than that. Erik knew me well; he knew without my having to say anything that it was my fondest wish to have Father Barbier perform our ceremony. It was a relief to learn that he had not changed his mind about marrying me, but I confess I was just a little, well, discomfited at the thought of being married so quickly. I had thought I would have a little more time to get used to the idea.

But why did Father Barbier think I was making such a grievous error? I frowned. Now that I looked back on it, I realized he had never really warmed to Erik; he always seemed to mistrust him. But he need not worry. I answered firmly,

"*Oui*, Father, I am absolutely resolved on this. Ever since I first met Erik, he is all I have ever wanted." And it was true.

He regarded me gravely. "He is not your cousin, is he, Sylvie?" He asked, his dark eyes grave and perhaps a little reproachful. Unprepared for his probing question, my eyes dropped to my lap, and I blushed.

"No, he is not. He is a friend." I looked at him anxiously. "I promise you, Father, that neither he nor I have behaved in an improper manner. I would not want you thinking that." It was a lie, but I delivered it with all the earnestness I could muster.

"But why did you invent that story about him being related to you?"

"Oh, it was necessary to account for him being with me. It is difficult to explain, Father, but there are some things about Erik that cannot be divulged. Suffice it to say that he is a very complex individual." Such an understatement! I looked pleadingly at him.

He shook his head and sighed. "Those are true words, *vraiment*. Well, he will not be gainsaid, and so I have agreed to his 'request'. I understand from our private talk earlier that some rather strange events have just taken place and that you have been through an ordeal of some sort, so I will not say anything that will further distress you, my dear." After offering him another heartfelt reassurance that I did indeed know what I was about, I took my leave of Father Barbier, for I was anxious now to speak with Erik.

I found him sitting at the piano under the beautiful clerestory windows. He was not playing anything, merely running through notes idly, and he was obviously expecting me. Without looking up, he made room for me to sit next to him on the bench.

"Tomorrow?" I ventured after a moment's charged silence between us. He looked at me sidelong, his eyes unreadable, his face solemn.

"There seemed to be no point in waiting." He said, his fingers still moving gently across the keys. I thought I detected a slight questioning inflection in his voice, and I wondered what he was thinking.

Where had this awkwardness between us come from? Biting my lip, I put my hand on his arm. His restless fingers stilled at once. He seemed to be waiting.

"Erik, I must ask you…if you have changed your mind, if you do not want to…you can tell me, you know. I would understand. We were, perhaps, not entirely ourselves last night." I was afraid to look into his face, frightened of what I might see there: confirmation of my worst fears perhaps?

I realized he had been holding his breath; he let it out now slowly. He put his hand under my chin and gently turned my face so that our eyes met.

"I was going to ask you the same thing, Sylvie." At the sight of my pained expression, he went on quickly, "Do not misunderstand me. *My* feelings and wishes have not changed in the slightest; it is only that, in the light of day, I might not look like a very good choice for a husband. I do not think that your Father Barbier wants me for you. And he would be right. You of all people know what I am capable of. You should always remember, Sylvie, that even though I may love you and be good to you, I am still the same man I was before." His eyes grew intense, holding mine.

"I believe that you could make even Attila the Hun reform his wicked ways, but you will never succeed in really taming me."

Perhaps those words ought to have frightened me; instead, my heart began to hammer in my breast. Relief made me giddy, and I smiled widely at him, my wild, uncivilized wolf.

"I do not want to tame you, Erik. I only want to direct your energy in a more appropriate direction. You need me; you know that, don't you?"

Erik did not return my smile. Instead, he looked down at the keys of the piano and frowned. "Marrying you seems like the most selfish thing I'll ever do, Sylvie." He said finally. "But I'm still going to do it."

"Selfish? I do not understand why you feel that way."

Erik was quiet for a moment, as though marshalling his thoughts. Then he turned to me.

"*Mon Dieu*, you have to ask?" He made a frustrated gesture with his hands, speaking in a rush. "I don't know how to do any of this. I have no idea how to be a husband; I don't know how to behave or what I'm supposed to do. I do not know how *not* to be selfish. I am so accustomed to simply taking what I want. You will have to be very patient with me - nothing in my life up until now has prepared me for anything except being alone. I don't want to let you down, Sylvie." His voice sank to a whisper. "You mean too much to me."

I touched his hand, seeking to reassure him. "I wish you would not worry so, *mon amour*. Don't you think I have doubts and worries, too?"

Erik turned on the bench to face me. "What do you worry about," he asked gently, "other than the possibility that your new husband will forget himself and commit mayhem again?" I felt myself colour under his intent gaze, for it wasn't mayhem I was worried about. I pretended to be fascinated by the stained glass window above us. Anything to avoid meeting his eyes; I now wished fervently that I had not confessed to any doubts. But Erik would not give up. He stroked my cheek encouragingly.

357

"Tell me your worries, sweetheart. I told you mine. Yours cannot be any worse."

I was not so sanguine about that. Unable to resist his gentle persuasion, but still not able to meet his eyes, I spoke hesitantly.

"I...I worry that...that you will tire of me, Erik. And that I will eventually bore you. After all, I do not know anything about music, I cannot sing or play an instrument, and I know how important your music is to you." Flooded with embarrassment, my voice fell almost to a whisper.

"And I don't...I am nothing like..." Although I could not bring myself to say the name of the girl who hovered like a specter between us, Erik read my unspoken thoughts.

"Like Christine?" His voice was tender and grave.

"Yes."

"Oh, Sylvie." Erik reached for me then and pulled me against his chest, tucking my head against his neck. He pressed his face into my hair and sighed. "How ridiculous you are." He said. "I will never tire of you, and I do not care in the slightest that you are not musical. That will never matter to me, I promise you. It is so much more important to me that...although I do not know what it really feels like to be happy, I think, I believe, I will be happy with you. It is a strange concept for me: such uncharted territory." Realizing that we had just reassured each other, I smiled a little into his shirt front before pulling back from his embrace and staring earnestly into his face.

"We'll do this together, Erik. We'll help each other. And if I cannot make you happy, I am no cook." I declared firmly. Erik laughed.

"We've nothing to fear, then," he said.

Dr. Gaudet was out most of the day; when I asked where he had gone, Erik would only tell me that he had entrusted the doctor with an important errand for him. The errand must have been a success, because they went off to the clinic together soon after his return, the good doctor chattering away like a magpie.

"Have the packages been delivered yet?" Was the only snippet of conversation I could catch before the door closed behind them, leaving me rather perplexed.

The rest of that day passed in a kind of blur. There was a dreamlike quality about it, as though I were an invisible observer and this was happening to someone else altogether. Father Barbier, Sister Chantal, Erik and several other nuns were quite busy with preparations for the wedding that would take place on the morrow. I have a recollection of sitting quietly while people spun around me. I was at the still center of a maelstrom of activity.

I had never seen Sister Chantal so outgoing and excited, or quite so dominating: she bustled about, face flushed, habit flying, giving orders to all and sundry. Flowers, comestibles, linen tablecloths, music: who would have known the quiet, shy Sister was so knowledgeable about these worldly things! I thought of the first day I met her, when she accompanied Dr. Gaudet to interview me that long-ago day. I could never have imagined that one day hence she would be arranging my wedding.

I might have ventured to express my opinion about their plans for my wedding if anyone had bothered to ask me, but no one did. And to be perfectly candid, I didn't care. The outcome was all that really mattered to me.

Sister Chantal did venture to inquire about what I was to wear; she knew I had come away with only a small valise to my name. I promptly reassured her on that point.

"I will wear one of the two gowns I brought with me." I told her firmly. "It is of no consequence to me, Sister. In fact, I am just as happy that I do *not* have a wedding gown. I am not a first-time bride, so it would not be appropriate or proper for me to do so." She was not entirely satisfied, but I was. I had another reason that I could not share with her: a vision of a different wedding ensemble, prepared in secret for a different bride. To see myself in such an ensemble would inevitably invite a comparison, and I was not ready for that. To make up for her obvious disappointment, I agreed to let Sister Chantal arrange my hair – another surprise – who would have thought she knew how to do that? But it turned out that Sister Chantal had nieces.

In the early evening Dr. Gaudet invited Erik and I to his private *salon* in his rooms on the third floor for a glass of wine and a chat. I had never been in his rooms before, and now I saw that they were warm and comfortable, if a little shabby and cluttered. Much like the good doctor himself. Several minutes were taken up in gathering various periodicals, books and papers from every surface so we could sit down.

Dr. Gaudet was brimming with excitement, overflowing with joy, and as we soon learned, it was not entirely due to our impending nuptials. After serving us dark, sweet wine in lovely old cut crystal glasses, he picked up a letter that had been lying on his desk and waved it around merrily.

"You were not here when this letter arrived, Mlle. Bessette," he said by way of explanation. "At first I was really very disappointed, for I could not see any way I could make the trip, and the Diocese could not give me the funds. The War…but now I am to go!"

Confused, I tried to follow the progress of the letter through the air in order to see who it was from, but could not discern anything. "What trip are you referring to, Doctor?" I asked.

He sat down in a large armchair, beaming. "Forgive me, my dear, I am carried away. It is from Dr. Hansen in Norway – you remember my telling you about his researches on leprosy there (indeed I did; there could be no escaping it). I have been corresponding with him for some time, and he wrote back shortly before you went away inviting me to come there and see his hospital and his work. But there was no money for such a journey, and, *bien sûr*, it would be a visit of some duration, and the Church would have to pay for a substitute doctor for St. Giles while I was absent. The war has made things so difficult…."

Running short of breath, Dr. Gaudet stopped and took a restorative sip of his wine. I sipped mine as well, feeling the need of it. Erik was sitting quietly studying the carpet on the floor. His thoughts looked to be far away. He must find the topic rather boring, as, indeed, did I.

"That is a shame, Doctor," I said sympathetically. "I am well aware of what an honor it must be for you to receive such an invitation, and how much you would wish to go."

Dr. Gaudet turned suddenly to look at Erik with an expression that was perplexingly brimming with affection.

"But I *am* to go, Mademoiselle!" The good doctor exclaimed eagerly. "I am going next week! The arrangements have all been made."

I looked from Dr. Gaudet to Erik. "But I do not understand…has the Church found the money after all?" Erik shifted a little in his chair. He was now earnestly contemplating the fire burning cheerfully in the grate.

Dr. Gaudet smiled at me, eyes sparkling. "I see M. Bessette has not told you; well, we have all been rather busy today. *Ce matin*, one of my errands was to a certain banking firm. Your cousin, Mademoiselle, has made me a present of the funds necessary for me to make the trip. In exchange, *naturellement,* for my assistance in performing one or two errands for him. It is all settled. I made the arrangements and sent a telegraph to Dr. Hansen on my way back. It has all worked out quite nicely." Beaming, he took a sip of his wine.

I looked at Erik. He met my gaze almost reluctantly, embarrassed at having his kind and generous gesture discovered.

"Well, after all, Sylvie, I could not present myself at the bank in person. And Dr. Gaudet should not have to miss this opportunity to further his knowledge," he muttered.

"That was…very generous of you, Erik. I did not realize you had a bank account." Somehow, the idea of Erik and a bank account did not go hand-in-hand.

"It is not in my own name, *bien sûr.* I simply gave Dr. Gaudet a letter addressed to my banker." He studied my blank expression, interpreted it correctly, and said gently, "did you think I kept the monthly salary I received from M. Poligny all those years stored in a boot, Sylvie?"

Ah. Now I remembered: Celestine had told me once long ago, he received the sum of 20,000 francs a month for years, his 'salary' for all that unsolicited advice on how to run the theatre. To me it had sounded like an astronomical sum. Erik smirked a little as he watched understanding grow on my face.

"*Alors*, you have…"

"Quite a lot of money, yes, mostly in various investments. Enough to take care of us for a good while, once we are settled safely somewhere, and I can get my hands on it."

I glanced at Dr. Gaudet; he was absorbed in rereading his letter from Dr. Hansen. It would appear that he was so pleased with the gift of funds for his trip that he did not even question why Erik had a bank account under another name, in a city he was not supposed to be living in. It was just as well that he was so oblivious. *Or was he?*

Turning back to Erik, I asked, "Well, we can talk about that another time, but I am still curious…" here Erik rolled his eyes at me, having heard that from me many a time…"what was the errand Dr. Gaudet performed for *you* today?" Erik's face was warmed by a satisfied smile. He raised his glass to me in a little salute.

"You will find out *demain*, Sylvie." He said, draining his glass.

"Hmph." Acknowledging defeat, I crossed my arms across my chest and glowered at him. But it was not much of a glower.

CHAPTER TWENTY-EIGHT

'True love always makes a man better, no matter what woman inspires it.'

A.D.

The next afternoon, I married for the second, and final, time. It was by necessity a very small wedding, as different from my first as can be imagined. When I married that first time, I was a *naïve* young girl, utterly dazzled by the dashing young man in his dress uniform standing next to me. And my mother! My mother had been there, discreetly dabbing her eyes with a handkerchief. Already thin from the wasting disease that claimed her three years later, that day she had radiated pride and happiness for her only daughter. And today? Today I was a wanted criminal about to marry another wanted criminal, something that would have been utterly unimaginable to me a year ago. Nevertheless, I had high hopes. The sun shone for the first time in many days, a good omen, *certainement!*

I cannot describe my wedding to Erik in any great detail, because I was in such a state of apprehension and nerves it was a miracle that I could even speak. Erik was in little better case; paler than usual, he was handsomely clad in a formal black tailcoat and trousers obtained for him by Dr. Gaudet. The mystery of the packages was solved, I thought with a little inner smile. Erik's black silk cravat was tied just a bit crooked, something I had never seen before. *Bien*, I reminded myself, it was the first time he had ever been married, after all. He was entitled to some nerves.

When I reached up to straighten his cravat for him, I realized my hands were trembling. The cravat resisted my efforts, and refused to straighten. This was what I wanted more than anything in the world, so why was I so nervous? I have never enjoyed being the center of attention; perhaps that was the problem. I do remember that the normally musty-smelling chapel was filled with a fresh fragrance. Somehow, Sister Chantal was able to obtain several bunches of early narcissus and *muguets* and their sweet perfume surrounded us. Ever after that day, the scent of those delicate spring flowers brings me right back to that chapel, and our wedding.

My beloved Father Barbier stood before us and recited in his sonorous and beautiful voice the words that would bind Erik and me together for the rest of our lives. I knew he was filled with misgivings

363

on my behalf, but he nevertheless performed his offices with grace and gravity. My vows when I spoke them seemed to come out in a sort of croak, barely audible, but Erik's voice was rough with emotion. I dared not look directly at him, for I knew he was struggling manfully to avoid shedding tears.

You may well wonder, Reader, how any sensible, respectable woman could marry such a man. I might have wondered that same thing, once upon a time. But by now it must be apparent to you that your narrator is both senseless and unrespectable, for she has just most willingly been wed to the Phantom.

While standing there gazing dazedly at my new husband's crooked cravat, I suddenly recalled that long-ago proposal from my mother's *notaire*, M. Blanc. I had declined him because I thought life with him would be quite dull, and I longed for a bit of excitement. But now, I thought with wry amusement, perhaps a little dullness would be welcome. But somehow I knew life with Erik would never be dull.

At the conclusion of the ceremony, I finally learned the secret of one of Dr. Gaudet's errands for Erik the previous day. When prompted by Father Barbier, Erik took my hand and pushed a heavy ring firmly onto my finger. I stared down at it in open-mouthed surprise. The idea of wedding rings had not been at the forefront of my mind, for obvious reasons.

The ring now resting on my finger was a very large, very red, heart-shaped ruby set in gold, like a faceted, frozen drop of blood resting on my finger. The symbolic heart seemed to weigh down my hand with the enormous responsibility that went along with the gift – as if I held his real heart in my hand. When I raised my suddenly wet eyes from the ruby to his face, Erik was watching me intently. I felt a tear course down my cheek, but I did not bother to brush it away. I also gave a silent prayer of heartfelt thanks that the glittering red gem was not cut into the shape of a skull.

Father Barbier placed my hand in Erik's, and suddenly I was his. Erik closed his large hand around mine, put his other hand behind my neck and brought his mouth to mine in a kiss that seared my lips with its fierceness. It was as if, with this kiss he was claiming me. I felt myself blush and Dr. Gaudet, behind us, cleared his throat loudly. Erik, smiling widely, released my lips, but not my hand, which was for the best, because I could not walk very well owing to feeling rather dizzy. There was a hot, feral glow in his pale eyes that I found most unsettling.

When we turned as man and wife to face the room, I was touched to see Robert standing in the back of the chapel behind the patients and nuns who had attended the ceremony. All the faces turned toward us radiated joy and happiness, except for Robert's. He looked extremely uncomfortable in an ill-fitting, hideous tweed jacket. He was holding his cap in his hands, exposing a bald head with a ring of grey all around, and his face wore its habitual scowl. I gave him a wide, happy smile, and to my amusement he turned beet-red.

The only melancholy moment on that day occurred as I scanned the small but joyful audience. I could not help searching for the face I missed among the rest of the smiling faces, though I knew it was not there. I missed the face of my friend Celestine. If there had been any possible way to include her, we would have done so, but the sad fact was that I did not expect to ever set eyes on my dear friend again.

We had a pleasant little party after the ceremony. Sister Chantal had caused some cold meat and salads to be brought in, champagne was poured, and Dr. Gaudet made a merry toast to our happiness. I believe Erik and I were both a little dazed by the sudden change in our marital status; we kept stealing wide-eyed glances at one another while we ate and sipped our champagne. Nevertheless, I smiled until my mouth hurt. My triumph was all the more complete when I thought back over all those months of yearning, loneliness and despair, all behind me now.

Shortly after the meal was concluded, Father Barbier came up to me. Indicating the doors to the outside with one thickly-bandaged hand, he said,

"Come take a turn in the courtyard with me, *ma petite*. The sun is out today, it is really quite pleasant."

"*Bien sûr*, Father," I acquiesced, and after casting one last adoring glance at my new husband, I tore myself away and followed the old priest out of the refectory into the courtyard. "Did Sister Chantal get her herb garden planted?" I asked, thinking that must be what he wanted to show me. Father Barbier only shook his head and smiled a little.

The sun was indeed shining; not a cloud could be seen in the brilliant blue sky. On the empty branches of the ancient sycamore, fresh chartreuse buds were forming. The green shoots of spring bulbs were just beginning to push up through a thin layer of snow lying here and there in the shadowed parts of the courtyard. Father Barbier led me to our favorite bench, and we sat down side by side.

"You are very happy, Sylvie, I can see that. I am happy for you."

"Thank you, Father," I said gratefully. "And thank you for performing the ceremony for us. It was beautiful, and exactly what I wished."

He smiled at me kindly. *"C-'était mon plaisir.* Your young man is truly fortunate; I can see that you will be very good for him. That you *are* good for him. I am glad to have had this chance to get to know him better – enough to see the potential for good in him."

He paused, and then turned his head to study me thoughtfully. "But there is something I wanted you to know."

I waited expectantly, puzzling over what he had just said about Erik, while he groped for a moment in the pocket of his cassock. He drew out a folded piece of paper. Carefully he unfolded it and spread it open, and then he placed it on the bench between us, so that I could read it without having to touch the paper. It was a page cut from a newspaper, much creased and worn, obviously having been folded and unfolded many times.

I glanced at him curiously, a little smile hovering on my lips, and bent my head over the fragile page. I studied it for a moment, and then time stood still. My smile died, and I ceased to breathe. I stared at the paper for a long, unseeing minute while the print swam like ants in a stirred nest, and then I looked up again at Father Barbier.

"Father," I whispered breathlessly, "you *know.* How...how long have you known?"

He answered calmly. "Since the first day you brought him here. I knew it must be the same man; it could be no one else. You see my dear, that morning, M. Didier's family paid him a visit, and they brought with them the first edition of the morning newspaper. They left it behind by mistake, so I picked it up and took it to my room to read. I was eager to have it to myself, for we get so few newspapers here. No one else had a chance to see it, which was for the best. Such a disaster as had just occurred at the Opéra Populaire merited the front page, and I read the entire story with great interest."

"Then on Monday you came with the mid-day meal and brought your cousin from Rouen. It was not like you, Sylvie, to suddenly bring someone here without giving us any warning. And then the description fit exactly; such a face could not be mistaken for anyone else. You remember all those questions I asked you that day..."

"Oh yes, yes, I remember. I wondered at the time."

366

He went on, "I watched the two of you closely, for I knew he could not be your cousin, and I was trying to understand why you, Sylvie, would lie. That was not like you either. Why were you protecting him? Had he some hold over you? And then in an unguarded moment, I saw your face, and I knew that you loved him."

I remembered that moment quite well. "Oh, Father! I am sorry I lied to you. And then the day I had to leave early, I could not understand why you said those things about Erik. I was angry with you, Father, and I spoke to you shortly, but I am heartily ashamed of myself now." I hung my head in remorse – how very observant was Father Barbier, how little those bright black eyes missed, yet how kind he was. Kinder than I deserved.

Father Barbier sighed gently. "It was I who convinced Dr. Gaudet to go to the police when Robert came back saying you were missing from your apartment. I was sure Erik had a hand in it somehow, and that something terrible must have happened to you. I can see I was quite wrong about that."

I turned quickly to him, eager to exonerate Erik from that accusation at least. "Something very bad did happen to me, but it was Erik who saved me. I would be dead by now if it were not for him. I cannot say more, but please believe me, *c'est vrai*."

"Gracious, my dear!" He exclaimed, his face full of shocked concern.

"But Father, I do not understand. If you knew the truth all along, why did you keep my secret? Why didn't you go to the police?"

There was a pause, during which a robin, that reliable harbinger of spring, began singing in the sycamore above our heads. Finally Father Barbier spoke.

"I do not know how *le bon Dieu* will view my silence, but I could not bring myself to betray you, Sylvie. It was obvious to me that you loved Erik, and I had to trust that if you loved him, he must be worthy. I did it for you." He finished simply.

Tears formed in my eyes as I listened to him, and I longed to embrace him, leprosy or no leprosy. All this time, unbeknownst to either Erik or I, this sweet, gentle man held both our fates in his hands. But because he loved me, and I loved him, he had kept my secret. I sat quietly for a moment, and wiped away a few tears with my hand.

Thinking back to the first time we met, I said, "Father, imagine that I have just given you a very big hug, and kissed you on the cheek."

He laughed, his eyes shining suspiciously. "*Merci*, Sylvie. This is a moment I will always cherish." Then his face grew serious again, and he went on, "I intend to have a little chat with your new husband in a few moments, because I want to make certain he always takes very good care of you in future. You will go away soon, and my heart tells me we will not meet again. I do not want to be worrying about you, Sylvie."

"You need not have any concerns about me, Father. I know he will take very good care of me. Erik *is* worthy. He is not perfect, but what man is? I think I can manage him, however."

"Spoken like a true wife!" With that, we rose from the bench and passed back into the refectory in amicable companionship. Father Barbier strolled over to the big open fireplace and stood in front of it, warming his hands. I believe I was the only person who noticed him nonchalantly take a piece of paper from his pocket and toss it into the flames, where it was immediately consumed.

I looked forward very much to telling Erik later about what had just transpired.

The rest of the afternoon and evening of our wedding day were spent in the refectory or strolling around the hospital grounds. I could not breathe enough of pure, fresh air, or feel enough warm sunshine on my face. We were forbidden to go upstairs; again, Sister Chantal put her foot down about that quite firmly. She was preparing a bridal chamber for us; not the small rooms we had spent the previous night in, but another, slightly larger room which contained, she explained, 'an appropriately-sized bed' for a married couple. I felt myself blush madly and Erik looked quite discomfited when she mentioned this.

There was a great deal that Erik and I wanted to talk about with each other, so the afternoon passed quickly. For my part, I requested an account of how he had spent his time after leaving me to escape Paris, as well as everything that occurred after his return. And it transpired that he had in fact returned to the city after only a few days, for he had been too concerned about me to simply abandon me and flee. His mysterious friend the Persian had hidden him away in his own rooms on several occasions, or Erik would have been forced to stay out of doors for many days in the freezing weather. I was beginning to realize I owed that strange man a debt of gratitude.

Erik, in his turn, wanted to know what happened to me while I was Gaston's prisoner. I was reluctant to share with him the details of my ordeal, for I knew he would be furious, but he insisted. I finally had to put a stop to my account because Erik grew so distraught and angry, and consumed with guilt. I did not want our wedding day marred by him becoming overmastered by his powerful emotions. At least, not those kind of emotions.

Hoping to distract him, I dragged Erik back inside the chapel, and bade him sit at the piano and play something for me. He obliged, reluctantly at first, and presently all his previous discomfiture vanished as he concentrated on his playing. I sat quietly next to him, listening. Rays from the setting sun slanting through the stained glass windows sent a kaleidoscope of colors over our hands and faces, and glittered upon my ruby ring. I stared at it, turning it this way and that, fascinated by its beauty and colour. Never in my life had I ever owned such fine jewelry.

"Do you like it?" Erik asked, having noticed my careful study of the ring.

I turned to him, frowning. "Oh Erik, I love it! You could not have chosen better for me. I only wish…"

"What, Sylvie? What is it now?" He sounded only mildly exasperated with me.

I sighed and looked at him. "I did not know you were planning to do this. If I had known…I had no ring to give to you. I would have liked to very much, Erik." I remembered my father always wore a thick gold band, which he took to the grave, and wore still. I wanted the same thing for my new husband – especially for him, as a mark of my possession.

Erik smiled and put his arm around me. "And so you shall, if it will make you happy. I will wear it proudly. You can get one for me later, once we are settled elsewhere."

"*Très bien*," I said grudgingly. "But it won't be a moment too soon."

Erik laughed and resumed his playing.

In the evening we were at last admitted to our little "bridal suite" on the third floor. I saw that it had been made ready to serve as our nuptial chamber. Sister Chantal had done very well by us. I would have to think of a suitable thank-you gift for her.

My valise and dressing gown had been brought from my old room. A cozy fire burned cheerfully in the grate, the 'appropriately sized' bed was made up with a pretty quilt. Candles burned on the mantle and the window ledge. There was even a little bouquet of lily-of-the-valley in a vase by the bed, next to a water-filled carafe. I was so touched by all this sweet thoughtfulness, my eyes filled with moisture yet again. I was not so sanguine, however, about having a painting of the Virgin Mary gazing down on us from the wall, her expression serene and composed. I wondered if I ought to cover the painting up. Moving further into the room, I turned in a circle to admire everything.

"Why, this is charming!" I exclaimed, looking back at Erik expectantly.

However, if he noticed all the sweetly romantic touches in our bridal chamber he gave no sign of it; following behind me, he crossed the room and stood stiffly by the fireplace. Saying nothing, he stared fixedly at me, a rather wild-eyed look in his eyes. He looked absolutely terrified. I had never seen fear on his face before, so it took a few seconds for me to recognize it for what it was. The charm of our room was forgotten as I came to stand before him and looked up into his frozen face.

"Erik, what is the matter?" I asked. "Are you all right?" I reached for his hand and took it in mine. At first his hand was lax, unresponsive, then abruptly it turned and squeezed mine so hard it hurt. I tried not to wince. With his free hand, he reached up and gently stroked my cheek, but he still did not speak. As I watched, the undamaged side of his face took on a rosy glow – I realized all at once that Erik was blushing! And then understanding dawned, and I was relieved and happy again.

"It's all right, you know. You can tell me," I said softly. "You must know that you can tell me anything, Love."

He sighed. "This is cursed difficult for me, Sylvie. For someone of my temperament, it does not come easy to admit to any weakness, but…" he paused, and slowly closed his eyes.

"Well, the fact is I *never* admit weakness." He laughed ruefully, and shook his head. "I want you more than anything, but, because of my face, I have never…this will be…you know this already; I told you once, do not force me to say it out loud." He groaned in frustration, blushing even more, and passed his free hand over his face in an agitated gesture.

I had to put him out of his misery, the poor man. He hated knowing there was something he might not be proficient at. Reaching up, I caressed his face gently.

370

"Do not worry, my love. I *have* done this before."

Erik scowled down at me. "*Oui*, but with a poor excuse for a man, unless I miss my guess. You may not know very much more than I do, Sylvie." His bravado made a smile tug at my lips, but I pushed it back and instead gave his hand a reassuring squeeze.

"That may be so, but you trust me, don't you?"

In spite of his obvious discomfort, his eyes warmed with affection. "All the times you asked me to trust you, Sylvie, do you remember? And I always did, in spite of all the reasons why I shouldn't." Erik put his hand under my chin, to hold my gaze to his. "You are the only person in this entire world that I trust completely, believe me. But you have to understand how awkward this is for me. And I am afraid I might hurt you somehow – that I won't know how to be gentle."

"You won't hurt me, Erik; I assure you I am quite resilient," I said, smiling up into his face. I was the only person in the world that he trusted! How his words thrilled me! To think that I, of all people, had won the trust of this dangerous, brilliant, half-tamed man. I felt the thrill of victory right down to my toes. *Mine-mine-mine* my heart sang when I looked at him. All mine.

Seeking to reassure him on the point of his lack of experience, I said a trifle breathlessly, "We both know you have a very masterful nature, *et alors, sans doute* it will not be long before you have full confidence. In fact I am certain of it. And we have the rest of our lives, remember?"

His eyes widened; I saw the embarrassment beginning to recede from them, to be replaced with something else. Those pale blue eyes glittered with anticipation.

"Yes, but I have a great deal of lost time to make up for." He murmured softly.

"You can start by kissing me." I said, giving him a gentle reminder.

"*Oui*, I can do that. *Viens, petite*," he said. Releasing my chin, he reached for me and gathered me into his arms.

CHAPTER TWENTY-NINE

'Who knows? Perhaps your love will make me forget all that I do not wish to remember....I have but you in the world,..., through you I again take hold of life.'

A.D.

I was having a lovely dream. I was sorry to wake, for as I came into drowsy wakefulness the lovely dream vanished like mist in the sun, as dreams often do. Almost reluctantly I opened my eyes, and wondered where I was, for I did not recognize my surroundings. Judging by the pale morning light, it was still quite early. I was lying on my left side and there was a weight lying across my waist, pinning me to the bed. It was warm and heavy but not particularly uncomfortable. I was content to lie quietly and to drowsily allow my eyes to wander...until they came to rest on an old painting of the Virgin Mary on the wall across the room. Oh. *Oh.*

Recognition arrived, and with it my memory returned in a rush. My eyes flew wide open and I sucked in my breath with an audible gasp. I remembered *everything*. I was married. I was in bed with *Erik*, and he was *mon mari*. And last night was my wedding night.

I glanced down, and the weight across my waist resolved itself into a heavy male arm, flung across me possessively. The warm body it was attached to still slumbered peacefully, spooned up against my back. I heard Erik's steady breathing, felt his breath softly stirring the loose and tangled hair at the back of my neck. It was no wonder he was still asleep, I thought musingly. He had made up for several lost times last night. I smiled to myself contentedly. I had not really been worried; I was sure we would manage perfectly well. It had, in fact, been wonderful.

I will spare you the intimate details, Reader, but I was confident that I was well on my way to making him forget about Christine Daaé - or the Comtess de Chagny, as I must think of her now. A warm, pleased feeling spread over me.

Eventually I was forced to rise in order to answer a call of nature, though I hated to leave the shelter of the bed and that warm, protecting arm. Finally I could put it off no longer; I carefully drew back the quilt and slipped out from under Erik's arm, wincing a little as I stood up. Reaching for my dressing gown draped over the footboard of the bed, I slipped into it hastily and started barefoot for the *en suite* bath chamber.

It was cold in the room; the embers of the fire had burned to ashes hours ago. But in spite of the cold I could not stop myself from pausing to look at Erik; he still slept, the quilt down around his waist, his outflung arm now lying across the bed. His face was peaceful in repose, but when I thought of how he had been last night, and the searing intimacies we had shared, I knew that a great weight had been lifted from him. How like a wolf he was, even now. Longing for love and connection had brought him to me the same way a wolf might circle a warm campfire, craving things he had no name for.

I briefly considered pinching myself to be sure I was not still dreaming; how could this magnificent creature possibly be mine? One side of his face might be disfigured, but there was certainly nothing the matter with the rest of him. A sigh escaped me, and I turned and went into the bath chamber.

A few minutes later, having attended to my personal needs, I stood before the small mirror in the bath chamber trying to tidy myself, not an easy task. My hair was in dreadful disorder and I was some time combing it out. And what was that blotch on the side of my neck? Setting my comb aside, I leaned closer to the mirror, peering at my reflection in the dim morning light. It looked like…like a *bite mark*, bruised and purple. A wild blush spread over my face and neck as I recollected how it came to be there, and I quickly pulled the ruffled lace collar of the dressing gown up tightly to hide the mark.

When I slipped quietly back into the bedroom Erik was awake. He was lying on his back, gazing up at the low beamed ceiling, a far-away look on his face. His fingers danced restlessly on the soft surface of the quilt. He turned his head and smiled at me, his expression warm and loving. My heart gave such a violent leap, I thought it would leave my breast.

"I was dreaming in music," he explained, his voice sleep-roughened. "Sometimes music just comes to me while I am asleep. I was trying to remember the melody so I can write it down later." He held out both arms in an irresistible invitation, and I hastened eagerly back to bed to lie in the shelter of his warm embrace.

"Tell me about your dream music," I murmured, nuzzling into his neck.

Erik's arm tightened over my shoulder. "It is about us – about last night," he responded quietly. "Only music could describe last night; no mere words could do it justice." Feeling shy and embarrassed and secretly pleased, I had to agree with him there.

"I am sure the nuns would let you use the piano in the chapel if you wished. They love to hear you play." I said, hiding my suddenly hot face by burying it against his chest.

Erik laughed softly; turning toward me, he drew me out of the safety of his arms and began pulling open the neck of my dressing gown with his free hand. He looked like a happy child about to unwrap a birthday present.

"Not just yet," he said, his voice a seductive murmur. Suddenly he froze and stared at my neck, exposed when the ruffles had fallen away.

"What is that?" He asked, his finger probing the purple mark gently, causing it to throb a little beneath his touch.

It was my turn to laugh. "You did that, although you may not remember. I am surprised there is but one."

"*I* did?" He sounded quite puzzled. "*Comment?*" I looked at him in astonishment. He really didn't know.

"You bit me, Erik. I think you were a little carried away."

Erik looked chagrinned. "Oh. I am sorry, Sylvie! I hope I did not hurt you."

"I cannot say that I remember, but I don't think so. I was also a little carried away." I blushed yet again; this time he saw it spread across my cheeks and it brought an answering smile to his face.

"Yes, you were; that I definitely remember. Let us get carried away again, and I will try not to bite you this time." And he resumed happily unwrapping his birthday present.

A little while later, I suddenly raised up with a gasp. "Oh!" I had just had the strangest feeling, *exactly* as if I had done this before.

Erik, who had until a second before been passionately kissing me, pulled back and looked at me, frowning worriedly.

"Did I do something wrong, Sylvie?" He asked anxiously. I hastened to reassure him.

"Oh no, Love, nothing is wrong. I just remembered…it is quite extraordinary…I dreamed this once, a long time ago it seems," I gazed wonderingly into his beautiful pale eyes. "Before I really even knew you very well, before you had taken your mask off for me, or anything." At first I had thought I was having a *déjà vu* experience, but then the memory of that long-ago dream came back to me. Even the light was the same.

Erik's frown smoothed out and he looked pleased. "You dreamed we were kissing like this?" As he spoke his hands were reverently stroking and caressing my skin here and there, warming it with his touch. I shivered with pleasure, but I forced myself to concentrate so I could explain.

"*Non, non*, I mean I dreamed *this*," I said, waving my arm around to encompass the room, the bed, ourselves. "This exact moment, with you. Only I didn't know when I was dreaming, that it was *this*. I wasn't sure where it came from at the time."

He was pressing little kisses to my neck softly. "If you had that dream so long ago, it must have seemed like a nightmare to you. I can hardly bear to think of how I treated you then," he murmured; I could feel his lips brush my skin softly as he spoke.

I was losing my concentration rapidly. "It was a wonderful dream. I could never remember feeling so happy, just as I do this moment." I gave up trying to think then, and reached for him, pulling his face to mine so I could kiss him soundly.

Sometime later, lying quietly with my head on Erik's chest, my hand resting over his heart so I could feel its steady beating beneath my palm, I listened to his soft breathing. I knew that I had never known such peace and happiness as at this moment. My thoughts kept returning to that prophetic dream. Perhaps it was just as well I did not know then that I was dreaming of my own future, *our* future, since I could not go back in time to change the course of events. What happened was over, and there was no going back, but if I had known.....

The room slowly grew light; sun brightened the rippled old glass of the window and warmed our little room. We would have to rise and face the day, but neither of us was in haste to do so. There was much to think about, so many dangers waiting for us outside the gates of St. Giles. We were now two fugitives from justice, bound together forever, and where one flew, the other would go. I closed my eyes; I must have made some involuntary little movement because his arm tightened around me, holding me close against him. Safe.

While I was lying there in quiet contentment, I found myself thinking, for some unaccountable reason, of the Count of Monte Cristo. There were, I thought, a number of parallels between his story and Erik's. There was even a physical resemblance: the description offered by Alexandre Dumas of his anti-hero would exactly fit the man now holding me in his arms, even to his ability to see in the dark like a cat.

And then something else fell in to place: something very important about myself. I experienced a very quiet epiphany, a monumental shift within myself that went completely unnoticed by Erik. I was *not* Kitty; I had never been Kitty. I had been imagining myself part of the wrong story all along.

Let me explain, Reader: in the novel the Count of Monte Cristo, a man who had started out life as the rather *naïf* and innocent Edmond Dantes, was falsely accused of a crime and confined to a dark, lonely dungeon where he was forced to live in misery and solitude for fourteen years. Upon escaping, he claimed a vast secret treasure and used the money to reinvent himself as a ruthlessly avenging angel, calling himself the Count of Monte Cristo. As this fictional person, he wreaked a terrible vengeance upon the enemies who had falsely accused him and ruined his life, thereby unleashing a cataclysm of violence and evil deeds. He believed himself to be alone in the world, without a friend. The girl he had been betrothed to prior to his false imprisonment was now married to one of his mortal enemies.

But he was not alone – he had Haidee. Unbeknownst to him, he was loved, admired, and desired by this girl who was, in fact, his slave. He was her master. When in the end he set her free, she confessed that she would die without him; he was her *raison d'être*. She had loved him all along, though he was completely blind to her regard. Once he comprehended the depth of her feelings for him, he understood he was being given a second chance at life, at happiness. He opened his arms and she ran into them, and the next day, they departed together to begin a new life, not as master and slave, but as equals. Thinking about this made me smile; feeling the curving of my lips against his skin, Erik asked drowsily,

"What are you smiling about?"

"You," I answered. "I was thinking about you."

The End

EPILOGUE

(Six months later)

*'There is neither happiness nor misery in the world; there is
only the comparison of one state with another, nothing more.
He who has felt the deepest grief is best able to experience
supreme happiness. We must have felt what it is to die,...
that we may appreciate the enjoyments of living.'*

A.D.

It was a beautiful late summer afternoon, the air still and a little hazy. On either side of our rolling carriage fields of grain were ripening. Stretching out beyond and above them, the soft hillsides were covered with neat rows of grape vines, their leaves a green counterpoint to the gold of the fields. We were deep in the French countryside. The road had narrowed to a mere lane, occasional farm carts and hay-laden wagons the only other traffic. Ahead of us taller hills rose, thickly covered in forests of chestnut and pine that looked cool and inviting.

Although the lane was rutted, the frequent jolts from the wheels had no affect on me. That would have been quite impossible, for I was cocooned and swathed in cushions and bolsters until you would think I was made of glass. Which was ridiculous; nevertheless, Erik could not stop casting worried glances at me every time we bounced over a rut. As for me, I could not seem to stop looking out the carriage window, for I did not know where we were going and my curiosity was getting the better of me. Much to my annoyance, our destination was a secret he steadfastly refused to divulge.

All our scant worldly belongings were fastened to the top of the carriage: only two small trunks. We'd traveled lightly these past six months, the two trunks and a few other bits and pieces being all that we had or could carry. We were constantly in motion, staying only a few days in any one place, always keeping to the roads less travelled.

I cast a brief glance out the open window at the short, stocky man sitting in the top bench of the carriage, holding the reins. I have to admit I do not know what we would have done without Robert, although truth compels me to admit he was not my first choice of a traveling companion. Indeed, when he made it clear that he was coming with us, I was quite cross with him. And yet, we never would have escaped Paris without his aid.

Robert had smuggled us out of the city six months ago on the floor of an old supply wagon; not the one belonging to St. Giles, but an old, rickety one he had managed to procure from heaven knows where. Best not to inquire. It was filled with hay; trust Robert to think it logical to carry hay *out* of the city, rather than in to it.

We originally thought it would be wise to slip out of the city via the river. The Prussian blockade had finally been lifted, so river traffic was continuing as before, but Robert insisted quite determinedly that leaving in a wagon would be quicker and safer. Not until we were out of Paris did I discover that he'd packed a bag and meant to accompany us, something he could not have gotten away with had we left by boat as originally planned.

Once we were safely away from Paris, sitting up and brushing bits of straw off my shoulders and out of my mouth and hair, I had confronted him about the valise which had been concealed in the hay. Casting a malignant look at Erik, also surfacing from under the straw, Robert had said petulantly,

"Someone has to come along with you and see that you are properly tended to, Madame. You will need me, you'll see."

Much as I hated to admit it, he had been right. Robert proved invaluable in fact; in the days that followed it was he who spoke to innkeepers, shopkeepers, hostelries and so forth, he who conducted all our business so that we never needed to reveal ourselves along the way. Erik's disfigured face would have been a shock just by itself; but we also had to bear in mind that even in the provinces the events at the Opera would be known. For a time, those events even superseded news of the war, owing to their sensational nature. Thanks to Robert's presence, we travelled as two perfectly respectable citizens and their servant, and no one ever suspected otherwise.

The three of us managed to get on tolerably well, considering. It certainly helped that Robert did not talk much. What had really surprised me, though, was Erik's gentle explanation: Robert, he explained, had grown fond of me during the many months he transported me and my food back and forth from the hospital. That knowledge softened me a bit toward Robert, even though he made no secret of his mistrust of Erik. Robert did not know Erik's true identity, but he did know that both of us were fugitives now and must remain undiscovered. He was also certain the blame for our difficult circumstances must be laid at Erik's feet (which I suppose is justified).

Erik explained that Robert thought of himself as my protector in case Erik should turn out to be a poor husband.

Erik was not, in fact, a poor husband, and I consider myself somewhat of an expert on terrible husbands. The irony was not lost on me: I had married a man I thought to be good, and found he was a scoundrel. Then I married a man I thought to be bad, and found he was good. Nevertheless I did not find it an easy matter to be married to that man.

It was challenging for Erik to adapt to always being with someone, after so many years of isolation. And it was frustrating for him at times not to always get his way, and to have to take others into consideration. A great deal of patience was required – from me, not him. And many times his sleep (and mine) was disturbed by horrible nightmares. Guilt over his wicked deeds often brought on tortured dreams, but worse were the nights when I awoke to hear Erik muttering Christine's name in his sleep. He never remembered his dreams in the morning, fortunately.

The burning of the Opera House and the Phantom's escape from justice was eventually overshadowed by far more serious matters, and we doubted the Paris police or *la Sûreté* were even spending any time attempting to capture him now. They were needed elsewhere, most urgently. We were shocked to learn, while staying at a travelers' inn along the south road, that revolutionaries calling themselves the Paris Commune had taken over the Tuileries Palace and tragically, Parisians were now fighting each other. Twenty thousand people would die before the insurrection was put down, and the Tuileries Palace would burn to the ground in September of that year. I gave thanks that I was not there to see it.

Erik's voice brought me out of my reverie. "Are you thirsty, Sylvie? Do you need some water?" I turned to see him once more watching me, a frown notched between his brows. All this unnecessary attention was beginning to get on my nerves, but I forced a smile and shook my head. I had just had a drink of water about five minutes ago. Smoothing my hand affectionately over my still relatively flat stomach, I replied patiently,

"I am fine, *mon amour*, but I do wish you would tell me where we are going, and when we might expect to get there. I am getting tired of bouncing around in this carriage."

Glancing out the window, he put his arm around me and pulled me close to him, not an easy feat considering the thick cushion between us.

"It will not be long now. Look, do you see those trees ahead of us?" He pointed out the window toward the front of the carriage. "It is two or three miles at the most."

I frowned at him. "But *Robert* knows where we are going. Why have you told him and not me?"

Feigning excessive patience, he replied, "Because it is a surprise, as I have told you at least ten times already. Are you certain you are all right, Sylvie? You do not need anything? You are well?" His expression again shifted to one of worry. Sighing, I patted him on the leg, shook my head, and turned back to the window. The land was gradually rising; we had left the golden fields behind and now there were vines stretching out on either side of the lane, dark clusters of ripening grapes hanging from their branches, and I could see an orchard of walnut trees in the distance. It was so beautiful, so bountiful here! Eagerly I drew another deep breath, simply for the joy of it.

Although his constant fussing over me tried my patience, I could not really blame Erik for being so worried. He would feel responsible if anything were to go wrong, and it would have been very difficult to seek medical attention under our particular circumstances. However, I was now, I reckoned, approximately four months along, past the worrisome stage, and there was no denying I was in a state of the rudest health. My skin was blooming like wild roses, my hair was growing luxuriantly. I felt wonderful.

A little secret smile crossed my face. I had always wanted a child; it was the one regret of my first, failed marriage, that the ill-fated union had not produced a baby for me to nurture and love. I knew perfectly well how a baby was conceived, but Erik, apparently, had not made the connection. It never crossed his mind that his new favorite activity, the exercising of his conjugal rights, might eventually produce the condition that was now mine. I would never forget the look on his face the night I told him of my (of *our*) expectations! My little smile of amusement faded then, for it was not a happy memory.

We were staying at a small inn on the outskirts of Sarlat at the time. I had not wanted to say anything until I was absolutely certain, but suspicion was now certainty. I waited until our evening meal was finished and we were alone in our cozy little private room, preparing to retire. Most new husbands, whose wives sat them down and said they had some news for them, would leap at once to the correct conclusion, but not Erik. His expression was merely expectant, mildly curious. I sighed; this, I knew, would not be a simple conveying of joyful news.

"I have something to tell you, Erik, but first let me assure you that I am quite well. The sickness I experienced last month was normal for a woman in my present condition." His expression shifted to confusion, so I hastened on, blushing and tripping over my words.

"*Vous voyez*, I am...we are...well, you are going to become a father, in approximately five months." My hand, moving of its own accord, rested on my stomach as I spoke.

Erik had stared at me, utterly speechless. It took several seconds for understanding to grow. His eyes darted to my stomach. Although I was not 'showing' yet, I would be soon. My hand covered it protectively, possessively. His eyes grew wide. He struggled to speak.

"*Condition*...what...you mean you are...you are with child?" He stuttered at last. I nodded, and ventured a hopeful smile. But I did not speak, because I was waiting with pent breath for what would almost certainly come next. For one brief moment, dawning joy could be seen in his eyes; he almost smiled back at me. And then even as I watched, a look of growing horror replaced the brief flash of happiness. All colour drained out of his face, leaving it as pale as when I first met him, before sunlight had touched his face. Even his lips went white.

"No," he whispered hoarsely, "no, Sylvie. This cannot be." Slowly, bowing his shoulders as though the weight of the world rested on them, he brought his hands up and covered his face. I reached out and took hold of his wrist, and tried to pull his hand away.

"Erik..." I began, but suddenly his hands dropped away and he raised up to face me. He was furious; a flush of ruddy colour now replaced the bloodless white. I flinched back from the anger that rolled off him in waves. But he was not angry with me.

"What kind of monster am I? How could I have...*mon Dieu*, I cannot bear this!" In an instant he had leapt to his feet and paced away from me, across the room, unable to sit still under the grip of his overwhelming emotions. I began to worry that he would do himself an injury, so great was his remorse and anger. It was as much my fault as it was his, and perhaps more, because I had kept quiet all the while, secretly hoping for this very thing to happen.

I rose from the bed and went to him. "Stop this right now! If you will let me finish speaking, you will see that your fears are for nothing. Please Erik, please sit down and listen to me." I stroked his arm gently; he was trembling from head to foot. Still he resisted.

"Please," I said, pulling at his arm. Finally he moved; like a sleepwalker he returned to sit on the bed, and I sat likewise, and took his trembling hand in mine.

"I saw my *maman* last night," I began. His eyes flashed to my face; I had his attention at last. "She came to me in a dream. She was very happy for me; she knew I had always wanted to be a mother. We embraced; it was so real, I felt as if she were really here with me." I gave him a warm, loving look. "She approves of you, by the way. She admitted to some misgivings at first, but you have won her over. Shhh." He had been about to speak, to no doubt contradict this.

"And she said, and these are her exact words, 'do not allow your husband to entertain any fears about his daughter; she will be as perfect and beautiful as a spring morning. I think you ought to name her after me.'" I raised Erik's hand to my lips and pressed a kiss into his palm. "I believe in my dreams, and so should you." I said firmly.

Erik was silent for a long time, thinking over what I had told him. I watched as anger slowly faded from his eyes, to be replaced with dawning hope and a yearning expression.

"Marie," he whispered softly, as if to himself.

"You remembered!"

"*Bien sûr.* So you think…you believe that there is no chance of this…" he made a helpless, pathetic gesture, indicating the disfigured side of his face.

"Absolutely no chance at all," I replied firmly. "If my mother says our *enfant* will be perfect, then she *will* be perfect. All I ask is that you feel happy, as happy as I am. I know it will change things, our lives will not be the same, but still…" I stopped, anxiously holding my breath, waiting for his response.

He took me gently in his arms, and I could feel that he was trembling all over. My heart wrenched.

"It must mean…that we will be a family," He said slowly. "I will try to be happy, Sylvie. You must give me time." I felt his chest expand with a deep breath. "A daughter," he mused. "Let us name her Marie Celestine. If she looks anything like you, she will be a beauty". His free hand stroked my hair tenderly.

"Tell me something though; does this mean we cannot…" he paused, and his wandering hand settled on a particularly convenient portion of my anatomy.

I laughed a little shakily. "We have a little more time for that, *mon amour*, do not worry. But once the babe comes, you will have to do without for a while." I took his head in my hands and gently drew it to my breast, where I cradled it against my heart. He slipped his arms around my waist, and as we sat together quietly, the trembling gradually stopped. The worst was over, I knew.

What I did *not* tell him, and never would, was that there had been no dream, no vision of my mother; I had needed no such reassurance that our *enfant* would be beautiful, but he had. And somehow, I was absolutely certain she would be a girl. Forgive me, Reader, but what else could I do?

Approximately three weeks after this conversation took place, Erik and Robert mysteriously absented themselves on several occasions from the inn where we were staying. All Erik would tell me was that he had business matters needing his attention. And then one morning I was instructed to pack my trunk *rapide*, and we embarked on our present journey, and he stubbornly refused to tell me the destination.

Peering out the open carriage window, I saw that we had drawn abreast of the walnut orchard; the land continued to rise, and we next entered the edge of a wild chestnut forest. We were slowing down; I glanced up at Erik and saw that his eyes were shining expectantly.

"*Nous voici*," he said softly. Finally!

We were turning left now, and our carriage passed between two old, lichen-spotted stone pillars. A long, curving gravel drive stretched out before us, lined with ancient sycamores that met in shady arcs above the drive. I gazed out in wonder; what *was* this place? It seemed a strange location for a hotel or inn, so deep in the country. We were skirting the side of a hill; suddenly Erik called out to Robert.

"Stop just there, Robert, on the curve." Obediently the carriage came to a halt. Erik leaped out and turned back to me.

"Sylvie," he said, reaching to take my hand and help me to descend after I had extricated myself from my cocoon of cushions. Oh, how wonderful it felt to be out of that carriage and on my feet at last! Once I was standing next to Erik, he took me by the shoulders and turned me to face away, down the drive.

"*Regardez*, Sylvie," he commanded.

Eager to discover Erik's secret, I looked as ordered. Nestled into the side of the hill we were skirting, I saw a two-story stone château. Vines grew up the sides, twining around windows with blue-painted shutters. In front was a courtyard, below was a wide, inviting stretch of green lawn, and running down into a small valley were fields of grape vines and brilliant yellow sunflowers. At the bottom of the valley the Dordogne River could be glimpsed, a silver half-moon of water curving along the limestone bluffs that rose craggily on the far bank. In the distance, the picturesque ruins of a castle could be seen perched on a rounded hill. There was not another structure in sight. It was utterly beautiful, as magical as something out of a fairy tale. I could only stare in wonder at first.

"What a beautiful place...what is it?" I asked; my voice scarcely above a whisper. "Is it an inn? How I would love to stay there." Erik and Robert exchanged matching smug expressions, Erik looking up, Robert looking down from his seat on the carriage bench.

Erik took my hand in his. "It is *not* an inn, but you certainly shall stay there. It is our home, Sylvie. We own this château, and all the land that you see going down to the river. We could not very well continue our nomadic existence. You needed to be settled somewhere, and soon, before...what do you women call it? Confinement. Before your confinement begins. Do you like it?" His voice held a little edge of anxiety.

I was dumbfounded, I confess. Staggered. "It is the most wonderful place in the entire world," I managed at last. "I must remember to make a little toast to M. Poligny for his generous monthly contributions to the Opera Ghost, without which this happy ending would not have been possible." Erik smiled, but then his expression became serious, even a little wistful.

"I always dreamed of living someplace where I could walk outside in the sunshine, with someone I loved beside me, like normal people do. A place where I would not have to hide my face. Such a simple thing, that most people take for granted." He slanted a pensive look down at me.

"Remember you asked me once if I missed the sun? I told you I didn't, but it was a lie. You cannot imagine how much I envied all the people who could walk beneath the sun without fear of the consequences." He gave himself a little shake, and became cheerful again.

"Come, Sylvie. Let us go on to the château – there is someone waiting for you whom I believe you will be very happy to see." Enjoying my quizzical expression, he assisted me back into the carriage and we continued on our way. Who could possibly be waiting for me? I wondered curiously.

As we drew into the courtyard, I leaned out the carriage window eagerly. Indeed there was someone, standing in the doorway of the château, observing our progress: a woman dressed in a black gown with jet beads glinting in the sunshine, and a thick red-gold braid hanging over one shoulder. At first I could not believe my own eyes.

"Celestine!" I cried joyfully, for it was certainly she, but how did she come to be here? She came laughing to the carriage door and when Erik helped me down, embraced me warmly. I did not scruple to hide my tears; they were tears of happiness.

"I cannot believe this…I never thought to see you again! How came you to be here?"

Celestine and Erik hugged in their turn. "Knowing of my current state of unemployment," she began, giving him a sly look, "Erik invited me to come and live with you and be your head housekeeper. It is a position that should suit me admirably. Meg is residing at a private finishing school, also thanks to Erik, so I am no longer needed in Paris." She held me at arm's length and looked me over, blue eyes sparkling.

"You look wonderful, Sylvie. I do not think I have ever seen you looking lovelier." Over my head, I saw her eyes meet Erik's, and they both smiled in mutual satisfaction.

Robert, having unloaded our two small trunks from the carriage with a loud groan, stood looking out over the lawn, his gaze sweeping over the land alertly.

"Who is going to take care of all those vines?" He asked finally, removing his cap and scratching his bald head.

"You are," said Erik, and then he took my arm and we walked up the steps and through the door.

He may have been making a little jest at Robert's expense, yet if one of us had happened to glance back at Robert, we might have seen the look spreading over his dour face that foretold a future in which Robert would be telling *us* how to run a vineyard (and how to do everything else as well). Unbeknownst to us all, Robert being a man of few words, his family had once cared for the vines, and winemaking was in his blood. It was good fortune for us, city-dwellers that we were.

I thought the château and Celestine would certainly be all the revelations in store for me this incredible day, but Erik had one more surprise up his sleeve. Putting his arm around my shoulders, he led me through several lovely, though sparsely furnished rooms. Celestine followed close behind, until we reached a small, pretty room with high ceilings and French doors opening onto the sunny courtyard.

"This is our music room," he explained. I looked about me, only vaguely interested, since it would in fact be Erik's music room, not mine. I was not surprised to see a stunning black lacquered grand piano dominating the room. My eyes travelled on. And then I saw it. My hand came to my mouth as I stifled an amazed sob. There, near the windows, stood my mother's beloved pianoforte. I turned to Erik with a dazed, uncomprehending look on my face.

"How...how did you...", but I could not go on. He put his arms around me and held me close. I could feel him smiling into my hair.

"Best not to inquire," he said. "By the way, there is a *petite* present for you on the pianoforte." He gestured with his head toward the instrument.

"A present? I can't imagine what more you could possibly..." my voice trailed off as I stepped toward the pianoforte and noticed a little box resting on the top. I recognized it instantly. Slowly I extended my hand and stroked my fingers gently over the lid and its black and white mosaic pattern. The yin-yang symbol. In that moment I knew I was married to a man who should never, *ever*, be underestimated.

Who now asked me wryly, "*À propos*, perhaps you would care to explain how my shirt came to be found inside your pianoforte, Sylvie."

Author's Notes

I must admit to my readers that I took some creative license in regards to *la Sûreté Nationale*. This semi-private crime fighting organization was founded by M. Eugene Vidocq, a former (and sometimes not so former) criminal, in 1811. Eventually it became part of the Prefecture of Police. Under M. Vidocq, it was a very colorful organization, for he hired many of his old criminal cronies to assist in his crime-fighting efforts. In conducting my research into this organization, I discovered many interesting facts but unfortunately, my story takes place much later and M. Vidocq had long since departed this mortal coil. The reader who wishes to learn more will find the research quite interesting, I assure you.

By the time of 'Disfigured', the latter part of the 1870s, the autonomy of its early days no longer existed. I have taken some creative license to extend its autonomy and rather "unusual" methods by some years in order to serve my story. Needless to say, Chief-Inspector Gaston is a completely fictional character, and I trust no one in charge of *la Sûreté* ever behaved so badly.

In researching Paris in the early 1870s, I discovered that during the time period covered by the Phantom of the Opera musical and movie, the Franco-Prussian War was in full swing. The only time the war is referenced at all in the musical and movie is when Raoul appears at the *bal masque* in his dress uniform. This is because the story takes place entirely within the confines of the Opera building and its immediate environs. However, I soon realized that the war would most definitely have an effect on Sylvie, so I felt it necessary to at least reference the war and what her feelings about it might be. I expect I took some additional creative license here and there, because the blockade went on for months and Christmas for Parisians would have been bleak, indeed. France was ill-prepared to start a war with Germany, and they ultimately lost the war and much else besides.

I conducted a fair amount of research on leprosy and the existence of leper colonies around the world, but no such place existed in Paris to my knowledge. St. Giles Hospital is my own creation, but Dr. Hansen in Norway and his researches on leprosy are entirely real.

For the meanings of most of the French language used in the book, I have included on my website a glossary of the words and their English translation.

Finally, all the quotes used throughout the book to begin the chapters are taken either from written works by Alexandre Dumas, or from direct quotes attributed to him. I was certain that a romantic creature like Sylvie would love his novels, and his work still resonates today. If you have never read the Three Musketeers, I highly recommend it to you.

Thank you!

Please visit my website @ www.disfiguredseries.com for blog articles, recipes from this book, and sneak peeks at the next book in the series, 'About-Face'.